DEATH UNDER THE CRESCENT MOON

Dusty Rainbolt

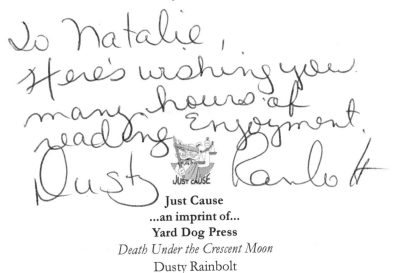

To Natalie,
Here's wishing you
many hours of
reading Enjoyment.
Dusty Rainbolt

Just Cause
...an imprint of...
Yard Dog Press
Death Under the Crescent Moon
Dusty Rainbolt

ISBN 978-1-937105-36-5
Death Under the Crescent Moon
First Edition Copyright © Dusty Rainbolt, 2013

Yard Dog Press
710 W. Redbud Lane
Alma, AR 72921-7247

http://www.yarddogpress.com

Edited by Selina Rosen
Copy & Technical Editor Lynn Stranathan
Cover art by Dell Harris

First Edition March 1, 2013
Printed in the United States of America
0 9 8 7 6 5 4 3 2 1

Acknowledgements

Death Under the Crescent Moon was a labor of love, but as with any creation, it didn't gestate in a vacuum. Writing a novel is like shooting a movie. The actress gets the accolades, but it was the behind-the-scenes crew that brings the show to life. *Death Under the Crescent Moon* had an amazing support staff.

Thank you to:

* My eternally patient husband, Weems Hutto, for coming up with the original idea for the book and for returning to the Crescent Hotel again and again.

* Tom and Linda Small, who made my most valuable Norman Baker research possible with their generosity and hospitality.

* Tom and Cindi Kautz, who shared their library and their Norman Baker collection with me.

* Selina Rosen and Lynn Stranathan—you're the best publishers in the world!

* My sister, Margaret Rainbolt for her medical knowledge and brainstorming.

*Susan Schaefer, for sharing her Eureka Springs research.

* Heike Hagenguth for sharing information on early 20th century cat care.

* Leslie Luza, for his expertise in forensics.

Also thank you also to Aunt Dot, Aunt Eva, Beth Adelman, Maggie Bonham, Ruthanne Brockway, Jean Broders, Pat Chapman, Sheila Chaudoin at the Musser Public Library, Boyd Church at the Crescent Hotel, Virginia Cooper at the Muscatine Art Center, Peggy Dee, Dusty Rose Herman Gea, Mary Hamilton, Donna Hawkins, Carroll Heath at the Crescent Hotel, Liz Lummus, Julia Mandala, Ruth McClure, Mary Anne Miller, Pairodocs Ivan the Terrible, Teresa Patterson, Cindy Rigoni, Marty and Elise Roenigk owners of the Crescent Hotel, Debbie and Bobb Waller, Laurence Woodruff, Norman Baker, the hanging man in room 424, Theodora in room 419 and in the annex the man who said to me, "I want you."

I couldn't have done it without you.

Disclaimer

This is a work of fiction in a historical setting. Some of the things that occurred in *Death Under the Crescent Moon* were appropriate for the 1930s, but are no longer considered acceptable. Never give your pet alcohol. Alcohol toxicity can cause seizures, coma and death in dogs and cats.

Dedication

For Mom…

And Weems and Dot.

You've had my back all these years.

Los Angeles, California—*Winter 1928*

Moonlight filtered through a lacy veil of leaves. In the breeze their shadows danced and swayed across the headstones as if moving to the rhythm of a macabre waltz. Rain began to fall—a gentle mist at first, then quickly swelling into a violent tempest.

Eva Dupree's breath hung in the air. She trembled; the cold air and her rain-soaked clothes wicked the warmth right out of her. Her flimsy gown clung to every curve of her body, while a bulky wool cloak pulled her down like quicksand.

A sheet of lightning flared above the graveyard just long enough to illuminate the entrance, Eva's only chance at escape. Her hands, numb from the cold, pulled the ornate gate latch. It gave a few inches, but seized, bound firmly by an equally ornate padlock. Eva drew a ragged breath as she gripped the bars and violently shook the gate back and forth. It held fast—so secure, so solid, it could have sealed the gates of Hell.

Maybe she had lost him.

She dashed toward a row of grave markers, splashing water as she ran. Eva took a few more steps, then she ducked behind a towering marble obelisk to catch her breath.

At eye-level, carvings of baby-faced cherubs stared back at her. With raindrops slipping down their chubby cheeks, she could almost believe the angels were weeping for her. Exhausted, she wanted to curl up inside a dry mausoleum and sleep. Instead, Eva leaned against the cold marble, then slid to the ground.

Her chestnut hair, meticulously styled into a bob by her personal hairdresser only a few hours earlier, lay plastered against her face, rain dripping from the ends. She closed her eyes. Her body ached. She needed to move on, but her muscles ignored her will.

To sleep. Perchance to dream.

Another sheet of lightning illuminated the graveyard for a moment. In that brief light, Macedonia looked like any other Gothic cemetery. Headstones lined up like soldiers awaiting that order to charge into a hopeless battle.

In another flash of lightning she caught a glimpse of a silhouetted figure moving steadily closer. Eva stood and ran. She only made it a few steps before the creature caught up with her. Grabbing the hem of her cape, he brought her escape to an abrupt stop, not unlike a dog running to the end of a chain at full speed. She slammed onto the ground.

Eva rolled over to face her attacker, and lifted her trembling hands—partly for protection, partly a prayer for mercy. "Please, please, don't hurt me," she croaked, her voice choked with laryngitis and fatigue.

The creature's fingers, with awkwardly long claws, formed a clumsy circle around her neck. She kicked and struggled to push him away, but he was too strong. Between the rain collecting in her mouth and his hands shutting off her air, her head grew light.

Through the trees the lightning flashed again. Then, as abruptly as the downpour began, it ceased—completely. Eva and the creature looked around briefly, then locked eyes again. The clank of metal against metal joined the howl of the wind, and finally the rain resumed with its former ferocity.

She took one last look at the creature's gray skin and bulging eyes. His large ears made him look more like a donkey than a man. She tried to loosen his grip on her throat, but her struggling only invigorated him. Her eyes grew wild—like trapped prey—just before her hands fell limp to the ground.

The creature ripped the cloak away from her throat, leaning closer, closer. But then he quickly recoiled, shielding his eyes from that most dreaded of signs, hanging from a slender gold chain and nestled in her bosom—the Crucifix. The creature dropped her in the mud and fled into the shadows.

"Cut! That's perfect this time," a male voice yelled through a megaphone. "We can edit out that little glitch with the rain machine. All right gang, that's a wrap."

Immediately the spraying water ceased and two giant fans wound down. Shivering, Eva struggled upright and massaged her throat. Red fingerprints appeared on her throat. "Lennie, you son-of-a-bitch," she wheezed at the man peeling off the creature's face, "That hurt! I thought you were going to kill me."

The prop master took the hideous mask with one hand and offered the actor a smoke with the other. Lennox Fitzroy held the cigarette in his carefully manicured claws and took a deep drag. "Sorry, kid. Roger wanted it rough."

The director, seated on a dry headstone a few feet away, handed his megaphone to his assistant, and turned to Eva. "Stop whining. When you win the Academy Award for this scene, baby, you'll thank me."

On the far side of the set, a gaffer in a heavy raincoat wiggled the switch on one of the giant fans that had produced the storm's gale-force wind. The fan kicked into high gear, spraying water from the set on both Eva and the director.

"Roger!" Eva yelled at the director as loud as she could with her failing voice. "Tell the grip to turn off that bloody wind mach…." Before she could finish the sentence she sunk to her knees and clutched at her chest. Her lungs burned. She broke into a coughing spasm.

Can't breathe. Can't breathe.

"Bravo!" The director applauded her. "Stunning, darling." He flicked his still glowing cigarette butt onto a new mound. "But really, don't you think that's pushing melodrama a bit too far, even for you? Perhaps you should have saved your performance for the camera."

Still coughing and gasping for air she collapsed into the mud. Eva was pale as a ghost and the stain of real blood smeared her lips, hands and gown.

Her costar, Fitzroy, threw down his own cigarette and dropped to one knee.

"We need a doctor," he screamed at the startled film crew. "For God's sakes, someone get a doctor!"

DAY ONE—*Thursday, August 31, 1939*
The Baker Hospital and Health Resort
Eureka Springs, Arkansas

"I was a ghost long before I died. A fossil, a life whose useful-ness had long since gone extinct." Eva Dupree returned the cap to her fountain pen and blew on the diary page until the last spot of ink had completely dried. She laid the pen down on a battered desk that had probably been around since before the turn of the century. *The desk may be well-worn, but at least it's useful,* Eva thought. She allowed her fingers to roam absently over the oak surface, so modest and out of place in her luxurious suite at Baker Hospital and Health Resort, where, as its brochure claimed, "Cancer is Curable."

She read over her entry and shook her head. "Self-pity is so unattractive," she told herself. "This sounds morbid—right out of the book of Lamentations." She abhorred listening to people wallowing in self-pity. "No," Eva sighed as she closed the diary, this wasn't like her. "I sound whiny, like Job."

In each of her film roles as the "vixen victim," she had enjoyed the scenes where the tears flowed. Of course, the tears were only glycerin. After weeping over the crisis *du jour*, her icy green eyes still looked striking—even in black and white. And miraculously, on screen her makeup never smeared. But tonight she didn't have a makeup artist to protect her image.

Eva rose from the old desk and wandered into the bathroom. Leaning over the sink, she looked into the mirror and contemplated the face returning her stare. She found it hard to believe that aging stranger was really her. She splashed water on her face, carefully dabbing her swollen eyes. Silver streaks now highlighted her chest-nut hair. Her manicured nails ran through her collar-length coiffure, permed into perfect finger waves. At thirty-nine, the once flawless, milky skin now wore more character than she cared to see—lines etched by a storybook life turned to tragedy. She'd been a tall woman with a full bosom, but since she had fallen ill she looked as if she'd put on flesh one size too small for her face.

"I don't know which is more depressing," Eva said to the image in the mirror, "the diary entry or looking at you."

She glanced around the room. She simply couldn't shake the feeling that someone else was standing behind her, watching her. Eva turned out the bathroom light and opened the side door to the large public balcony adjoining her suite. It was dark outside, and the patients who usually lounged out there had long since gone to bed. As an afterthought, she grabbed a magazine, then slipped through the door.

Eva sat down on a wicker chaise lounge near the guardrail, beneath the light of a gas lamp. The muted golden light from the pole-mounted lantern cast a series of long, irregular shadows across the balcony. She flipped through the latest copy of *Hollywood Magazine,* September 1939. A photo of Clark Gable, so dashing in his Confederate captain's uniform, dominated the cover. Inside, Clark and Vivien Leigh shared a passionate kiss. Eva touched Vivien's face. With a rueful smile she whispered, "Enjoy it while you can, honey."

Had it really been ten years since her own face had graced the pages of this same magazine and dozens of others just like it? At that time, Vivien Leigh had just celebrated her sixteenth birthday—a nobody. Had things gone differently, it could have been Eva in Clark Gable's arms. Eva thought about her reflection in the mirror. Granted, Rhett Butler wouldn't have had much interest in a nearly-forty Scarlett O'Hara. Still, had it not been for the pneumonia she caught while filming *Caught in a Web*, she might still be starring in movies—albeit, in more mature roles. "Enjoy it while you can."

Eva looked over the balcony guardrail. Compared to bustling Dallas, where she now made her home, the Baker Hospital sat in the middle of nowhere. She'd arrived by train late that afternoon, and hadn't yet had much time to orient herself to the surrounding countryside. From this vantage point on the fourth floor balcony, she could see the lights from Eureka Springs' homes and businesses in the valley below. Directly across from her stood East Mountain. On this night, the peak blended into the backdrop of a pitch dark sky, with a sliver of crescent moon just showing above the center rise.

Only a few hours earlier, Eva had entered the lobby of the Baker Hospital. Throughout her life, she'd sat in many hospital waiting rooms. Her husband, Edgar, had died at St. Paul's Hospital in Dallas just two years ago. Eva herself spent an entire month at Hollywood's gloomy Good Samaritan Hospital struggling for each breath after filming *Caught in a Web*. And at the height of her movie popularity, Eva donned a large-brimmed hat and sunglasses to sneak into a sanitarium to visit silent screen star Pola Negri. Her diva friend had suffered a nervous breakdown—unpublicized, of course—after the sudden death of her lover, Rudolph Valentino. Even the best room Pola's money could buy, filled with more blooms than a florist shop, was still as white and impersonal as a mausoleum.

Every one of those clinics could have all been interchangeable—stark white walls, (except for the vomit green wall tiles) and a veneer of white marble tiles covering the floors. Nurses wore glaring white, from the soles of their old-lady shoes to the tops of their starched caps. The doctors, too, swaddled themselves in bleached white. Surrounded by all that purity, one might have imagined that they were in heaven. Except Eva's image of heaven didn't include sharp instruments, hypodermic needles, and antiseptic odors that seared the nasal passages. It was a wonder all that lack of color didn't drive already sick people insane.

Fortunately, the Baker Hospital didn't have that sterile look. Every wall in the cancer center was painted brilliant purple or lavender

Even her own suite wore a fresh coat of lavender with purple wood trim. Despite the colorfulness of the place, Eva still felt very alone and very far away from home.

In the distance, crickets chirped and the deep bark of a large dog echoed through the valley. Birds called hauntingly, taunting the dog and inspiring another round of howls. It reminded her of a scene from *Frankenstein*.

A gust of icy autumn wind whipped off the Ozark mountains. She shivered. Edgar had loved cold weather. He was a mountain boy at heart, at home on the ski slopes of Mt. Baldy. But he lived without a peak on the flat plains of Texas because that's where his father established his oil empire. Edgar once told Eva, "When we have children, I want to take them to the mountains so they can have snowball fights."

Only the children never came...and Edgar died. So, tonight Eva Dupree sat alone in the frosty mountain air that Edgar loved. Eva shifted in the chair, trying to find a comfortable position...and failing, as usual. Her doctor had warned her that those sharp jabs were common symptoms of her cancer. She squeezed her eyes shut, as if that would squeeze out any thoughts or fears about her illness. That, too, failed.

Below her, a gray fog settled into the valley. The mist slowly grew heavier and denser, descending into the basin's depths. Slowly, misty tentacles of fog extended, swallowing the town lights. Eventually the fog reached her and rose up through the guardrail as if someone was trying to cover her in a burial shroud. Funny, her old film producers would have killed to duplicate this atmosphere.

Norman Baker had promised her a new beginning, a cancer cure. Eva looked out over the vista wondering, *is this the Valley of the Shadow of Death, or is it a sign that I have nothing to fear?* The wind from the north picked up and the fog temporarily receded.

She turned her wedding ring, still stubbornly displayed on her left hand. Alone...Eva Dupree, the once-famous darling of the silent screen, alone and under attack by a monster that, unlike those in her films, could not be banished by a director yelling "Cut!" She shut herself away from the world—except for her sharp-tongued maid, Rose, and Edgar's cat, Ivan the Terrible.

Without warning, the hair on her neck lifted and a glacier of goose bumps spread across her arms—a deeper cold than mere weather. This chill sank all the way to her bones. She closed her chenille robe and knotted the tie.

An icy hand brushed Eva's shoulder. Alarmed, Eva dropped the magazine into her lap and whipped her head around. Only a few feet away stood a young woman. The woman—a girl really, surely no more than sixteen—was wearing a shapeless white dressing gown and stared at Eva. Long, dark hair tumbled about her shoulders. She, too, had been crying.

Eva let out a breath. "Oh honey, you really startled me."

With all her time in and out of hospitals, Eva had learned they weren't just lonely places for her alone. That explained why at any time of the day or night one could find patients or even visitors roaming the halls looking for escape or comfort. Even Eva was out on the balcony in search of solace—and perhaps this young patient simply needed to clear her mind of the pharmaceutical fog of painkillers. There was a learning curve to facing mortality as Eva was beginning to understand.

"I didn't see you come out here." Eva loosened her grip on the chair. "I'm sorry. You caught me at a bad moment."

The teenager didn't say anything; she just looked back at the older woman with eyes so sad, they broke Eva's heart. The long silence grew more awkward. Eva finally decided the girl was too heavily medicated to respond—the poor thing probably didn't even know where she was.

"No harm done." Eva pointed at a chair next to hers. "You can sit here with me for a while if you like." She laughed nervously. "I know it sounds crazy, but when I looked up just now and saw you there, I was sure I'd seen a ghost." Eva's brittle laugh faded into the wind.

The girl moved closer to the guardrail. She stared down for a moment and then gazed over at Eva. Suddenly her expression changed. She looked around as if she expected someone to storm onto the deck. Suddenly, Eva feared for the girl's safety.

"Are you all right?" Eva stood up from the lounge chair and took a step toward her.

The girl placed her hands on the railing. She cocked her head, staring at the ground four stories below.

Eva reached out her hand then pulled back, afraid her advances might urge the young patient over the edge, literally. "What are you doing? Sweetie, come away from there."

This girl shifted her unblinking gaze from the ground to Eva.

"Sweetie, I know how bad you feel. But you've come here to get well. Why don't you sit over here and tell me what's bothering you?"

The girl pulled herself up and balanced on the rail. She looked like a thin, sad pixie, poised on a toadstool of death. Eva froze, paralyzed by what she was seeing. "No, don't do it!"

The girl's eyes met Eva's for a final moment. She reached out her pale, delicate hand, a sad ethereal invitation, and said in a wispy voice, "Why don't you jump?" Then she swung her legs over the railing.

Eva lunged toward the rail, stretching for the girl's hand. At that moment, the girl released her hold. Eva grabbed only a handful of air while the girl plummeted silently toward the earth.

Eva watched her fall halfway, then fled into the hall shouting, "Oh, holy Jesus! Somebody help me! She jumped. She killed herself. Isn't anyone around?"

In moments a nurse appeared from the stairwell, and Eva pulled up short of crashing into the immovable object that was Nurse Mary Turner. In her pressed white uniform, the hospital's head nurse couldn't have looked more the part if they'd sent her from central casting. Most of her ashen hair was tucked beneath her starched white nurse's cap. She was in her late forties, and harsh frown lines framed her face.

Being a nurse in a cancer hospital, she had seen too much suffering. Each lost patient had etched her creases just a bit deeper. Those thin lips were unpracticed at smiling. She wouldn't be the nurse to seek out for comfort. "What's wrong?"

"A girl just jumped off the balcony!" Eva screamed.

"Not again," the nurse muttered under her breath. Then, more audibly, she said, "Surely you must be mistaken." Nurse Turner finished making notations on the clip board in her hands, snapped the metal cover shut and urged Eva down the hall. "Come with me," she said with the cold finality of reason. She ushered Eva back to the balcony.

Eva dabbed her eye. "If I'd grabbed her a second sooner, she'd still be alive." She hung back in the doorway, afraid to look at the girl's broken body below, but Nurse Turner went straight to the front of the balcony and bent over the rail.

A breeze picked up, momentarily thinning the fog.

"Just as I thought." Nurse Turner reigned herself in from the railing. She placed an intuitionally reassuring arm around Eva's shoulders and tried to maneuver her patient back into the hall. "There's no one there. I think you should return to your room and take your medicine."

Eva stared back at the nurse for a moment, then broke free, running back onto the deck. Nurse Turner watched from the doorway.

"She's right down here!" Eva craned out over the edge, steeling herself for the grizzly scene below.

More gas lights illuminated the hospital's rear entrance. Beneath Eva a couple sat casually chatting on a bench in a well-tended rose garden. They broke off their conversation and looked up when they heard Eva's frantic voice.

Eva felt like someone had punched her in the sternum. "But I saw her. She told me to jump too. Then she climbed over the guardrail. I thought I had her hand. If I'd just been a second sooner…"

Wearing a deadpan face that read more like annoyance, the nurse asked, "What room are you in?"

"I'm in four-nineteen."

Nurse Turner pulled out a list from her pocket. "Mrs. Dupree?"

Eva clenched her teeth. "*Miss* Dupree," Eva corrected gently. "I go by my professional name." She smiled and gave a little chuckle.

"Mrs. Dupree is my mother."

"Well, *Miss* Dupree, let's get you back to your room. We don't want you to disturb the other patients." Nurse Turner began moving toward Eva's room.

Eva didn't budge. "You don't understand." Eva took care to pronounce every syllable. "A girl jumped off of the balcony."

"You looked down and saw no body," Nurse Turner said stiffly. "You're just letting your nerves get the best of you." The nurse herded her patient down the hall and around the corner to room four-nineteen. "Sometimes the treatments can cause people to think they see things, Miss Dupree. You wouldn't be the first. I'm sure you'll be fine in the morning." The nurse opened the door and switched on the light.

"Look, I may be taking painkillers, but I don't start my cancer treatments until tomorrow morning. I know what I saw. A girl just killed herself."

Nurse Turner let the subject drop. Her attention turned to Eva's pillow and the white cat that sprang to his feet, hissing at the nurse before disappearing under the bed.

Nurse Turner shifted her gaze from the cat to Eva.

"You know," Eva said, "it's damn aggravating that my cat can stay with me in my room, but not my maid."

"Who told you that cat can stay here?" Nurse Turner snapped, her thin lips settling into a grim line. "We have rules about that sort of thing. A hospital is no place for a filthy animal."

"Nurse Turner, was it?"

The nurse nodded.

"That cat is probably cleaner than many of your patients. My maid sees to all of his sanitary needs, so your nurses will be neither inconvenienced nor contaminated. I can assure you, he won't be a problem. Besides, I'm paying handsomely for the privilege of keeping him here." Eva stood a little taller. "He's staying here with the blessings, of both Dr. Baker and Mr. Bellows, the hospital administrator. If you have an issue with it, I suggest you take it up with them." Eva glared at the nurse. She really wanted to add "bitch!" but checked her tongue.

Still hovering just outside the door to her room, Eva peered around the doorframe and instantly regretted arguing with Nurse Turner. Eva couldn't shake the image of the girl falling to her death. Despite Turner's less-than-compassionate disposition, Eva really didn't want to be left alone. She hesitated, then looked at Nurse Turner and said shakily, "Nurse, I know this sounds childish, but can you stay here for a few minutes?"

Nurse Turner gave a snort. "I'm not a babysitter, Mrs. Dupree."

"I don't want to be alone right now. All I'm asking is a few moments."

The nurse frowned at her, arms folded. "That Shirley Temple act won't wash with me. I have two nurses out sick tonight. I don't have time for games." Her tone softened slightly. "Now please, just get into bed. You'll feel better in the morning."

Eva, her bravado deflated, climbed into bed and pulled her blanket up to her chin. Right now she felt like a little girl asking for a drink of water to stall being left alone.

"Good night, Miss Dupree."

"Please leave the light on."

The nurse hesitated for a moment, then switched off the overhead light and closed the door behind her.

Eva gave an exasperated gasp at Nurse Turner's audacity. She closed her eyes, but her mind continued to replay the image of the girl balanced on the rail.

The cat jumped back up on the bed and butted her hand with his head. Large with heavy, dense muscles, he had the white cashmere-like fur of an Angora, but with a red tail and two red spots on his head. Eva pulled him next to her. Rocking back and forth, she whispered, "Oh, God! Oh, God! Oh, God!"

Over and over in her mind she played the scene on the balcony, like watching herself on the dailies at the end of the filming day. Unlike the vampires and other monsters that once plagued her, that pathetic child really scared the hell out of her.

She leaned her head against the cat's chest to listen to him purr. Ivan the Terrible had been Edgar's cat. Until Eva grew ill, woman and beast never really saw eye to eye. But tonight, she was glad she'd paid the extra twenty-five dollars a week for the right to bring him along.

Eva looked around her suite. She threw back the covers, climbed out of bed and hurried into the adjoining room. She tested the door that led to the balcony. She cracked the door open then quickly shut it. She needed a key to lock the door. Tonight, however, the key was missing in action. Eva then scoured the room for something to use to wedge the door. The chair at the oak desk would work. She jammed the chair back under the doorknob and tested it. That would have to do for tonight.

The admissions nurse had told Eva that this suite was the nicest room in the entire hospital. Nice or not, she wanted to get the hell out of here. Tomorrow she'd ask for a different room.

Eva got back into bed and gathered the cat and the covers closer. Without thinking, Eva began to scratch him. "Oh, God, Ivan. Am I losing my mind? I know I saw that girl. She asked me, 'Why don't you jump?'"

Tonight wasn't the first time she felt like she was losing her grip on reality. After Edgar died, every aspect of her life seemed to be reeling out of control. She misplaced her keys, her purse, even important papers—something she'd never done before. Things turned up in places she'd swear she had never put them. Edgar's absence smothered her like a heavy blanket; she began to drink more, and just getting out of bed became a struggle.

Even two years later, Eva would sometimes wake up in the middle of the night and think she saw Edgar out of the corner of her eye. When she sat up, of course, no one was there. Lately, it seemed, this happened more and more. Once she even thought she felt someone on the bed. Except for Ivan, she really was alone. Between the apparent hallucinations and her inability to concentrate, she feared she was going insane.

So was the balcony girl a product of her imagination or a real girl whose broken body had vanished? The third option was so much more frightening that she couldn't even explore the possibility: Had she seen a ghost? For the star of so many horror films, that was too ridiculous to fathom.

Yet, even here in her suite with all the lights on, she couldn't shake that feeling that someone was watching her from a corner of the room. Tomorrow she'd have to ask her maid to drop by the package store and pick up some scotch. Hospital rules or no, she couldn't sleep without a little something to relax her nerves.

Eva looked at her bedside table and stared at the last photograph taken of Edgar. She picked up the silver frame. He looked happy and his graying temples were so distinguished. And his eyes...how Eva missed Edgar's eyes.

She looked at her hand and recalled the way she'd felt that night when Edgar first kissed it. Turning her palm over, all she saw was a lifeline that was so short, she was living on borrowed time.

She was nineteen and new to Hollywood. Her friend Desdemona Evans, who was a mature twenty-three, had been invited to a party hosted by Charlie Chaplin. Of course, all the directors and producers would be there. Imagine that—two babes among Hollywood wolves.

That night at Chaplin's home, Desdemona went on and on about a movie producer she wanted to meet. "He's so dashing," she said. "I hear he finances his movies with oil money. That's him—over there."

She pointed to a tall, dark-haired man in his forties. He held a cigarette between his thumb and forefinger, the way Eva had seen European men do. His other hand held a glass of champagne. For an old guy, he was handsome.

"I'm going to see if I can get Charlie to introduce me to him."

"Oh, it's *Charlie*, now," Eva teased. "I thought you begged an invitation from a friend of his cousin."

"A friend of his *niece*," Desdemona corrected.

"So you're just going to walk up to the most famous star in Hollywood and ask him to introduce you to a producer? Dese, you're going to get us kicked out of here."

"Eva," Desdemona said as she discreetly edged her way over to the screen star, "if you're going to ride the horse, you're gonna have to take the reins." She struck a pose just a few feet away from where the Little Tramp was engaging movie legend Pola Negri in a spirited conversation about the sacrifices she'd made on the location of her latest film. Eva began an idle conversation with her back to the mark, allowing Desdemona to fully showplace her God-given gifts. Desdemona patted her raven hair, flashed her eyes seductively and breathed deeply a couple of times to accentuate those well-rounded bosoms.

Pola's voice jumped three octaves when she realized Charlie's eyes were no longer focused on her. "Charlie, what are you staring at?" Pola screamed with tyrannosaurus ferocity. For a silent movie actress, she could really project. She spun around and caught a glimpse of Desdemona practicing her heavy breathing. "How dare you ignore me and stare at a common street prostitute!" She flung her champagne in Chaplin's face, stomping away and swearing in a combination of Polish, English and Gypsy.

"I will send my tiger over to eat you both for dinner!" Pola slammed the front door behind her with such force, a few guests braced themselves for an aftershock.

Chaplin stood there with champagne dripping down his face. One drop hung at the end of his nose, shimmering whenever he moved his head. He removed a monogrammed silk handkerchief from his pocket and dabbed up the amber liquid. This was not the first time Pola Negri had baptized him in champagne.

Then he gave Desdemona one of his trademark smiles. "So my dear, what can I do for you?"

For the first time ever, Desdemona stood speechless, embarrassed at the scene she had just caused. She turned to make her escape when Eva grabbed her by the arm and gave her a nudge in Chaplin's direction. "Dese, this is your chance," Eva whispered.

"Oh, my. Mr. Chaplin, I'm so sorry. I, uh…"

Eva pointed at the tall man. "Mr. Chaplin, she'd like to meet that gentleman over there."

Chaplin looked around Desdemona at Eva. "So, you're the brave one? Very well." To Eva's shock, Charlie Chaplin put his arm around her waist and led her toward Edgar, with Desdemona in tow.

"Edgar," Chaplin pulled Eva up to see the producer face to face. "I want you to meet someone. This is…" Chaplin looked to Eva.

"Uh, Eva Dupree.

"Yes, this is Eva Dupree. Miss Dupree, meet Edgar Foxworthy."

"…And this is my friend Desdemona Evans."

Desdemona rushed up and offered her hand to Edgar. He took it and squeezed it briefly, but looked past her at Eva. "Eva did he say?" Edgar reached down, wrapped his fingers around Eva's, and slowly brought her hand to his lips, as if savoring the moment. Holding the pose, she gazed up into his eyes, so blue—like pools of water, so liquid she was drowning.

His touch and his lips were so gentle yet commanding, Eva felt like an electric current had snaked right up her arm from where his lips touched her.

"Good evening, Eva Dupree. What are you doing at such a boring party?"

Chaplin winked at Eva as he walked away. "It *was* a boring party." He walked away wiping his stained shirt with the handkerchief.

Eva couldn't stop staring at Edgar's engaging eyes, a combination of child and devil rolled into blue orbs that seemed to be laughing at her and kissing her at the same time.

That night signaled the beginning of her success. Finally, she had it all: choice parts, adoring fans, a husband who worshipped her and whom she worshipped.

The fans had long since abandoned Eva for younger starlets with sultry voices. Gone too were the movie roles and the fair-weather friends who profited from the Foxworthy-Dupree partnership.

Above her ceiling, thuds and footsteps pulled her back to the present. It sounded like horses loping above her head. In the morning she would most definitely ask the hospital administrator to move her to another room.

Eva returned the silver frame to the nightstand and retrieved the latest copy of *Screen Play*. Beside her, Ivan snoozed on his back with his feet sticking up in the air like a dog. Upstairs, the Kentucky Derby had finally ceased. Only the sound of the wind softly whistling past her windows and Ivan's snoring remained. Eva, too, dozed off, allowing the magazine to slip from her fingers. Suddenly, she sat upright when the near silence was broken by a faint noise down the hall. Squeak, squeak, squeak...

She took a deep breath and listened harder. It grew progressively louder, then gradually faded. Squeak, squeak, squeak...

Her sudden movement had disturbed Ivan, who stood up, circled and then laid down again.

"Sorry, Ivan." She lay back down, but sleep eluded her. In hidden corners of the room, and of course under her bed, she imagined the same monsters and bogeymen she'd feared as a small child. Every creak of the building's wooden interior, every whistle of the wind outside, promised another creature bent on her destruction. She slipped out of bed and turned the bathroom light on, leaving the door wide open as her mother used to do. At least if there was a bogeyman, she'd see him coming.

Eva finally drifted off into a restless sleep again, but shot straight up to the sound of Ivan's Halloween cat yowl. His back arched and fur erect, Ivan stared at the wall. The cat's guttural wail gradually faded, followed by yet another gentle round outside the room of "squeak, squeak, squeak."

DAY TWO—*Friday, September 1, 1939*

Eva's surgeon, Dr. Setzer, raised his eyebrows as he looked at the X-ray mounted in the light box.

Eva stared at the mysterious map of her insides.

"We're going to carve you up like a Thanksgiving turkey," Dr. Setzer said. "But it doesn't matter, because you're dying." His head transformed into the evil face of the Creature of the Night, but Dr. Setzer's hazel eyes glared right through the clumsy monster mask. He repeated, *"You're dying!"*

Suddenly, Eva found herself strapped down to an operating room table. The Creature stood over her wearing a white surgical mask. He held a carving knife in one hand and a serving fork in the other. Next to him stood smaller creatures masked just like him, who also wore nurses' caps and held empty meat platters.

"I want a drumstick," one of the little monsters said.

Another said, "I want the breast."

"Now for our main course," the Creature said with knife and fork poised. "Kidney pie… But before we start, Miss Dupree, we just need you to sign this release form. It entitles us to your immortal soul." He made an X on her left arm with a fountain pen. "Sign here."

"I don't want to sign it," Eva cried.

But without her lifting a finger, her elaborate autograph appeared on her forearm and drops of red ink began to flow from her name.

"Very good." The Creature removed her arm from the socket and handed it to one of the small monsters. "Nurse, file this with the others, will you?" The little monster threw it into a pile of other arms of varying shapes and sizes. Then the Creature said to Eva, "Nothing to worry about, Miss Dupree. This will only kill you."

Suddenly she was blinded by a tube of bright light.

"Good morning, Miss Dupree." The nurse ripped open the curtains, inviting a stream of bright sunlight to flood the room.

The vamp in Eva recoiled, shielding her eyes with the back of her hand. For a few moments, dream and reality merged.

"You have a spectacular view, don't you think?" the nurse said.
Eva sighed. *No one should be that cheerful this early.*

Nurse Gracie Cavanaugh looked to be a normal human being in her late twenties with short, wavy hair the shade of semi-sweet chocolate. Her finely defined eyebrows arched above large, expressive hazel eyes. She wore a mostly straight-tooth smile beneath her white nurse's cap, sans the mask of the Creature.

Eva rubbed the small of her back with her fingertips. It felt like someone wearing golfing cleats had been dancing a waltz on her backside all night. This was no way to greet the morning.

Next to her, Ivan woke up from Eva's pillow—his favorite sleeping spot. He yawned, stretched and then slid back down underneath the covers.

Nurse Cavanaugh made small talk. "This is the nicest room in the whole hospital. You even have a radio and a walk-in closet. Lucky you, don't you think?"

Eva took a closer look at the radio. It had a dark oak finish and a metal nameplate that read, "Tangley."

Eva's was certainly not a typical hospital accommodation; the suite had two large rooms, not unlike her guest house at home. The Victorian furnishings weren't as ornate or expensive as her own art deco furniture, but they beat the heck out of what she would expect to find at any other hospital.

The first room had a couple of chairs and a large fainting couch with a small mahogany coffee table. The table was actually of higher quality than the rest but it had a few nicks in the wood marring the finish. A mid-size bed claimed center stage. Across from it an oak vanity with an impressive mirror awaited a beauty to gaze into it. Next to the window stood the battered oak desk and chair.

Despite the view and fixtures, Eva didn't want to spend another night there. She took a deep breath. "Yes, the room is wonderful, but…"

Pounding and footsteps above her distracted her thoughts. Both Eva and the nurse looked up.

"Is someone racing elephants up there?" Eva asked.

"Mr. Baker's penthouse is right above you. It'll quiet down once he's gone downstairs to his office…How did you sleep last night?"

Eva shrugged. "Not very well. I kept having bad dreams."

Nurse Cavanaugh nodded sympathetically. "It's always hard sleeping in a new place. It's nice that you have a three-quarter-size bed, not a hospital bed. You'll enjoy your time in this suite. It's more like a hotel than a hospital, don't you think? Everyone who stays here speaks highly of it."

"I didn't feel very comfortable in here last night." Eva started to mention the girl who jumped to her death, but wondered if it had just been a bad dream. She took another tack. "In fact, can you ask the admissions clerk if I can have another room?"

"I'm afraid we're full right now. You can ask to be put on a waiting list." The nurse spied the chair lodged under the knob of the door to the balcony. "What happened here?"

Eva hesitated, then pointed to the deck. "I heard noises out there and couldn't find the key to lock the door."

Nurse Cavanaugh dragged the old oak chair back to the desk. "I'll see if I can find the key so you can lock it. Sometimes patients go out there late at night to think. I promise you, nothing's going to hurt you."

"Thanks." Eva eyed the door, unconvinced.

Returning to her patient, the nurse pulled the rolling table to Eva's bed. On it was a white enamel medical tray that held a shot-size glass filled with liquid the color and thickness of molasses, and a juice glass of fresh orange juice.

"Can I have some breakfast?" Eva asked. "I could really use a cup of coffee."

"I doubt that you'll want to eat beforehand," Nurse Cavanaugh said. "You might experience some nausea."

"I'd still like a scrambled egg and a couple of slices of bacon. It's not for me." She nodded at Ivan, who had popped his head out from under the covers and let out a long, loud meow. He arched his back, stretched his legs forward and yawned wide enough to expose his enormous canine teeth. After stretching, he sat properly and expectantly. It was breakfast time.

"Oh, my! What have we here?" Nurse Cavanaugh crouched down to get a closer look at Eva's roommate. The cat gazed at her with piercing amber eyes.

"Meet Ivan."

The cat responded to the mention of his name by kneading his paws and gazing up at the nurse with a "come hither," or rather, "feed me hither" expression.

The nurse patted his head like a dog's. "Don't worry. I won't say anything. But some of the other nurses will."

Eva smiled. "Believe me. Everyone with any say already knows." She smiled recalling Nurse Turner's reaction to Ivan. "We're actually paying for a double."

The nurse flipped open the chart and scanned it. Nurse Cavanaugh nodded. "I see you are." She read further. "It looks like you get the oral dose today. My patients tell me it tastes nasty, so I brought you some orange juice to rinse the flavor out of your mouth. After that, you can do anything you want: shop, go into town, whatever. After your stomach settles, you can even check out some of the quaint little restaurants." She looked down at the cat. "I'll go ahead and order *your* breakfast."

She handed Eva the glass of dark liquid, then Nurse Cavanaugh headed into the bathroom to wash off some of the sticky Baker Cure that had dripped on her hand. Next to the bathroom sink she found Ivan's facilities for his hygienic needs and his dirty dinner plate from the night before.

"Oh my!" the nurse said from the bathroom. "Aren't we fancy? I can't believe he's got a lace placemat. And is that real china?"

"My husband wanted only the best for Ivan. My maid follows his wishes...often to extremes. Rose sent some of the cat's posh accessories ahead with me so Ivan can be properly outfitted. I didn't have time to get everything done on such short notice. Rose'll be along in a few days after she ties up some loose ends at the house." Eva glanced at a crocodile hide trunk in the corner of the room containing only her (and Ivan's) bare essentials. "Thank goodness."

Nurse Cavanaugh returned from the bathroom drying her hands, to catch Eva sniffing the glass. "I wouldn't do that. It's much easier to take if you don't smell it first."

"You have some scotch to wash the taste away?" Eva sounded hopeful.

Nurse Cavanaugh leaned against the small oak desk next to the window. "Sorry, alcohol is strictly against the rules. At least, the drinking kind. That's what the juice is for. It goes down better if you hold your nose and gulp it."

Eva steeled herself, took a deep breath, and slammed the goo down her throat just as she had done shots of fiery alcohol with her friend, Desdemona, at some of the celebrity parties. But the liquor slid down the throat quickly and only burned for a second. This stuff moved at a snail's pace and had about the same slimy consistency—maybe even the same flavor.

"Here." Nurse Cavanaugh handed her the juice as soon as Eva had emptied the medicine glass. A thick brown coating clung to the inside of the used glass. "This will help clear out that aftertaste, don't you think?"

"I think I'm going to throw up," Eva gagged.

"That's why it's best to wait on your breakfast. You'll get used to it." Nurse Cavanaugh gathered up the empty glasses. "I see you came in yesterday evening, so I'm not sure what the night nurse had a chance to tell you. The dining room is on the ground floor next to the lobby. Lunch is at eleven-thirty and dinner at five."

"I've asked that my meals be served in my room," Eva informed her nurse.

Nurse Cavanaugh once again pulled the chart from its bracket mounted at the foot of the bed. "I didn't see it on your chart. I'll let the chef know. Speaking of food, it's pretty good here, overall." Nurse Cavanaugh looked around in a conspiratorial way. "Don't tell anyone I said this, but on the nights that they serve Mr. Baker's Fried Mush with Soybean Curd, I'd go into town. I'm sure even the worst food in town is better than that, don't you think? Oh, yes. Watch out for the Chop Suey with Bean Curd, too. It's almost as bad."

Eva nodded quietly, trying to imagine what fried mush with soybean curd must taste like. She shuddered.

Nurse Cavanaugh nodded at the door to the balcony. "In a little while I want you to spend some time in the sun breathing our fresh mountain air, because that helps your circulation and aids in removing poisons from your bloodstream. If you're out and about you can also get out to the balcony through the hall like the rest of the patients."

"Nurse," Eva hesitated, "did you hear anything about a woman jumping from that balcony last night?"

Nurse Cavanaugh smiled. "No, not last night. Do you need some pain medication?"

Eva touched her back gingerly. The guy wearing the cleats was still doing a jig on her. "In the worst way."

Nurse Cavanaugh held up the water pitcher. "Let me refill this and I'll be back with a little something for the pain." Apparently the balcony discussion was over.

As the nurse closed the door, another series of loud thumps and thuds banged above the ceiling. "If you need anything, you can push that button and it will page a nurse."

A few minutes later Nurse Cavanaugh returned with a breakfast tray and set it down on the rolling bedside table. She removed the graniteware cover and breathed in the aroma. "Mmmm. That smells pretty good, don't you think?" The morning cuisine: coffee with cream and sugar, lightly buttered toast and orange marmalade with a very small side order of scrambled eggs and several slices of bacon.

Ivan placed his paws on the table and watched as Eva cut up the bacon and mixed it with the scrambled eggs. "You hungry?"

He prompted her to hurry with an anxious cry.

"Here." She pushed it next to Ivan.

With his paws on either side of the plate, he worked on his breakfast. It wasn't quite as good as Rose's kitty concoctions. But before long the meal was history and Ivan was giving the dishwasher a hand by cleaning the plate with his tongue. Even after it had been thoroughly washed, he continued to polish it until every last streak of grease had vanished. When he'd finished, he sat back, looked at Eva and licked his nose.

She sipped the coffee cautiously—enjoying the warm feel of the cup against her fingers and the fragrance of coffee steam rising into the air. This was just the way she liked it. Nothing beats a really hot cup of coffee first thing in the morning. Thank goodness the nurse's prediction of nausea had been blown out of proportion.

As Eva sipped, she watched the cat amusing himself on the floor.

If anyone had told her two years ago that she'd let a cat sleep on her pillow, she'd have said they'd lost their mind. If they'd said she'd take one to the hospital with her and let him eat off her table, she'd have had them committed to a lunatic asylum. Although she wasn't completely comfortable in her role as kitty caretaker, she was beginning to adapt. My, how things had changed!

The nurse returned with the refilled stainless water pitcher. "If you don't plan on walking around town, I want you to drink a big glass of water then go out on the deck."

"Water?"

"When the Baker Cure starts dissolving the tumor, the water will help cleanse the poisons from your system. Water from Crescent Spring has healing ingredients in it. I read that Indians used to walk all the way from South America to drink from this spring. You're lucky your cancer's in your kidney. You don't want to know where the water goes in the patients with cancer of the intestines."

Absently, the nurse ran her hand across the surface of the old oak desk. In a far corner someone had carved the words, "I love Jack."

Seeing the graffiti, Eva said, "I saw that yesterday. I wonder who Jack is?"

"I've often wondered the same thing," the nurse said. "This used to be a girl's school, and a hotel before that. I guess one of the students left a mystery for you. Exciting, don't you think? The center drawer doesn't open." Nurse Cavanaugh tugged at the handle. "The key was lost before the hospital moved in." She opened the side drawer and held up a dog-eared copy of *Gone with the Wind*. "I noticed that our last patient forgot his book. Maybe you'd like to read it. And here's a pencil someone left behind, in case you'd like to write something down." She headed for the door. "I'll be back in a little while to check on you."

Eva nodded and took another sip of coffee, which also helped rid her mouth of the aftertaste from the Baker Cure.

When her stomach settled, Eva drank the water, then stood up and slipped on the red and white silk kimono Edgar had brought her from Tokyo. She cracked the door open a few inches to watch the patients on the deck. A few sunned themselves from the comfort of their hospital beds. At the opposite end of the deck, two older men in wheelchairs played checkers. Over by the notorious guardrail sat a female patient in a wheelchair. Lined up next to her were a number of empty wicker patio chairs and the chaise lounge Eva had sat in last night. A few seats down, a couple of ladies chatted. From a distance everyone acted so casually Eva knew no one had jumped off the deck last night. Still, it seemed so real.

With the copy of *Gone with the Wind* in hand, Eva opened her side door and straightened her back as much as she could without the internal pitchforks gouging her insides. She headed for one of the available outer chairs. Everyone looked up from their respective conversations, books or games.

In the center of the deck stood a round table occupied by an interesting assortment of people playing the latest rage, Monopoly. A squirming six-year-old girl with blond pigtails had just bought the Reading Railroad. Like a good little miser, the young investor added her new deed to a healthy portfolio of earlier purchases.

"Now I own all of the railroads," the child announced with all the compassion of Ebenezer Scrooge. "If anyone lands there they'll have to pay me *two hundred dollars* in rent."

"Aren't you the little robber baron!" a female competitor said as she rolled the dice.

An older gentleman sitting next to the little girl carefully stroked his graying beard as he examined the Monopoly board. He put out his cigarette, looked up over his glasses, and stood when Eva walked up. He gave a little bow. "Janowitz," he said in a thick Polish accent. "Stephan Janowitz." He offered his hand.

He was in his fifties with graying temples, an advancing forehead where there had once been dark brown hair, and a slightly ragged salt and pepper beard. He wore a sweater with a hole that had been repaired with a slightly different shade of yarn. By the wear on his old black fedora, it had been a favorite of his for many years.

Eva returned the handshake, and nodded. "Eva Dupree."

"And 'dis entrepreneur is Trudy," Mr. Janowitz said.

"Hi, Trudy," Eva said.

Trudy was busy counting her Monopoly money.

"Trudy, say hello to Mrs. Dupree," Mr. Janowitz instructed.

Mr. Janowitz seemed like such a sweet man, and in a strange new land. She decided not to correct him about her title. Instead Eva smiled warmly.

Below her, the little girl played it shy, choosing to answer with a smile and a wave.

The woman playing the game offered to Eva, "Would you like to play in my place?"

"No, thank you," Eva said, easing over to the railing. "I've never been very good at making investment decisions. I think I'd just like to read." She held up the tattered book.

Eva took the vacant rocking chair, leaving an empty seat between herself and the lady in the wheelchair. The woman looked vaguely familiar. By the way the woman studied Eva's face, it was obvious the feeling was mutual.

Eva opened her novel.

"That's a good book." The woman was well-rounded—perhaps even bloated—and about fifteen years Eva's senior, with once-golden hair that had faded to an old newspaper yellow. "It's going to be an even better movie if they ever get the damn thing finished." She had a Boston accent. She was sunning herself in one of those fancy wheelchairs that could recline almost into a bed. "Clark Gable can carry me up to his bedroom any time."

She stuck her hand out toward Eva. "Mossell Knight."

Eva shook it. "Knight? A long time ago I worked with a director named Roger Knight."

"Yes, I thought I recognized you. Roger was my husband."

Their conversation broke off when a middle-aged gentleman strode out on the porch and sat down to the right of Mossell. He set aside his tools for tying fishing flies and shook Mossell's hand. "Good morning, Mrs. Knight. You're looking well today."

"And you, Mr. Reilly." She noticed the man staring at Eva, and finally said, "Miss Dupree, I want to you meet Cooper Reilly. He's here from San Diego, I believe. Mr. Reilly, this is Eva Dupree."

Cooper reached across Mossell to shake hands with Eva. He stopped mid-shake and his eyes widened as he studied her face and her slightly crooked smile. "Eva Dupree? The actress? Oh yes, I'd recognize those eyes anywhere."

"You've heard of me?"

"Heard of you?" He seemed to be taking in the texture and feel of her fingers. "I fell in love with you when I was a young man. I never thought I'd actually get to meet you."

"Oh." *When you were a young man,* Eva thought. Her hand stiffened in his. She put on that noncommittal smile reserved for fans who had the uncanny ability of saying all the wrong things.

"I'm afraid that came out wrong." Cooper stumbled over his words. "When I was a young man, you were hardly more than a girl. You haven't changed at all. Forgive me. I'm afraid my words simply aren't coming out right."

Though a handsome man, he momentarily seemed as awkward as a teenage boy asking a girl out for the first time. Still, his Howard Hughes mustache, dark hair and graying temples gave him an air of sophistication that reminded Eva a little of Edgar ten years ago. He wore a class ring from University of California, Davis.

"I can't believe after all these years that I'd meet you in an out-of-the-way place like Eureka Springs," Cooper went on.

Eva smiled self-consciously, easing her hand from his grasp. "It's been a while since I've made hearts spin, Mr. Reilly. I haven't appeared in a picture in years."

"Only ten years, Gumdrop," Mossell said tartly. Then she turned to Cooper and warned, "Be careful, Mr. Reilly, she can hypnotize you with those eyes."

"Too late," he said to Mossell, and turned to Eva to finish his answer. "She already has."

Mossell patted his hand as it returned to his side. "Puddin', all the men loved her. Believe me, I know."

Ignoring the older woman in the wheelchair, he continued, "I couldn't believe you stopped making movies. Maybe you should get back into it."

Eva touched her wedding band. "I'm afraid I've lost all my contacts."

"I know some people," Cooper offered. "Maybe after you get out of here you might consider returning to the screen."

Mossell rolled her eyes and asked Eva's admirer, "What are you here for, Mr. Reilly?"

"Nerves, I'm afraid. I just needed to get away for a while." He removed a pack of Lucky Strike cigarettes from his coat pocket, thumped it against his hand and pulled one out with his lips.

"Hey, Cooper, got a snipe for a lady? I'm dying here," Mossell asked.

Like a gentleman, Cooper offered her a smoke and lit it with his Zippo lighter. He had some sort of insignia engraved on it, but Eva couldn't make it out.

Mossell closed her eyes and blew the smoke out of her nose, looking like a Chinese parade dragon. "Ah, that's better."

A few feet away at the Monopoly table, the game was in the process of disintegrating. The little girl arranged all the cards face up before returning the property deeds to the game box. In a few moments the woman who had already liquidated all her Monopoly properties sat down in the empty seat between Mossell and Eva.

"I want you to meet Gazetta Smith," Mossell said. "This is Eva Dupree."

Eva and Gazetta nodded. Cooper held his cigarette pack out toward Gazetta, offering her a smoke.

The Monopoly washout shook her head and pulled a pack of smokes out of her purse. "I only smoke Marlboros." She held the cigarette up to her lips waiting for Cooper to light it. "It's designed especially for ladies. See the red tip? Hides my lipstick."

"But, lambcakes, you aren't wearing any lipstick," Mossell observed.

Gazetta let the cigarette droop in her lips as she glared at Mossell.

"Eva, care for one?" Cooper held the pack in her direction.

Eva smiled. "Thanks, no." She coughed. "I had to quit about ten years ago."

Everyone settled back into their respective conversations when Trudy grabbed her Orphan Annie doll and ran up to Cooper, stumbling the last few steps. "Mr. Cooper, swing me."

"Are you sure?" he asked. "I don't want to hurt you again, Trudy."

"It's okay." The little girl held out her arms and showed him some fading yellow and purple bruises around her wrists. "My bruises are going away and I don't have any new ones. See?"

Cooper shook his head regretfully. "I don't want another tongue-lashing from Nurse Turner for hurting you."

The little girl grabbed his hand. "I know it won't hurt this time. Please, please, please? "

Cooper hesitated, then sighed. "All right, but let's try it a different way." Instead of picking her up by the arms, he scooped Trudy up like a large baby and swung her around three or four times. Then he set her down and winked at the other patients as he asked, "Trudy, where is she?"

"Right here." She pointed at the empty space beside her. "Only he's not a girl."

"I thought your invisible friend's name was Catherine," Cooper said.

"She was, but she's not here anymore. I have a new friend now."

"Hi, young man," Cooper said, reaching down to shake the invisible hand of Trudy's imaginary friend. "He's a very handsome little boy."

Mossell whispered to Eva, "Isn't she a cute little girl? Trudy's always got a new invisible friend. This is the third one since she came here a few weeks ago. I believe she forgets what she names them."

Eva watched the girl dance across the deck with her "friend." Despite her enthusiasm, her eyes betrayed her condition. Gray shadows encircled them. Her dance only lasted a minute or so before she flopped to the deck on an open blanket, played out.

Eva returned her attention to Mossell. "So, you're Roger's wife."

"*Was*, my dear. 'Was' being the operative word. But we both graduated from that university of mutual abuse. I got tired of all the starlets in his life and he got tired of me breaking bottles over his head. You were in his *Caught in a Web*, weren't you?"

"You have a good memory."

"Well, I was on the set while you were making the movie."

Mossell took a puff of her cigarette and blew out the smoke. "Roger's an S.O.B, but he's one helluva director for bad horror movies on a tight budget."

Eva nodded. "Yes...on both counts."

The restless pigtailed child lay on her blanket for a few minutes, then apparently refreshed, got up, wadded up her blanket and turned to her imaginary playmate, "Let's go have some tea, okay?" She waited a moment, cupped her ear as if hearing a secret and smiled. "Okay." She ambled up to Eva and Mossell and said, "We're going to have tea with the King of England and all the princesses and Orphan Annie." Then she looked directly at Eva. "You want to come with us? He says it's okay."

Eva brushed her fingers through Trudy's blond bangs. "I'm a little tired this morning. Maybe later."

"Okay." Looking at empty air, she shrugged her tiny shoulders, and then like a whirlwind in Mary Janes headed for the door to the hall.

Mossell took a last puff, stubbed out the cigarette on the arm of her chair, and flicked the butt out over the deck railing. "You married Edgar Foxworthy, didn't you?"

"Yes," Eva said quietly.

"How is Edgar?" Mossell wanted to know. "He was a decent sort."

Eva felt her throat tighten.

Mossell eyed her. "Oh, dear. Did I say something wrong?"

"Edgar died a couple of years ago."

Mossell's face fell. "I'm sorry! What a shame. I can think of someone a whole lot more deserving."

Eva pulled herself back together. "How's Roger?"

"Still living, dammit."

Eva laughed.

"Paying lots of alimony. And torturing his fifth wife. Poor thing. She still believes he's human. She'll find out what a skunk he is soon enough. You know the bastard left me because of the starlet in that movie *Caught in a Web*. They had a thing going."

Eva smiled weakly. She'd heard about rumors that she had been sleeping with Roger. She thought Roger himself probably started them because his ego couldn't stand being turned down.

Eva looked over at her deck door and saw a hint of Ivan's face in the window. He must have been standing on his hind feet because only his nose and eyes were visible.

She waited for a pause in the conversation and said, "I'll be right back." She left the door ajar, allowing the cat to venture out if he so desired. Ivan stood in the door, torn between venturing out onto the balcony and hiding under the bed.

By the time she returned to her chair, the conversation had moved on to more current topics. Eva laid her novel on her lap. The view from her own suite paled in comparison to the daytime vista of East Mountain from this section of the deck—not a treat normally afforded a hospital patient. But of course, this was not a typical hospital. In both his "Cancer Is Curable" booklet and his radio broadcasts, Norman Baker touted the vast differences between the Baker Hospital and a big city hospital. Not only was Norman Baker's treatment center in what had once been a luxury hotel, but patients were treated more like guests than sick people. There was no mandatory bed confinement. Unlike other medical centers, the Baker Hospital never boasted a modern operating room; in fact, no surgery ever occurred there. With the Baker Cure, surgery was never necessary.

Within a few moments, Eva felt something down at her feet. With the balcony empty except for Eva, Mossell, Cooper and a few others, Ivan had mustered the courage to venture out. He looked at the pine-filled valley and the tree-lined hospital grounds with pupils so dilated that the amber of his eyes appeared to vanish. Ivan held his nose up, his little nostrils quivering, testing the air. His ears twitched independently listening to the calls of black birds in the distance and the sharp chirping of a cardinal hidden in a tree near the balcony.

"Hello," Cooper said to the cat.

The cat froze mid-step, and gave Cooper an unblinking stare.

"Come here, fella." Cooper patted his leg, then wiggled his fingers provocatively.

Ivan didn't show his paw too quickly. He waited a few seconds before easing over to his new admirer, sniffing Cooper's fingers from a safe distance. Cooper leaned forward, running his hand through the cat's coat. A hand full of cottony fur clung to his fingers. Cooper held up his hand and let the fur waft away on the wind.

Embarrassed, Eva apologized as a puff of white cat fur drifted past her face. "Sorry about that. With everything that's been happening, the maid hasn't had an opportunity to comb him in the last few days."

"That's no problem." Cooper shook his hand to release the last few strands into the breeze. "If the hospital runs out of cotton he could make a contribution."

Ivan responded by bumping his head against Cooper's ankle.

Mossell eyed Ivan suspiciously. "I've never seen a cat at a hospital before."

"I convinced Dr. Baker I would only keep him in the health spa." Eva rubbed her thumb against her middle and forefinger implying an exchange of money. "Edgar found the kitten in a garbage can while he was on a trip to the Middle East shortly before he passed away. I promised I'd take care of Ivan for him." She watched as Cooper massaged the cat's chin. "I keep my promises," she added unenthusiastically.

Ivan's interest in Cooper quickly faded. He trotted off to monitor some pigeons sitting on the iron guardrail.

From her seat two chairs away Gazetta's attention switched from the cat to Eva. She stared at Eva's face as if trying to memorize a 'wanted' poster. "You look very familiar. I'm trying to remember, have we met?"

"I don't think so." Eva hated being *almost* recognized.

"Yes, but I know I've seen you before." Gazetta's stare could have bored a hole in wood. "I remember: You used to be in movies, weren't you?"

Eva shrugged. *Here it comes.*

"You were in those silly horror movies, always sucking blood or being sacrificed or something." With silent movie melodrama Gazetta shielded her jugular vein with her palm. "The movies about ghosts were the scariest. Do you believe in spooks?"

Eva gave her a polite smile. "No, Mrs. Smith, ghosts are a figment of Hollywood imagination."

Mossell followed the exchange with amusement. She leaned her head in Gazetta's direction and said, "She used to work with my ex-husband."

"Oooh."

Somehow, thankfully, that explained it all...until Gazetta asked, "Did you and Roger have nookie? It seems all the women have."

Eva stared at her for a moment before realizing that all eyes were focused on her. Eva's lips formed a nervous smile. "I was happily married, and have much better taste in men than Mossell." After the words escaped her mouth, Eva wished she had not sounded so sharp.

"Touché, gumdrop," Mossell said with an indifferent smile. "Touché." But she maintained challenging eye contact for a few seconds more.

Eva broke Mossell's stare and asked Gazetta, "Mrs. Smith, how long have you been here?"

"About six weeks." Gazetta ran her hand through her hair, which looked like steel wool piled carelessly atop her head. "I was so sick when I got here." She leaned over to Eva and whispered so Cooper couldn't hear, "I had female cancer. I was starting to look pregnant. Look at me now. I can't wait to get home to my children." She bit a hangnail. "To tell the truth, I didn't think I would ever go home. I could barely walk when I got here. Mr. Baker's a miracle worker."

"That's comforting to hear," Eva said. "I hope I have the same outcome."

"You will. I can feel it," Gazetta pronounced.

"Oh, so you're a psychic?" Mossell piped in.

"Let's just say I have a sense about some things," Gazetta said. "Like the ghost in my Aunt Alice's outhouse; I was the only one who knew it was there. It was creepy sitting on the throne and hearing moaning."

Mossell winked. "That sounds like my ex-husband, only it was really more like grunt, groan, sigh. There were other scary sound effects, but you don't want to hear about them."

They all laughed.

Nearby Ivan jumped to full alert at the sound of a swallow's wings. In a blur of motion, Ivan leapt several feet in the air. At the apex of his leap, he left behind a small cloud of feathers settling slowly onto the deck. His quarry may have escaped, but he still had his minor trophy. All that remained of his observation deck safari was a single breast feather clinging to the moisture of his gums.

Cooper laughed. "Behold, the Mighty Hunter."

Eva laughed. If he could have spoken, the cat probably would have held his paws a foot apart and told the story of the big one that got away. Instead, Ivan bristled as the wind brushed his whiskers and focused on a pigeon landing only a few feet away from Eva's chair.

Eva scooped up the cat. "Come on, Mister. No squab for you today." She deposited him in her room, then returned to the other patients.

The door at the other end of the deck opened and a dapper

gentleman in his late sixties appeared. The scattered conversations stopped, and all eyes followed the newcomer.

Dressed in a hospital–white business suit, the man stopped to speak with the two checkers players. He leaned over to shake their hands, nodding his head back and forth as they spoke.

"Who's he?" Eva whispered to the group.

"That's Norman Baker," Gazetta whispered back. "See his shirt. He always wears purple. *Always.* Once he even wore a purple suit and white shirt." She placed her hand over her mouth and tittered.

Eva's medical messiah was not at all as Eva had pictured him. She imagined a towering, muscular type, with dignified graying hair in a white doctor's smock. While she got the white attire right, she missed the other Baker details. Since all the patients were sitting, she couldn't begin to guess his height, but he was certainly shorter than most men. His trademark attire consisted of a purple imported silk shirt and a lavender silk necktie with purple and red swirls. In some ways he resembled a bald eagle: his aquiline nose, white hair, deep set piercing blue eyes hidden behind wire-rimmed glasses, and wide thin lips that spoke "the naked truth" to thousands, tens of thousands, even hundreds of thousands of radio listeners.

Baker stopped and spoke to each patient as he worked the deck like a host at his party. Eventually he made his way to Eva's group.

"Good morning, ladies," Baker nodded at each of the women. "Mr. Reilly." Baker extended his hand, but instead of returning the handshake, Cooper waved briefly with the hand holding a pair of pliers. He had set up his fly-tying rig and his hands were occupied manipulating feathers and thread.

"Dr. Baker, have you met Eva Dupree?" Gazetta asked.

He reached out his hand. "Not in person." Norman Baker's cognac-smooth voice greeted her. "I heard that you arrived late yesterday. Welcome to the Baker Hospital." After a brief, all-business exchange, he released her hand.

"She used to be a famous movie star," Gazetta interjected.

Eva smiled and let out a long sigh. *Damn.*

Mossell looked at Gazetta, and shared a sly grin. All eyes returned to Eva and Norman Baker.

"You have remained as lovely as I remember you on screen."

Eva lowered her eyes. "You lie very well, Dr. Baker. You could have been quite an actor had you not gone into medicine."

"Don't let her suck your blood, Dr. Baker," Gazetta teased.

A master of diversion, Eva said, "I noticed a grand piano down in the lobby. Can the patients play it? I'm a bit rusty and certainly could stand to practice."

A broad smile played on Baker's thin lips. "I didn't know you played piano."

"Organ, really. I play the pipe organ at St. Michael's in Dallas."

"We can certainly do better than an out-of-tune baby grand. If you feel up to it, come upstairs with me. I'd like to show you my instrument."

Gazetta almost rammed her elbow through Mossell's ribcage and snickered, "I bet she's heard that one plenty of times."

Mossell cried out and winced from the punch, but nodded in agreement.

Bitch. Eva ignored the verbal jab and nodded at Baker with a smile.

"Excuse us, will you?" Baker said to the other seated patients.

He reached down, offering Eva a stabilizing hand. Accepting the help, Eva struggled to her feet. As she did, those internal pitchforks jabbed her insides with such ferocity that she couldn't breathe. Between the pain and her lack of balance, she squeezed Baker's hand with such intensity Eva almost expected to hear his bones snap. She knew her grip had to hurt, but he never let on. Baker's pleasant smile never wavered.

Once she stood upright and steady, Eva glanced at the chair she'd occupied last night. The light of day had chased away most of the eerie feelings, but she still couldn't help but wonder what had really happened. "Could we wait just a moment?" She eased over to the railing and looked down.

"It's a beautiful view, isn't it?" Baker said.

She gave an obligatory glance out at the horizon. "Yes. Beautiful." But she examined the pavement beneath them. No indentions. No pesky, inexplicable bloodstains. No trampled flowers, and no dead body.

As he led her to the public door, Eva glanced back one more time, and could almost see the girl balancing precariously on the railing. She shuddered, then stepped into the hall.

"It's a Calliaphone," Baker said.

"What is?"

"My instrument. It's called a Tangley Calliaphone."

"Calliope?" She was still focused on the suicidal girl.

"Calliaphone," he corrected her. "I'll show you." He held her hand and led her to a locked staircase near the elevator. He took her elbow to steady her as they climbed the private staircase slowly, a few steps at a time until they reached another locked door. The highest point in the hospital was an open air turret on the roof in the center of the building.

Baker held the door and motioned her ahead with his free hand. She'd only taken a step or two when someone shoved a machine gun muzzle in her face. She gasped and froze. Wielding the weapon was a very tall, muscular man with arms the thickness of tree limbs, looking much the part of Al Capone. Once again she felt as if she were playing out a scene in a movie, except the reflection of the sun gleaming off the gun barrel hinted that this was not a prop, and she'd bet the bullets weren't blanks, either. Instinctively she kept her hands very still. The man looked past Eva to the hospital owner and his demeanor instantly switched from class bully to naughty boy sweating it out in the principal's office.

"I'm sorry, Mr. Baker," the armed man said in a gravelly voice. "I didn't realize it was you." He quickly disappeared up another flight of stairs.

When Eva didn't move, Baker placed his arm around her shoulders and led her away from the door. "I'm sorry. He's one of my guards," Baker explained. "I have a lot of influential people here at any given time. Right now, we are treating a prince from Sweden. They asked us to step up our security."

"Where'd he go?"

"He's heading back to the roof." Mr. Baker led her to the brattice, an open structure that looked like a belfry or a gazebo. In the middle of the open room stood something that resembled a big fire engine red pipe organ, but not exactly. A brass nameplate bore the words, "Tangley Company of Muscatine, Iowa." Another plate further claimed that, "Tangley is the World's Largest Calliope and Calliaphone Builder."

Eva ran her left hand across the red case. Her other hand was busy counting the brass pipes.

"This is my Calliaphone," he said proudly as if he were introducing his first born.

She smiled. "You own it?"

"I invented it."

Recalling the radio in her room, she thought, *Ah, Tangley is his company.*

She pressed one of the silent keys slowly, and then again, but more quickly to get a feel for the keyboard action.

Baker turned on the Calliaphone's electric compressor and allowed the pressure to build. "All right. You're ready to play."

Within a few moments Eva treated the entire valley to the elegant notes of Beethoven surrealistically played on an air-driven calliope.

"This is wonderful," Baker cupped his hand and shouted to her. The instrument almost completely drowned out his voice. "This is the first time a professional musician has played here."

"What?" Eva shouted back, barely audible over the circus clown rendition of the classic "Ode to Joy."

"The town is going to love this. You can hear the Calliaphone for miles!" Then he shouted, "Miss Dupree, do you feel up to eating dinner with me this evening in my penthouse?"

"I'd like that very much." Perhaps if she plied him with liquor she might learn more about what she'd seen the night before and why she'd seen it.

"Wonderful. My penthouse is directly above your suite. Come by at six."

Rose Freeman set down her tattered tweed suitcase. The leather corners wore the scars of many a trip she had taken accompanying Mr. Edgar and Miss Eva on their world travels. She eyed the scuffs and drew a deep breath. She had a lot in common with that old suitcase. It had been a decade since either of them had gone someplace fun, and the miles they'd both traveled were really starting to show.

Eva Dupree's maid was a short, robust woman with sable skin and eyes as dark as onyx. Well into her forties, her hair was sprinkled with more white than black. She wore it pulled up into a ponytail wound into a bun.

Yesterday, before sunrise, Miss Eva climbed aboard a sleeper car bound for the hospital in the Ozarks Mountains. Staying behind, Rose spent the day packing Miss Eva's two remaining travel trunks with everything a grand lady would need for next month, the period she'd planned to stay at the Baker Hospital. There were all sorts of piddling things Rose had to do around the house like clean out the refrigerator, stop the newspaper, and pay the neighbor boy in advance to tend the lawn and water Miss Eva's rose garden. Then late last night, Rose took a taxi to the train terminal.

After a thirteen hour ride, Rose arrived in Eureka Springs. Hospital employees picked up Miss Eva's trunks from the train station, while Rose located a place to stay. *Easier said than done.* Rose was having a dickens of a time finding a place to stay.

She rubbed her wrist. Packed in that suitcase were all of Rose's worldly possessions, at least for this trip: four cotton dresses—pressed, of course, four pairs of white cotton panties—large, a brassiere—D cup, four pairs of socks, a tin of Lucky Brown Negro Hair Pressing Oil, and a brilliant red silk hair ribbon from China that Mr. Edgar had given her for her birthday the year he died.

Her hand felt like it was being pulled off at the wrist as she lugged her suitcase and her canvas tote bag around hilly Eureka Springs. Although her rheumatism hadn't given her much trouble before now, her knuckles throbbed with a dull constant ache that felt as though her forty-six year old joints had been set afire and left to smolder. A modern-day beast of burden, she clutched a small red Persian rug under her left armpit and struggled to keep her heavy purse stable in the crook of her right arm.

She set her burdens down and flexed her fingers. *I'm getting too old for this sort of thing.*

At her age, she ought to be able to keep the house straight and cook the meals. Period. World travel was a little more than she bargained for.

But then, you do what you have to. Miss Eva needed her, now. Ivan needed her. For once in her life, it seemed everyone needed her. It was a burden she didn't want, but a responsibility she would honor.

Rose sighed and picked up her luggage. She followed the path back down the street.

Soon she would be able to sit down, at least for a little while.

The limestone blocks that paved the sidewalks in Eureka Springs came from the side of a nearby mountain, so she had been told. The frequent rainstorms had worn indentions and holes in the stones. It gave the walks a beautiful rustic look, not unlike Miss Eva's flower rock garden. But those same indentions made the walk uneven and, in some places, downright treacherous.

Rose entered the Wadsworth Hotel. Before she could ask for a room the clerk said, "We don't have any vacancies." That seemed to be the standard answer.

Rose shuffled back down the uneven steps to the street, yet again. It was getting late. She was hungry and at the hospital poor Ivan probably needed to have his facilities spruced up.

"Hey, you," a woman's voice called from behind her. "Hey, wait." A chubby white woman about her own age waddled up to her waving her hand in a friendly gesture.

Again, the maid set down her baggage and turned to face the woman. She had a kind face, although well-tanned and weathered.

"Look, I don't want to meddle, I happened to overhear what the manager said at that hotel. The Congress Hotel is the only one in town that welcomes colored folk. They have a colored section in the back. If they're full, there's a Negro family that lives on Montgomery Street. Andy's the elevator operator at the hospital. His wife, Zola Mae, cleans my house. They're a nice family. They might be able to put you up for a while, especially if you can pay them a little something. They've been visited by some hard times."

The woman drew a crude map on the back of an old envelope with a dull pencil she'd pulled out of her purse.

Beneath her fatigue Rose smiled faintly. "Thank you, kindly." She hoisted up her bags and moved in the direction of the hotel.

Rose tried the Congress Hotel but all the colored-only rooms were already let. She made her way to the other place on the map. It really wasn't much more than a shack, but the roof looked solid and the yard had a well-groomed fall flowerbed with yellow and purple chrysanthemums, snapdragons and clusters of fading irises.

Rose knocked on the door to the house. A lean black woman in her mid-twenties answered the door. "Yes?"

"I'm Rose Freeman from Dallas. I'm looking for a place to stay. Do you have a room to rent? I can pay seventy-five cents a day."

"Seventy-five cents?"

Rose nodded.

The young woman opened the screen door and invited her in. "I can't rent you a whole room, but you can stay in the room with my daughter and son. I'm Zola Mae."

Rose looked around the house. It was nothing fancy. Not nearly as well-furnished as her own modest house in Dallas, but it was clean and smelled of red beans simmering on the stove.

"I'll still pay seventy-five cents."

"Really?" Zola Mae smiled.

Rose set her bags on the floor and began rummaging through her purse. Holding her hand out, she held up a quarter and half dollar. "I'll pay you the first night, upfront."

The woman's eye widened. She took the coins and slipped them in her pocket. "For seventy five cents, I'll include dinner. Would you like some bean soup?"

"That'd be mighty fine."

Rose stepped down from the electric trolley car and moved slowly across the parking lot toward the rear entrance of the Baker Hospital and Health Resort. In addition to her purse she carried a large canvas tote bag. With each step, her bag made a metallic clink.

She shifted her load, and angled away from a concrete island covered with bloomed out irises. Amidst the green leaves stood a small-scale facsimile of the Statue of Liberty. The faux Eiffel statue greeted patients arriving at the hospital the same way the Ellis Island icon received newcomers to the New World.

Rose snorted. "Liberty, my hiney."

She took a last look at Lady Liberty before she scaled the concrete stairs.

When she opened the hospital door, Rose noticed the waiting area smelled more like a hotel than a hospital, with the aroma of spices and simmering food wafting from a nearby kitchen.

Setting her heavy canvas burden on the floor, she drew a deep breath and dabbed the perspiration trickling down the side of her face. Her eyebrows lifted as she scanned the room.

Over the arched main entrance on the opposite side of the great room hung a sign that read, "Quacks are those who do things enemies can't do."

Huh?

Rose rushed out of the way as a nurse scurried past her pushing a patient in a wheelchair. The woman, garbed in pristine white, stood out against walls of purple. The Baker Hospital didn't have that sterile, stark appearance other hospitals had. It certainly seemed like a more inviting and personal place.

The entire lobby was washed in brilliant circus colors of purple and lavender. The interior had a carnival atmosphere, except for the high ceilings and suites of elegant furniture that looked out of place.

"My, my," Rose said to herself. "Someone must have bought a paint store."

She stowed her hankie back in the side pocket of her cowhide leather purse. Weighted down with personal necessities she'd need during her long stay, it felt as though she was lugging around an entire cow.

Rose approached the admissions desk; it looked like a typical hotel check-in, but instead of dark stained wood, it too was painted purple. Natural pink marble insets broke up the large spaces of rich color. Spanning to the ceiling, the lobby support columns were colored in shades of purple and lavender. Even the thigh-high ashtrays wore that same streaking. However, high above, the ceiling still showed bare, natural wood.

The receptionist, also dressed in medical white sans the nurse's cap, looked up at Rose. "Yes?"

"Where is Miss Eva Dupree's room?" Rose asked.

The woman flipped through a bunch of pages bound together with brass brads. "She's staying in four-nineteen. Take the back staircase at the end of this hall just before the dining room. Go all the way up. It's on the fourth floor at the far end of that hall."

Rose nodded as she mentally jotted down the directions. "Thank you, kindly." Her aging muscles protested as she picked up her bags and made her way to the stairs. Naturally, Rose had been directed to the side stairway, not the formal staircase. Holding her purse in one hand and large canvas tote bag in the other, she scaled the steps to the fourth floor. Between the clanking metal, the squeaky stairs and Rose's occasional groaning, her ascent sounded like a one-maid band.

She found room four-nineteen just as the receptionist had directed. She paused for a moment, assumed her happy face, then gave the door a polite knock.

"Come in," Eva called listlessly through the door.

When Eva recognized Rose, the actress' face came to life. "Rose, come in! Come in."

Rose closed the door behind her, and gazed around the room. "Oooohh, Miss Eva! Ain't this fancy!"

Miss Eva sat up in bed wearing her pink silk nightgown and, naturally a matching silk robe. She didn't look like the pathetic thing Rose had put on the train yesterday.

For the moment Miss Eva could have been one of the women she had portrayed so many times on the silent screen, beautiful and at times a little helpless.

In the past Rose would have said, "Helpless, my foot." But

since Eva's pains began a month ago, she had appeared less and less Eva-the-"helpless" actress, and more Eva, a woman frightened by approaching death.

Rose dropped the rug roll and her heavy bags on the floor with a loud wooden clunk. "How you're feelin'?"

"Like I have *some* hope," Eva said from her bed. "But I'm still so scared. I'm so glad you're here, Rose."

Ivan jumped down from the bed and trotted over to the maid, rubbing his side against Rose's ankles, depositing white hairs on her black socks. He meowed loudly, insistently.

Smiling, Rose squatted down and gave him a gentle scratch under his chin. "You hungry, boy? I imagine you hate that canned cat food, don't you?" She looked up at her boss. "Where are Master Ivan's dining facilities?"

"In the bathroom, so it's easier to clean up after him."

Rose glanced in the direction of the bathroom, then back at the cat. She pulled a can of Kit-E-Ration cat food and a silver-plated soup spoon from the bag and said, "Sorry, boy. The pickings are a little slim today. I'll make it up to you tomorrow."

She walked into the bathroom and quickly came back out. "Oh my. He's really made a mess in here, hasn't he?"

"I tried to scoop," Eva apologized, "but when I bent over, I felt like someone was gutting me with a hunting knife."

"Don't you worry, Miss Eva. I'll manage it. You rest."

After dishing out the cat's dinner, Rose pulled a few more cans of "the supreme cat food" from her tote and said, "I'll put the extra cans and the can opener in the top drawer of dresser just in case you need to feed him when I'm not around."

"Ivan thanks you."

"Of course, he does." She closed her eyes for a long moment.

"Rose." Eva motioned to the chair next to the desk. "Sit down. You must be exhausted."

"Miss Eva, you have a gift for understatement." Rose dropped into the chair.

"If you want to smoke, go ahead," Miss Eva offered.

"Thank you kindly." Rose retrieved a pack of cigarettes and her lighter from her purse, then scooted the oak chair near her employer's bed. She lit the Kool, closed her eyes and inhaled deeply. After a long exhale, Rose opened her eyes and stared at the slender sterling silver lighter in her hand. The corners of her mouth crept up sadly.

Her initials 'RLF' were engraved longways in fancy scrolling script—a gift from Mr. Edgar and Miss Eva for her twentieth anniversary in their employ.

Rose took another puff. "I brought you something." She leaned toward Miss Eva's bed to pass along a thin newspaper that had been previously read, then folded into a quarter-length. "I know you like to stay up on what's happening in the world."

"*The Daily Times-Echo.* How thoughtful."

"They didn't have the *Dallas Times Herald.* It was the best I could do."

"That's okay, thanks." Miss Eva unfolded the paper. The above-the-fold headline read, "Funeral Home Buys Crematorium."

"I'm afraid it's a tad short of news unless you consider the opening of a funeral parlor a news flash," Rose observed. She rummaged through her canvas sack and handed Eva a book. "In case that doesn't satisfy your need to know, I brought you a book. Here."

Eagerly Miss Eva took it from the maid. Her obvious excitement dimmed, however, when she looked at the title: *A Practical Cat Book* by Ida Mellen.

"You brought me a book about cat care?"

"That book was written by the lady who worked with that puss on Mr. Edgar's movie *The Black Cat.* She sent it to him a couple of months ago. I guess she didn't know about his passing. Besides, Mr. Edgar would want you to know all about how to take care of Master Ivan properly. What if something happened to me? Or what if you fired me?"

"Don't be ridiculous." Eva dropped her arms and the book into her lap. "There's no way I could let you go. And if you even think about going to your great reward, I'll dock your pay."

"I'm no arithmetical genius, but half of not much is still not much."

Miss Eva's smile faded. "You know, if this treatment doesn't work, you'll be the one to take care of Ivan."

Rose stood up and dismissed her boss with a wave of the hand. "Don't you be talking foolish. Now, if you'll excuse me, *someone* needs a clean bathroom."

Eva forced a smile and returned her attention to the newspaper.

Rose inspected Ivan's toilet facilities. A white enamel baking pan had changed occupations and now, filled with muddy fireplace ashes, functioned exclusively as Ivan's sanitary pan. A few stray gray footprints managed to make it onto the white tiles, which Rose wiped up with a used bath towel. She emptied the sludge from the pan into the commode and rinsed the pan with hot water. When it was nice and dry, she untied the string securing a cardboard box she'd brought with her from the Brown's home and dumped a fresh load of ashes into the pan. Rose finished the process, as was her ritual, by placing the baking pan on the tiny Persian carpet.

Just out of arms' reach Ivan monitored the cleanup process. When Rose had finished tidying up, he immediately jumped in the pan and emptied his bladder.

She took a deep breath. *A woman's work is never finished.* Armed with a fry strainer, she scooped the newly soiled ashes and wiped the tile floor. She smiled. The crimson carpet displayed a new feline-inspired pattern: ashen paw prints.

When Rose emerged from the bathroom, she found Miss Eva, dozing, still holding the *Echo* in her limp fingers.

Quietly Rose hung up the clothes from Miss Eva's travel trunks and straightened up the room. Within a short time, everything seemed to be under control. With Miss Eva still sleeping, Rose slipped quietly out of room four-nineteen and shut the door behind her.

It was a few minutes before five o'clock. She had plenty of time before dinner. Eva turned on the Tangley radio on her nightstand. Within a few minutes, a deep-voiced announcer invited Eva to enjoy the lively tunes of the Viking Accordion Band. She absently listened to the music, tapping her foot to the rhythm. When she'd had more of the Vikings than she could take, she played with the dial until she could hear what she recognized as the *CBS World News Roundup*. She began applying her makeup about the same time the announcer returned from a commercial break. Things were heating up in Europe.

The newscaster said, "At approximately four-forty five a.m. some million and a half German troops invaded Poland along its seventeen-hundred-mile border with Germany."

Eva dropped her powder puff and stared at the cloth-covered speaker as if she expected the newscaster's face to appear. "Oh, no." She dashed out her private door to the deck, and blurted out to the assembled patients, "I just heard on the news that Germany has invaded Poland."

Stefan Janowitz's looked up from his book. "What did you say?"

"I hope we don't get into it," Gazetta said as she counted her crochet row. "Damn." She tore out two rows of stitches. "Those people over there are worse than a bunch of spoiled kids who need a good spanking. Besides, look at all our boys that died in the Great War. What a waste!"

Stefan ground out his cigarette in an ashtray, twisting so hard the stub crumbled. His voice cracked. "That madman! Can I listen to your radio?"

"Certainly." Eva opened her door wide, inviting him in. "Whoever wants to listen can come...as long as you don't mind my cat."

"I've never had a cat," Gazetta said merrily. "I've got a dog at home. A beagle. She is so loud sometimes I can't hear myself think."

Janowitz and Gazetta filed into Eva's room and left the door wide open.

Eva worked the tuner knob back and forth until she tuned into the sharpest reception, or at least the voice with the least static. When it sounded as clear as she could get it, she turned up the volume.

"...At five-forty five a.m. a German training ship anchored off Danzig fired the first shell, scoring a direct hit on a Polish ammunition dump."

Eva could hardly believe what she heard.

"Oh, Judyta!" Janowitz cried.

"Who's Judyta, Mr. Janowitz?" Eva asked gently.

"My wife."

Nurse Turner followed the blaring news show through the open balcony door to find Eva, Janowitz and Gazetta hovering over the radio.

"Miss Dupree, turn down the radio and please keep your door closed! You're disturbing the other patients."

Eva, with her hand over her mouth, turned from the radio to face the nurse. "Oh, it's so terrible. They say the war has started in Europe."

"It's none of our concern." Nurse Turner held Eva in her gaze. "Now turn it down."

For show Eva reduced the volume a little.

Nurse Turner's appearance had sent Gazetta back to the deck, but Mr. Janowitz hovered next to the door, hopeless. A tear trickled down his cheek and became trapped in his beard. "My poor little Judyta." He took a handkerchief from his pocket and blew his nose. He seemed to have aged twenty years in just a few moments. His shoulders slumped and his nose looked red and swollen from blowing. "I must go to my room and think," he said. "Mrs. Dupree, I don't have a radio in my room. Let me know if you hear anything."

"Of course. Your wife is there?" Eva asked.

He turned around to face her again. "Yes, my wife and my son." He pulled off his glasses and polished the lenses with his white cotton shirt, leaving a wrinkled spot just above the beltline. "I came ahead to America to make money so they could join me soon. Then I got sick. I wanted to bring them over, but in her last letter Judyta wanted me to come here and get well. Then I would be able to work and send them money for the boat passage."

Eva's eyes began to tear. "Mr. Janowitz, I'm having dinner with Dr. Baker this evening. I'm afraid I have to get dressed. Why don't you take the radio to your room? You can listen to it in private. I'll come get it later."

"That is most kind of you, Mrs. Dupree." He unplugged the radio and left with the cord trailing behind him like a tail.

Poor Mr. Janowitz. She understood all those emotions he was feeling.

She lay back on the fainting couch and took in a deep breath. The world was going from bad to worse. First Edgar died in her arms, then she found out she was terminally ill. The war that Edgar feared would happen had finally started, and now poor Mr. Janowitz had to worry about whether his family was still living.

She had not felt so helpless since that horrible night two years ago when she found Edgar on the floor fighting for breath. Rose had already left for the day. Somehow Eva managed to drag him to the Cadillac by herself.

Edgar gasped and clutched his chest as he lay on the front seat with his head on her lap.

"Take care of Ivan."

"Jonathon Edgar Foxworthy, you stop that! You're going to be fine."

His face drew up in a spasm of pain and he groaned. "Promise."

"I will."

She screeched up to St. Paul's Hospital and leaned on the horn. In seconds an orderly dressed in white charged through the swinging doors pushing a gurney. She followed the gurney through a set of double doors to a treatment room.

"I'm sorry." A nurse blocked her way. "You need to go over

there and fill out some forms," the nurse instructed. "When you're done, the waiting room is right over there. We'll come get you."

After she had finished the paperwork, Eva collapsed on the couch in the smoky waiting room. As she waited, she wrung her hands and inspected the lace trimming on her silk hanky. Edgar had bought her a whole box of the handkerchiefs, handmade by nuns in Austria. She blew her nose. Silly her! No need to worry. He'd be fine. He always had little aches and pains. And he was always fine.

Finally, the doctor walked into the waiting room and the nurse pointed to Eva. He wore a grim expression, and he shifted his eyes away from Eva.

The doctor sat down beside her. He explained a lot of things to Eva, but all she heard was, "I'm sorry Mrs. Foxworthy. We couldn't save him."

Those words felt like a fist to her gut. She looked helpless like a lost child. Her eyes were distant and uncomprehending.

When she could finally speak, she told the doctor, "Edgar's got to be all right. He's got to feed the cat."

After the doctor rushed off to handle another emergency, a nurse sat down beside Eva and handed her a glass of water.

While even today Eva couldn't believe Edgar's last words were about that damn cat, she had made a promise. And this week, when she was ready to give up, her words "I will," haunted her. She had promised him "I will" twice—once on the day she and Edgar married, and at the last moment of his life. She never dreamed that her final, frustrating promise to Edgar would make her want to fight for *her* life.

The mountain cast long shadows as Eva slipped into the brocade gown that nipped and tucked in all the right places, giving her just the right *je ne sais quoi*. The cobalt floral dress had always been one of her favorites. Its intense blue turned her eyes the most soulful shade of jade. Now all she needed was a delicate stone around her throat, gilding the lily.

Her life up until recently had been all about illusion. Tonight was no different. Although she really didn't want to impress Norman Baker romantically, slipping into something a little *less* comfortable and hiding behind a façade of makeup gave her the illusion of control, and—she gazed at the alluring face in the mirror—health. Movie magic at its best. Well before midnight, the illusion would fade. She would exchange the brocade gown for a hospital gown and, with her makeup removed, the dark circles would return to her eyes.

Eva glanced at her watch as she stepped into the hall and locked the door to her suite. She had five minutes or so to kill before making her grand entrance, so she decided to take in the sunset. She headed to the west end of the hall, wading through splashes of red and gold light seeping through openings in the heavy velvet drapes. Two rocking chairs had been placed next to the window, perfect for lounging and soaking in the healing warmth of the afternoon sun. The large single-hung window revealed the front of the hospital, the parking lot and a thicket beyond.

Facing the window, a seventy-something woman knitted in cadence with the purple wicker rocker moving back and forth. A pattern of age spots dotted the woman's sagging skin, and she'd pinned a pile of yellow-gray hair on top of her head in an out-of-date Gibson Girl bun. With her free needle, she counted her purls. The old woman smelled like Mentholatum. Under her breath, the woman hummed a doleful melody, a series of runs in B minor. Though familiar, Eva couldn't quite recall the title of the tune. Beside the knitter, the second rocking chair sat vacant.

"Do you mind if I share your window for a moment?"

"My friend is sitting there." The woman's voice wavered as she spoke. When she noticed Eva eyeing the empty seat, she added, "She'll be back soon." She returned her focus to her knitting needles, and counted the same row of stitches two or three times. Satisfied that the stitches were correct, she started a new row, knitting as if by instinct. In a few moments she resumed her humming.

Eva gazed out the window into the parking lot below. Black Cadillacs, Fords and Chevrolets filled a third of the spaces. The rest were empty, except for one car parked well away from the others: a gleaming sports car with an orchid paint job. In Hollywood Eva had seen Rolls Royces, Bentleys and Mercedes, but nothing that looked like this futuristic luxury car. It might have been used as a prop in the 1926 science fiction thriller, *Metropolis*. The stretched body and large exhaust tube bespoke, or at least implied, speed, as did the whitewall tires and dog dish hubcaps. It had no radiator grille as such, but rather a series of chrome-accented horizontal slats wrapping around the sides of the hood.

With a lavender paint job to match the hospital décor, Eva had no doubts about the car's owner. It stood out like royalty amid peasants. Edgar would have loved it.

Ignoring the old woman's disapproving stare, Eva eased between the vacant chair and the window. "I just want to stand here and enjoy this view for a moment." Looking down, Eva spied the trolley stop, where an electric train car paused momentarily to unload passengers. Rose would be back soon, hopefully with Eva's shopping requests.

Nearby, a few fall hold-out blooms graced a chain of once-colorful rock-lined flower beds. Above the faded garden, a mixture of pine trees and yellow-tinged oaks surrounded the hospital grounds. Beyond the trees, hues of crimson and coral lit up the sky. This was the Magic Hour; movie directors and cameramen love the few minutes right before and after sunset (and sunrise) when the light is softer and warmer in hue, shadows are longer and the women are more beautiful.

Behind her, the old woman provided the musical score as she resumed humming softly. Listening closely to the song, Eva finally identified it—one of the more pleasant passages of Chopin's Piano Sonata No. 2 in B-flat minor. Most people instantly recognized the introductory bars of the third movement as Chopin's Funeral March. Eva knew the more obscure sections because she had recently played the sonata at the funeral of one of Dallas' past mayors. She'd also heard the stereotypical four notes—dun, da dunnn, dunnnnnn—the first time she'd heard Norman Baker's voice on the radio, a voice that countless thousands tuned in to hear "the naked truth."

It was the same day she found out about her cancer. She'd thumbed through a pamphlet she'd found in the wastebasket at Dr. Setzer's office. That evening she searched the dial for the radio station mentioned in the brochure.

"It's the bottom of the eight o'clock hour," the announcer interrupted a cheerful string performance, "and you're tuned in to XENT, nine-ten kilocycles in Nuevo Laredo."

Heavy organ music, Chopin's famous dirge, followed the station identification. The music faded and canaries began to whistle and warble over the airwaves. "Hello folks," said a smooth voice.

Eva moved her hand away from the dial. "I'm Norman Baker. You know it, and I know it. You can't sleep soundly knowing you may have cancer. It can eat the life right out of you. I have the cure, the only cure for cancer. Come to me...come to me. Let me save your life."

He paused, for theatrical effect, then continued, "Patients may live at the hospital and health resort or in private homes and hotels. The cost of treatments depends upon the severity of the case. Come to the Baker Hospital in Eureka Springs, Arkansas, where sick folks get well. Call me tonight at 2221. I'll make arrangements for you personally."

That night Eva made the call and prayed to God Norman Baker was a man of his word.

A few moments passed in silence before Eva glanced back at the older woman. "Have you been here long?"

The old woman's lips pressed into a grimmer frown. She might as well have said, "The new ones were always so impertinent."

Eva cringed at her *faux pas*. Of course, asking a total stranger about her slow, painful death was in no way socially acceptable. "This time I've been here two weeks. I was here last year for a month and a half. They said I was cured, but the cancer came back. They're treating me for free, just like they said they would do in that book, *The Baker Cure*. You look familiar. You were here last year too, weren't you?"

"No, I only arrived yesterday." She hesitated. "My name's Eva."

The woman stopped knitting and said, "Ruth Harrington."

"That's odd," Eva said.

The lady looked up from her needles and gazed at Eva over the top of her glasses. "What's odd?"

"The chair seems to be rocking on its own," Eva observed.

Ruth glanced sideways at the chair. "Must be a breeze," she said with a knowing smile, then returned to her knitting.

"Must be." Eva looked down at her watch. Her time was up and she didn't want to be late for her dinner with Baker. Eva turned around and headed back down the hall, calling over her shoulder, "It was nice meeting you. Have a good evening, Mrs. Harrington."

"Evening," Ruth grumbled without looking up.

Eva passed her own suite, then paused at the unlocked door to Baker's private staircase. She slipped off her shoes. If she had to walk up that long, steep flight of stairs to the penthouse, she was going to do it without her stiletto heels.

She'd read in the brochure that contemporary engineers deemed the Crescent Hotel to be an architectural wonder when its doors first opened in 1886. Before the town of Eureka Springs even had electricity, the hotel pampered its guests with electric Edison lamps, electric bells and a state-of-the-art hydraulic elevator.

You'd think that the architects of the luxury hotel would have installed a lift to the owner's fifth floor penthouse. Holding her shoes in one hand and pressing her aching back with the other, Eva climbed the stairs, stopping for a moment after each step. At the landing in front of Baker's door, she paused to put her shoes on and pulled on lace-trimmed white gloves. She hesitated before knocking.

She wondered what he'd be like. Would he be a gentleman or an octopus? It had been more than twenty years since she'd been out with a man who wasn't her husband. This wasn't a date—or was it? She smiled. She probably didn't have to worry about a guy who had such an affinity for purple.

Eva took a deep breath, then tapped at the door. Norman Baker answered almost immediately. He must have been impressive when he was younger, with his prominent nose and a wide mouth with thin lips. His alabaster hair reminded her of a snowy mountain top. Striking lapis eyes hid behind round wire frames.

He had changed clothes. This time he wore a crisp lavender suit (probably European), with a white shirt (most likely French), and a dark purple silk tie (possibly Italian). In place of a tie tack he wore a gold horseshoe pin inlaid with diamonds. Baker wore it upside down—with the ends facing down, so luck would drain out. *Perhaps,* Eva thought, *in Eureka Springs he had found something more and he didn't need luck.*

"Come in," he said, then, "I have a couple of friends I'd like you to meet. Bruno, Bertha, come down here."

"Do you have children?" she asked.

"In a sense."

Thundering down a set of stairs from an upper floor came two small horses—well, Great Danes, but they were almost the size of horses. The female wore a brown coat with a dark, thoughtful face and short, military-cropped ears. The male had a white and brindle coat, a hodgepodge of light and dark browns as well as white. He had one brown eye and one blue eye.

"They're beautiful," she said. "Are they friendly?"

"When I tell them to be." He tousled the female's head. "Sit." Both dogs promptly assumed an alert sitting position. They looked up to Baker for further instructions. "This is Miss Dupree. Bruno, say hello."

Bruno, with his eyes still glued to Baker, lifted his front leg as if to shake hands. The paw covered Eva's whole palm and fingers. "They're huge! How big are they?"

"Bruno weighs almost two hundred pounds; Bertha is only a hundred-thirty."

Eva looked at the wood floor. "Well, that certainly explains all the commotion above my ceiling."

Baker placed his hand on Eva's back, and guided her into the room. The dogs shadowed each step. "I'm sorry. I hope we don't disturb you."

"It's a bit noisy in the morning. But they stay quiet most of the day. Although they do seem to get excited every now and then."

"I'm glad they settle after I go down to my main office downstairs," Baker said. "They always look forward to my houseboy taking them out for romps throughout the day."

Bruno closed his eyes and yawned wide.

Eva stroked Bertha's head as she stared at the male's aperture. *What enormous jaws!*

Baker patted Bruno on the shoulders. "They're actually very gentle for their size, but I do have them for protection."

She looked around cautiously, expecting to see another black-clad thug wielding a Tommy gun. "Dr. Baker, who do you need protection from?"

He motioned her over to the couch that gave her a fading view of East Mountain.

"Please, it's *Mr.* Baker. I'm not an M.D.—I'm afraid the American Meatcutters' Association and I aren't on very good terms."

"Mr. Baker, all right. You need protection from the A.M.A.?"

"Of course. They're afraid I'm going to put them out of business. Someday I will."

Nodding in agreement, she said, "If all doctors treat their patients the way mine did, they should be."

She looked around the room. Baker's penthouse looked smaller than she had expected. Like the rest of the hospital, he'd painted his quarters in shades of lavender and violet. Along the west wall was a small, disused kitchen. A series of picture windows facing the east provided a spectacular view of the mountains and the town—even more breathtaking than the view from her room because of the higher elevation.

As they sat down on the couch, he continued, "The A.M.A. resents my success with cancer treatment. Haven't you noticed that more and more, they are trying to take control of treatment out of the patient's hands? They outlaw procedures that prove successful in other countries. They want to deny you herbs that Indians have been using for thousands of years to treat disease. Treatment outside their union deprives the association and their members of income."

Yes, she nodded. "They do like the control they have over us; I've noticed that doctors tend to treat us as the unwashed masses. I practically had to twist my doctor's arm just to learn the diagnosis."

He pulled a silver cigarette case from his jacket pocket, flicked it open and offered her one.

"No thank you." Unconsciously, she coughed.

Baker nodded, removed a smoke from the case, placed it between his lips, and then flipped the case over to use the self-contained lighter. He puffed a few times, inhaled deeply, and finally focused his thoughts back to those scoundrels at the A.M.A. "I have a signed check for five thousand dollars in my office right now and I've offered it to the first person who can prove that the Baker Cure doesn't work," he paused to exhale. "That check is ten years old. Nobody has been able to prove anything. The simple truth is, the Cure works...Would you like some water?"

He poured them each a glass of ice water.

As if proposing a toast to her health, Eva held the stemmed crystal water glass up, then took a sip. She'd never been a fan of drinking water without at least a little alcohol to kill the flavor, but this water tasted so pure, so refreshing. She could get used to this.

"Here's to your health," Baker said as he too took a sip. "I have to admit, I couldn't believe it when my secretary said you called. I recognized your name immediately."

"I'm surprised."

"Why?" He looked over his glasses at her. "Every young man wanted to steal a kiss from the beautiful Eva Dupree."

Eva laughed and primped at her hair. "Not many people remember my movies these days."

"I'll never forget *The Spider Web*." His expression grew distant, as if he were envisioning the movie in his mind.

"*Caught in a Web*," Eva corrected.

"That's right. That was my favorite, but I loved *The Mortician's*

Wife, too. I cheered aloud when you thrust your sword into Mortimer the Murderer."

"Dr., I mean Mr. Baker, you're betraying your age."

The corners of his lips crept up. "I spent many an enjoyable hour watching you escape maniacs and evil monsters. You might say I had quite a crush on you."

"That was a long time ago."

"Not that long ago." He took a puff up his cigarette. "What did you do after you made *Caught in a Web*?"

"I retired—but not by choice." She shivered unconsciously. Her hand traveled to her throat. "I caught pneumonia during the filming and wound up spending the next month in Good Samaritan Hospital. I thought I was going to cough up a lung. Turned out, I damaged my vocal cords. Even though my director had signed me to do his first talkie, he cut me loose. For years I sounded like Donald Duck...No, worse than that—Donald Duck with a Texas accent."

"You have a lovely voice now," Baker said. "It's very rich. Rather reminds me of Marlena Dietrich, but more feminine." He inhaled deeply from his cigarette, held the smoke for a moment as if to savor the taste and then blew it out through his nose. He laid the cigarette in the Baker Hospital ashtray and ignored it, allowing it to smolder out.

She smiled and took another sip of water. Just talking about the illness made her throat feel scratchy. "Thank you. But by the time I was healthy enough to make movies again, I'd lost my box office appeal. Younger actresses had replaced me." She sighed deeply, painfully, then quickly changed the subject. "Where are you from, Mr. Baker?"

"I'm from Iowa, Muscatine."

"What brought you to Arkansas?" Eva asked.

"The healing properties of the water and the clean air." Norman Baker held up his water glass, and pointed to the nearly dark picture window with it. In doing so, he sloshed a couple of drops of water onto the tablecloth.

The room grew quiet and Baker returned his attention to Eva. He gave her neckline an appreciative leer and started to say something when Eva cut him off.

"You said you're 'Mister' Baker, not 'Doctor' Baker. How did you end up running a cancer hospital?"

"When I was very young, I learned I had the power to overcome illness. I survived pneumonia and then later tuberculosis." He lit another cigarette, puffed on it and watched the smoke curl up toward the ceiling.

Eva laughed. "It's amazing. You survived both pneumonia *and* tuberculosis. People told me how lucky I was to survive pneumonia."

"Just think how you will further amaze your friends and family, Miss Dupree, when you survive both pneumonia *and* cancer. They will think you're a walking miracle. You must simply believe you will recover. Envision it. Know it. Your belief and the Baker Cure will return you to the picture of health."

"Really?"

He leaned closer to her. "I'll teach you to believe. You asked about my cancer cure. My interest in healing brought me into contact with a man who sold me the cancer cure I use today. I've saved thousands of people that the Meatcutters wanted to cut up or just forget."

As Baker took another puff from his cigarette, Eva looked around the penthouse. Every inch of wood was covered in lavender with amethyst trim. The furniture upholstery, even the dogs' collars, wore shades of amethyst. It had very much the feel of an old lady's house.

"While watching the sunset a few minutes ago, I saw the most amazing car in the parking lot. It had such long, graceful lines. It made those chunky black Fords alongside it look like a bunch of clumsy adolescents next to an Olympic athlete. I've never seen a car like it before." She nodded at the lavender walls in his penthouse. "That wouldn't be your car, would it?"

Baker's chest swelled slightly. "It's my 1937 Cord 418 convertible."

"I didn't see any headlights. Can you drive at night?" Eva asked.

"There are cranks on each side of the dash that raise and lower the headlamps."

"It's incredible." She hesitated. If there was ever a time to ask him about his purple fetish, this was it. "Mr. Baker, I've noticed that you have an affinity for all shades of purple. I must say, it is certainly better than being surrounded by sterile white. But it's not a color commonly appreciated by such a, uh, strong man."

Baker smiled. "Miss Dupree..."

"Please call me Eva."

"Eva, have you ever read Edgar Cayce?"

"Edgar Cayce." Eva frowned. "I must confess, I haven't studied his writings. He's a little esoteric for my taste."

"Nonsense. Edgar Cayce had an intuitive insight into the human psyche. He wrote that color is but vibration, like the overtones of music. Vibration is movement. Movement is activity of a positive and negative force. These overtones should be used in attuning the body's consciousness. Purple is a healing color, which…" Baker reached over and took her left hand, stroking it slowly, sensuously. "…helps the mind heal the body."

Oh, dear. He's not a queen after all.

A knock at the door interrupted Baker's quiet advances as well as his dissertation on the power of color. Eva repossessed her hand as a large black man dressed in white carried in a massive covered tray.

Baker pulled his hand back. "Our dinner has arrived. I hope you're hungry."

"I'm famished," Eva lied. Her stomach churned and at the moment nothing sounded appealing. Was she nauseous because she was nervous, her illness or the Baker Cure? She couldn't tell. Either way, this would be a long evening.

The server set the tray down in the kitchenette. As if by rote he rummaged through the cabinet and found a pair of silver candle holders with slightly used twelve-inch beeswax candlesticks. Eva could tell by his routine demeanor, this wasn't the first time the man had served Mr. Baker and a lady friend. The orderly-turned-waiter lit the candles with his cigarette lighter. Eva watched as the tiny flickering flame took to the wick and suddenly realized Mr. Baker may have misinterpreted her nervous smile. She took a deep breath, and hoped he didn't expect her for dessert.

When the porter finished setting the table, Eva and Baker moved from the sofa to the small dinner table set up for a romantic dinner for two.

The dogs obviously thought they'd been invited.

"Sorry, sports," the server said to the dogs as he dished out some appetizers. "This is for the boss, not you."

"Bruno, Bertha, go lie down," Baker commanded. The big dogs trotted loudly across the room. Between their weight hitting the wood floor and the clicking of their toenails, they made quite a racket.

Baker held Eva's chair as she sat down, then joined her at the table. He nodded to the porter. "Chester, you can serve us now."

Chester placed the plates down at the table. The first course was a lettuce and carrot salad.

Eva took a bite. "This is…" She groped for the right words, but they escaped her. "It's, uh, good. What is this dressing?"

Baker straightened his glasses. "It's whipped soybean milk. You can find the recipe in the Baker Hospital Recipe Booklet."

She smiled broadly, as she had done on screen just before someone tried to murder her. "Oh, so this is *your* recipe."

Eva took a few more small bites and then nodded for the server to take her salad plate. When Baker noticed, she said, "I haven't been able to eat much lately. Sometimes when I eat I get queasy." She gingerly touched her belly. At least she didn't have to fib. "I'd like to save room for my dinner."

She looked around as Chester placed a bowl of vegetable soup in front of her. The aroma actually made her hungry. "What are we having for the main course?

"Chop suey."

She recalled the nurse's warning about the Chinese dish. *Oh, no! I'd better enjoy the soup, just in case.* "I can't wait." She took a sip of the soup. It had a bold flavor. "Mmmm. This is very good!" She sounded a little surprised.

He smiled. "This was my mother's recipe."

"I believe it…" *…because it doesn't taste like swill.*

Ignoring the server, Baker resumed the conversation. "You know, when you first asked about bringing the cat to the hospital, I confess I was concerned about how the other patients would react. Rather than receiving complaints, patients who have seen him are delighted. Two patients have already thanked me for having him here. After you return home, I'm considering adding a cat to the staff. It never occurred to me that animals would cause such a positive reaction. I hope you'll allow him…"

"Ivan."

"I hope you'll allow Ivan to visit more of the patients, if they desire."

"He's a little shy right now. I'm sure in another day or so he'll feel more outgoing."

Baker dabbed his lip with the white cotton napkin.

"Mr. Baker, your letterhead said you had hospitals in the U.S., Mexico and Australia."

"Yes, we have a hospital in Laredo—Laredo, Texas. There's a hospital in Australia and of course, here in Eureka Springs." He sipped his tea. "I may expand it by opening a second office in Texas. I moved my radio station to Nuevo Laredo, just across the border from Laredo, so we don't have the broadcasting constraints of the Federal Radio Commission. Now I'm looking at another hotel in the Texas community of Mineral Wells. Ever heard of it?"

"Mineral Wells? Of course, everybody in Texas has heard of Mineral Wells. My aunt went there on one of her honeymoons. I think she stayed at The Baker Hotel. Why, that must be another one of your hotels, isn't it?"

"No, unfortunately The Baker isn't for sale. I'm looking at buying an interest in the Crazy Water Hotel across town. I'm supposed to meet the owner in Little Rock in a couple of weeks to discuss it. I wish I could acquire The Baker Hotel. It's very nice. Catchy name."

"That's exciting, Mr. Baker." Eva blew on her steamy soup to cool it down. "I imagine you're anxious."

"I'll be there on the sixteenth of September. I trust everything will go well."

Since he was being talkative, she took her chance to get some answers. "Mr. Baker, have you ever experienced something logic couldn't explain? Since I arrived, I've seen some things that might be described as odd."

"There's much about this world we don't understand," he admitted.

"I'll say. Last night I was on the fourth floor observation deck. I thought I saw a woman climb over the rail and fall. When I looked at the ground, there was nothing there."

Baker must have been a terrible poker player. He looked at her with the surprised expression of a kid whose mom just caught him stealing cookies, as if he had something to hide—or maybe not. "Really?"

"Really."

The lights above them sparked, interrupting his words, then the chandelier went dark, leaving only the candles flickering between them. "Excuse me, Eva."

Baker stumbled across the darkened room, slamming his knee into a piece of furniture. "Son of a bitch!" He found the front door and opened it, allowing light to flood in from downstairs. "I'm afraid we blew another fuse. See, the rest of the hospital is okay. Chester!"

he yelled to the servant waiting outside the door. "Track down the maintenance man."

"Yes sir, Mr. Baker."

Poker player or not, he acted odd for an innocent man. He sounded too irritated. His voice had too much of an edge. Somehow, Eva knew Norman Baker had something to hide.

Worse still, her platonic dining experience with a charming homosexual gentleman had suddenly evolved into a candlelit dinner with a one-hundred-percent heterosexual male. Things weren't going at all according to her plan.

"Mr. Baker, what about the strange things I saw?" She asked. The flicker of the flames cast odd shadows around the room.

"I wouldn't worry about them." He waved his hand dismissively. "I've heard patients sometimes experience, uh, things during the treatments. Imagination is an extraordinarily creative tool. People in general imagine what they most fear. An unfamiliar setting can intensify fear and imagination considerably."

"That's what Nurse Turner said. But I've only had one treatment—a glass of cold tar just this morning—after the girl jumped. Mr. Baker, I know what I saw. It was no hallucination."

He just nodded.

"I also heard some very strange sounds in my room, and a squeaking late last night out in the hall. I have to admit, it makes me a little nervous."

Baker stopped in the middle of a puff, held his breath for a moment, then let out a lungful of smoke. "This is an old building, Miss Dupree."

Hmmm. Back to "Miss Dupree" again. The tension drained from her body and her knotted belly untied. *Whew!*

Baker vigorously tamped his half-smoked cigarette into the ashtray, several more times than he needed to extinguish the ember. "And as I'm sure you know, old buildings make some very strange sounds."

Eva sipped some ice water. As she set her goblet down, Baker reached across the table to take her hand. "I assure you nothing in this hospital will hurt you. I'll ask the nurses to give you something to help you sleep."

As he brushed his fingers up her arm, the candle flame grew long then flickered out. Eva quickly pulled back her arm.

"Well, Mr. Baker, I believe that's my cue." *Thank goodness.* "I'm afraid this has been a very long day, and I'm simply exhausted." Eva pushed back her chair, slipped off her pumps and headed for the door. "Thank you for a lovely dinner." She rushed past him and out of the penthouse.

As she descended the stairs, her bare feet made hollow thumps against the old wood. A couple of steps creaked when she put her weight on them. When Eva left the staircase and approached her room, she found the radio Mr. Janowitz had borrowed on the floor next to the door. Eva picked up the radio and turned the doorknob. The door opened. *Funny.* She stared at the knob. *I'd swear I locked the door.* As she entered the room, Eva ran into a wall of air cold as an icebox. Her stomach suddenly tightened and gooseflesh rose all over her body. A faint hint of menthol hung in the air.

The room looked as though it had been struck by a tornado. The closet doors stood agape and every drawer in the suite hung wide open—all of them, the dresser, the wardrobe in the second room, even the desk drawer with the missing key.

Eva tossed the radio on an overstuffed chair next to the door and stormed out of her suite toward the nurse's station. There she found Nurses Turner and Johnston involved in an animated discussion.

Miss Johnston said, "I don't know what to tell them when they say they see or hear things."

"Just say..." Nurse Turner broke off when she saw Eva approach them. She took off her reading glasses. "Yes, Miss Dupree? Do you need something?"

"Someone's been in my room!"

Turner frowned at her. "This is a hospital. People go into rooms all the time to tend patients."

"I wasn't in my room, and one of your nurses has been rifling through all my belongings. I want to know who it was."

Nurse Turner folded her arms like an Indian chief. "I've been the charge nurse for this floor all evening. No one has been in your room."

"Everything's been opened up and inspected. I could smell menthol. Look, if it wasn't a nurse, maybe it was another patient. Whoever it was, they had a key. I locked the door when I left. I want some answers. I want them now!"

Nurse Turner laid her glasses down on the desk. "Very well. Let's take a look."

Together they walked into the room. The light was still on, but now the air was warm. Her dresser and desk drawers had been neatly closed and the closets shut. Everything looked exactly as it had when she left for dinner.

Eva felt as though someone had poured ice water on her. Nurse Turner's lips thinned. "I don't see a problem here. Do you?" She glared at Eva, then left without another word, slamming the door behind her.

After Nurse Turner left, Eva just couldn't bear to sit down. She paced, then dropped onto the vanity bench. She tested the keyless drawer. She couldn't budge it.

What the hell had happened in here? Even if it had been one of the nurses, how could this room have possibly gone from shambles to tidy in less than a minute? Was she going crazy? Could she be seeing things after only one treatment?

How the hell did they get the desk drawer open? She gave the drawer a vicious tug, breaking her nail in the process.

Ivan jumped up on the vanity and bumped his head against her hand. Unlike Eva, whose eyes darted nervously around the room, Ivan sat confidently before her staring at a single point in the middle of the room as if watching a film.

She eyed him curiously. "What are you looking at?" She saw nothing—no insects, no spirits, no imaginary friend—just empty space.

For a moment Ivan turned back to her, then refocused on the same point in the center of the suite.

"You know I hate it when you do that," she told him.

But he simply continued to stare.

Damn inscrutable beast! She picked up the hand-tinted photo of Edgar on the vanity and stared into his eyes. "Why did you stick me with him? I want *you!*" She didn't mind the adoring fans vanishing, or the fair-weather business associates disappearing after Edgar's death. None of them mattered as long as she had Edgar.

Not that life with Edgar was perfect. Just before they met at Charlie Chaplin's, Edgar had gone to a psychic who warned him he would die young. Since that day he knew that every headache, every sneeze, every smoker's cough was going to be the big one. So he worried and complained about everything. If only she'd taken him to the doctor sooner that afternoon—in time to save his life. If she'd listened to his complaints of indigestion, he might be holding her hand now.

Then suddenly, the pain hit her. "Damn! Not again." She leaned against the vanity and sucked in a long, deliberate breath, letting it out slowly. Her folded arms across her waist offered no comfort. She felt as though a bare-knuckles fighter had just punched her in the back. She couldn't breathe.

Eva fell to the floor on her hands and knees. Wave after wave of pain radiated up and down her back, followed by nausea. She broke out in a cold sweat, and she lost her dinner.

These episodes had grown much more frequent recently. At first the volcanic pain arrived every few weeks. Then every few days. It increased until her dull fatigue was disrupted by searing pain every couple of hours. Breathing slowly and deeply helped some, but as the pain escalated, the breathing helped less and less.

Eva closed her eyes, trying to wish away pain that would have brought an English rugby player to his knees. But it hung on and on. She tried to ignore the disgusting taste in her mouth. Slowly, the wave of pain ebbed away, leaving her weak and drained. When she could finally speak, Eva pulled herself up and pressed the call button for help.

In a few minutes Nurse Turner appeared. She helped Eva to her feet and into the bathroom. "Here, let's get you into the shower," she said in a rare moment of compassion. "Can you stand on your own?"

Eva nodded her head yes, but she feared that might not be true.

"I'll clean up out here," Nurse Turner told her. "Call me if you need help."

Eva let the water heat up and stepped into the tub and turned the shower on. The warmth washed over her but did not sooth her as a bath usually did.

"Miss Dupree," Nurse Turner called into the bathroom. "Are you all right?"

"Yes."

"I'll be back in a few minutes," the nurse said.

Eva kept peeking out of the shower. Everything felt wrong— like someone was hidden somewhere in the room watching her, waiting to jump out when she least expected. Her brain knew that except for her and the cat, the room was empty. But still...

From nowhere she felt something gently brush against her leg. Gasping, she slipped and tumbled. Before she hit the tub floor, Eva grabbed at the towel rack, catching the ceramic brace. It held, and stopped her fall.

Below her, Ivan had poked his upper body underneath the shower curtain. Dewy drops of water spray clung to his face and whiskers. One paw extended into the spray, catching droplets. Some he licked from his paw. Other times he shook the paw, sending the water drops flying everywhere.

"Ivan," she yelled, still clutching the towel bar. "You scared the shit out of me!"

He looked up, as if to say, "What?" He went back to playing with the water by biting the spray as if it were prey.

After she dried off, she tapped some dental powder onto her toothbrush and gave her teeth a good going over to rid her mouth of the foul taste. Much better.

Still naked, Eva staggered into her bedroom. The cold mountain air invaded her room through the windows and glass door. She shivered. Tonight she would forego the sexy nightgowns she loved so much in favor of something less attractive but more practical. Eva slipped on her oriental silk pajamas. Patterns of flying birds and tiny sailboats had been intricately woven into the bronze fabric. Eva envied the little silk boats. They seemed to have purpose and someplace to go.

Her life had no purpose. There was nothing she could do for anyone, least of all herself. Here she sat, trapped in a cage waiting to either live or die. With its beautiful gardens, unorthodox color scheme and come-and-go policy, the Baker Hospital was a lovely place for the afflicted. But the lack of bars didn't change the fact that she was still trapped in a cage.

She retrieved the radio from the chair and set it back on her nightstand. A little music would cheer her up. She plugged it in, and turned it on. Turning the knob, she scanned up and down the dial hoping to find some music, but it seemed as if the only thing on was news—bad news about the German invasion. She turned the radio off and tried to read.

That failed too. Who could concentrate on the Civil War when real war threatened to engulf the world?

Still cold, she turned the radiator up a bit to warm the air and pulled the rocking chair and lamp closer to the warmth. Finally, when she could no longer keep her eyes open, she climbed into bed.

She had almost slipped off to sleep when Ivan walked across her chest. "Come on, Ivan. Settle down."

That's when she heard it again.

What time is it? She looked at her clock. It was three minutes before eleven.

Squeak, squeak, squeak.

"What *is* that?" she asked the cat.

Squeak, squeak, squeak.

It seemed as if she lay in bed for hours, only half asleep. Even with Ivan sharing her pillow and his comforting purr, she'd wake up startled for no reason. Later that night, she awoke unable to breathe or move, immersed in an airless, frigid void. Her body felt heavy, as if she were completely encased in mud—smothering. Her heart hammered so hard she feared it would explode or that she would simply pass out and die. But at the last moment, as consciousness had begun to slip away, her arms broke free, then air returned to her lungs, and finally her voice.

She screamed.

In her movies it would have made her director nod with satisfaction, and it certainly brought Nurse Turner rushing into the room. Flipping on the light she demanded, "Miss Dupree. What in the world is wrong with you?"

Eva gasped for air. "I couldn't breathe. I couldn't move. I thought I was going to die."

Breath hissed out through Turner's nose. "This is ridiculous! Try to act like an adult! I can't remember when I've had a patient who was this much trouble. Your condition has nothing to do with breathing difficulty."

"Nurse Turner, I want another room. There's something wrong with this place. I will not sleep in here."

"Miss Dupree, you have an overactive imagination and you're letting it get the best of you. Even little Trudy isn't afraid of a boogeyman."

Eva set her jaw. "I'm not kidding. I am *not* sleeping in here. I don't care what you have to do, find me someplace else."

"I'll see what I can arrange." She left and returned with a syringe. "Give me your hip."

"I don't want a shot, I want out of this room!"

Nurse Turner's lips thinned almost to invisibility. "Don't make this any more difficult than it already is. I'm going to give you something to calm you down."

"What is it?" Eva demanded.

The nurse pronounced every syllable individually. "Some-thing-to-calm-you-down." Nurse Turner must have been a bear wrestler in her past. She heaved Eva onto her side and stabbed her with the hypodermic before Eva could protest further. "There." The White Dragon left Eva in a fog, where every motion took so much effort, she felt she was underwater.

Eva felt all the strength drain from her body, as though her bones had simply dissolved.

When the nurse came back, a minute or a year later, she checked Eva's pulse and found it slow, strong, and steady. "That should keep you quiet," she muttered. "Now maybe I can get some work done."

DAY THREE—*Saturday, September 2*

The next morning Eva stared out her window as she sipped her coffee. An empty plate of bacon and eggs licked squeaky clean, awaited the nurse to pick it up. Somehow things felt different. The room felt strange—even sinister.

What was I thinking? Maybe I should just save my money and go back home.

Above her the creaking floorboards told her Norman Baker and the dogs were up and about. Did he know about Nurse Turner drugging frightened patients into insensibility?

Eva had arrived at the Baker Cancer hospital just two days before out of desperation—only a few days after her own physician discovered what he called carcinoma of the kidney, a day she would never forget.

Eva had gone to Dr. Setzer for what she feared was appendicitis, mind-numbing pain in her right side and nausea. The doctor poked and probed her abdomen, and listened to her swear when he hit the sore spots, then sent her to the hospital for X-rays.

When Eva returned to his downtown office, Dr. Setzer claimed the rolling leather chair next to an oak roll top desk. He dropped his stethoscope into a coiled pile beside a yellowed human skull and a black leather medical bag.

Eva slowly eased onto an uncomfortable wooden chair, shifting a number of times to find that golden position that left her free of pain. Of course, these days that position didn't exist, so she settled for an angle that didn't feel like she'd turned her insides out.

Dr. Setzer's private inner sanctum looked like any other physicians' office. It had a clean, impersonal look. Saffron-covered walls, no doubt painted that way to elicit feelings of cheer and tranquility, looked more like someone had smeared baby poop on it. Three framed diplomas from different universities hung from those cheerful walls, while a white thumbtack impaled a vision chart at eye level.

A large cherry wood barrister bookcase held thick cloth and

leather bound copies of *Diagnostics of Internal Medicine*, and *Differential Diagnosis and Treatment of Disease* and numerous other medical books. At the other end of the room a corner supply cabinet displayed an assortment of drug bottles of amber and cobalt. Knowing how bitter most medicines tasted or how sharp they stung, Eva cringed. Hopefully she wouldn't have to suffer through too many doses of Dr. Setzer's vile potions before he cured her.

Eva handed Dr. Setzer the large manila envelope holding her X-rays.

Lifting his eyebrows, he said, "Let's see what's going on inside your body, why don't we?" He opened the envelope and slid the film into the light viewer. "Hmmmmm. Uh huh. Mmmmmm." He brushed his mustache with his forefinger. "Hmmm." He sighed, then inserted the second film. Another sigh and another, "Hmmm." But he said nothing directly to Eva.

After a few minutes, Eva waved her hand in front of the doctor. "Excuse me, Dr. Setzer. I don't know if you remember me. I came here for a consultation. There's not much consulting going on here. I can't have a conversation with myself. I suppose I could, but you'd call a different kind of doctor and send me to an asylum. Now, what do you see in your magic pictures?"

"Ah, there it is," the doctor said as if he hadn't heard her.

"What? Where?" Eva asked.

He picked up his fountain pen and used it as a pointer. "There." He pointed at a couple of smaller splotches that showed up white against the light. "Right there. That's your kidney. Now, do you see these spots here?" He made a smaller circle inside the blob.

She focused on the fuzzy picture. "I think so."

"Those are growths on your kidney," Dr. Setzer casually told her. "We have to remove them as soon as possible. Tomorrow we can go in and cut them out. That will give you some time."

Eva clenched her hands. "I thought I had appendicitis."

"No, it's a growth."

"And 'growth' means what?" she demanded.

He ignored her question. Instead he pointed the pen at the other kidney. "You have another on your left kidney too. It's smaller, but still there."

"You said that will buy me some time. What do you mean by that?"

"We don't want to tell you anything that might cause you to

worry needlessly."

"Too late," she said. "I'm already worried sick." When she was upset or excited her East Texas drawl grew more pronounced and the word 'I'm' sounded like 'ahm.' She sounded very Texan today. "I'm weak, nauseous. I can't eat. My back aches. I have pain in my gut that feels like I have a hundred Alabama coal miners picking their way out through my skin. I've vomited more today than I've eaten in a week. And you're afraid you're going to worry me? What do you mean a growth, Dr. Setzer? Are you talking about a cyst or an abscess?"

He remained silent with his hands on his desk, then finally said, "Your X-ray was blurred so we weren't able to confirm the diagnosis..." His voice trailed off for a moment. "We won't know until after the exploratory operation."

She slammed her fist down against his desk. "I hate you doctors because you always use sanctimonious medical jargon. You never just come out and say something. You doctors and your subjective ethics!"

"All right, Miss Dupree." He nervously tapped his fountain pen on his desk as if he were playing percussion. He had no particular rhythm, and the tick-tick-tick-ta-tick-tick was irritating as hell.

"Are you sure you want the whole ugly truth?" he pressed.

She took a deep breath. "Let's cut right through the crap, Doctor. For God's sake, I paid for those tests. I have a right to know."

"You have a serious tumor," he said avoiding her gaze.

Eva swallowed hard. "Are you telling me I'm dying?"

He hesitated, shuffled a few papers and finally said, "From your symptoms—and from those shadows on the X-rays—you most likely have carcinoma of the kidney. *Cancer*."

She gasped and covered her mouth with her hands. The shock of hearing the word was not unlike one of her kidney attacks, sharp, painful and it took her breath away. It made her feel like she had to vomit. "Cancer?" Maybe there was something to be said for code language after all.

"You wanted me to be blunt." His voice sounded like he was saying, "Told ya so!"

"So I did." She forced a laugh, then dropped her head in her hands. After a minute or so, sniffed, then fumbled through her purse for her hankie. "My God!" She dabbed her eyes. "You've just pronounced my death sentence, haven't you?"

"We won't know until we operate." Tick-tick-ta-tick.

We? Eva wondered. *Who is "we"? Why the hell does this guy refer to himself in the plural?*

"If you'll step into the waiting room, we'll finish the paperwork. You can drop it by the hospital today. You can check in tomorrow afternoon about two..."

"If I have this operation, will I live?"

"I don't know." Ticky-tick, the pen continued to tap against the table top.

She grabbed the pen out of his hand and slammed it down on the desk next to him. "Goddammit. Can't you just be straight with me? Am I dying?"

Eyeing his pen, but not daring to touch it, Dr. Setzer let out a deep sigh. "We believe you are."

As Dr. Setzer described the operation in more detail, a disturbance broke out in the waiting room.

"Get out of my way," boomed an angry male voice outside the office door.

"The doctor's with a patient," the nurse protested. "You can't go in there."

"The hell I can't!" A mountain of a man with sun-streaked hair and dirty fingernails stormed into the doctor's private office, pausing for just a brief moment to look at the door's textured glass insert. 'Joseph K. Setzer, M.D.' had been carefully hand-lettered on the smooth side of the glass facing the hall. The man read the name aloud and spit on the floor as he turned the doorknob. He left it ajar as he blasted into the doctor's office. "Setzer, I want to talk to you!"

The man paused and glared at the doctor. His eyes were insane, otherworldly. They looked like the eyes of a bull squaring off with a matador, rage mixed with desperation.

The color drained from the doctor's face. Now he was the one feeling the fear. His hand shook as he motioned to Eva to leave. "Miss Dupree, you'll need to get some paperwork from the nurse to take to the hospital." He glanced at the man towering over him. "I'll see you over there tomorrow afternoon."

Eva hurriedly clutched her purse and started to rise from her seat, but midway up a work-calloused hand grabbed her shoulder and pressed her gently back down to the chair. Eva shrunk back, shielding her face with her hands.

"Ma'am," the blonde man said in a distinct east Texas drawl, "don't you go nowhere. I ain't gonna hurt you, but I want you to hear this. I'm gonna save your life. I wish someone had done that for my wife."

Recognizing her terror, the man's eyes softened. For a moment he must have seen someone else in Eva's face. He gave her shoulder a tender pat. "I'd never hurt you, Mildred."

He then turned his full attention to Dr. Setzer and returned to his bull-in-full-charge posture. "You!" he said only slightly louder than polite conversation, then his voice quickly crescendoed. "I oughtta kill you, you worthless college-boy. You're so much smarter than everyone else. You convinced her that you could save her."

Dr. Setzer spoke to the man using the same voice he'd use to quiet an aggressive dog. "Mr. Taylor, we know you're upset, but you need to calm down."

The man's voice exploded. "Don't tell me to calm down. My wife's dead because of you!"

"At least have the courtesy to close the door," Dr. Setzer begged.

Even despite the hot August afternoon a sudden chill filled the air and the overhead light flickered.

"Okay!" He slammed the door behind him with such force the glass insert shattered, spraying fragments throughout the office. Tiny fragments of glass shrapnel pinged against the windows and settled to every surface in the room like anger-driven snow. A cloud of papers flew into the air and then settled all over the floor—at the same time the light bulbs in the doctor's reading lamp also shattered.

The man approached the desk, crunching through the scattered shards. The air held an eerie stillness...until one last fragment of glass fell from the door insert, smashing to the checkerboard linoleum floor.

"There." The blond mountain leaned close to Dr. Setzer's face. "It's closed. Are you happy?"

The physician gave a shallow nod, then closed his eyes slowly, deliberately. "Don't hit me!"

The distraught man backed away. He dropped his head and pinched his brows together, as if he bore all the world's troubles. Maybe he did.

"I tried to get my Mildred to go to that Baker Hospital, but you talked her out of it." He held his arms out, pleading. He wiped his nose with his sleeve as tears rolled down his face. "You convinced her Dr. Baker was a quack. Who's the quack here? You cut her open for nothing. My wife's dead cuz of you. She'd still be alive if you had told her the truth. My two boys are orphans cuz of you, you lying bastard."

"No, she wouldn't," Dr. Setzer countered as unemotionally as if he were lecturing a college class. "She was dying when she came to me. No one could have saved her. Not even your miraculous Dr. Baker..." The doctor's voice broke off.

Mr. Taylor held his hands up as if in prayer. "Why did she listen to you?" He looked at Eva. "Why?"

The man's voice hardened again. He fumbled into his shirt pocket and removed a tattered photograph with worn corners. A longing filled his face as he gazed at the photo, tracing his forefinger along the pale hand-tinted cheeks and wavy yellow hair. He set it gently on the glass-blanketed desk. "I brought you a picture of my Mildred. You look at her."

The doctor continued to stare wide-eyed at Mr. Taylor.

"I said, "Look at her!""

Setzer shook as he picked up the photo.

"I want you to see her face every day...in every patient you kill. If I weren't a Christian, I'd be sending you to St. Peter right now!" He reached into his pocket and threw a booklet in the trash can. "Don't you never walk on the same street as me, cuz if I see you again, I'll tear your head clean off." Turning around, he grabbed the picture out of the doctor's hand and crunched through the glass, sobbing, "If she'd gone to that hospital she'd still be alive. Damn you!" Within a few steps his cries were muffled into silence.

Dr. Setzer shook his head. "I'm sorry you had to see that, Miss Dupree. Sometimes the spouses of patients who have died get upset. He shouldn't have forced you to sit through his display."

She shrugged, not knowing what to say or to think. Should she run? Should she stay?

The nurse rushed into the office—the sound of shattered glass grinding beneath her feet. "Doctor, are you alright?"

"Nurse Studer, get us each a wet towel." His right eye tightly squinted.

It would take more than a moist towel.

Eva reached into her purse to get her hanky again. As she did she wrapped her fingers around a sharp shard. "Ow!" She pulled it out and watched a drop of blood rise from the cut. She sucked her forefinger.

"Excuse me, Miss Dupree." He placed his hand over his eye. "I'll be back in a minute. I think I've got some glass in my eye."

While he was gone, Eva retrieved the booklet from the garbage. The cover said, "The Baker Hospital and Health Resort. Where sick people get well." She shook the glass from her alligator handbag and Eva stashed the booklet in a side pocket. She struggled to her feet and walked out the door. As she sneaked through the waiting room, the receptionist's window opened. "Miss Dupree."

Eva straightened her back, resolutely.

"Eva Dupree," the woman repeated, more forcefully this time. "I have your paperwork...Miss Dupree!" the nurse called after her. "Here are your admissions papers."

Eva hesitated at the door.

"Miss Dupree, you'll need..."

The door closed behind her, cutting off the nurse's voice.

Only days later, Eva boarded a train bound for the world famous Baker Hospital in Eureka Springs, Arkansas, where according to the brochure, "Cancer is Curable." And soon she'd receive her second treatment of the Baker Cure. Now all she had to do to get better was to drink water and take medicine, and, as Nurse Cavanaugh told her, get plenty of sun.

A couple of pigeons landed on the brickwork just outside her window hoping for a handout. Patients feeding pigeons seemed to be a common pastime around here. They cooed impatiently when she ignored them; obviously they were used to better-trained patients.

From below Ivan honed in on his potential prey. He leapt up on the windowsill to get closer to the action. At the sight of the predator through the glass, the birds fluttered backward. They hovered for a moment before flying off in search of safer snacks. Ivan sat still until another bird landed. With ears erect and whiskers flared, he crouched motionless in his attack stance, his eyes fixed on the bird. The cat's bottom wiggled and the tip of his auburn tail twitched like a rattlesnake. He chattered softly, and when the pigeons seemed sufficiently distracted, he made his move, smacking headfirst into the glass and sending the birds scattering.

Eva laughed out loud at his antics. Who'd have believed that an ailurophobe like her could actually enjoy the presence of a cat? The night Edgar showed up with that scruffy white and red kitten she almost threw both of them out on their tails. It was only after Edgar died that she came to appreciate his pet's personality and sense of humor.

Someone tapped low on Eva's door. "Mrs. Dupree?" asked a small voice Eva recognized as Gertrude Trent, yesterday's Monopoly magnate.

"Hi, Gertrude."

"Everyone at home calls me Trudy. I only get called Gertrude when I get in trouble or when a doctor talks to me."

Trudy took a step inside and hovered shyly by the door.

"It's okay, Trudy. Come on in."

She closed the door behind her. "Can I see your cat?"

"I bet he'd like that."

The youngster's smile broadened. At the end of each pigtail, Trudy wore a pink satin bow. Her huge round eyes, the shade of bluegrass, were bloodshot and accentuated by gray circles—a tell-tale sign that she was a sick little girl.

Ivan trotted to the center of the room, his eyes fixed on Trudy. He purred, shifting from paw to paw.

"How'd you know I have a cat?" Eva asked.

"My friend told me," she said.

"My, news travels fast," Eva laughed. "Which friend?"

"Him." She pointed to empty space right beside her.

"Oh, I see." Eva smiled.

Eva's cousin had an imaginary friend when she was little. Unlike Trudy, Marnie had the same companion throughout her childhood, until one day, shortly after she'd turned ten, invisible Betsy simply disappeared. Marnie always seems sadder once the Betsy stories stopped. Eva wondered when Trudy would tire of her companion.

Ivan flopped down on the oak planks and looked up at the child.

"Hi, Mr. Kitty." Trudy dropped to the floor much like a rag doll hitting the ground, and began petting Ivan. "I've never seen a cat at a hospital before." She laid stomach down—getting nose to nose with her new friend. He responded by bumping her cheek with his fore-head and tickling her nostrils with his whiskers. Trudy rubbed her face, rolled over on her back and giggled.

Eva pressed her hand against her back as she lowered herself to an ottoman to watch Trudy and Ivan play—both appeared to be in Heaven. The little girl whispered something in his ear. He twitched it once and then settled back to the floor.

"He's a really nice cat. I wish he was mine. Mommy won't let me have a kitty."

"Why not?"

Trudy patted his ribcage. "She said it would give me worms."

Funny, that was the same excuse Eva spouted when Edgar came home with the kitten, those two amber eyes peeking out from within her husband's leather jacket.

As a child she suffered months of smelly ringworm treatments as a result of a brief encounter with a neighbor's tabby. Even after thirty years, the sight of a strange feline still made Eva shudder. All these decades later she could still smell the sulfur and formaldehyde her mother coated her skin with to get rid of the fungus. A hell of a punishment for petting one cute little cat. Eva unconsciously scratched her forearms.

"Don't worry," Eva said. "Ivan doesn't have worms. He's lucky to be so healthy."

As she watched them play, Eva thought about Edgar. If they'd had a little girl would she have been like Trudy? Without thinking Eva leaned over and ran her fingers through the child's bangs. A cowlick punched through as if trying to peek around its peers.

Trudy ran her hand along Ivan's body from his head to the end of his tail. "I've never seen a kitty like this before. It looks like God ran out of white tails and gave him a red one."

"It does, doesn't it? My husband was in a faraway place called eastern Anatolia when he found Ivan in a trash can. He said he saw cats just like Ivan swimming in the nearby Van Lake."

Trudy's eyes grew wide, then squeezed them skeptically. "A swimming cat? Does Ivan swim?"

"Not really. But he does like to dip his paw in water. One lady, who lives nearby, told my husband Ivan was a Vankedisi cat, named after Lake Van. There's even a local legend that the Vankedisi were the cats Noah took on board his Ark."

"Wow. Noah's Ark!"

Eva glanced at the blue sky and puffy clouds through the window. "Trudy, it's such a nice day. Why don't you two go out on the balcony and play? You know the nurse wants us to get lots of sun"

"I don't wanna."

"Why not?"

Trudy hid her face. "Promise you won't tell anyone."

"I promise."

The little girl sat up and whispered in Eva's ear, "Some of the people smell real bad—like something dead. You don't smell like that."

"Thank you."

Trudy began petting Ivan again. "Besides, I'm supposed to get my shot in a little while. I hoped they wouldn't find me here."

"I see. Your secrets are safe with me. Are your parents here? I didn't see them yesterday."

The little girl's expression dropped, and she shook her head. "They're at home. Daddy has to work and Mommy takes care of my brothers and sisters. I miss my mommy."

"I bet you do."

Poor little thing. All alone in such a scary place. No wonder she needed a make believe friend.

Were Trudy's imaginary conversations with her "friend" any different from Eva's discussions with the cat? Perhaps.

"Are you scared?" Trudy asked.

"What?" Eva was blindsided by the girl's bluntness.

"Sometimes I hear a lady screaming. Is it you?"

How to answer that innocent question?

So Trudy hears her screams. Eva never thought about how her own fear affected others, especially such a brave little girl. Eva tried to smile reassuringly. "Everyone gets scared sometime."

"Even grownups?"

"Even grownups. Are you scared?" Eva asked.

Trudy thought about it for a moment, then admitted, "I'm scared of Nurse Turner."

"Really? That's all?" Maybe Nurse Turner and Mr. Baker were right. Maybe all the strange goings on were in Eva's own mind. "You're very brave. I'd think being here alone would be kind of scary without your mom or dad."

"I'm not alone." Trudy pointed at the air beside her. "*He* takes care of me."

"That's good. It's nice to have someone look out for you."

"You don't have to be scared either."

"How do you know?"

"He watches you all the time, too."

Eva's back stiffened. She tried to smile. *That's creepy.* "He does?"

"Uh huh. He really likes your perfume."

Before Eva could respond further, the door opened and Nurse Cavanaugh walked in carrying a covered medical tray. "Trudy, you're not bothering Miss Dupree, are you?"

"No, ma'am. I just came by to tell her not to be worried about her shot." She turned to Eva. "It's not too awful."

"Thank you," Eva said. "I feel much safer now."

"Trudy, run back to your room. Dr. Hutto is already there. And he's not happy that you made him wait on you."

Not budging, Trudy put her arms around the cat and kissed him on top of the head. "Can't you tell him you couldn't find me?"

The nurse grabbed her by the forearm, dragging her toward the door. "Come on, Trudy. Stop wasting time. Miss Dupree, he'll be by in a few minutes with today's treatment."

"Bye, Miss Eva," Trudy said in a plaintive voice. "Bye, Mr. Kitty."

Eva watched the pair disappear behind the closing door.

"Poor little girl." She sat on the bed and quietly stroked Ivan's fur. She picked up the newspaper Rose had brought by yesterday. The headline, "The Mayor Promises More Jobs," showed above the fold. There was no mention of the entire world outside of Eureka Springs unraveling.

In a few moments, the silence was shattered by a child's scream piercing through the wall. "No, no, no! Please don't. Pleeeasse don't!" she screamed loud enough to make the dead in the cemetery tremble with fear.

"Be still, Gertrude," Eva heard through the wall. "It wouldn't hurt so much if you'd just be still."

Ivan worked his way under the sheets as if the bed covers could protect him from whatever was happening to Trudy.

"Doonn't." Then all that could be heard was muffled sobs.

Eva joined Ivan between the sheets and sat in silence, hoping that she would be braver than her little next door neighbor.

Was the shot so bad? Of course not.

Trudy was a little girl, all alone and a long way from home. Everything was going to seem worse than it really was. Eva relaxed. Poor little Trudy was just overreacting.

As promised, a few minutes later Dr. Hutto knocked at her door.

"Come in," she answered weakly.

Whatever trauma Trudy had suffered now awaited her. She shuddered.

"Good morning, Miss Dupree. How are you..." He stopped mid-sentence when he spied Ivan's nose peeking out of the sheets. "What is that?" he demanded staring at Ivan through narrowed eyes.

Ivan, an accomplished stare-er himself, returned the favor without blinking.

Dr. Hutto was an older man, almost elderly, certainly mature enough to retire from practice. His closely cropped white hair made Eva wonder whether his hair was short or just sparse.

"That, Doctor, is my cat," Eva said.

"I've seen cats before. I used to dissect them. What is it doing here?"

Eva cringed. Great bedside manner. Not feeling the need to explain yet again, she simply said, "See my chart."

He flipped open the chart and scanned it. On the second page, hand-scribbled in all capital letters, was simply, "CAT OK. NORMAN BAKER."

"You don't have a problem with that, do you, Doctor?"

"I do, but I guess that doesn't matter. If Mr. Baker approved this..." His words trailed off, and he returned his attention to the medicine tray. "Has anyone explained the Baker Treatment to you?"

"I get a treatment every day."

"That's right. We give you three different medicines. Yesterday you received an oral dose. Tomorrow, you'll get a shot in the hip." He set his covered enamel medical tray down on the nightstand and opened it ceremoniously, like a chef serving a gourmet meal. "Today's injection goes in your intestine."

The color drained out of Eva's face. "Where?"

"In the intestine. It's absorbed into the system faster."

Eva took a deliberate breath and steeled herself. The needle looked huge, like something that should be used on a horse. It wasn't supposed to be like this. She thought The Cure was supposed to be one hundred percent successful and pain free.

"Can't you use a smaller needle?" she asked.

He frowned. "Mrs. Dupree, in the amount of time you have been stalling we could have finished. Please lift up your shirt."

Eva raised her pajama top and pulled her waist down far enough to expose her abdomen for the doctor. She felt the cold tease of the alcohol as the cotton washed across her skin. It brought back memories of that month in the hospital fighting for every breath. She dropped her head back against the pillow, squeezing her eyes closed, as if it could shut out the impending pain. At the first hint of the needle, she tensed up. "Oh God!" she cried when he had slid the needle into her belly. She gripped the sheet in her hand crushing it into a little wad.

"Just a little longer," Dr. Hutto said as he slowly depressed the syringe plunger. "Just a moment more."

In that moment it took him to empty his syringe, God had time to create the universe and make man. The plunger delivered its last few CCs of liquid lava and he finally withdrew it. But the vibrant aching lingered on and on. It felt like she was burning from the inside out. She rolled over into a fetal position and moaned.

"You'll feel better in a little while. Now, get some rest." Dr. Hutto pointed at the call button. "Just call the nurse if you need anything."

Eva rolled up into a tighter little ball and clutched her aching abdomen. This was different from the pain she normally experienced from her diseased kidneys. Instead of stabbing and spreading across her back like a hornet's sting as she felt from the cancer, the injection burned and throbbed along her entire lower belly. Everything from the ribcage down felt afire. Oh, God, she needed another pain shot. She reached out for the call button, but it hung just out of reach, taunting her.

A few minutes after the doctor left, Ivan crawled out from his hiding place and joined Eva, trembling on the bed. He curled up beside her, pressing his back next to her stomach, his warm plush body comforted her like a purring hot water bottle. "It's just not worth it," she whimpered as she patted his head. "I want to go home. If I'm going to die, I want to die at home." Within a few minutes, she drifted off to sleep.

Rose Freeman shifted her bags and boxes as she climbed the side stairs to Miss Eva's fourth floor hospital room. The elevator would have made her life so much easier, but it didn't need to display a sign saying, "Whites Only." It was understood. Balancing one sack on her knee, she tapped lightly on the door of room four-nineteen and entered without waiting for an answer. After all, she didn't want to wake Miss Eva if she was sleeping.

"Miss Eva?" she said softly as she pushed the door ajar. The room smelled sour and bitter.

From her bed Eva moaned, "Rose, help me!"

The maid dropped her bags in the open doorway and dashed over to her employer's bed. Eva was drenched in sweat and was as pale as a swan's back.

"Sweet Jesus, save us all! Miss Eva, what have they done to you?" Rose grabbed a washcloth from the bathroom towel rack, wet it under the faucet and began bathing Eva's face, throat, hands and arms.

"I'm going to be sick," Eva moaned.

Rose looked around, for the emesis basin but didn't see it. She reached for the next best thing. "Here you go, baby." Rose held the bronze wastepaper basket next to her employer, and dropped her cotton hanky over the recycled scrambled eggs on the floor. "Don't you worry. I'll clean up that little mess in a minute."

Eva held her hand out. "I tried to call for help. I hurt so badly, I couldn't reach the button."

Rose fetched a glass of tap water from the bathroom. "Have a drink of this."

Eva took the glass and sipped slowly.

"How long have you been like this?" Rose asked.

"How long has it been?" Eva shrugged. "I don't know."

"You hang on. I'll be right back." Rose picked up the pitcher, and stormed down to the nurse's station where Nurse Cavanaugh and another nurse laughed and talked as they sharpened hypodermic needles with an Arkansas wet stone. Nurse Cavanaugh eyed the point, then ran it across the wet stone a couple of times to remove a barb. Between viewings she described a costume she'd made for her second grade daughter's upcoming performance in *Sleeping Beauty*.

Rose interrupted her description. "Which one of you debutantes is supposed to be taking care of Eva Dupree?"

"Excuse me?" the other nurse said.

"Which one of you is Eva Dupree's nurse?"

"I am," Nurse Cavanaugh said. "Is there a problem?"

"Yes, ma'am. There's plenty of problem. While you two are having a party out here, Miss Dupree is burning up with fever and urping all over the floor. When's the last time you bothered to check on her?" She raised her eyebrows as if scolding a child. She handed the nurse the pitcher. "I'm certain you were fixing to take her some ice cold water, weren't you?"

Nurse Cavanaugh passed the pitcher to the other nurse. "I'll be right back. Would you fill this up for me?"

When Rose and Nurse Cavanaugh entered the room, Eva was swabbing her face with Rose's moist washrag.

"Miss Dupree, I'm so sorry." Nurse Cavanaugh rushed over to

feel her head.

"I tried to call, but I couldn't reach the button," Eva said weakly.

"I'll get you some ice water."

"She could do with a little soup, too," Rose added.

"Of course. A little soup," Nurse Cavanaugh echoed.

As the nurse headed for the door Rose called to her, "We could use a cup of hot water too."

When the nurse left, Rose cleaned up the mess on the floor, and then refreshed the warm washcloth with cool water. In a few minutes, Nurse Cavanaugh returned with an order of chicken soup in an invalid feeder. The feeder looked like a teapot except the spout extended at an angle from the base to allow a patient to drink while lying flat on her back.

"I think she can handle a spoon," Rose told the nurse. "I'm sure she'll be telling you where that spout could go if you try to feed her with that thing."

Down at Rose's feet Ivan meowed insistently, winding in and out of her legs. "Master Ivan, you'll just have to be patient."

Miss Eva closed her eyes and dropped her head into the pillow. "I'm feeling a little better. Go ahead and feed him before he wastes away."

"Yes, Miss Eva." Rose picked up the paper sack blocking the door and headed for the bathroom with Ivan in tow. Ivan jumped up on the lavatory to supervise Rose as she washed out Ivan's bowls in the bathroom sink. As she worked, he stuck his paw in the water, splattering it all over the mirror, the walls and the floor. Then he licked the moisture from his foot or shook it to watch the droplets fly through the air. Rose knew exactly what he wanted. She turned the pressure to a slow steady stream and stood back as he lapped water directly from the faucet. As he drank, she dried his Nippon dining essentials.

"Here you go, Master Ivan," she said as she emptied the freshly prepared minced chicken contents from the one-quart glass Mason jar onto the clean saucer. Ivan smacked his lips appreciatively as he licked at his dinner.

While he dined, she used the fry strainer to scoop the pan. Once again, she freshened the pan with a shoebox full of clean ashes.

As Rose emerged from the bathroom, Nurse Cavanaugh handed Miss Eva an ivory colored soup bowl inscribed with "Baker Hospital" in burgundy.

"You need anything else, Miss Dupree?" the nurse asked.

Eva shook her head and blew on the soup. "I'm better for now."

After some soup, a bit of color filtered back to Eva's face. "Thank you, Rose. What would I do without you?"

"You'd have to do your own fussing again. As much as you like fussing, you'd enjoy that."

Eva dropped her head against her pillow. "Not right now. I prefer you handle the fussing for a while."

"I'll do that." Rose handed her boss a steaming cup with the instructions, "Drink this."

Eva sniffed it suspiciously. "What is it?"

"Something that will make you feel better." She turned her back to Eva and headed back to the bathroom. The discussion about the cup's contents was closed.

"This is foul," she called into the bathroom. She pushed the cup away.

"I'll see if I can't buy something to improve the flavor," Rose returned to Eva with the tote bag in hand. "Until then, finish it up."

"I'm feeling better. Why don't you go on and explore the town? See if you can find a package store."

Rose shook her head. "Not just yet. Let's see some more color in your face, first."

Eva ignored her and continued, "If you're up for shopping, could you pick up a few things for me when you get into town?"

"Yes, ma'am. I saw a market not far from where I'm staying."

"Great." Eva jotted down a list of necessities, including Scotch whiskey and oil of wintergreen. As an afterthought, she wrote down a beer. After all, she might find someone else who needed a drink as badly as she did. She handed the list to Rose. "Do *you* need anything?"

"I've been looking for a rich colored man to take care of me, but I hear Louis Armstrong is married." She placed the list in her purse.

"I'll keep an eye out for one. What age?"

"Rich, honey. Rich is the age...I could use a new set of feet, too."

"I'll see what I can do...Do you have your medicine?"

Rose dug around in her bag, pulled out a brown bottle and held it up.

"Thank you, Rose. I need you here. I know it's hard on you. You didn't have to come."

Rose rested her hands on her hips. "Yes I did. Mr. Edgar would want me to take care of you...and Master Ivan."

They awkwardly stared at each other. Rose broke eye contact and headed for the bathroom. "I need to finish cleaning up after His Majesty, and then I'll check out the shops."

Rose sang under her breath as she washed the dirty kitty dishes.

With Ivan resting by her side, Eva dozed lightly to the melody of, "Ain't got Time to Die," as Rose's mellow alto voice drifted out from the bathroom. Lulled to sleep, Eva never heard Rose quietly shut the door behind her

Rose left the hospital and walked toward Spring Street. She guessed her kinfolk back home in Dallas were still suffering with ninety-something temperatures. Just the hike four blocks from her home to the A & P Grocery Store would have had her swimming in her own sweat. Here, high up in the mountains, it felt like a late Texas autumn, almost long sleeve weather. This brisk afternoon, she could walk all over town without drawing so much as a bead of perspiration.

Today she was a woman on a mission, several missions, actually.

One of the items on Miss Eva's shopping list was right next door to the hospital at St. Elizabeth's Catholic Church. One of the strangest churches she'd ever seen, Rose entered the church through the belfry and walked through the courtyard toward the gift store.

Although Rose, herself, wasn't big on saints and medals, Miss Eva had asked her to pick up a medallion and prayer card for St. Peregrine, the patron saint of cancer victims. Not entirely convinced of the doctors' diagnosis, Rose studied other options. Reading all those cards took more time than she expected. After all, they didn't pay much attention to saints at the Living Waters Gospel Church. She gathered up some other cards, too. St. Michael defended against evil. Who couldn't benefit from protection again foul forces? Marina of Antioch was the patron saint of kidney sufferers. There was only one medal left of St. Alban; he must be good. After all, people had bought all but one of his cards. Maybe one of these saints would take pity on Miss Eva. She smiled as she took a final card, Gertrude of Nivelles. An artist depicted her with a mouse scurrying up her staff. Ironic since Gertrude represented the patron saint of cats. Mr. Edgar would be pleased that there's a saint to look after his Ivan.

Rose paid for her treasures, then headed downtown.

After a while the shops all blurred together, and Rose stepped back into a recessed store entrance to get her bearings. She toyed with a wild strand of hair visible in her reflection in the shop's front window. A wide smile crossed her face. Basin Liquors, was painted on the window. Miss Eva sure would be glad to see her tonight.

Her blissful moment was short-lived. She picked up her bag. She'd have to walk all the way around the block so she could enter through the back door. Rose sighed.

Out of the hundreds of alcoholic beverages, she saw only one of interest to Miss Eva, Haig and Haig Blue Label Scotch. Mixed with mineral water, it ought to bring a smile to her boss' poor strained face. A splash of the Haig would make Rose's herbal concoctions considerably more tolerable. Rose recalled Miss Eva mentioning running into an old friend at the hospital. That lady might not be interested in that lighter fluid Miss Eva drank. Rose also picked up a six-bottle bag of Blatz Old Heidelberg Beer just in case Miss Eva's company had more discriminating taste in refreshments than Eva did.

After Rose left the package store, she entered the butcher shop. The smell of meat hung in the air while a half-butchered beef carcass dangled from a meat hook behind the counter. A large cleaver stuck out of a wooden chopping block next to a couple of naked partially dismembered chickens.

She examined the poultry displayed behind the glass while the butcher finished serving a customer. Another customer or two trickled in, white customers, and Rose waited in the back of the store until their orders had been filled. Only after they left the shop did she dare approach the counter.

"Do you have any chicken giblets?"

The butcher nodded silently.

"I could use some liver, gizzards, heart and lungs for my boss lady's cat."

The butcher was a squat but solid man. His arms, with weight-builder's muscles, looked almost as thick as most men's thighs. His apron wore brown blood stains from wiping his hands. He grabbed a hand full of giblets and tossed them in a square of white butcher paper.

"And I need one of those chickens, that big fat one back there." She pointed to the one in the back of the case.

"Forty cents." His first words to her.

Rose handed him the change and took her two white packages. "Thank you, kindly. I'll be back tomorrow for Master Ivan's dinner." She dropped the parcels into her canvas bag.

Her shopping finished, Rose returned to her temporary home to chop up the chicken parts and sweep up the fireplace ashes into a box for Ivan's commode.

Her host, Zola Mae, kept a tidy home. The smell of dinner simmering on the stove filled the house. Seventy-five cents a day rent included dinner. Tonight it smelled of boiled ham and greens, mostly greens.

"You hungry?" Zola Mae called from the back of the house.

"Oh yes." Rose joined Zola Mae in the kitchen.

"Andy'll be home from the hospital soon. Sally, our neighbor's daughter is eating with us tonight. Her mama's got to work late cuz her boss lady's sick."

"I'll just take care of a few things and get cleaned up."

Rose expertly chopped the chicken parts into bite-sized pieces, at least bite-sized for a cat.

Zola Mae crossed her arms and said bitterly, "I'll say, that cat eats better than most folks I know. If that was my cat I'd make that varmint live off his own work killing mice and rats."

Rose dried her hands on the apron that Zola Mae lent her. "When other employers treated their colored help like criminals, Mr. Edgar treated me kindly. And he loved that cat. He ain't here to care for him now, so the least I can do is take care of something he loved. Besides, unlike most people, Master Ivan appreciates when I do something for him and he shows it."

Rose wiped the paring knife on a wet rag and wrapped the giblets back in the butcher paper.

"I brought you a little something." Rose nodded toward a white butcher package sitting on the kitchen table.

At suppertime they all sat around the table, Andy, Zola Mae and their two children, Henry and Ruthie and their neighbor's teenage daughter, Sally.

With the fragrance of fried chicken hanging in the air, Andy, still dressed in his Baker Hospital elevator operator uniform, folded his hands and said grace much more enthusiastically than the night before. After 'amen' he nodded at Zola Mae to serve dinner.

Sally bit into a thigh. She closed her eyes as she chewed. "Miss Zola, I don't think I never tasted chicken this good. I can't remember the last time I had chicken."

Zola looked at Rose and started to say something, but Rose shook her head as if to say, "Don't ruin it." Instead of explaining where the windfall came from, Zola Mae simply said, "The Lord provided us with this good food." Across the table the two younger kids bickered over a drumstick.

"Where you from, Miss Rose?" Sally asked.

"I'm from Dallas."

"Why you here in Eureka Springs?

"Miss Eva, the lady I work, for is sick. She's at the Baker Hospital."

Everything stopped. Ruthie, who was in the process of laying a right jab into her brother's shoulder, froze mid-punch. Zola Mae and Andy exchanged cryptic glances. Andy went back to cutting a piece of meat that didn't need it. Zola Mae stirred the vegetables, then offered Henry another helping of greens.

"Is something wrong?" Rose asked.

After a long pause, Sally finally said, "I wouldn't stay there."

"Why not?"

The girl glanced sideways at Zola Mae who gave her the keep-your-mouth-shut stare.

Finally, Sally asked, "Don't she know?"

"Sally, this ain't none of our business," Zola Mae snapped. "Hush now."

Rose put her fork down. "What's wrong with that hospital?"

The girl answered, "My mama says that it's a good place to die."

"Ouch." Sally rubbed her shin and looked at Zola Mae. "Why'd you kick me? I was just telling the truth. My mama said you shouldn't tell lies or you'll go to Hell."

Rose put her fork down. "What do you mean? Dr. Baker told Miss Eva, that she was guaranteed a cure."

Andy took another bite of ham then pointed at her with his fork. "When Mr. Baker opened his cancer treatment hospital in November of thirty-seven, there was only four funeral parlors in town. Now, we have us eight. The burying business has been good."

Twelve year old Henry squirmed in his seat like he was sitting on hot coals. "I heard that the hospital is haunted."

"Henry!" Andy scolded.

"It's true, Papa," the boy protested. "I ain't the only one who says so. Dexter at church says he and one of his friends went and crawled into that furnace what the hospital got and pulled out a hand."

Andy thumped Henry on the top of the head. "What you talking shit for, boy?"

"But Daddy, I ain't talking shit." Henry ducked as Zola Mae, too, cuffed him on the top of the head. The boy rubbed his head. "Hey, he said it first." The boy pointed at his dad. "Mama, I was only repeating what he said. Besides, I seen the hand. Dexter says they burned the bodies in there. I wouldn't go near there for nothing."

Ruthie piped in her two cents worth. "I heard that there was spooks there. You ever seen any, Daddy?

Andy unconsciously shivered. "I never seen one, sometimes I feel so scared I could swallow my heart and don't know why. Now, don't you go telling folks that. I'll lose my job. You hear?"

"Yes, Papa," the kids said together.

That ended the conversation. The six people sitting around the table finished their meal in total silence. As Rose dished herself another spoon of greens she replayed the conversation in her mind. She said a silent prayer and hoped that St. Albans could protect her and Miss Eva against whatever spirits dwelt at the Baker Hospital.

After dinner, Rose returned to the hospital with her purchases in hand. Surprisingly, Ivan wasn't at his usual place—at the door awaiting her arrival. After all, it was mealtime.

"Miss Eva," Rose called as she walked through the door. Rose stopped, set down her bags and rested her fists on her hips. "My, my." Rose smiled at Miss Eva and her guest. "I see you're feeling better."

"Thanks to the world's best nurse." Eva pointed at Rose.

Ivan snoozed on an overstuffed chair in the corner. He opened his eyes the moment he heard Rose's voice, which was the same as sounding the dinner bell. After taking a long, invigorating stretch, he rushed over to Rose weaving in and out of her ankles.

Eva stood up slowly from her couch and approached Rose. "Did you get it?" She had her hand out in expectation and took a bottle-shaped paper bag from her maid. Eva could smell cigarette smoke on Rose's clothes as the maid leaned closer.

"Mossell," Eva nodded to Rose, "This is my bootlegger, Rose."

"Hi there, Rose, I'm Mossell. How's the world treating you?" she asked from her wheelchair.

"Pleased to meet you," the maid answered on the way to the bathroom.

After Eva pulled the scotch out, Mossell called to Rose, "Didn't you bring anything good to drink?"

"Is this what you are waiting for?" Rose walked into the living area and handed Mossell a large canvas bag and a bottle opener.

"Ooooh girl," Mossell held up the bottle opener. "Where I come from we call these church keys. Praise the Lord. Hey, Rose, get a glass. Join us."

Rose hesitated and looked at Eva.

"You heard the lady," Eva said. "Get a glass."

"Really?" Rose smiled a broad smile, and held up the white package of giblets. "Let me tend to Master Ivan or we won't have a moment's peace."

A few minutes later, she joined them, meekly at first.

Eva and Mossell sat on a flower-patterned sofa in the sitting room. Each lady held her beverage of choice—Mossell clutched a bottle of Blatz Old Heidelberg Beer while Eva sipped Scotch and Eureka Springs water out of a Baker Hospital water glass. Rose sat down on a nearby stuffed chair, albeit a little uncomfortably.

"Name your poison, sweet pea," Mossell said to Rose.

Eva raised her eyebrows and shrugged her shoulders. "Would you like a drink, Rose?"

"How about one of Miss Mossell's beers?" Rose asked.

"That's my girl," Mossell popped the cap off with the church key with one motion of her experienced beer-drinking hand. "Here." She handed Rose the brown bottle.

She took a long drink. "My, oh my. That's no Shiner Beer."

"Shiner Beer?"

"A Texas brand," Eva explained. "Roughly the same flavor as some bodily waste."

"Miss Eva is certainly entitled to her opinion," Rose said, "but she has been known to be wrong on some form of refreshments."

Mossell took a long sip and savored the taste in her mouth before swallowing. "God, that's good. I thought I'd die never getting to drink another beer. Now I can die happy. I don't know how Eva drinks that paint thinner of hers."

Eva held up her glass. "This is eighteen-year old paint thinner.

Thank you, Rose."

"Yes, ma'am. The best Eureka Springs has to offer." Rose took another sip of Old Heidelberg.

"Roger used to drink scotch." Mossell said. "Tried to get me to drink it. I knew, then, that man hated me. That's when I learned that he was just one giant trouser snake."

Rose started laughing so hard beer spewed out her nose. Embarrassed, she jumped up and wiped her face with her hankie, which she had conveniently stored between her cleavage.

Still licking the dinner off of his whiskers Ivan eased out from under the bed and followed her back into the bathroom.

"What's so funny about that?" Eva asked.

"Nothing, Miss Eva."

"The ironic thing about Roger," Mossell explained, "is that although he was the world's largest dick, he had the world's smallest equipment. Only about this big." She held her fingers about an inch apart...Here, Rose. Have another beer." She opened another bottle and handed it to the maid. "But then," she said to Eva, "I don't need to tell you that, do I, sugar?"

"I'm afraid I wouldn't know," Eva said firmly.

"It's kind of funny the affection he had for his little, uh," she looked at her crotch, "friend. Much ado about nothing, if you ask me. What do you have to say about it, Rose? You were laughing a few minutes ago. Sounds to me like you're a woman with something on her mind."

"It ain't one of those things I can talk about in polite company," Rose admitted.

"Well, hell, Cumquat. Who says you're in polite company? Come on. Confess. What was so damn funny?."

Rose again looked at Eva.

"Go ahead, Rose," Eva said. "I'm intrigued, too."

Rose took a long swig from the bottle, a little liquid courage. "You'll never guess what I saw today on Spring Street."

They stared at her. "Tell us."

"My, oh my. This is embarrassing." She giggled. "But, I must have seen Miss Mossell's former mister cuz I saw a prick that must have been twenty feet long."

"Rose?" Eva stared at her.

"Do tell, dumpling." Mossell lit a cigarette and took a long drag off of it then flicked the growing line of ashes in a square glass

Baker Hospital ashtray.

"Really, Miss Eva." Rose jumped up and pulled a postcard from one of the shopping bags. Handing it to Eva with a sly grin she said, "It was a sign for the Palace Hotel and Bathhouse. It looked like a twenty-foot tall old fellow. I'm telling you it was even Jewish."

Sure enough, Eva passed Mossell a full color postal card of a hotel, not unlike cards she had seen of the Baker Hospital, except the outline of the sign in front did resemble the shape of an enormous penis complete with testicles, a circumcised penis. Besides the sign, the corners of the roof display big, but not that big, bronze old fellows without any accoutrements.

"Where did you get this?" Mossell asked with a mischievous twinkle in her eyes.

"It's a hotel on Spring Street. They tell me it used to be a house of ill repute."

Eva eyed the postcard. "Who'd have guessed? What kind of services did they provide, there?"

"What you see there…to the ladies." Rose giggled like a college girl telling a dirty joke.

"To ladies?" Mossell asked still wide-eyed.

"Loosely speaking, Miss Mossell."

"Now, see, Eva," Mossell instructed. "I told you that you should drink with the servants. It creates loyalty and you'd be amazed at what you learn. Who would have thought Rose would have presented us with such a flattering likeness of Roger?"

As if on cue, Ivan jumped up on the chair, snuggling closely to Rose. Although her attention was firmly fixed on the photograph, she stroked his fur absently.

"I always said he thought with his head," Mossell said. "I just never said which one."

"How long did you stay married?" Eva polished off the last few drops of scotch.

"Too long." Mossell took another drink from her bottle. "Did you know that eternity consists of seven years?" She held up Rose's postcard. "After seven years he said he wanted one of his starlets…" she eyed Eva briefly. "…and said goodbye. All I got was the house, the Rolls, alimony and his mother's priceless Ming vase."

"You must have been close to his mother," Eva said, her voice warm with sympathy.

Mossell screwed up her face as if she had just smelled a skunk.

"Oh, precious, I hated the old bat. She was spiteful, self-centered, and miserly. Come to think of it, she was just like her son."

"Miss Mossell, why did you keep her vase if you disliked her so?" Rose wondered.

"Because he wanted it. Simple as that. He got everything he ever wanted. So when we got our divorce, I insisted on the vase. It's five-hundred years old...just like his mother."

"My, oh my. It must be worth a fortune," Eva said.

"It is." Mossell agreed. "But I'll never part with it. Not as long as there's breath in my body. Maybe not even then." Mossell focused on Eva. "I tell you, cookie, I want to be buried in there."

"You won't have to worry about that for a long time."

Mossell raised her eyebrows. "We'll see." Then she turned to Rose and said, "Rose, you're a beer behind me. Let's get us a refill."

Rose placed her long thin fingers over her mouth to cover a polite burp. "I don't think so, Miss Mossell. I still got to make it back to town. You have one and I'll pretend I'm drinking with you."

"Good enough." Mossell took another sip from her bottle.

Mossell turned to Eva. "Roger's *Caught in a Web* was your last movie, wasn't it?"

"I caught pneumonia filming the cemetery scene. Damaged my vocal cords. Roger said I sounded like I was going through puberty."

"That's not so bad. Is it?" Mossell cocked an eyebrow.

"I sounded like a *boy* going through puberty."

Mossell grinned. "Oh, that *is* bad."

"His next movie was going to be his first talkie, and the female lead wasn't a deaf-mute," Eva said. "I'm afraid Donald Duck isn't very sexy. Roger wasn't very tactful."

"That's Roger. He was as subtle as, well, a twenty-foot tall penis...Funny..." Mossell drew deeply from the bottle, swallowed and finally continued, "I thought he fired you because you quit screwing him, muffin."

That again? Eva sighed. "Mossell, I...never...slept...with...him."

Suddenly there was a rattling at the door. Rose jumped up, yanked the bottle out of Mossell's hand and dashed to the bathroom.

"Good evening, ladies," sang Nurse Noreen Johnston, the youngest nurse Eva had ever seen. She looked about fifteen years old, although she surely must have been older, with sandy hair worn up inside her white nurse's hat. She had a pleasant smile beneath lipstick that was way too pale to be stylish. "It's almost bedtime, Miss

Knight."

"My, where has the time gone?" Mossell said looking at her watch. She tapped out her cigarette in the ashtray sitting on her lap.

"I need to take you back to your room." Nurse Johnston grabbed the wheelchair handles. "Tomorrow's a big day."

"Mossell...I..."

"Night, Eva. Don't worry. Everything's fine."

"Goodnight, Mossell," Eva echoed. Then to the nurse, "I'll turn the light off in a few minutes. I'd like to freshen up before I go to bed."

When the nurse had gone, Rose came out of the bathroom with a couple of sacks in hand. "I'll dispose of the evidence for you, Miss Eva."

"Thank you. It makes me feel like I'm back in high school raiding my mom's liquor cabinet."

"Where I come from, what you're drinking isn't just paint thinner, it's cough medicine." Rose smiled. "When I was little, my grams used to cough something awful. *Poor Grammy*. By the way Miss Eva, I thought you might need a little help." She handed her boss the thin paper sack from the church gift store. "You know, I prefer talking directly to the man upstairs, but if you'd like to talk to those saints too, I thought I'd introduce you personally."

Eva shuffled through the prayer cards, and looked up. "There's a saint for cats?"

"That's what it says. Maybe St. Gertrude can ask Master Ivan to wipe his paws before he steps on the floor...Oh yes, while I was walking around downtown I found something you ladies might enjoy." Rose handed Eva a bag with a large printed envelope inside. "It's kinda silly, but it tickled me."

Eva smiled. "What would I do without you?"

Rose had always been around. She worked for Edgar long before young Eva ever met the love of her life. And before that, young Rose helped her mother Opal Freeman, tend the Foxworthy home. When Opal grew too old to work, her daughter began maintaining the Foxworthy home. Rose was part of the family. Eva couldn't imagine running the house without her.

"You'd have to hire three just to replace me." Rose slid an envelope out of the sack. Fitch's *Hollywood Try-On Hair Styles*. Inside she found cardboard squares, each with a different hairstyle and color printed on it. One had a platinum blonde up do, another had black braids. A brunette hairstyle sported a Marcel wave. The last had a short curly red style.

"I got this when I bought a bottle of Fitch Shampoo." Rose picked up the redhead hairdo. "It's a cut-out." She poked her fingers through the perforation. "See?" She held up the haircut. Instantly, Rose became a redhead with soft wavy curls.

Eva placed her fingers over her mouth and giggled. "Oh, Rose, it's you!"

Rose dashed over to the mirror and gazed at the redhead staring back at her. "I always wondered what I'd look like with red hair. I guess I know now. It would look a might more natural on Master Ivan. You and your ladies will have a fine time playing with your hair."

"Thanks. This will be a fun diversion." Eva slid the saint card into her pocket.

"Can I get you something else, Miss Eva?" As she often did, Rose wiped her hands on her apron.

Eva glanced out the door to the balcony. "What?"

"Do you need anything, Miss Eva? You look sort of lost," the housekeeper said.

Eva shook her head. She started to tell Rose about the girl on the balcony when the maid checked her watch and said, "I'd better get going. I don't want to miss the last trolley." She picked up her tote bag filled with the empty contraband beer bottles and headed for the door. "Night, Miss Eva. I'll see you in the morning."

"Goodnight, Rose."

The sound of the door closing behind Rose felt like the sealing of a crypt. A few minutes ago the jokes and alcohol flowed like a Roman fountain. Now, Eva sat in her chair alone listening to every creak and groan of the building. Were those sounds the natural sounds of an aging building or something more sinister? Eva hesitated, but climbed into the shower. If something happened to her, at least she would go out clean. Eva slipped into the clean nightgown and climbed into bed. Ivan jumped up beside her and rested his head on her thigh.

By the rhythmic pounding above her, Eva could tell the dogs were trotting up and down the stairs. Norman Baker must still be in his office. After her Haig and Haig, she didn't face the rest of the night with the same trepidation. Within a few minutes, Eva fell into a troubled sleep.

Eva awoke with a start. A chill filled the room and Eva with dread. She trembled as she looked around. It took a few moments before she recalled where she was. *Was a nurse in the room?* Although she saw no one else in the suite, she felt someone's stare. She pulled the blanket up a little closer to her throat.

After a while she decided she really was alone. She nestled her head back into the pillow and closed her eyes. Suddenly the hair on her arm stood up on end and, quite distinctly, a man's voice whispered in her left ear, "I want you."

She froze, paralyzed and unable to move or even breathe, like being mummified alive. Finally the invisible force released her and she screamed.

When Nurse Turner entered the room she found Eva pale and trembling. "What's wrong *this* time, Miss Dupree?"

She hesitated. "Someone whispered in my ear. He said, 'I want you.'"

"You were dreaming."

Eva clenched her fists. "Don't patronize me! I wasn't dreaming."

"Miss Dupree, if you continue to disrupt the patients in this hospital, I will have to isolate you." Nurse Turner stormed out the door.

Once she had shut the door behind her, Ivan jumped back on the bed. He tapped Eva with his paw. When that failed to get her attention, he bumped her hand with his head. Ivan was persistent, forcing her to rub his forehead.

"I know I heard someone whisper something in my ear." She began to cry. "I'm going crazy. Oh, God, I'm going crazy." Eva turned the reading lamp on and folded herself into a fetal position. Rocking back and forth, she softly sang, "*A mighty fortress is our God, a bulwark...*No, let's try the third stanza. *"And though this world, with devils filled, should threaten to undo us, we will not fear, for God hath willed...his truth to triumph through us. The Prince of Darkness grim, we tremble not for him; his rage we can endure, for lo, his doom is sure; one little word shall fell him.*"

Eva turned the radio on, then returned to bed. She leaned back against the headboard and tried to read, but even with the light on, she eventually dozed off with the book on her chest.

Shortly, she opened her eyes, caught in that twilight between waking and sleeping. She heard sounds in the hall—the metallic clanging of keys, a door closing, and, after a brief pause, the soft, "squeak, squeak, squeak." She recalled her first night at the Baker Hospital. She heard the squeak twice within a few minutes. Maybe the nurse would come back again. She climbed out of bed and slowly approached the door.

She placed her ear against the wood and waited. A few minutes later, she heard it again. Once more Eva cracked the door and saw Turner coming out of the fourth floor annex pushing a gurney. A white sheet covered an outline that looked like a female body.

DAY FOUR—*Sunday, September 3*

"Good morning, Miss Dupree," said Nurse Cavanaugh. As usual she opened the curtains with a blinding yank of the cord. "It's a beautiful morning, don't you think? Here's your coffee and your treatment." She rolled the bedside table over and placed the coffee cup in front of Eva. "Ummmm. That coffee smells so good. I could use a cup myself."

"And Ivan, here's your breakfast." She carried another plate into the bathroom. On a Baker Hospital plate was turkey cut into tiny cubes and a scrambled egg. Apparently the chef didn't realize his diner was a cat because he garnished the plate with a sprig of parsley. Nurse Cavanaugh reached down and patted Ivan's head.

The cat pounced and swallowed the first piece without chewing then settled down to enjoy his morning feast.

Nurse Cavanaugh smiled mischievously. "I stole the turkey off of another patient's plate. He'll never miss it...After your treatment, I want you to get some sun."

"I don't feel like it. I'd rather stay in here. I haven't been sleeping well."

"Don't worry. Today's shot is in the hip. It's not bad at all."

Eva sniffed her coffee before taking a sip. "If it's that easy, then you can take it for me."

"Sorry, Miss Dupree." She opened the door to leave. "I'm not the one who needs it."

After the fact, Eva had to admit that compared to yesterday's shot in the abdomen, this injection was barely noticeable. Afterward, obeying Nurse Cavanaugh's demand, Eva dressed, dabbed a couple of drops of oil of wintergreen inside her nostrils and dragged herself onto the deck to survive the bright morning sun.

Out in the center of the deck, a patient soaked in sun rays while reading in her hospital bed. After all, fresh air and sunshine could work miracles. Eva didn't recognize either of the sunbathers resting in the lavender chaise lounge. One snoozed despite the bright light. Another patient shielded her eyes from the sun with her hand.

In the center of a klatch of somewhat more mobile patients,

Gazetta blabbered on. Around them gathered swallows fluttering and darting up and down, squealing as if they were on a predator's dinner menu. Sparrows and pigeons landed on the guardrail. Patients who were more desperate for a taste of nature brought slices of toast or biscuits and tossed crumbs to the birds.

Today a faint haze separated East Mountain from the observation deck. Treetops swayed in the soft breeze.

As Eva approached, the birds scattered, fluttering a few feet away. They eyed her with wait-and-see looks. Once she settled into her seat, the bolder pigeons began to coo, then returned to their panhandling.

Gazetta, who must have been afraid that she would catch lockjaw unless she kept her mouth moving constantly, held captive an insecure young woman Nurse Cavanaugh had introduced as Irma Shivers. Irma sat with her arms crossed across her chest, staring into space and nodding occasionally while Gazetta babbled on and on.

"Strange things happen in my room," Irma confessed in a brief moment when Gazetta paused to take a breath. "I don't want to be alone in there. Sometimes it's so cold I can barely stand it. It feels like someone's watching me all the time."

"It sounds like your room's haunted," Gazetta said. "I've never told anyone before, but I have a ghost in my home. Sometimes I'm so scared I almost tinkle on myself. My bedroom gets so cold you could store meat in there."

Eva scanned the deck. Alone at the far edge of the balcony Mr. Janowitz had drifted off with his head propped up on his hand. He had a couple of days of whisker growth, making him look sloppy and unkempt—not at all the sweet, vibrant man she first saw playing Monopoly with Trudy.

Seeking out a few familiar faces Eva sat in the only vacant chair near Mossell...between Cooper, who was busy tying horsehair fishing flies, and Gazetta. The Human Mouth reminded her of champagne, bright and bubbly. Her body was even shaped much like a wine bottle, with bountiful bosoms and an even more ample posterior. According to Gazetta, her late husband was ambassador to Venezuela. And in her younger days she'd probably been quite a showpiece. Today, husband-hunting, she still dressed in too-low, too-tight blouses that gave the impression that one deep breath would violently free her abundant assets, giving those around her more view than they probably cared for. She might as well have had her vanity mirror surgically fastened to her hand and she was constantly fussing with her hair or checking her lipstick.

Eva smiled at Cooper. "Good morning, Mr. Reilly."

He looked up from the fly he was tying, and took off his reading glasses. "Good morning, Miss Dupree." She couldn't tell whether he was glad to see her or not. He looked down at the deck and said, "Hello, Ivan."

Cooper looked jaunty in a silver brocade smoking jacket.

Eva turned around and saw the cat. "I didn't realize His Majesty had graced us with his presence."

"I hoped he'd show up." Cooper ran his hand all the way down Ivan's back and down his tail. "I have something for him." He pulled a long brown wing feather from his breast pocket. He held it in front of the cat and wiggled it seductively.

Ivan leapt straight up for the swallow's feather, spearing it with his claws. Cooper, an experienced cat teaser tore the feather from Ivan's grasp. With hind legs like steel springs, Ivan pursued it with the graceful persistence of a ballet dancer.

Eva watched Cooper tease the cat. Amused, she asked, "So Mr. Reilly, what do you do?"

He led the cat around in a figure-eight. "I import French wine."

"What did you do during Prohibition?"

"Let's just say, I was a broker."

She smiled knowingly. Broker, that translated to bootlegger. "If there's a war in Europe, will that hurt you?"

He dropped the hand with the feather, letting Ivan capture his prey. The cat padded off with his prize in mouth finally settling under one of the deck chairs to chew on his quarry without interruption.

"I'm sure it will," Cooper said.

Mossell made clicking sounds with her tongue and tossed a couple of breadcrumbs onto the floor. Answering her invitation, the birds waddled over to partake in the feast.

Silently and motionlessly, Ivan waited under the chair. The tip of his tail twitched, his bottom wiggled in anticipation of his pending meal. Fat and indifferent, the fowl nibbled at the tidbits on the floor. Suddenly, a white and red flash appeared in the midst of the birds, and they scattered. The score was Hungry Birds-one, Hungry Cat-nothing. However intimidating an adversary, the cat merely scattered them. A couple of them sought refuge on the guardrail.

"Ivan!" Eva cried out.

He jumped up on the guardrail, wavering and tottering like a tightrope walker with four unsteady feet. The birds simply moved out of reach. As he neared, they fluttered away.

Eva leapt to her feet.

Her husband's cat moved slowly and precariously along the one-inch rail, sixty feet above the ground. He stumbled, slipped from the rail, dangling by his front claws. As he hung there, Eva's stomach knotted and her chest froze. She held her breath.

After what seemed like hours, Ivan reached up with his hind foot and thrust himself back on top of the guardrail. Once he regained his footing, Eva could breathe again. He walked a few more feet, to prove he could, and then hopped down as if it were no more eventful than jumping down from the sofa.

Eva stood up to retrieve her cat when he trotted out of her reach. Ivan was ready for a round of catch-me-if-you-can, but Eva returned to her seat. She simply didn't have the energy to chase him this morning. Once seated again, she turned to Cooper and asked, "You were saying something about the war and the wine business, Mr. Reilly?"

As Cooper went into more detail about the war's devastating effect on the family business, Trudy bounced onto the deck. One hand clung to her Orphan Annie rag doll, the other gestured occasionally to her invisible friend. "They" withdrew to a quiet corner of the deck. Immediately Ivan trotted over to greet Trudy.

"Mr. Kitty," she called out and threw her arms around him.

The grownups watched Trudy play with Ivan for a while. She teased him with his feather making him run and jump for it. Once, in the middle of Ivan's Olympic leap, Trudy stopped and turned to empty air. She cocked her head for a few moments, nodding her head and adding a few words. To those around her it appeared she was actually conversing with a pal. She'd giggle or answer questions. She'd even ask questions and nod at the answers. A couple of times she even responded by looking puzzled.

"I bet I never told you, I had an imaginary friend when I was her age," Gazetta said across Eva to Mossell. "A little gladiator."

"Really?" Mossell said. "What'd he look like?"

"It was a girl. She looked just like me."

"Really?"

"Uh huh."

"I think she was the ghost of a gladiator. Maybe she was me reincarnated."

Mossell asked the question for everyone who was present. "How can you be your own imaginary friend?"

"I don't rightly know. But adults couldn't see her. Kids are always better at seeing ghosts. I know I was."

Eva snickered. *Gladiator, indeed!*

Before long Norman Baker made an appearance on the balcony to greet all the patients.

He had just left the observation deck when Gazetta asked Mossell, "Did you see that?"

"See what, Sugar?"

Gazetta pressed her hand to her collar bone. "Why, the way he was looking at my breasts."

Mossell shot a sideways glance to Eva.

"Who, lamb chop?" Mossell turned slightly and winked at Eva. "Who was looking at your tits? I'll call Mr. Bellows and have that man confined to his room. How rude; staring at a woman's mammaries!"

"Don't call Mr. Bellows." Gazetta blushed. "I'm talking about Dr. Baker."

"Mr. Baker was staring at your breasts?" Eva gasped, fighting to squelch a belly laugh.

Gazetta primped her too-black hair back. "Didn't you see? He wants me."

"Of course, he does, angel." Mossell rolled her eyes at Eva. "Imagine that. Gazetta and Mr. Baker. How does Gazetta Baker sound to you, Eva?"

"I think it has a ring. I hear he's available."

"Stop it." Gazetta pushed away the embarrassment with her hand. "I didn't say anything like that. I can just tell that he's attracted to me. Did you see that motorcar of his? My, oh my! I have never seen anything like it. He picked me up in it."

"Really. I hear he picks up all his important patients with it," Mossell said. "Didn't he pick you up, Eva?"

Eva played along with Mossell. "Yes, he did. Nice car."

"Did you know those headlights disappear into the car?" Gazetta asked. "There are cranks on each side of the dash that raise and lower the headlamps. So does the roof."

"Do tell."

"Eva, it looks like something Buster Crabb should have been driving. I hear he paid $7000 for it. And with all the leather, it smelled like a tack room. I had a dream about Mr. Baker last night. You know what we were doing? He took his hand and he was stroking my—"

Eva jumped up, and headed over to where Trudy and Ivan were playing. "I need to get back to my room." She picked up Ivan and said to Trudy, "Sorry, Trudy. We have to go take a nap." Eva moved toward her door. "I'm starting to feel that ache in my side."

Mossell glared at Eva with that don't-you-dare-leave-me-here-with-her look. "Call me when Rose gets back."

"I will," Eva sang. "You'll need it." She closed the door to the deck behind her.

Eva put Ivan on the floor and dropped into her bed. She picked up the September *Movie Story Magazine* that Rose had left for her and sat on the overstuffed arm chair. There was a two-page spread on Madeleine Carroll and Fred MacMurray in *Honeymoon in Bali*, and six pages devoted to Judy Garland and the newly-released *The Wizard of Oz*. Eva scanned the table of contents for friends. None to speak of, Claudette Colbert, Lana Turner, Constance Bennett, John Wayne, Eddie Albert, Jane Wyman and finally young Mickey Rooney. All newcomers, so to speak.

She opened to an article about Claudette Colbert. There was a photo of Claudette, with her painted-on eyebrows, wearing a slinky, shiny gown reclining on a fainting couch. *That could have been me,* Eva thought sadly.

Suddenly the door opened and Miss Johnston, the very young nurse, came in.

"Good morning, Miss Dupree. Have another glass of water." She handed her a full glass. "Do you need anything?"

Yes...Edgar, their old life, the cancer gone.

Eva shook her head and placed the glass on the side table. "I'm fine."

Moments after the door closed behind the nurse, someone knocked. Eva thought Miss Johnston had returned, but instead Cooper Reilly peered in. "Hello, Miss Dupree."

The moment of self-pity seeing the picture of Claudette Colbert evaporated into pleasure. "Mr. Reilly, come in."

"Please, call me Cooper."

"All right, but only if you call me Eva. Please, sit down." She motioned to her sofa in the suite's living area. "Would you like something to drink?"

"What do you have?"

She smiled devilishly. "I can offer you scotch and water."

His brows rose in mock shock. "I didn't think they allowed alcohol."

"This is medication." She rose and pulled the bottle of Haig out from beneath her nightgown in the dresser. She hid in the bathroom for a moment and retuned with two glasses of "water."

He raised his glass. "Here's to your health."

"To health."

They clinked glasses and took a drink.

"Do you ever miss being on the screen?"

His question caught her off guard. "I can see myself whenever I want; I have a screening room at home. I used to watch them, but I don't anymore."

"Why not? I'd think it would be fun to see yourself with Lon Chaney again."

"Lon's gone, and I'm so much older." Eva pursed her lips and said sadly, "I don't like to see myself as I was."

"I could watch them over and over again. Some of those moving pictures scared me so badly, I checked my closets and looked under the mattress before I went to bed."

"Really?" Her voice sounded uncharacteristically raspy—her throat, scratchy.

"Really. Even though they scared the willies out of me, I watched them over and over again. And when your new movies came out, I was first in line to buy a ticket. I still have some of the ticket stubs."

They chatted for a few more minutes about a little bit of everything, movies, the wine business and drilling sites in west Texas. Finally Cooper said, "You need a change of scenery. Why don't you let me take you to dinner in town?" He lit a cigarette and took a deep puff. "I know this great little diner."

Eva looked up for a moment, and hesitated. *Why not?* "That sounds like fun…" she started, but a mental horror movie interrupted her.

In her mind a scene played out. A line of people wandered up to her table, 'Don't I know you?" "Didn't you used to be a teller at my bank?" and worst of all, "Didn't you used to be Eva Dupree?" Another image followed in which a romantic dinner was suddenly interrupted by explosive pain and projectile vomiting.

"…but…Thank you, Mr. Reilly. I'd like to go…I really would. But right now I'm feeling rather weak. Could you give me a rain check?" She struggled to get to her feet.

"Can I help you?" Still holding his drink, he jumped up and ran around the chair. "It's all right." He wrapped his arm around her waist.

"I'm sorry. Right now, I'm not feeling well. Maybe some other time. Really," She tried to smile.

"Do you need anything?" he asked, leading Eva to her bed.

Did she? Did she need someone to keep her company, or someone to confide in? Would he believe her if she told him about the strange happenings in her room? He'd probably think she was a kook taking her own movies too seriously.

Cooper steadied her elbow as she flopped onto her bed with all the grace of Trudy's Orphan Annie ragdoll.

"Some other time," he repeated. After draining his glass, he set it on her nightstand and headed for the door. He hesitated, smiling at her for a moment, then closed the door behind him.

She struggled to the bathroom, poured a scotch and water then went back to bed.

Miss Johnston came in to check on her. "Oh good. You're drinking."

"Oh yes."

"Would you like some more?" She reached for Eva's glass.

Eva tightened her grip. "No, thank you."

The young nurse's eyes narrowed. She wrestled it from Eva's grasp and sniffed the contents. "What's in here?"

"Hey, one of the patients gave that to me. What's the problem?"

Johnston poured the contents into the toilet and flushed. "Alcohol is against the rules at the Baker Hospital. When you go home you can drink. You will not have alcohol here."

Eva stared hard at her. "*You* have alcohol here."

She filled Eva's glass with water and handed it back. "That's to sterilize the instruments, not to drink."

Eva sighed and sipped. *Busted.* She turned on the radio. The notes of *Moonlight Serenade* danced around the room. When she heard it for the first time earlier in the year, she thought it was such a beautiful song, the melody romantic and poignant. It called up memories of Edgar and her dancing the hours away on the polished floor at the Fairmont Hotel to Gershwin's *Someone to Watch Over Me*. She could almost feel him, almost touch the roughness of his stubble at the end of the day. She remembered how his scent hung in the air when he left the room. And yet, pieces were missing. What she wouldn't give to have him back, or to forget him entirely. This limbo was too painful to bear.

Ivan joined her in bed and bumped his massive head against hers. It was like being head-butted by a small bulldozer. That was it. At those times when Edgar forced her to pet the cat, she could smell Edgar's pipe tobacco on his fur. Eva so resented the cat's invasion into their intimate moments. She certainly complained about the bushels of cat hair he seemed to shed year-round. Now, Ivan was her sole connection to her one true love—Ivan, the Terrible had become her lifeline. The rumbling in the back of his throat echoed the band's percussion.

He crawled up into her lap, resting his head against her breast as *Moonlight Serenade* played its final notes. Childlike, his enormous amber eyes gazed into her face. She slid her arms around him, closing her eyes and rocking him.

More love songs followed, but the mood vanished with the broadcast of the afternoon news of a world going insane. She tried to blot out the words of the announcer. The only thing that existed was the purr of Edgar's cat and the cashmere softness of his fur. That and that slightly sweet smell of Ivan. Together they napped. She wondered what people would think about her, embracing a silly cat like that. But it didn't matter. They could all go to Hell.

A few hours later, as Eva and Ivan slept, Gazetta Smith tiptoed into the suite. She took one last glance around outside the door before closing it—like a spy trying to make sure the enemy didn't spot her.

"Hi," Gazetta said as Eva cracked one eye.

"Hi, Gazetta. Do you need something?"

"I was so excited to learn you were going to be staying here," Gazetta said, rubbing her hands together. "There's something I need to tell you. Something I could never tell anyone else."

She was momentarily distracted by the appearance of Ivan.

"What's it about?" Eva prompted

Gazetta reached over and stroked the cat's fur. "Have you noticed that Mr. Baker is a little...strange?"

"I have to admit, I don't know many men who wear lavender,"

Eva confessed. "What are you getting at?"

"Nothing, really. I just think some of the things he does are strange. Did you know he won't touch a yellow vegetable? It's at the opposite side of the color wheel from purple. He even had me sign some silly letter to my niece."

"What did it say?" Eva asked.

"I don't remember, but it just seemed odd to me. I asked a couple of the ladies about it and none of the married ladies had to sign one."

Eva sat up. The one disadvantage to her suite was that the bed was a regular hotel bed, not a hospital bed that could be cranked into more comfortable positions. "That *is* strange."

Gazetta started to say something when the rumble of Great Danes trotting around overhead interrupted her thoughts.

"Speaking of strange," Gazetta said. "I need to tell you about the ghost I have in my bedroom back home. I've never said anything to anyone about it before, but you'd understand since you were in all those pictures." Her voice lowered. "He lives in my underwear drawer. Whenever I open the drawer he's moved everything around. He especially likes my pink lacy panties."

"Really?" Eva tried in vain to think of an escape. She was trapped in her own bed.

"He talks to me. Every now and then you can understand what he's saying but most of the time he mumbles or says things that don't make sense. You know they do that. Or they can't finish what they want to say. Kind of like my late husband—God rest him—he could never finish a sentence."

It's no wonder he couldn't complete a sentence.

"They only have so much strength for communicating, you know," Gazetta said.

"Who has only so much strength?" Eva asked.

"Ghosts, of course," Gazetta said.

"Really." Eva fought to keep her tone polite. "How do you know the ghost is a man. A female spirit might just think you have good taste in lingerie."

"I know it's male because he has sex with me."

"Really?" Eva tried not to gape or laugh.

"Oh yes. It's the same every time. First he pulls down the sheet. Then he raises up my nightgown..."

That was too much. She had to get away! "Oooh, uh, Gazetta,

that's fascinating, but my goodness, look at the time!" Eva slid off the bed. "I didn't realize how late it's gotten. I'm supposed to practice the piano every day at the same time. I should be practicing right now. If I miss it, even by a few minutes, my rhythm is off for days. I've got to go down to the lobby, right now."

"But I'm not finished."

"Yes, you are." *Oh that was so harsh.* To sound a little less abrasive Eva added, "Gazetta, that would make a great book. Why don't you write it all down and I'll read it when you get it finished. Okay?" Eva grabbed her robe and rushed past her guest toward the door. "Maybe you can tell Ivan about it."

After she practiced, Eva went out to the observation deck where she found some of the other patients. Mr. Janowitz was nowhere to be found. Unfortunately, Mossell was missing, too. However, Irma Shivers chatted and played Gin Rummy with Lillian Hundley and Corinthia Shipp.

Eva chatted with the ladies for a few minutes, then said, "Anyone want to go to the hair dressers?"

"We could all use a hair appointment," Corinthia confessed, pulling some stray dishwater bangs off of her forehead.

"Well, I can't take you to the beauty shop," Eva smiled, "but I have the next best thing."

Irma smiled weakly, then answered with a hoarse voice, "I'd love to, really. But I just need to get back to my room. I'm afraid I could use a little lie down."

Eva smiled. "Why don't we meet down in your room in a little while. If you don't feel like it, then we'll go back up to my room. You'll love it."

"My room's a bit drafty," Irma complained. "I don't know where it comes from. It always seems to have cold spots."

"That's all right," Eva countered. "I'll wear my sweater."

"Are you sure you want to come to my room? I'm always having problems with the electrical," Irma complained. "Sometimes the light flickers on and off. When the janitor checks on it, it always works just fine when he gets there."

Lillian patted her on the shoulder. "We'll light a candle if we need to."

"Okay, my room. By the way, Miss Dupree, could you bring your little friend?"

"Trudy?"

"No, your roommate."

At two that afternoon the little party filed down to room 218. Compared to Eva's suite, it was a shoebox, with only room for a bed, a chest of drawers, a vanity and a small writing desk crammed in with a shoehorn. The entire room could fit into the smaller room of Eva's suite. As Irma promised it was colder than Eva's.

Eva dropped Ivan on the vanity and set her makeup carrying case down on the desk. Ivan hissed at the mirror, jumped down and made himself comfortable on Irma's twin bed. Eva shrugged. Who could explain what sets a cat off?

"I guess he doesn't like the cat in the mirror," Eva said. "Who's thirsty?"

Lillian shook her head. "No thanks. I've had enough Baker Hospital water to keep me peeing until God comes back."

Eva opened her crocodile makeup bag. "I'm not talking about water." She held up a half-full bottle of scotch and a couple of semi-cool bottles of beer. Corinthia snatched the scotch bottle out of Eva's hand and poured a little into a Baker Hospital glass, then handed the bottle to Lillian Hundley who sniffed the bouquet as one would a fine wine. Irma took an Old Heidelberg and opened it on the corner of her oak desk.

Eva raised one eyebrow. "You've done that before!"

"That's right, Miss Dupree. I learned how to do that at Miss Clairemore's Finishing School for Young Ladies."

"I knew you popped that cap with a touch of class."

"Now, down to business." Eva laid out the twelve Old Fitch hairdos on the bed so they could all be seen: silver hair with a Marcel wave, raven with a braid piled on top, bleach blond pin curls that framed the face, loose chocolate curls reminiscent of some of Katherine Hepburn's styles, short, soft auburn hair, an ebony-ivory blend worn by middle aged ladies, an ash blond updo, and Rose's red hair. Since Ivan had claimed the center of the bed for himself, Eva arranged them around him. Unimpressed, he laid with his head resting on his paws, his eyes half-opened.

"What's your pleasure," Eva asked Irma.

Irma coughed and then replied in her husky voice, "I've always wanted to have mysterious black hair." She hacked some more.

They all circled Irma, who sat in front of the mirror of her vanity. Irma Shivers was in her early twenties, thin and pale. Her face and neck were so swollen they looked like they had been stuck on the wrong body. She'd piled her acorn-colored hair in a haphazard manner atop her head and her bangs hung down stringy and oily.

Eva pulled her hair back and tacked it up with hairpins. She slid the cardboard hairpiece over her face like an Easter bonnet. Irma looked like a completely different woman. Beneath the empty eyes, she glowed. For a moment, just a fleeting second, she felt pretty, maybe even glamorous. She giggled like a schoolgirl.

"Let's see what you look like as a brunette." Lillian handed her the Hepburn look.

She tried on the other styles, but Irma always went back to the elegant coal black braids.

Next Lillian sat before the mirror, tittering. "Mirror, mirror on the wall..." she said. "Who's the fairest one of all."

They all laughed.

"Which one do you want to try?"

"I'd like to have fiery red hair," Lillian said.

"I bet you would," Corinthia said.

"What would your husband think of you with red hair" Irma asked.

"He'd say he'd gone to the wrong home."

"Ooooh, that could be fun." Irma chuckled naughtily.

Lillian slipped the cutout over her own hair. The red hair made her look sultry, but with her fair complexion she seemed more natural as a blonde.

"That's just peachy."

"Wait a minute," Irma said. "I need to get a picture of this. She pulled her Baby Brownie out of her dresser and removed it from the corduroy case. "Smile, Lillian."

Lillian turned toward the camera, smiled and froze. Irma snapped the picture and turned the knob until number four appeared through a little window in the back.

After everyone got their turn, Irma said, "We haven't seen you with your hair done, Eva...Is anyone else cold in here? I'm a little chilly."

Eva looked down, blushing. "I just brought them for y'all. I'd feel silly."

"Then feel silly," Corinthia said. "You saw us. It's only fair we get to see you. Besides, I understand you used to do this sort of thing all the time."

"I did?"

"When you dressed up for your movie parts."

Eva sighed. "So I did. All right." She hesitated before she sat down in front of the mirror. She remembered when she was being made up for *Dying Tomorrow*. Doris the makeup girl—a mid-thirties woman with a missing front tooth and a waistline almost as big as her butt and bust put together, had the enviable job of turning beautiful women into zombies. Eva remembered the first time Doris transformed her from a nineteen-year-old beauty into the pallid undead.

"I want to be blonde," the new actress said excitedly when Doris first sat down to do her magic.

"And blonde you shall be."

By the time the makeup girl had finished, Eva had traded in her stylish dark curls for a frizzy white wig that looked like she had stuck her tongue in a high voltage socket.

Eva found herself once again saying, "I want to be blonde."

Granting her wish, Irma slid the blond updo onto her head. Eva turned around to face her audience.

"Oh, my dear, that's you!" Lillian said.

Corinthia just sighed. "You look so good as a blonde. I'm sure you look good in all of them. It's just not fair."

"What do you think?" Eva turned to ask Irma, who was staring back wide-eyed. Irma's face drained of color, and she screamed, dropping hairpins all over the hardwood floor.

Suddenly the hair on the back of Eva's neck stood up and she felt like she'd been doused in ice water.

Over on the bed Ivan instantly transformed from a sleepy feline to a spitting demon cat with every hair standing on end. From his throat arose a shriek that sounded as if it came straight from the pits of Hell.

Eva jumped up and tried to lead Irma to the vanity chair. "Come on, Irma. Why don't you sit down?"

"No, I can't!" Irma looked like she'd seen a ghost. Eva poured her a scotch and water, a little stronger than normal.

"What's wrong?" Eva handed Irma the glass.

"Are you all right?" Corinthia asked.

Irma drained her drink in one gulp. Staring at the vanity, she stammered, "I saw a pair of hands reach for you through the mirror."

"What?" Lillian asked. "That's silly."

"No, I'm telling you, when Eva turned around to look at us I saw two hands reach out of the mirror for her."

"Irma, you must have seen the reflection of one of us. There's no one else in here," Lillian said.

Irma's hands shook as she held her glass out for a refill, then took another long sip of Scotch. "I'm not imagining it. I really saw it."

"Dear, Nurse Turner told me that sometimes the medication makes you see things. I think I see things every now and then, myself," Lillian said.

Irma trembled, sloshing some of her drink on the floor. "That's not all. Once, out of the corner of my eye, I saw someone outside the window looking in."

"That couldn't be," Lillian said. "Hon, this is the second floor. He'd have to be floating."

The terrified woman slowly shut her eyes. "I know."

Eva poured the last of the Scotch in Irma's glass and dropped the empty bottle back into the makeup carrying case. Lillian and Corinthia picked up their bags and headed for the door.

"We'd better get back to our rooms," Lillian said. "If they find out we've got alcohol in here, we'll all have to deal with Nurse Turner."

"That would be a fate worse than death," giggled Corinthia.

Irma sat on the edge of her bed. "I know you think I'm crazy, but I'm not, Eva. This room scares the peewaddle out of me. I always feel like someone's watching me."

"Irma, it's all right. There's nobody here. We're the only ones in the room."

Irma grabbed Eva's wrist and held on tight. "You believe me, don't you?"

"Yes, Irma. I believe you." Eva worked her arm free. "More than you know. Now listen to me. Nothing is going to hurt you. Nothing!" Eva let out a deep breath. *I wish I really believed that.*

Eva rifled through the hairstyles until she found the black do. "Here. Keep this. When you get scared, just remember how pretty and strong you really are."

Irma clutched the cut out, but it held none of its former joy. "Thank you," she said quietly.

"Ivan and I need to get back to our room. Irma, have you told anyone how scared you are?"

"I did," she said as a tear rolled down her cheek. "Nurse Turner said I was behaving foolishly. That I should grow up."

Eva smiled. "I guess Nurse Turner doesn't know what it's like to be afraid. Why don't you ask Mr. Statler to switch your room? I bet if there's ever a room available, he'll move you."

Eva gave Irma a reassuring pat on the shoulder. Gathering up her makeup case and cardboard hairstyles in one hand and Ivan in the other, Eva said, "It'll be fine."

Irma clasped the cutout to her breast. "I really don't want to be alone."

"I know, but I have to get back to my room." Eva dug into her pocket and pulled out the saint cards Rose had brought her. "Here, this has the St. Michael's prayer to protect you against evil. Just take it out and read it whenever you get scared. You'll feel better. I promise."

Back in her suite Eva switched on CBS news. "German radio reported thousands of civilian casualties yesterday in a Luftwaffe air raid over the town of Sulejowek, Poland. Earlier today, German soldiers set fire to a predominantly Jewish section of the town, shooting many fleeing the inferno. The number of fatalities is unknown." "Sulejowek," Eva repeated to herself. "Isn't that the town that Mr. Janowitz comes from?"

She fed Ivan the last few scraps of meat that Rose had brought for him earlier. She watched him delicately nibble at the giblets. "I'll ask Mr. Janowitz tomorrow. It won't change anything, and at least he'll get one good night's sleep."

Timid rapping at her door interrupted her thoughts. "Yes?"

The door opened ever so slightly. "Mrs. Dupree?" Janowitz's voice shook a little.

She held her breath for a moment. "Come in, Mr. Janowitz."

He stuck his face inside. "I don't wish to disturb you."

"You're not disturbing me. The truth is: I'd like some company."

He grabbed an old spoke back chair and set it down next to the radiator.

"I have a feeling something has happened to my Judyta. Have you heard any more about the war?" he asked

She hesitated. Goose flesh crawled up her arms and back. At first she was tempted to lie and say no, but instead she averted her eyes and said nothing.

"Ah, I see," he said. "The news—it is not so good, eh?"

She shook her head. "No, Mr. Janowitz. I'm afraid it's not." Again, she hesitated. Eva remembered what it felt like when the doctor said the words, "He didn't make it." She chose her words carefully.

"I'm afraid it doesn't look good."

"And what does this mean: It doesn't look good?"

She tried to avoid the stare of those dark eyes—dark and lonely in a strange country. Now, probably alone in the entire world.

"Mr. Janowitz, the Germans have bombed most of Sulejowek."

He wouldn't let her eyes escape his.

"But there's more, isn't there?"

Silently, she looked down.

"What is it you are not saying to me?"

"CBS News reported that German radio broadcasts were bragging about burning down the Jewish neighborhoods in Sulejow..." her words broke off.

Quietly, like a hollow voice in a mausoleum, he said, "And yet, there is even more; is there not?"

Even if she had wanted to, she simply couldn't speak.

"I must know, Mrs. Dupree. No matter what; I must know what my *kochany* has gone through. You see, I know she is dead. She told me," he pointed at his temple, "in my mind."

She pulled her handkerchief from her pocket and blew her nose. "They shot the people fleeing the fires."

Janowitz nodded his head, yes. His eyes gazed at the wall, but what horrors he saw thousands of miles away she could only imagine. Things she'd pretended to feel when playing scenes in movies. Now she understood. She saw it in the vacant eyes of a lonely little man. "Yes, I know this."

He forced a smile and patted her hand. "I must think what to do next."

"Are you all right?" She cringed at her own words. What a ridiculous thing to ask. *Of course, he's not all right.* "Mr. Janowitz, I'm so sorry."

He closed the door behind him so quietly she couldn't even hear the lock catch.

She put the hankie down and stared at the door. How she wished she could have said something meaningful to him. But she knew there were no words that could comfort Mr. Janowitz right now.

Early that evening Eva chewed her food and listened to the NBC Nightly News. It was all bad. She dozed off listening to the latest of horrors inflicted by Hitler's forces. Eva woke up from her nap to the sound of a knock at the door. "Hi, Dumpling," Mossell said as she rolled her wheelchair over to Eva's bedside. "It's party time."

Eva sat up.

A strong knock came from the door and Rose came in. "I'm sorry, Miss Eva. I was running late." She walked into the room carrying her customary packages: Ivan's dinner, and six cold Old Heidelberg's in its traditional brown handled bag for Mossell. Rose had concealed the bag of beer inside a paper box.

"You need some help, Miss Eva?" Rose asked.

Eva shook her head. "No. Go ahead and feed Ivan."

"Okay. Let me just give you this." She pulled a new bottle of scotch from the sack and walked over to give it to Eva. But Ivan, circled her legs and sent Rose tumbling to the ground, bottle and all.

"Rose!" Eva screamed. "Don't move. There's glass everywhere."

Eva and Mossell moved the shards out of the way and helped the maid to her feet.

"Rose, you're cut!"

"It ain't nothing, Miss Eva. Just a little scratch."

A trickle of blood ran across her ankle into her shoe. "Please don't fuss over me."

Mossell instructed Rose to sit in the comfy chair, while Eva swabbed up the runaway scotch and picked up the shards of glass.

"Hush, pumpkin." Mossell dug around in the sack, found the bottle opener, and handed the opened beer to the flustered maid. "Drink this and let us clean this up before the nurse comes in."

"I'm so sorry, Miss Eva. You didn't even get your smidge to-night."

Eva tried to conceal her disappointment; after all, she had been looking forward to her evening "smidge" of scotch all day. Since there hadn't been enough for her and the ladies, she had a glass of water on the rocks, while the others drank high octane.

"That's all right..." She waved her hand as if brushing it off. "This time I'll drink some of Edgar's favorite. If it's good enough for you and Mossell, then I can buck up and drink it, too."

"Ooooow, thank you Rose. Now, I get to see Sugar lower herself to my level. Don't worry sweetie, you'll never notice that it's not that nasty paint thinner."

"I will notice that it tastes like something Ivan leaves in his sanitary box." Eva tossed the broken glass in the bathroom wastebasket. After the mess and evidence was safely hidden, Eva completed the trio and shared the contents of the beer bag.

Before Eva knew it, Mossell had finished a fresh bottle of Old Heidelberg. The alcohol was loose and the tongues were looser. After Ivan had finished his dinner, he trotted to the bed and proceeded to take his nightly spit bath.

Mossell pooped out early that evening. "Sorry ladies, I just can't stay up any longer. I feel like they stuck one of those needles in me and took out all of my energy."

For the first time since she'd arrived at the Baker Hospital, Eva saw Mossell for the aging woman she was. For all her animation, she didn't have the same spark she'd had even a couple of days ago.

Mossell handed Rose a half drunk bottle of beer, then turned to Eva. "I think you ought to look out for Mr. Baker. I don't think he's everything he claims to be...Rose, could you wheel me back to my room? I just don't have the energy to do it myself."

"Sure, Miss Mossell."

When Rose returned to Eva's suite, she said, "Miss Mossell don't look too good." Ivan came out from under the bed and met Rose at the door. She began gathering all the bottles, stashing them in her canvas sack. "I need to get out of here," Rose said. "The trolley stops running soon. It may already be too late."

"If you missed it, have the admissions clerk call you a cab. Do you have money for it?"

"Yes, ma'am."

She wanted to beg Rose to stay a while longer. She couldn't stand another night alone in this hospital room. It was damn ridiculous that she could keep a cat in her room, but the black maid wasn't welcome to stay at the hospital.

Rose picked up her bags and paused at the door. "'night Miss Eva."

"Rose, wait."

Rose froze with her hand on the door. "Yes, Miss Eva?"

"In your travels around town, did you hear any talk about a suicide that happened here recently?"

"I don't think so."

Eva hesitated. "I heard a patient say she saw someone jump from the observation deck, but no one was there. She must have been hallucinating."

Rose recalled the dinner conversation with the Brown family. "I didn't hear anything about a *suicide*."

Eva sighed, too tired to pursue it. "Goodnight, Rose."

And suddenly, with the exception of Ivan, Eva was once again alone. She tried to keep her mind occupied by scanning a movie magazine or a book, but she simply couldn't concentrate.

A couple of hours passed. Eva still wasn't feeling sleepy and she simply couldn't stand sitting in her room alone any longer. She ran a brush through her hair, grabbed a book and left the room. The elevators didn't run this late, so she went down the south staircase next to Mr. Janowitz's room to the lobby. As she passed his room a chill rushed past her. At the end of the hall an empty rocking chair softly swayed back and forth.

She quietly crossed the lobby and took a purple wicker chair next to the piano. None of the medical staff were in the reception area—only the receptionist behind the glass appeared from time to time to make sure no new patients arrived.

Now that she had finished *Gone with the Wind*, her only reading options were *Finnegans Wake* and *A Practical Cat Book* by Ida Mellen. She had grabbed the cat book. She opened it. Scribbled on the inside page was the inscription, "To Edgar, Congratulations on your new cat. Best wishes, Ida."

Eva thumbed through the book. The author's name sounded familiar. She must be the same woman who trained animals for Edgar's movies. She vaguely recalled Ida, but Eva definitely remembered the most stunning ebony cat for the filming of Poe's, "The Tail of the Black Cat." He looked like a miniature panther, fierce and evil, with large fangs jutting below his upper lip. But he was gentle and personable and the entire crew oohed and aahed over him the way they would with a new baby. Eva had watched, dumbfounded, as the cat mostly obeyed the woman's commands. Ida had taught Rufus to walk on a leash like a dog, to put his paws together and pray, to roll over and even shake hands. During filming he flattened his ears as if in a rage. He swatted and arched his back like a scaredy-cat. Edgar, who became enchanted with the cat, caused the filming to fall behind schedule because he'd take the film's star off to play with him. Edgar so wanted a cat. How unfair that she let him keep one only the year before he died.

Eva took a deep breath to try to dissolve those pangs of guilt.

She recalled that March evening several years ago when Edgar came home from the Middle East with the funny white and red kitten.

Those two amber eyes peeked out of Edgar's jacket.

"Put that diseased animal outside," Eva demanded.

"He's not diseased," Edgar answered. "He's just cold. Someone tossed him away in a trash can."

"You're not bringing it into my home."

"My darling," he said in that smooth baritone voice that always made her melt. "We do share this home. The kitten will simply stay in my half."

Eva fixed her jaw and crossed her arms like a mother scolding her naughty child.

He continued to scratch under the kitten's chin and called out, "Rose!"

During the argument, Rose had been conspicuously inconspicuous. She peered in the bedroom. "Yes, Mr. Edgar?"

"Go check the temperature."

"Yes, sir." When she reappeared she said, "That blue norther's blown in. It's forty-four."

"Thank you."

She didn't answer, but quickly left the room.

"Forty-four," he repeated. He slowly drew from his pipe. In moments, a smoky haze filled the room with musky cherry. Edgar held out his hand. "Come my dear; let's go outside."

"Why?"

"Your beauty overwhelms me; I'm overcome by desire. Let's shed our clothes and go make love by the pool."

"Edgar, you're crazy. It's almost freezing out there. I'm not going to strip naked out there. Besides, you'd catch your death of cold."

He raised his eyebrows. "So will he. I can't put him outside to die. If you want him outdoors, you must throw him out yourself. " He held the white and orange wad of fur up by the scruff of the neck and tried to hand the kitten to her. "Can you?"

"All right, Edgar, you can keep him, but if I get ringworm you're both sleeping outside."

That's where the plan fell apart. It had begun to rain and there was no dry dirt for the kitten's bathroom. Instead, Edgar placed the kitten in the guestroom and gave him a wooden ammunition box filled with fireplace ashes for his lavatory. Rose provided a little leftover chicken and water served in a gold-trimmed Nippon saucer making little Ivan a king of cats.

The next morning when Edgar checked on him, sooty paw prints peppered his dead mother-in-law's white linen bedspread.

"Ivan, my friend," he said trying to pound the paw prints out of the bedspread, "I'd say we're both in the dog house."

And they were. But Eva could never stay mad at Edgar for long and she knew she either had to accept the new package deal or dig in for a long War of the Kitty.

"Pet him," Edgar begged. "He's soft."

"He's got diseases," she protested, her arms rigidly at her side.

"Look at him," Edgar said. "He doesn't have any diseases."

She watched him bathe his face by licking his paw then wiping it across his cheek.

"See how clean he is."

Eva finally screwed up the courage to touch him. She patted the top of his head.

"He's soft," Edgar said. "Like cashmere. Pretend he's one of your sweaters. He'll keep you warm if I'm not around—if I have to go out of town."

He dropped the kitten in her arms.

"Edgar, what are you doing? I don't want to hold it! When I was little I had a dog. He smelled so bad. I don't want a stinky cat underfoot."

"Smell him, Eva. He doesn't have a doggy smell."

Indeed, he had no offensive odor at all.

"He smells a little like your cherry pipe tobacco," she conceded.

"You didn't like the tobacco at first, did you?"

She shook her head.

"Give him a chance. He'll grow on you if you'll just give him a chance."

She loved Edgar because of his compassion. Her big-hearted man would never have left even a rat to die. As much as she disliked his new best friend, he wouldn't have been Edgar if he hadn't pulled the kitten from the garbage.

Now, Edgar was gone and the cat she had rejected was all she had left of him.

She sighed and opened the cat care book to the forward. Eva craved reading, even to the point of reading the cereal box when eating breakfast alone. Even a book about cat care was better than nothing, and she did promise to take care of Ivan.

Eva read until she started dozing. *Not much of a plot.* Time seemed to melt away. Her head dropped forward until she woke with a jerk—startled by the touch of a hand on her shoulder. She gasped.

Nurse Turner stood above her. "Miss Dupree, you should be in bed now."

Eva took a deep breath. "Nurse Turner, I simply can't sleep in that room. I just want to read a little longer."

Nurse Turner picked up the book from Eva's lap. "I notice you weren't doing much reading. You need to go back to your suite. We can't have patients sleeping in the lobby." She grabbed Eva by the elbow and helped her to her feet. "Go back to your room. I'll check on you in a little while."

"That's okay, Nurse Turner. Don't go to any trouble." She took her book from the nurse. As she headed up, she passed an older man in a black coat heading down to the lobby.

Odd, Eva thought. His clothes looked out of fashion, almost like a costume from an old movie.

Then the air turned icy. Her chest knotted and her heart began racing. She turned toward the old man again, but he'd vanished. Eva ran back down to the lobby. He was nowhere to be found.

She shivered. It looked like she was facing another long, sleepless night.

On the way back to her room, she decided she should check on Mr. Janowitz. His room was just the other side of the stairs.

"Mr. Janowitz?" She knocked on the door.

No response.

"Mr. Janowitz, do you need anything?"

Still no answer.

Eva cracked his door open and peeked inside. The light was off, but light from the hall faintly illuminated the room. The room wasn't much more than an L-shaped shoebox. An ugly under-stuffed chair sat next to the window. She opened the door wider. The bed was in the other leg of the L, next to the hall. That area was so small, there was little room to move around. Still, no Mr. Janowitz. In the silence, something was odd. Eva took a closer look at the bed.

On his still-made bed, Janowitz's fresh pair of nightclothes had been laid out neatly waiting for him to put them on. But next to the wall his spoke back chair lay on its side as if thrown there. She flipped on the light switch, and pushed the door open. A night slipper lay upside down on the floor next to the chair.

Even though the room appeared empty, she still had a feeling that she was being watched. She opened the door even more and looked up. What she saw sucked the air out of her lungs.

Up in the recesses of the room's story-high skylight dangled striped men's pajama legs and feet, one of them bare. Above them, Eva could make out limp arms, then Mr. Janowitz's head, with the belt from his robe stretching between his neck and the truss inside the room's story-high skylight. His face glowed bluish in the faint light. His mouth gaped open, his swollen tongue protruding.

Eva fled blindly from the room, and turned the corner running into Nurse Turner, head on. Turner's tray of medicine cups and syringes of Baker Cure flew into the air and rained down on both of them.

Turner glared at her. "Miss Dupree, what in the world is wrong with you, *this* time?"

"Mr. Janowitz," Eva gasped. "He's dead!" She grabbed Turner's arm and pulled her back toward the room.

Turner tried jerking loose. "Don't be foolish. He's probably just asleep."

Eva stopped short and sniffed. "Silly me. I should have thought of that myself. I'm sure *you* see sleeping people hanging by their necks all the time."

"Hanging by their—" She pushed Eva aside and ran into the room. Eva arrived moments later to find her staring up at Janowitz. Then she focused on Eva with narrowed eyes. "What were you doing in here?"

"Earlier he heard that the town where his wife and son lived was bombed," Eva said. "I was just checking to see how he was doing."

"I should say, not so well." Turner looked up at Janowitz and for a moment Eva thought she saw a hint of sorrow in Nurse Turner's eyes. As quickly as the gentle moment came, it vanished behind the professional mask again. She eyed Eva. "Well, as long as you're already here, I want you to stay here. Lock the door and don't let anyone in until I return with the janitor."

"You're not leaving me in here alone with a dead man!"

Turner's lips tightened. "Miss Dupree, don't be childish. He's dead. You've nothing to fear from him."

Turner closed the door behind her.

Poor Mr. Janowitz. Eva glanced up. The body turned so slowly as if surveying the room. She moved away from him, but looked back again, feeling drawn by an unseen force. She took a few steps toward the body. On the floor beneath him next to a puddle smelling of urine lay, an old photograph of Mr. Janowitz with a woman and young boy. *His wife and son?* He must have had it in his hand when he kicked the chair from under his feet. She picked up the picture and moved back away from the body.

She studied the photograph. Mr. Janowitz was much younger, just a tinge of gray at his temples and a full head of hair. The woman had her hair piled atop her head and wore a stoic expression on her face. Next to her, a teenage boy had dark hair and that skinny adolescent look.

From behind a hand reached up and touched her on the shoulder.

Eva screamed and whipped around. "Holy Mother of God!" She crossed herself.

"Miss Dupree, control yourself," Nurse Turner chided. "I don't want you disturbing the other patients."

"For God's sake, Nurse Turner. If you don't want me to disturb anyone, then you shouldn't sneak up on me." Eva moved out of the way and made room for Turner and a young blond maintenance man with a ladder and a tool belt. The man set up the ladder and pulled a large hunting knife from his belt.

"This oughtta do it," he said, and cut the thick cloth robe belt with a quick slice.

Mr. Janowitz's body crashed to the wood floor with a thud and, sprawled like a discarded ragdoll, his legs and arms splayed in unnatural directions.

"Mr. Kelly, please be careful!" Turner said.

"He ain't feelin' nothin', Mrs. Turner. Don't know if you noticed, but that old feller, is dead." He snickered. "He don't feel it cuz he's dead, get it? An' I'd guess it ain't been long cuz he ain't 'tall stiff yet."

Eva felt as if she were watching one of her own horror films. Her breath quickened and her eyes seemed as though they could pop out of her head.

Turner led Eva out into the hall. "Thank you, Miss Dupree. You should go back to your room, now. And I don't think you should mention this to any of the other patients. We wouldn't want to alarm them, would we?"

"Of course, we wouldn't. But don't you think they're going to wonder where he is when he doesn't come out on the porch in the morning?"

"Go to bed." Turner went back into room four-twenty-four and closed the door in Eva's face.

Eva stood there for a moment and then trudged down the hall to her room. Images from the scene behind her replayed over and over in her mind like the daily rushes at a movie studio. She could almost hear the director say, "I just don't think the way she responded was believable. Try clutching your hands for a better effect."
Why was Nurse Turner so insistent that Eva keep quiet about this?

Eva switched the radio on and patted some cold cream on her face to remove her makeup as she listened to the latest developments in Europe. Eva climbed into the shower. She hoped the hot water would wash away her vision of Janowitz's bugging eyes and blue face. Even with closed eyes she saw that dead stare seemingly focused on her.

She dried off, slipped into her nightgown and switched the radio on. Eva unwrapped the towel from her head and ran her fingers through her damp Marcel waves. As she glanced through the door at Ivan snoozing with his head comfortably nestled on her pillow, she mused, "I look like something the cat dragged in."

Eva opened her door a crack. She peered out until she saw the door to room four-twenty-four open. Turner held the door for the janitor carrying his ladder and the knife. He turned the corner heading for the elevator, but Turner stayed behind. She disappeared into the room for a few minutes and then finally reappeared. She looked around, quickly locked the door, tested it and straightened her starched white dress before heading to the elevator, as well.

It seemed everything had resumed an air of calm. But a few minutes after she lay down, she heard a familiar sound in the hall. Squeak, squeak, squeak.

Eva willed her legs to move, forcing herself out of bed, and grabbed her satin robe. Through the crack of her door she saw a nurse with a gurney entering Mr. Janowitz's room down the hall.

"That's what it is," she said to herself. "It's a gurney."

She sneaked out into the hall, but stayed close to the wall to evade detection as she had done in a movie where she played a spy fighting for France in the Great War. Naturally the on-screen war heroine sucked the blood out of the enemies' bodies every chance she got. It was an enjoyable way to reduce enemy numbers and get a meal at the same time.

Before long, the door to four-twenty-four opened. Eva shot back to her room and cracked the door so she could continue her surveillance.

Nurse Turner was pushing the cart closer. And closer. Finally, she turned down the hall toward the elevator. Eva listened to the sound of the squeaky wheels. The elevator rang as the doors opened.

Eva moved to the corner for a better view.

A sheet covered something on the gurney—Mr. Janowitz, presumably. Within a few seconds the elevator swallowed them up.

Back in bed, Eva tried to sleep, but she dozed off in only fits and spurts, awakening with a start. Once again she had the feeling of someone watching her. Finally she fell into a fitful sleep.

DAY FIVE—*Monday, September 4*

She woke up numb, unrested...and on edge. The Baker Hospital felt ominous—finding Mr. Janowitz's body, the eerie goings on in her room. She wanted to hide under her bed. And given that her doctor decided because of her cancer's location, she needed to receive another abdominal shot, hiding under the bed this morning didn't seem like such a bad idea.

Before the treatment, Nurse Cavanaugh checked on Eva and handed her a cup of coffee. "I'm afraid your treatment will be late today. Dr. Hutto is off, so Nurse Turner's pulling a second shift and giving the abdominal shots."

Torturing patients. That ought to put her in a good mood.

"There's no reason for you to have to sit here and wait," Cavanaugh continued. "If you want to go out and sit on the porch, we'll come and get you when we're ready for you."

Eva grabbed her book and joined Mossell in one of the wicker rockers on the observation deck. Although Mossell was fair in complexion, today her face lacked any color at all. She could barely keep her eyes open. Mossell's book, *Snows of Kilimanjaro*, lay on the deck, as if she had dozed off and dropped it.

"Morning, Sleepyhead." Eva patted Mossell's hand gently.

Mossell smiled weakly. "Good morning."

"How are you feeling today," Eva asked.

"Like birdseed."

Eva blinked. "Birdseed?"

"After it's eaten, it's shit." Mossell tried to smile, but just sighed instead.

Eva laughed. Even sick Mossell could make her smile.

Mossell sighed again. "I don't think these treatments are working for me, angel."

"I feel that some days, too," Eva said. "Then other days I feel pretty good."

"Obviously this is one of those pretty good days for you. I'm glad, dovie." Mossell began scribbling a note on a page of her book. "This is my niece's address and phone number. If anything happens to me, I want you to write her. Make sure that vase goes to her. I don't want it getting back to Roger."

Eva was speechless. "Mossell, nothing's going to happen to you. You'll be fine."

"No, sweetie, I won't be." She tried to smile, but obviously lacked the energy for it.

Nurse Cavanaugh walked up to them. "Can I get you anything, Mrs. Knight?"

"Yes, sunshine, I could use a big strong dose of that pain killer."

"I'm sorry," Cavanaugh said. "I'll talk to the doctor about getting something for the discomfort."

"No, cupcake, discomfort is something you feel after drinking a bottle of tequila alone. This hurts like hell. Tell the doctor I need something, *now*!"

The nurse forced a smile. "I'll be right back."

After she left, Mossell finished scribbling on the book page, ripped it from the binding and handed it to Eva. "Here's my niece's address."

Eva stared at the page. "This is a page from your book. What's going to happen when you get to that page?"

"You'll have to tell me how it ends, puffin. I just don't have the strength to finish it. I'll just pretend the butler did it."

"You're reading a romance."

"Okay the butler did the rich lady." She winked weakly. "He did at my house."

Eva folded the page and used it as a bookmark in *Finnegans Wake*, a book she had found in the lobby.

Mossell was right. It looked like the treatments weren't working. Mossell had looked weaker and thinner every day.

Cavanaugh put her hands on the back of Mossell's wheelchair. "Come along, Mrs. Knight. Let's get you back to your room so I can give you your shot. You can return when you feel better."

Mossell nodded and leaned back heavily into the headrest.

"See you later, pudding." She waved weakly to Eva.

Eva watched as Nurse Cavanaugh rolled Mossell away. "Poor thing," she said aloud.

"Wow, she looks bad," Gazetta said.

The remaining patients nodded in agreement.

Before she could say anything else, the main door to the deck opened and Norman Baker walked outside. Clad in a plum linen suit and white silk shirt, Baker straightened his wisteria tie. "Hello Folks," he said cheerfully to the group. He walked across the porch and began greeting patients. "Good morning, Mrs. Shipp and Mrs. Smith. How are you feeling this morning?" He moved along before Gazetta could start a recitation of her ails and aches.

He reached down and shook hands with an elderly man. "Hello, Mr. Dye. I think you've put on some weight. Haven't you? That's great!"

As he spoke to Mr. Dye, Ivan trotted up to him with his tail held high and his whiskers forward, as if to introduce himself and give Baker permission to access the deck.

"Ah," Baker said to the cat. "You must be the famous Ivan."

As if to confirm the suspicion, Ivan squeezed his eyes closed and stretched open his mouth in a full-blown yawn.

"Watch this," Cooper said as he wadded up a scrap of paper. He crinkled it between his fingers to make a crunching noise then tossed it across the balcony.

Like a shooting star with a red tail Ivan leapt across the deck in pursuit of the still fleeing paper wad. Before it had stopped sliding, Ivan flipped to his back, claws ready. It would be a fight to the death. The paper prey didn't stand a chance. He held it between his paws, issued the death bite right between the creases and then finally returned to Cooper, dropping the dead paper at his feet.

"Now aren't you clever," Baker said to the cat. "I've never seen a cat play fetch before."

"He's quite dog-like," Eva said.

"That he is." Baker smiled at Eva. "Hello, Miss Dupree."

"Hello, Mr. Baker."

"How are you feeling today?"

"Fairly well, thank you."

Mr. Baker pulled up a chair. "Do you mind if I join you?"

As Baker sat down, Ivan dropped the paper at his feet. He picked it up and gave it a good toss. Baker ran his thumb over his fingers, smiled and said to Eva, "The paper was not as gooey as when I play ball with Bruno. Cat fetch is quite a pleasant diversion. I'm starting to understand the charm of the cat and why the patients seem to enjoy his company."

As Baker wound up for a paper pitch, Mr. Dye snapped a photo. "I want a copy of that one, Mr. Dye," Eva said as Ivan dashed across the deck. "Please have a seat." Eva laid her book down on the table.

Dye took a chair. He pulled out a package of Lucky Strike cigarettes, offering a smoke to everyone in the group. Several people took him up on it, including Baker. Dye smiled at Eva knowing she'd decline, then took out a lighter and lit everyone's cigarette.

"Thank you," Baker said. He slowly inhaled and then returned his attention to Eva. "How are you enjoying your stay?"

Oh, fine. Aside from feeling like something is watching me in my room, and finding poor Mr. Janowitz dead as Hamlet? she thought, but instead said, "The room and the nurses have been wonderful. The food is delicious."

"You look like you're feeling better." Mr. Baker flicked a growing line of ashes into a Baker Hospital ashtray on a nearby table.

Without thinking, she rubbed her back where she felt the constant pressure. "I think I am." She sounded a little surprised.

"I'm delighted to hear that," Mr. Baker said. "I knew we could help you."

"I have to admit, I really thought it was too good to be true. I guess I was mistaken."

"And this is one time I'm glad you were." He smiled warmly.

"I'm afraid I can't say the same for my friend, Mossell Knight. She hasn't looked very well for the last couple of days."

"That's not uncommon." Baker looked around as he said it, clearly meaning the statement for everyone. "The treatments dissolve the tumors and release poisons into the system. With that many toxins circulating through the bloodstream, patients are susceptible to ill health until it's been passed out into the toilet. In a few days she should bounce back."

"That's good news. I was a little worried about her."

He tapped the back cover of her book, *Finnegans Wake*. "Is it any good?"

Eva grimaced. "I'm afraid James Joyce must have been smoking opium while he wrote it. If this is an example of his work, I understand why he's writing about a wake. It's so bad; I believe Ivan would be inspired to bury it. It's, well, it's silly."

"I have one in my office called *Gone with the Wind*," Mr. Baker said. "You're welcome to borrow it if you like. Or there's a nice selection of popular books in the gift shop."

"Thank you, Mr. Baker. I'm afraid I've already read all about the tragedies of Tara."

"Now, if you'll excuse me, Miss Dupree..." He extended his

hand. "I'm afraid I have an appointment in a few minutes. Enjoy this beautiful day."

Shortly after he left Nurse Cavanaugh walked out on the deck and scanned the patients. Eva felt like a turkey in mid-November with the farmer eyeing his flock, ax in hand. Unfortunately, Eva drew the short feather and got the nod. "Miss Dupree, Mrs. Turner's ready for you."

"Great."

Eva took her bookmark and intentionally left James Joyce on the deck. She'd let someone else throw it away. She picked up Ivan and went back to her room.

While she waited for Nurse Turner, Eva watched the cat. He must have known something was up. He paced the room nervously. Then, he scaled the curtains and climbed to the top of the curtain rod. It was the perfect vantage point for spotting a scary predator—like a needle-wielding nurse. And even if he couldn't save Eva, he was safe.

In a few moments Nurse Turner entered the suite with the ominous covered enamel tray in hand.

"I guess it's time for my scene," Eva said getting into bed. "I wish I could say I was glad to see you," she told the nurse, "but..."

"I get that reaction."

"Aren't you here early today?" Eva knew why, she just wanted to delay her treatment.

"I'm afraid I'm working a double shift, again." Nurse Turner removed the tray lid. "The injection in the intestine has to be given by a doctor or myself. Now, please pull up your gown."

"I just don't think I could bear to have my stomach poked one more time. Couldn't you give this one in the hip? I'll pay you ten dollars."

"I'd be rich if I had taken all the bribes I'd been offered to move the injection spot or even forego it. I could retire today. Now, quit your stalling and pull up your gown!"

While a woman sang "You hurt me" mockingly over the radio, Eva raised her gown, exposing yellowing bruises from her treatment a few days earlier.

"I hate needles," Eva said.

Her complaint fell on deaf ears. Nurse Turner produced her syringe from the tray and pushed an air bubble out with the plunger.

Eva closed her eyes and felt the volcanic serum fill her belly.

She took short shallow breaths that made her head feel it was float-ing away. Compared to her first belly shot this one was a breeze. Nurse Turner, despite her brusque manners, gave a far less painful shot than Dr. Hutto. Slowly the flames ebbed away, replaced by exhaustion, and Eva slipped off to sleep.

After Eva heard the nurse leave, Ivan jumped down from his perch and joined Eva in bed. He shared her pillow as she slept until Rose arrived with his lunch and clean toilet. In a repeat of her treatment days earlier, Eva mostly slept while Rose fed the cat and straightened the room. Even the side effects were milder: her fever caused only a mild sweat and the nausea was tolerable.

Eva dozed into the evening. She awoke suddenly, enveloped by a cold draft of air and the feeling of someone lying next to her. Her flesh rippled at the sensation of breath as someone whispered into her ear. Her gut twisted violently and she broke into an icy sweat. Screaming, she bolted upright in bed.

Miss Johnston ran into the suite. "Miss Dupree, what's wrong?"

"There was someone in here, lying on the bed with me!"

A frown replaced the nurse's anxious expression. "I came as soon as I heard you. There is no one else here. If there had been, I'd have passed them. I can see your deck door is locked, so no one went out that way."

Eva grabbed Ivan and clutched him tightly to her. "I'm telling you, there was someone here."

"Well, they're not here now," The nurse tried to sound comfort-ing. "Do you want to get up for a while or just go back to sleep?"

"I'm afraid to go back to sleep."

"Have it your way." The nurse picked up *A Practical Cat Book*. "Maybe you can fall asleep if you read a while."

"I'll try." Eva let go of Ivan and took the book.

Before the nurse left she turned on the light on her night stand.

Eva wasn't really in a mood to read, but that way she didn't have to admit she was afraid of the dark, or at least the dark at the Baker Hospital. She looked beside her. Ivan had commandeered her pil-low, snoring rhythmically.

She flipped through the photos of the cats. "Take care of Ivan." She repeated her husband's last words in this mortal life. She sighed deeply. Although she loved him so, she hated him for leaving her, especially without saying he loved her. At the time, for his final words to be about the very cat she loathed, seemed like a betrayal.

But she had to admit that the promise to care for Ivan gave her a reason to go on living.

She lay back on the bed, and listening to the cat's gentle snore, drifted off to sleep…and dreamed of Edgar. A younger Edgar, the one she first met at Charlie Chaplin's party. He grasped both her hands in his as he had that night and his eyes stared deep into hers, bewitching her all over again. "Eva, I— "

"Edgar, I miss you, too!" she said.

"No, listen." His grip on her hands tightened. "I want— "

"I'm taking care of Ivan, just like you asked."

"Yes, but I want— "

But as he spoke his voice faded. He turned to a mist that drifted away from her.

She ran after him. "No! Don't go! What is it you want? Edgar!"

But he had disappeared.

DAY SIX—*Tuesday, September 5*

The next morning Eva sat alone on the deck and inhaled the fresh mountain air, but all she could smell was the overwhelming scent of wintergreen oil she'd dabbed inside her nostrils before she came outside. In the distance the clouds hung low, shrouding the mountaintops. The air was so clean and clear that it seemed like Heaven came down and embraced the Earth.

Nature certainly had audacity to look so cheerful when she felt so exhausted. Last night's dream continued to haunt even into the morning. Perhaps she should have stayed home and accepted her fate, rather than struggle so hard to live…alone.

Eva's book lay in her lap. She kept reading the same page over and over, cut off by dozing, or her attention wandering to the scenery. She glanced at her watch, too. Half past ten and still no Mossell. Maybe she had problems sleeping too. Eva managed to read a few more chapters and checked her watch again. Another thirty minutes had crept by.

One by one, patients filed out into the open air. Gazetta and another woman sat down to Eva's right. Gazetta pointed at a middle-aged woman sitting beside her. "Eva, have you met Lizzie Albright? She just got here yesterday. Lizzie, this is Eva Dupree. She's killed more men than Al Capone."

Lizzie stared wide-eyed at Eva. "You've killed people before?"

Eva smiled. "I've died several times, too, but only in the figurative sense."

"You died?"

"She used to be a screen star," Gazetta explained. "She was in those old-fashioned horror movies."

"I thought you meant it," Lizzie said. "After last night, I'd believe anything."

"Why is that?" Eva asked.

Lizzie wrapped her robe tie around her forefinger, then unwrapped, then twisted it around again. "I woke up in the middle of the night and saw a dead man hanging from the rafters in my room."

Eva felt the hairs on her arms stand on end.

"You were dreaming," Corinthia Shipp said, as she too sat down.

"No, I wasn't. I turned on the light and saw him for a second or two before he faded away," Lizzie insisted.

"Come on. That didn't happen," Corinthia insisted. "If it did, he'd still be there."

"Are you in room four-twenty-four?" Eva asked.

"Yes." A look of terror overcame her. "How did you know?"

A tear collected in the corner of Eva's, eye. She dabbed it with her knuckle and forced herself to smile. "Lucky guess."

Corinthia snickered. "Well, if a man was hanging in your room, what did he look like?"

"I couldn't see him." Lizzie closed her eyes as if reliving the event. "He was just a black silhouette. He was gone before I could see any more. Not that I'd want to!"

"Are you telling me you're seeing ghosts?" Corinthia's belly laugh ended in a nasal whistle. "There ain't no such thing as ghosts."

"I used to live in a haunted flat in Venezuela," Gazetta said. "I took a picture of the house and it looked like someone was smoking a cigarette in front of the lens. I'd wake up in the middle of the night and this smoke would be swirling around me. It scared the pee out of me."

"I know what that feels like," Eva said.

"Come on, Eva. You said you don't believe in that silly stuff," Corinthia said.

Eva glanced sideways at her door. "I didn't until I came here."

"She's teasing you," Corinthia said. "Don't take her seriously."

Eva debated with herself mentally. Should she tell Lizzie about the gentle man who died in that room? A man who wouldn't hurt any of God's creatures? Who wouldn't hurt Lizzie? A man who simply wanted to end the hurt? Or would the woman be more terrified to learn about the lonely ghost who now resides in room four-twenty-four.

Eva reached across and patted Lizzie's hand. "We'll talk later...when we don't have an interpreter."

Lizzie nodded back, looking confused.

Eva returned to her book and read a while longer, occasionally glancing at her watch—still no Mossell.

Without Mossell to liven things up, the balcony was boring as an oil company annual meeting. There were only so many minutes one could devote to reading a book about cat care, looking at East Mountain and listening to Gazetta gossip. When Eva feared her brain would liquefy and pour out her ears, she excused herself and returned to her room.

A few minutes later, when Nurse Cavanaugh came to the suite to check on her, Eva asked, "Have you seen Mrs. Knight this morning?"

"I'm sorry. No," the nurse said. "I'll check on her in a few minutes."

Eva settled back into her bed to try to catch a catnap. Out on the deck she heard Trudy's giggle and then a shriek. Eva smiled. Someone must be tickling her. *Hopefully she'll come by and visit later.*

Eva turned on the radio and listened to the music. So far, they'd only mentioned the fighting in Europe during newscasts. Today would be a more cheerful day, at least entertainment-wise.

Eva dozed off and on, awaking to a knock at her door. She grabbed her shoulder. "Come in."

Cooper Reilly with his face gleaming, walked over to her bed where Eva struggled to keep her eyes open.

"I didn't know you were sleeping. I didn't mean to disturb you."

"Oh, no, Cooper, it's all right." Eva fastened the top button of her bed jacket. "You'll excuse me if I don't get up."

"I just took a walk around the grounds and into town," he said. "I hope you don't mind, but I brought you a little something." Cooper hid one hand behind his back. He looked a little like a boy bringing his mom a special gift.

She smiled weakly, not knowing whether she minded or not. Eva's nephew was especially fond of bestowing frogs. She found that out the hard way. It had been a long time since a man had given her a gift. Looking down at Ivan, she hoped it wasn't a frog...or another cat.

He brought his hand out from behind him and presented her with a crude arrangement of leather fern fronds and a half dozen sausage-shaped brown cattail spikes.

She took them, feeling suddenly more numb than sleepy. Her throat constricted. But somehow she forced out, "Why, thank you so much, Mr. Reilly." She neither sounded convincing or grateful.

"Remember, it's Cooper."

"Thank you, Cooper," she said hollowly. She brushed a finger across the wild cattails.

"I know you like cats." He nodded at Ivan hogging her pillow.

"I would have loved to have given you pussy willow, but of course it's the wrong time of year. When I saw these, something just told me to cut them for you."

"I see." Her grip felt frozen around the unconventional bouquet.

He shrugged. "This time of year it's hard to find complete ones. Most of them have gone to seed already. Did you know if you were starving, you could eat these?" He leaned over to kiss her, but she pulled away.

Above them, the ceiling light flickered off and on, settling on off for a while then popping back on for good.

She clutched the bouquet around the woody stems, until her fingers turned pale. Burying her face in the cattails, she smelled moist and earthy fragrance. This late in the season, the cattail had grown scratchy and fragile. One spear broke, releasing fluffy little puffs of cottony material in her hands. Should she embrace them or throw them away?

Poor Cooper. Seeing her less than enthusiastic reaction, his schoolboy grin fell. He looked like the kid whose mom yelled, "*Why'd you bring me these weeds?*" His chin flinched. "I guess I should have gone into town and bought something elegant and expensive; something more representative of your regal nature, like a room full of roses. I didn't mean to insult you."

"No, Mr. Reilly, I mean, Cooper. I'm not insulted and I don't want expensive. These are so perfect; you just don't know how perfect they truly are. I just—" She pulled one cattail out of the arrangement and rubbed the velvety head across her cheek. Tears welled in her eyes. Quickly, she turned her head away so he wouldn't see. "You just don't know—"

"I'm sorry. I shouldn't have presumed. Forgive me for intruding." She heard him walk out and close the door quietly behind him.

For a moment Eva considered dropping the bouquet in the trash, but instead dragged herself out of bed, and filled up her water pitcher so it could double as a vase.

Every now and then she peeked through the balcony door to the deck to see if Cooper was lounging on the deck or if Mossell had shown up. Noon came and went and Mossell still failed to appear. Since she'd been feeling so badly yesterday, Eva decided to trek down to her room. A strange voice answered her knock. Inside, a man, only slightly younger than Eva, lay in Mossell's bed.

Eva stopped short. "I'm sorry. I thought this was Mossell Knight's room."

"They moved me in here a little while ago," the man said.

"I'm sorry I disturbed you," Eva said, and after backing out returned to her suite. She turned on the radio and laid down on her bed, listening absently to the music. It was a jazzy little number and she found herself tapping her fingers on her thigh in time with the tune.

Where was Mossell? What was going on?

She climbed into her bed. The Tommy Dorsey band was playing his theme song, *I'm Getting Sentimental over You*. She drifted into a troubled sleep. When she awoke it was late afternoon and the melancholy melody of *Stormy Weather* floated through the air. She sang quietly along with Billie Holiday.

> *Life is bare, gloom and misery everywhere*
> *Stormy weather, just can't get my poor old self together*
> *I'm weary all the time, the time, so weary all of the time...*

Billie's dulcet voice floating over Cooper's unique bouquet, reminding her how alone she truly was.

She needed to go to the bathroom, but as soon as she climbed out of bed, the kidney pain suddenly hit her. "Damn! Not again."

She leaned against her desk and sucked in a long deliberate breath and let it out slowly. Her arms folded across her waist offered no comfort. She felt as though a bare-knuckle fighter had just punched her in the back. *Can't breathe. Can't breathe.* She backed herself back to bed, and dabbed the perspiration from her face with the sheet. She groped around the drawer of her bedside table for her emesis basin. When she was done, she pushed away the table so she wouldn't have to smell the bile. She tried to ignore the disgusting taste lingering in her mouth. She lay back, just trying to wait out the pain's passing. The attack lasted only a few minutes, then ebbed away leaving her weak and drained. When she could breathe again, it was only shallow gasps for air.

She'd been feeling so well. It had been days since she'd had a full-blown attack. Maybe she wasn't doing as well as she believed. Maybe she *was* still dying. Perhaps in her own desperation to live she had fooled herself and her body...at least for a while. Despite the treatments, she was really right back where she started, in bed and miserable.

Eva pressed the call button. She needed a painkiller and someone to clean up the puke.

Eva awoke to the sound of knocking at her door.

"Hi, Mrs. Dupree." Trudy Trent cracked the door open and poked her head around. "Can I play with Ivan?"

"Of course, Trudy," Eva said from her bed. "Come on in."

Trudy climbed up on Eva's bed next to Ivan. She covered his face with little girl kisses complete with, "Mmmbraw" sound effects. Today, instead of wearing pigtails, her hair hung down straight. She held out a thin clump of hair and dangled it before Ivan. He pawed at it occasionally grabbing it out of her fingers with his claws.

"I didn't realize your hair was so long" Eva observed. "It certainly makes a great cat toy,

Trudy giggled. "Uh huh." Then she turned serious for a moment. "I bet Mr. Kitty misses Rags."

"What rags?"

"The mouse made out of the sock," Trudy said. "You know, with the catnip in it."

Eva stared at her. Ivan did have a toy called Rags. It was an old sock of Edgar's filled with dried catnip. Edgar tied a knot at the top end and Rose had embroidered a pair of black eyes and some whiskers down at the toe. The cat carried it everywhere. It had turned green from kitty slobber and catnip juice, but it was a well-loved companion. Rags' name used to be Harold, but Ivan loved him hard. Unfortunately, in the rush to get packed, Rags had been left at home probably under the sofa. Ivan would have to make do with Trudy's hair.

"How'd you know about Rags?" Eva asked.

"He told me." She continued to tease the cat with her hair. After a few minutes, Trudy switched gears quickly. "I have a surprise for you."

Eva sat up a little straighter. She pressed her palm into her side and forced a smile. "What kind of surprise?"

"Do you want to have a tea party?" Trudy asked.

"A tea party?" Really Eva would have given anything for Trudy to take Ivan back to her room and let Eva sleep some more, but she had already hurt Cooper's feelings when he was trying to do something nice. She didn't want to wound Trudy while she was trying to do a good deed.

Besides, some of the few happy memories Eva recalled after her father's death revolved around tea parties with her mom. Every couple of weeks Mama would take time off from her seamstress work and set up her version of a high tea. Sometimes her Mama would treat her daughter with the teabags made of muslin rather than having to mess with straining loose tea. On special occasions mom would make scones and serve them with butter. The tea gave little Eva something to look forward to.

Trudy, alone in a strange scary hospital, had no friends or family and nothing to look forward to except playing with Ivan.

Eva swung her legs around and dangled them off the bed. She put on her best happy-actress face and said with a lack of enthusiasm, "Why not?"

"Okay, I'll be right back." Trudy rushed out the door.

While the youngster was gone Eva grabbed her flowing orchid satin robe trimmed with velvet and went into her living area to wait on her couch. Trudy returned in a just few minutes dragging a big wooden box full of toys.

"It'll take me a few minutes to set up. Where can I plug it in?"

"You need a plug? I think there's an electric socket over there." Eva pointed to a nearby wall plug.

"Okay. Don't peek."

Eva turned her head away from where the party was being set up and covered her eyes with her hands. She heard the clanking of tin, the clinking of porcelain and the pouring of liquid.

"Ouch!" Trudy cried out.

Eva opened her eyes and rushed over to Trudy who had stuck her tiny forefinger in her mouth.

"You hurt?"

"Uh huh. Burned my finger. I'm okay." Trudy sucked on her finger for a few moments then went back to her party planning. "Okay, open your eyes."

Eva turned her head toward Trudy and uncovered her face. "Oh, my! Isn't that something?"

On the coffee table Trudy had laid out a lovely arrangement. Four Orphan Annie teacups and saucers, a creamer containing real milk and sugar bowl. A teapot bearing a picture of everyone's favorite ragamuffin was warming up on the Orphan Annie electric play stove. Also on the table Trudy had carefully arranged four oatmeal cookies on a Baker Hospital dinner plate.

Once Trudy had everything set up to her satisfaction, she tried to pick up the teapot, but jerked her hand away with a cry of pain.

Eva unplugged the stove, which felt very hot. "Did you burn yourself again? Where are you hurt?"

Tears welled up in Trudy's eyes. "I wanted my surprise to be perfect, and I can't pour your tea."

Eva said quickly, "Trudy, it *is* perfect. You do know that etiquette requires the oldest person in the room to pour the tea, didn't you?"

The little girl looked up at Eva with those enormous blue eyes and wiped the tears away with her sleeve. "Really?"

"Really. At least that's the way I've always done it. So, see, everything is perfect." Eva scanned the spread. "Where did you get those lovely cookies?"

"Nurse Cavanaugh said she'd get them for me if I didn't throw a fit when I had my shot today. I was good, so she got them for me."

"Good for you!"

Eva retrieved a dry washcloth, wrapping it around the handle before picking the pot up. She poured some steaming tea in all four cups and placed the pot on the miniature stove. "Wow. You really are brave."

While she spoke, Ivan jumped up on the desk to inspect the party refreshments. Trudy held up a cup to his mouth and pretended to let him drink.

"I see four place settings?" Eva asked. "Who all's coming?"

"You and me and Mr. Kitty," she pointed to Ivan, "and my friend. You don't mind that I invited him do you?"

"Of course not. I'll be glad to have your little friend around. When is he going to get here?"

"He's here right now." Trudy sighed impatiently. "I guess you can't see him."

"I'm sorry. Tell him "Hi," for me."

Trudy frowned. "He can hear you, you know."

"Okay."

Impatience gave way to excitement. "We have a present for you."

Eva took a bite of the cookie. It was soft and crumbly, just baked fresh. It would be a recipe worth having. "A gift for me? How sweet!"

Trudy handed her a wad of tablet paper. She had scribbled little cartoons on it in pencil—little stick figures of a curly headed girl and something that must have been a dog who said, "Arf." Unfolding the clump of paper, she found a circular brass pin with a five-pointed star in the center of it. "Ooohh. This looks exciting. What is it?"

Trudy took the trinket from her and twisted a knob. "It's an Orphan Annie's Telematic Decoder Badge. We can send secret messages back and forth. See here's where you set it for the special code." She turned it until the number four appeared. "Then you take the code I send you and look here to see what it really says. See?"

"But what about you? Don't you need it?"

"Nuh uh. I have a new one. See?" She held up a second badge about the same size. "This is the new Mysto-Matic Decoder. It's even better."

Indeed, it was new shiny brass, embossed with a bald eagle in front of an American flag—an impressive decrypting device if Eva ever saw one. "You're going to send me secret messages?"

"Uh huh."

She pointed at the crumbled piece of paper. "There's a message here for you."

Eva carefully set her decoder and the dispatch on her table.

There was a knock at the door and Nurse Cavanaugh walked in. "Gertrude, it's time for your nap. Pick up your stuff and go back to your room."

The little girl got to her feet. "Bye, Mrs. Dupree. Bye bye, Mr. Kitty." After Trudy gave Eva a goodbye hug, she picked up her now-cooled play stove and moved toward the door slowly, like a man walking to a noose. "I'll come back for my tea set later."

"Thank you for the gift, Trudy."

Before Nurse Cavanaugh could close the door, Eva said, "Nurse Cavanaugh, earlier you were going to check on Mrs. Knight. Have you?"

Cavanaugh hesitated. "No. I think someone else did."

"I looked in her room. There was someone else in her bed."

"Excuse me?" The nurse kept her back to Eva.

"Someone else was assigned her room," Eva insisted. "I want to know where she is."

"Sure. I'll check for you."

On the way back to bed, she picked up the decoder and Trudy's secret message. The message read, "Turn to Code 4. Here's your message..." That was followed by a series of numbers and spaces. Eva worked the little contraption. The note said, "I am glad you're my friend."

She smiled and worked the dial, jotting down a coded message of her own. If Trudy deciphered it correctly, she should see, "I like you too." Eva would give it to the nurse in the morning.

When her task was completed, Ivan jumped up and lay across her belly—a furry hot water bottle. Between his purr and the music, she drifted off to sleep again, napping for the balance of the afternoon.

That evening Nurse Johnston called into the room, "Dinnertime, Miss Dupree." She walked in with a covered tray of food. "Hmmm. It smells good. Roast beef."

Despite the savory cloud of pot roast steam wafting in her direction, Eva had no appetite. Eva took the napkin from the nurse, but without enthusiasm. She sat in silence for a moment, then pushed the tray away. She didn't want to eat and she didn't want to hear any more news about the horrible things happening in Poland or romantic music or foolish dramas on the radio. She was worried about Mossell. Where was she? Why didn't anyone know what happened to her?

"Would you please give this to Trudy?" She handed her the secret message.

"Oh, that reminds me—I almost forgot." Nurse Johnston pulled a folded piece of paper out of her pocket. "Trudy asked me to give this to you."

Eva placed it unopened on the rolling table beside the white graniteware food tray.

When Nurse Johnston returned Eva asked again, "Did you learn anything about Mrs. Knight?"

"I asked about her." She picked up the food tray.

"And...?"

"I was told that she was transferred to the isolation ward for some aggressive treatment. She's being isolated because sometimes these treatments make you more susceptible to contagious viruses."

"I see. How long will she be isolated?"

"Usually a week or so. Sometimes longer, sometimes shorter. I'll tell her you were asking about her."

"Thank you." She snuggled back into the bed. "Tell her I miss her."

"I will," the nurse promised closing the door behind her.

Poor Mossell. She had to get sicker to get well. *Of course, if I get better I'll have to go through the same thing.* But if the Baker Cure successfully fought the cancer, a week in isolation would be a small sacrifice.

When the nurse left, Eva pulled the bedside table closer. She unfolded Trudy's note, which was written on lined tablet paper in pencil. It said, "Set your decoder to 19." It then listed a series of numbers that were sometimes separated by spaces. The decoded message read, "Nurse Turner sure is mean."

Eva couldn't agree with her more. She got a clean piece of paper and wrote in code, "You are a very brave girl."

Rose dragged herself up the final stair to the fourth floor landing, a climb of seventy-nine exhausting steps in all. She paused for a moment to catch her breath. Today, her climb seemed more rigorous than usual—like the steps had been moved farther apart and her black leather pumps had suddenly turned to lead. As she walked through the door, she said breathlessly. "Hello, Miss Eva. How are you feeling?"

Eva lay limp in her bed with Ivan resting his head on her thighs. Rose's heart dropped. Eva's eyes had that fearful doe expression again. She'd been doing so well. Now, Miss Eva looked just helpless and hopeless as she did the day the doctor handed her the death sentence.

Ivan leaped up and dashed to his bathroom-based dinner bowl but Rose didn't follow. "What's happened to you, Miss Eva. What's wrong?"

Unable to answer, Miss Eva dropped her head into her hands and sobbed, her shoulders shuddering uncontrollably. When she finally gathered her composure, Eva told her maid about finding Mr. Janowitz. Miss Eva finished her story with, "You need to look for another job, Rose."

"Huh uh, baby. I'm too old for that." Rose retrieved a fresh hankie from her purse and handed it to her boss. "I've been working in this household for thirty-five years. I'm not looking for another job. That is, unless you're firing me."

Eva slumped deep into the pillows. Her emerald eyes were swollen and red. "I'm dying. I know I'm dying. I can feel it."

"Because a sad little man killed himself? Hogwash! Is that what that high and mighty doctor here told you?"

"It's what Dr. Setzer in Dallas told me. I'm afraid he's right. The Baker Cure isn't working, Rose. I've had two attacks just today. I thought I was getting better. I'm not."

"Honey, those doctors don't know half as much as they think they do, especially that butcher in Dallas. He was just trying to make a payment on that brand new nineteen-forty Cadillac." As Rose spoke, Ivan twined himself around her legs.

Eva said nothing, but nodded again.

Rose made her voice forceful. "Baby, I could probably guess as good as they could using chicken entrails and some dirty dishwater, but Master Ivan would be upset about me wasting all that good meat. Miss Eva, it ain't your time. My whole church is praying for you. You ain't going to die. Not yet. Now you tell them dumb ass doctors to go take care of someone who's really sick." She tried to move toward the bed but Ivan continued to block her path with linebacker determination. She stared down at him. " 'cuse me Master Ivan. I got work to do." She winked at Eva. "Cuz that boss lady of mine, she don't have a heart in her body. If she catches me goofin' off, I'm gonna have hell to pay."

"I think it's time to run up the white flag and feed Ivan." Eva dabbed her eyes.

"*I think* it's time to look in the mirror and fix yourself up while I feed Master Ivan. You look a mess. You'll feel better with your hair brushed and your makeup on." With the cat almost attached to her ankle, she headed for the bathroom.

Rose laid down a clean bowl and filled it with a concoction of boiled and minced chicken gizzard, lungs, liver, heart and some thigh meat thrown in because Ivan liked dark meat.

"Where's Mrs. Mossell?" Rose asked as she headed to the bathroom.

"In an isolation unit receiving special treatments."

"Why's she in isolation?"

"The nurse told me she's going to be more susceptible to other illnesses until she's done with the treatments," Eva explained glumly.

"That don't sound good." Rose came out of the bathroom with Eva's hairbrush. "Here, brush your hair."

Once Ivan was happily eating at his dinner, Rose left the suite and returned a few minutes later with a cup of steaming water to steep some herbs in. She set the cup of piping amber liquid on the stand beside Eva.

"You might want to drink some of this," Rose said. "It'll make you feel better."

Eva eyed it suspiciously. "What is it?"

"It's hydrangea tea. My people drink it when we have a little pink in our water." She stood there expectantly.

Eva knew Rose wouldn't leave until she tried the tea. She took a small sip. It had a slightly bitter flavor and an unexpected kick to it. "What else is in it?"

"It's hydrangea tea and Scottish whiskey. *My* prescription. At least part of it's good for you. And I ain't saying which part." Rose grinned broadly. "I added just a little lemon juice. But I knew you wouldn't throw out good scotch even if it was in tea."

Eva sighed, smiling weakly. "Rose, you know me too well. Why don't you go on home? I'll be all right in the morning. I just miss Mr. Foxworthy."

"I know you do." Rose said. "But you know Mr. Edgar wouldn't want you feelin' sorry for yourself."

"I know. But, I should have listened to him when he said he felt puny." Eva could almost feel the weight of his head on her lap as she drove him to the hospital.

"He wouldn't want you feeling guilty, either."

"I do, though," Eva said. "He said he felt bad and I didn't pay attention to him."

"You know it and I know it—" Rose assumed her lecture stance, with her fists resting on her hips. "—Mr. Edgar always felt bad. If you'd taken him to the hospital every time he thought he was going to die, you'd have had to get a new address at St. Paul's. His last bout didn't seem anything different than before. Even his doctor thought he'd live to be a hundred."

"I should have listened to him."

"If you were home, Miss Eva, he'd tell you to put on that pretty red dress of yours and go dancing."

Rose loved to give a lecture.

Eva shook her head slowly. "You know I can't do that."

"I know." Rose softened her tone a bit. "If we were at home, and if Mr. Edgar could, he'd tell me to burn your dinner so you'd get out of the house and get some decent food."

Eva smiled. "You two were always conspirators. I can almost picture Edgar's ghost appearing before you with the day's marching orders." Eva paused and raised her eyebrows quizzically. "Do you talk to him often?"

Rose smiled slyly. "Not sayin' I do, an' not sayin' I don't." She wiped her hands on her apron and returned to the bathroom to finish cleaning up after Ivan. "Speaking of such things," Rose called from the bathroom, "I asked Mr. Brown about that jumper. He said ain't no one killed his self that way in years. But there was a girl that went to school here. I think they called it Crescent College, then. Anyway, she got in a family way by one of the professors. They said she killed herself, but Andy says some folks think he might of pushed her. He says the sheriff used to get called out real regular cuz people thought they saw someone jump. But, but there's never no one there."

Eva felt a little weak. "Are you telling me I saw a ghost?"

"I'm telling you, you ain't crazy, like you thought you were. You keep drinking your tea."

Eva took the tea and sipped it slowly. "What else did Andy say?"

"He says the professor got to know a number of the girls in the biblical sense. What did Andy say his name was? Swann I believe."

"Do you recall his first name?"

"I think he said "Jack.""

"Jack." The name raised the hair on her neck and spine. She glanced at the oak desk with "I love Jack" carved into it. "What happened to Mr. Swann?"

"Mr. Brown says one of the girls' daddies was hopping mad and stabbed him. He didn't die right away, but he got infected and passed away a few weeks later. I don't think too many of the daddies in town missed him. Sounds like he wanted 'em all."

"Wanted who?"

"All those girls. I reckon he fancied himself quite the Valentino."

She went back in the bathroom to check on Ivan's progress. He had already licked the Nippon bowl clean as it was when Eva brought it home, and left a gift in his formerly clean sanitary pan.

Rose washed the plate and put it away, and scooped up the smelly new deposit.

"Since Miss Mossell ain't here tonight, I think I'm going to head back to my room in town. I'm feeling a bit peaked."

"On your way out, could you tell the nurse to call the electrician? I think there's a short in the wiring. The lights keep flickering."

Rose's heavy shoes clomped to the front of the suite. "Yes,

Miss Eva. Good night."

Eva watched silently as the door closed behind Rose.

There was something so final about that sound—like a prison cell closing forever. Permanent solitary confinement. No human contact except for nurses and doctors. Feeling so utterly alone, Eva needed to hear a human voice. She turned on the radio, twisting the dial to rid the signal of static. Today it seemed like that was a futile cause. Most of the melody became garbled in hissing and scratching that had nothing to do with Ivan.

She looked at her watch. It was almost time for the news. Finally she tuned in to the station, scratchy though it sounded.

"Good evening. This is the CBS Nightly News with William L. Shirer reporting from Vienna. In response to Hitler's invasion of Poland, Britain and France, both allies of the overrun nation declare war on Germany. Earlier today, the British passenger ship, *H.M.S. Athenia*, was sunk by a German U-boat, killing thirty Americans and 82 other passengers of the 1,100 on board. U.S. President Franklin D. Roosevelt reiterated America's neutrality during a fireside chat."

So there it was: The world at war—at least most of it. But in a sense, she was locked in her own private little war. She felt her outcome was as unsure as the outcome abroad. No longer able to bear bad news, she switched off the radio.

She got up and looked at the oak desk. "I love Jack."

Suddenly she felt nauseous, with heaviness in her chest, the kind of feeling she got before influenza.

Recalling that first night, she remembered the sadness on the girl's face before she jumped. Those eyes. That poor girl bore the weight of the world, as well as Jack's baby, while that bastard went out and leapt between the sheets with any girl that he could. Had she really jumped, or did he push her to save his honor? She shrugged. His honor. That's a paradox if she ever heard one.

Suddenly her blood turned to ice as a distinct voice whispered in her left ear, "I want you..."

Eva spun around. No one—not a blessed soul was in the room. Yet she heard every syllable, "I want you." Who could it be but that bastard Jack Swann, like the swan who raped Leda in the myth?

What does he want with me?

Why would he come here, except it had once been the girl's room? Did he think Eva was that confused child he molested? Or did he know she was someone else but wanted to possess her, too? It was too terrifying to contemplate. As tired and achy as she felt, she couldn't spend another moment in the room.

Trembling, she grabbed Ivan and held him tight against her. She wanted to go home to Dallas, even if it meant dying.

Like a former resident of this room, she, too, was frightened of Jack. Now she understood why the poor girl had jumped.

"I wish a director would shout cut," she cried.

But the scene didn't end there. Both she and the cat looked toward the hall to the arrival of the eleven o'clock hour and, "Squeak, squeak, squeak. Squeak, squeak, squeak."

She left Ivan in the bed and opened the door slightly. She could see the nurse push an empty gurney into the annex and close the door. A few minutes later she reemerged rolling the loaded cart covered with a sheet, moving it toward the elevator.

Eva closed the door, shut her eyes and slid to the floor feeling as if her bones had liquefied.

But even in her fright, Eva couldn't help being curious about the secrets that lay beyond the annex door. None of the patients she'd met were assigned beds there. She seldom observed anyone going in or out during the day. Yet almost every night the gurney passed... squeak, squeak, squeak. She waited a few minutes, crept into the hall and looked around. Everything was quiet—no squeaking gurney, no footsteps.

Eva tested the annex door. Locked! Placing her ear against the door Eva heard something but couldn't quite make it out.

Back in 1926 she made a movie called *Righteous Indignation*, where she played a wife with an unfaithful husband. In the movie she discovered his affair using a glass against the wall to amplify the sound. She smiled at the irony of using this technique in a silent film.

Eva dashed to her room, grabbed her drinking glass and returned to the annex door. With the bottom of the glass against the door and her ear pressed against the lip of the glass, she heard what sounded like groans. She moved the glass a few inches to see if she could hear more clearly. Still, all she could hear was something that could best be described as Halloween moans. The moan became a shriek and then a scream—an eyeball popping, blood chilling, dying-breath scream. Eva closed her eyes for a moment to block out her other senses.

When she opened them, she found herself staring into Nurse Turner's eyes. She froze.

The nurse had her arms folded and wore the scowl of a high school principal catching someone smoking in the girls' room. "Miss Dupree, what are you doing!"

"I—I thought I heard... someone cry for help."

Nurse Turner tore the glass out of Eva's hand, grabbed her roughly by the elbow and dragged her back to her room. "We can't have you wandering around disturbing the other patients. You must stay in your room."

"I'm sorry, Nurse Turner," Eva said sweetly and as an after-thought added an innocent smile. "I thought someone was in trouble. I must have forgotten y'all use those rooms for storage. Silly me."

Nurse Turner's eyes narrowed as she stared, unblinking, at Eva, and shoved her into her room. "Good*night*, Miss Dupree!" Nurse Turner slammed the door in Eva's face.

Eva cringed. Was she going to pay for this little prank next time Nurse Turner gave her a shot!

Eva took a couple of steps toward her bed when behind her she heard the doorknob rattle then click. Only silence followed. Eva froze. *Oh, no!* She rushed back to the door pulled on the doorknob. The knob turned, but the door was locked as tight as a bank safe.

Her heart race furiously, her face heated up. Nurse Turner had trapped her inside the room with the ghost of Jack Swann. She rattled the door with every bit of strength she could rally. Other than making a lot of noise, she accomplished nothing.

Eva banged on the door with her first. "Let me out! Let me out!"

Trembling, aching and exhausted she slid to the floor. What would happen to her if Nurse Turner had to return to shut her up? Sedatives? Restraints? Or worse? The nurse could, and possibly, would make life, short as it might be, hell.

She glanced at the door to the balcony. If she needed to, she could always escape that way.

Eva struggled to her feet and made her way to bed. *Maybe it's time to go home.*

DAY SEVEN—*Wednesday, September 6*

The next morning Nurse Cavanaugh brought Eva a breakfast tray and a message. "The elevator operator asked me to give this to you." Cavanaugh paused for a moment and ran the back of her fingers across the cattails in Eva's water pitcher. "This is certainly an interesting flower arrangement."

"A gift from a friend."

"He must have known you like cats," Nurse Cavanaugh said. "That's very clever, don't you think?"

"Yes, very clever," Eva said. "Nurse, where exactly is Mrs. Knight?"

Nurse Cavanaugh had begun taking Eva's pulse. "She went home a few days ago. Don't you remember?"

What happened to the story about aggressive treatment and isolation? Alarm rose in Eva. Where was Mossell really? But she said, "Oh, that's right. The medicine must be affecting my memory. Odd she didn't even come by to tell me goodbye."

"People are often so happy to get a clean bill of health, they leave without much fanfare. You'll see how it is soon, don't you think?"

"I guess I will," she said but her voice was full of incredulity.

When the nurse had left, Eva opened the folded paper. The note was written in Rose's scrawl. The note read: *"I am sick with the urps. Please try to take care of Ivan for me. There are a couple of cans of Kit-E Ration in the closet. I will be there tomorrow. I don't want you to catch this. Rose"*

She read it, then set it down on her bedside table. "Well, Ivan, I guess we're on our own today."

Eva got the can opener out and stared at the can of Kit-E-Ration. She squeezed the can opener handles together and twisted the T-handle and the cute kitty face turned. It would almost be easier to chop up fresh chicken than to open the can with the cranky opener. Finally, after running the dull cutting wheel back and forth, back and forth, it made it full-circle, and the can was open. Inside was a solid gray chunk of cat food. She pulled it out in one solid piece with a thunk as it slammed into the delicate china.

"That smells awful. If I were you, I'd hold out for Rose's chicken mixture. But you'll have to wait until tomorrow for that."

After a few bites he'd eaten enough to take the edge off of his hunger. Ivan sniffed the gray blob on his plate and pantomimed covering it with his paw just like he would the poop in his sanitary pan.

"You're nothing else if not subtle," she told him. "I'll see if the nurse can bring you something more acceptable."

When Nurse Cavanaugh returned, Eva ordered some bacon and a piece of chicken to indulge Ivan with breakfast. A few minutes later Nurse Cavanaugh arrived with Eva's breakfast and a saucer of bite-sized bacon and chicken bits.

"Bacon sounds good, don't you think?" Cavanaugh asked the cat as she offered him the meal.

As he nibbled on the tidbits, Eva took a moment to watch him eat. He was a delicate eater, taking a little bite, chewing it, sitting for a second as if letting it digest before taking another bite. Occasionally he would lick his lips or wipe his whiskers with his paw to remove a chunk of clinging meat.

This was the first time Eva had ever just watched him eat. The little smacking noises he made as he chewed brought a smile to her face. "What a sweet sound."

He looked up at her and blinked as if to say, "Rose's known that all along." And of course, so did Edgar.

After breakfast, Eva went into the bathroom and inspected Ivan's commode. Rose was so inventive. She put fireplace ashes in a large white enamel baking pan and removed the poop with an old fry strainer. Almost all the ashes were soggy, more like mud. The bathroom had taken on an aroma—and not a pleasant one. Ivan needed to have his facilities freshened before Rose could make it back tomorrow.

What could she do? It wasn't like she could send anyone to the store for cat ashes or sand. By agreement, she couldn't ask her nurse for help. When Norman Baker gave her permission to bring Ivan along she promised she wouldn't ask the nurses to mess with Ivan's facilities.

Maybe she could talk some of the patients who like to tend the hospital's flower gardens into digging up some clean dirt. She thought about it further and dismissed the idea. While Ivan would probably enjoy getting his paws dirty, Eva wouldn't be able to flush dirt as she could ashes. As soon as she finished dressing, she'd go downstairs on a fact gathering expedition. When she'd first arrived at the Baker Hospital Eva had noticed a furnace chimney at the far end of the building. Besides, after last night she wanted to get out of the room now more than ever.

Once she was decent, she slipped her wallet into the pocket of her cherry and white floral cotton day dress. She also grabbed the paper bag that Rose kept the fry strainer in and took the elevator down to the lobby.

"Morning Andy," she said to the elevator operator.

Andy Brown hesitated, then as he closed the elevator door and the inside cage, said, "Morning Miss Dupree. How are you, today?" He kept his eyes on the elevator doors to monitor the passing floors.

"I'm feeling well enough that I think I want to take a little walk," she answered.

"Rose is feeling a mite puny today. Maybe something she ate didn't agree with her."

"Thank you for taking care of her," Eva said. "I'm glad she found a nice family to stay with. Let me know if she needs anything."

"Rose talks real fondly of you and the cat," he said cheerfully.

"Tell her to get better."

"Yes, ma'am. I'll do that." Andy opened the door. "Enjoy this fine day."

Eva nodded and left the elevator. Even this early, a number of patients lounged around the lobby and visited with their visitors.

On her way outside Eva found Cooper Reilly chatting with some ladies down in the lobby. "Cooper, can I talk to you for just a moment."

"Certainly." He rose and turned to the ladies he was speaking with. "I'll be back shortly."

Clutching her paper bag she said, "I owe you an apology."

"No." He shook his head. "I should apologize to you. The cattails and ferns must have been an insult to a woman of your refined taste."

"I told you they weren't an insult at all. I reacted that way because..." She broke off to blink back a tear. "I didn't want to tell you this, but my husband died two years ago."

"I'm sorry."

"Thank you. One of the sweet things he did was bring me flowers he found while walking around our neighborhood. This time of year he'd bring cattails. A few weeks after he'd first given them to me, he heard a kitten— Ivan—in a trash can. He said the flowers must have been an omen that a kitten would be coming into our lives. I dried those flowers. I still have them. So it was just overwhelming when you gave me cattails, too. I wanted you to know, I do appreciate them."

He looked down into her eyes. "Maybe he wanted me to give them to you for him. Edgar was a very fortunate man to have such a lovely and sensitive wife. Perhaps someday, when the time is right, you will honor me with your company for dinner." He smiled warmly at her.

She wanted to say something else to him, but she felt like she'd left her script at home. "Thanks for understanding. I'll see you later."

She walked to the center of the lobby and looked around. Across from the elevator was Norman Baker's office. At the other end of the lobby, next to the admissions desk sat a tiny gift store that she'd never noticed before. Remembering Mr. Baker said it might have books, Eva ventured inside.

The shop wasn't much larger than eight-foot by twelve but it was packed full of Baker Hospital memorabilia. A bookrack held Baker Hospital Cookbooks, the KTNT Magazine, an XENT program guide, Cancer Is Curable pamphlets and some sheet music for piano, violin, guitar, and accordion. She even found some music for Norman Baker's invention, the Calliaphone. Shelves held other items like Baker Hospital glasses, measuring cups and bouquets of artificial flowers made from feathers in a glass vase. One rack offered stationary, an assortment of greeting cards and picture postal cards, while another stand showed off flowery and humorous get-well cards. Rows of shelves held some knickknacks from fifteen cents to five dollars. The top shelf had a small selection of radios from a Tangley radio/phonograph combination to a battery-powered radio for a whopping forty dollars.

Eva looked at the postcards. She was drawn to one with a drawing of a pharmacist holding a medicine bottle. The message read, *"If thoughts and good wishes could banish your ills, You'd have no more need of physicians and pills: And if love, like the sunlight, could drive away gloom, T'would brighten each spot in your sick-a-bed room."*

None of them said anything about being "Glad you're feeling

better."

She picked up a linen postal card with a color photograph of the hospital that had an oval inset depicting Norman Baker's face. The caption read, "Where sick folks get well." Finally she decided on the postal card that said, "I'm feeling better at the Baker Hospital." It had a picture of the hospital from the valley below looking up at the 'Castle Atop the Ozarks'. She paid three cents for it and another thirty cents for a fountain pen and a bottle of purple ink. As an afterthought she picked up some one-cent stamps. Now, she needed to find some ashes for Ivan.

Outside the sun shone brightly, casting crisp shadows against the sidewalk. She'd picked a perfect day to venture out. She closed her eyes and inhaled deeply. Without the oil of wintergreen in her nose she could smell the greenness of the trees and grass hanging in the air. It was fresh and had a chilly bite. It was certainly nothing like her Dallas neighbors were experiencing. Most likely they were suffering through ninety-degree afternoons.

Maybe I should spend more time out here.

Eva found herself immersed in an emerald pool of vines and pines. The hospital's limestone facade wore a lacy veil of dew-covered English Ivy and brilliant pine trees covered the grounds.

Immediately outside the front and back hospital entrances lay lovely gardens with asters brightening the walk in shades of autumn blooms in shades of pink, purple and burgundy. Rose bushes in reds and pinks filled the air with a scent. She inhaled deeply. Though fragrant, it smelled fresh and clean—not a synthetic perfume used upstairs to poorly disguise the odor of decaying flesh—but a fresh sweetness. She missed her own flower garden so much. Despite the aching in her side and pressure in her back, Eva felt a sense of aliveness. For the first time in ages she longed to get her hands dirty.

She made her way down the steeply sloped grounds rather than walking all the way to the steps. Tall pines towered above her and shielded her from the sun. She wandered into a thicket to enjoy the shade and the solitude.

"Hey, you. Stop," yelled a male voice. A man wearing a rumpled suit appeared from behind a massive pine tree brandishing a Tommy gun. He had the barrel pointed down, but he kept his right hand close to the business end. "I'm sorry, ma'am. I didn't mean to frighten you."

She stared at the gun in disbelief.

He glanced around and lowered his voice. "Sorry, ma'am. No trouble. There's a, uh, dignitary from Austria being treated. Mr. Baker increased the guards while he's here. There's nothing to worry about. I'm sorry if you were startled." He tipped his hat to her. "Hope you enjoy your day, ma'am."

Eva smiled, but walked quickly away.

Austria? I thought Mr. Baker said the dignitary came from Sweden.

She picked up her pace when she spied a tall brick chimney on the south side of the building. When she reached the smokestack, it turned out to be a steam escape for the boiler. But just a few feet away from the boiler smokestack stood a large furnace with a shorter chimney. It should have what she needed. If there weren't any ashes, Ivan would have to dirty his paws on just soil. And she'd just have to figure out what to do with the mud later.

Eva wandered past the laundry, an area that also apparently doubled as a delivery dock. A produce truck had backed up to a large open garage door. A couple of black dishwashers carried wooden crates of fresh vegetables to the kitchen.

Amid the chaos, an elderly woman walked through the delivery door with an armful of groceries. She called back over her shoulder, "Thank Mr. Baker for the food."

Clearly, this was not where she needed to go to take care of the cat's latrine. About twenty feet away, she found what she was looking for. The incinerator was larger than most, red brick matching the stack to the boiler.

The rusty iron door squeaked as she opened it. Good! Inside she found a huge drift of ashes. She scooped them into her bag. Ivan would be happy with her and Rose would be delighted that she took some initiative. Of course, her hands and dress were dusted with soot. It was a small price to pay to keep the cat happy and using his bathroom.

Back in her suite, she poured the cinders into Ivan's baking pan, tossed the sack into the trash and washed her hands. These ashes weren't like fireplace ashes she had seen before; they felt a little sticky. Instead of soft gray flakes there were lots of little hard white pieces. Doubtless Ivan would not care.

She placed a towel under the pan and tried to wipe up the ash that had fallen on the white tiles. Ivan would soon show his gratitude by immediately dirtying the spotless sanitary pan, as he did after Rose cleaned up.

When she reached for a stray clump of cinders a few feet away, the internal guy with the pitchfork gave her a tremendous jab. Eva closed her eyes and took a long deep breath, waiting for the aching to subside.

Make it stop. Make it stop.

Finally the wave of pain passed. Before she could further inspire the wrath of the kidney, Eva quickly filled the water bowl and stood up.

As Eva washed her hands the cat ambled into the bathroom. But he did not climb into the box and dig around as usual. Instead he checked it out from six inches away. Tentatively sniffing the ashes then letting out a guttural yowl, the likes of which she had never before heard from him. He arched his back, hair sticking out on all directions. After staring at the enamel baking pan for a moment longer, he hissed. Ivan screeched, hopped sideways for a couple of steps, then fled the bathroom in a terrified white streak. Eva found Ivan sitting on her bed, his tail lashing against the blanket so hard she could actually hear it. He stared at the bathroom, his pupils dilated as big as his eyes.

Why would he react that way? she wondered. He never did that when Rose prepared his toilet.

A few minutes later there was a knock at the door. A black woman half Rose's age stood there holding Rose's tote bag.

"Are you Miss Eva?" the young woman asked.

Eva nodded.

"I'm Zola Mae Brown. Rose asked me to bring this up to you." She added with a touch of contempt in her voice, "She said your cat needs his dinner."

Eva glanced over at the bed. Ivan continued to stare warily at the bathroom.

"Yes, he does."

"Rose's got a terrible stomach upset. She said you might want me to clean up the cat's bathroom?"

Eva nodded. "I just freshened his toilet up, but I wasn't able to clean up thoroughly."

"Rose said you wouldn't mind paying me."

"No, of course not. I'll pay you extra for taking care of her while she's sick too."

"Really? Mighty fine." She peeked around the bathroom door. "Lordy, honey. You did make a mess. Where'd you get these ashes?"

"When I got Rose's note saying she was sick, I went downstairs and got some of the ashes out of the furnace next to the building."

The woman pulled her hands away from the pan as if her fingers were on fire and flew out of the bathroom. "You got this out of the furnace *downstairs*?"

"Yes. Why?"

"Huh uh," she said wiping her hands on her dress. "I ain't touching that. I don't touch no dead people. Not for no one. Not for no money." She dropped the canvas bag filled with fresh fireplace ashes and Ivan's dinner. "Here. You'll have to take care of this. I just don't touch no dead people. Good day to you."

As fast as she appeared Zola Mae disappeared. She didn't even wait for Eva to pay her.

What did she mean she doesn't touch dead people?

Eva went into the bathroom. She poured the lumpy ashes into the commode. Small white chips floated in the toilet water, circling the bowl in a vicious whirlpool until they finally disappeared. It took a couple of flushes to completely clear the bowl of all of the ashes and white floaters. Eva washed the sticky residue off with a washrag and dried it with the bath towel. She poured Zola Mae's replacement ashes in the container, wiping down the entire bathroom as best she could. But the restroom was pretty much still a mess.

When the nurse's aide came in to change her bed Eva asked, "Could I have some extra clean towels? I'm afraid I made a terrible mess."

"Sure," the young woman answered.

When the woman returned with more towels, Eva offered her a nice tip if she would go in and tidy the place up without telling anyone. She left out the part about where the ashes came from. After a few minutes the bathroom was once again sparkling.

Up on the observation deck, Eva gazed out across the mountains. The valley seemed bigger and emptier than it had before. Three days without Mossell's company seemed like forever.

Eva took out the postcard that she bought in the hospital gift store and circled the fourth floor porch where she and Mossell always sat together.

"*I miss you,*" she wrote. "*Glad you're feeling better. I hope we get to-*

gether after I go home. Evie."

She pulled out the page from Mossell's book and copied down the niece's mailing address. She'd ask a nurse to drop Mossell's card in the mail for her later.

Eva poured her own scotch and Eureka Springs healing water, stirring it with her forefinger. Then to keep from wasting even a drop, she licked her finger. *Ahh, the nectar of the gods*. What a shame she had to enjoy it by herself. If the nurses would just put in her special ingredient, she wouldn't complain about all of the water they made her drink.

Outside a starry evening had replaced a bright day. Inside her room, the death of another day brought anticipation of another night of her waking nightmares.

Since Edgar's passing, each lonely night spanned an eternity. Nights at the Baker Hospital lasted longer than that. Everything seemed to be amplified: the sounds of the mountain wind howling through the trees, the creaking of the old wood floors as the nurses walked through the halls, even Ivan's purr sounded louder.

She turned the radiator up a bit to warm the air and pulled the rocking chair and lamp closer to the warmth. She avoided her bed, preferring to doze on the rocking chair. Somehow she felt safer there. The bed felt more ominous. She could visualize the older and wiser professor violating that sixteen-year old girl, and convincing her how fortunate she was. In Eva's mind she saw him caress the pale skin, as he satisfied himself. He explored her body. She heard his moans of satisfaction; she felt the sensations. That poor girl felt so grown up.

The beginning of a life and the end of a life, really three lives lost, all a result of Jack Swann's selfish pleasure.

Eva imagined when she'd missed her period, she nervously met him on the fourth floor balcony. The night couldn't have been more perfect. A chill hung in the air and a crescent moon was suspended in the cloudless sky. It was just cold enough that she could snuggle up to him for warmth. He was so wonderful; he would understand. No, better still he would marry her. And like every storybook tale, they would live happily ever after.

But that's not the way it happened in Eva's mind. He screamed at her, blaming her for ruining his life. Jack might just as well have ended her life then, after all, his rebuke had pierced her heart.

The creaking of the suite door jerked her out of the daydream and made her yelp.

Nurse Johnston rushed over. "Miss Dupree! You all right?"

Eva looked around. She and Nurse Johnston were alone. No student, no Jack Swann. "I must have been having a bad dream," she said sheepishly.

"Just wanted to check in on you. Need anything?"

"Some ice water."

Nurse Johnston nodded. "Be right back."

She returned with a glass of ice cubes floating in a bath of water. "Here. Anything else?"

"No, I'm fine."

The nurse headed for the door.

"No. Wait." Eva got up and reached into the desk. "Could you put this in the mail for me?"

Miss Johnston took the card addressed to Mossell, glanced at the picture of the photograph of the Baker Hospital and stashed it in her pocket and patted it. "Sure. Be happy to."

When the nurse had left, Eva poured out some of the water and replaced it with her Haig & Haig Blue Label. She quickly drained the contents, leaving only a trace of the ice. No, she wasn't numb enough. She needed another drink before she could attempt to fall off to sleep.

With empty Baker Hospital glass in hand, Eva walked carefully to the nurse's station. There she found Nurse Johnston telling Nurse Turner about her father's broken leg. She held a pencil in her hand that was scarred point-to-eraser with tooth marks. "It was so nice of Mr. Baker to help my folks out. You know he paid my parents electric bill while Papa couldn't work? Mr. Baker didn't say anything to anyone. When Mom went to pay the bill, Mrs. Koontz at the electric company said he'd been in to pay it. He was a real lifesaver..." Nurse Johnston looked up and stopped mid-sentence. "Need something, Miss Dupree?"

Something in the trash can caught Eva's eye—a postal card exactly like the one she had just handed Miss Johnston a few minutes earlier. She peered closer and recognized the circle of ink on the fourth floor balcony.

"I said, 'You need help?'" the nurse repeated.

Eva glanced down at the trash one last time just to make sure it was her card. She had no doubt; Nurse Johnston never mailed it.

"Uh...yes...I'd like some more ice."

"I'll bring it to you. As a matter of fact, I'll bring you some extra ice, but I think you best go back to your room. It's too late for you to be out." With a hand on Eva's shoulder Nurse Johnston steered her back to her room. Ivan stood by the door waiting for her. Within a few minutes Nurse Johnston returned with a glass of crushed ice.

"Good night, Miss Dupree," Nurse Johnston said, and closed the door behind her.

Eva added a little water and a lot of scotch to the glass and took a long drink.

They never mailed the card? Why not?

Eva turned on the radio and listened as she tried to read *A Practical Cat Book*, but haunted by the postcard, she could not concentrate. Finally, when she could keep her eyes open no longer she turned off the radio and climbed in bed.

She had almost slipped off to sleep when Ivan walked across her chest. And that was when she heard it again.

Squeak, squeak, squeak.

What time was it? She looked at her clock. Five minutes after eleven.

DAY EIGHT—*Thursday, September 7*

"Good morning, Miss Dupree." Nurse Cavanaugh yanked the drapes open as usual. "It's a beautiful day, don't you think?"

Blinded by the brightness of the morning sky, Eva squinted and blinked uncomfortably. What she wouldn't give to show up some morning at Cavanaugh's house and blind her with a spotlight as *she* was trying to wake up.

"We're running a little behind today. I hope you don't mind that I can't give your treatment for a while. I'll get you some coffee." She scratched Ivan's forehead. "And I'll get you a snack. But don't worry, today's going to be an easy day. You'll only be getting an oral dose this morning."

"That's certainly good news," Eva said as she stretched everything right down to the fingertips. The guy with the pitchfork was showing restraint today.

Nurse Cavanaugh left and returned a few minutes later with coffee and breakfast for Ivan.

The nurse started to close the door, then changed her mind. "Oh, I nearly forgot. Another secret message." She handed Eva a piece of paper.

Eva recognized the extra-large block letters as Trudy's handwriting. She smiled. Despite the fact that the notes were hardly world altering, they certainly made a bright moment in her day. She had started looking forward to the messages.

When she was alone, Eva retrieved her Orphan Annie Telematic decoder and turned it twelve. "Here's todays secret message."

Eva turned the dial, one character at a time, then scratching down the letter. She was confused until she wrote down the final two letters. Cute as she was, Trudy wasn't the best speller in the world. The message said, "Will you pleas brade my hair".

She smiled as she worked out the code for her response. "Come over after your treatment. I will braid your hair."

Eva went outside to the observation deck to get some sun. She took her cup of coffee along with one of her magazines. The air was a bit nippy, but it felt good. Instead of reading *Picture Play*, she reclined and shielded her eyes with it. "It's time, Miss Dupree." It was Nurse Cavanaugh. "Time for your medicine."

"Already? I thought you gave me a reprieve?"

"Only a short one. I'm afraid you need to get back to your room. I'll bring your cocktail in just a minute."

"Don't forget the scotch."

"Oh, right." Cavanaugh winked as best she could but it was actually more of a blink.

If she only knew.

"All right. You win." Then as an afterthought Eva held up the note and asked, "Can you give this to Trudy?"

Cavanaugh glanced at it, smiled and said, "Of course." She slid it in her pocket.

A few minutes later the nurse dropped off the tar and went on with her day. As soon as she had left, Eva added a little Scottish preservative to the medicine to help get it down. An ounce of alcohol helped immensely. It thinned the mixture and made the flavor much less offensive. The scotch burned as it flowed down her throat.

A short time later, Eva heard Trudy's tiny knock.

"Come in, Trudy."

The little girl peeked around the corner. "How'd you know it was me?"

"I know your knock."

"Kinda like a secret knock?" Trudy asked.

"Exactly like a secret knock. You're very clever."

Trudy smiled proudly. As she entered the room Ivan jumped down off the bed and greeted her by weaving through her legs. Giggling, she plopped down on the floor and carefully laid her Orphan Annie doll down next to her. "Hi, Mr. Kitty." She scratched him up and down his back.

"So you want me to braid your hair?"

"Uh huh."

"Come on over here in front of the mirror." Eva patted the bench next to the vanity.

Trudy climbed up on the bench. She turned around and faced the mirror, her feet dangling way above the floor. In her hand she clutched two pink hair ribbons. Her furry shadow jumped up on the glass vanity top so the little girl could continue to pet him. Eva got her brush out and slid it though Trudy's sunny locks. Apparently the nurses hadn't had time to comb the girl's hair, at least not recently. Eva had to work through a number of nasty tangles. Occasionally Trudy would grunt or cry out when Eva tugged a little too hard.

"You look like you're feeling better," Eva observed.

"Uh huh. I do."

Finally the comb ran smoothly through the girl's shoulder-length hair. "Do you want two pigtails or a single ponytail down the center of your back."

"One. Don't you think one would make me look grown up?"

"Of course, it will. Okay. One grown up braid it is...I bet you miss your mom." At the crown of her head Eva divided the blond hair into thirds.

"Uh huh."

"Aren't you lonely here?" Eva asked.

"A little. But I have friends here." Trudy picked up Eva's tortoiseshell comb and ran it through her bangs. The cowlick right in front wouldn't lie down no matter how many times she combed it.

"You do? That's wonderful. Who are your friends?"

"Annie and you and Mr. Kitty." She patted Ivan.

"Why, thank you."

"And Johnny."

Eva twisted the hair on the right over the middle section. "Who's Johnny?"

Trudy pointed to empty air beside her. "He's right here. He thinks you're pretty. He spends a lot of time in your room."

The hair stood up on Eva's arms and her stomach knotted. She stopped braiding. Suddenly her room seemed even less safe than it had before. "Are you sure his name isn't Jack?"

The little girl shrugged her shoulders. "Nuh uh. He told me he was Johnny."

The knot in Eva's belly grew dense as a bowling ball. "Why don't we finish your hair outside on the deck?"

"I want to stay here and pet Mr. Kitty. I miss my dog, Sandy."

Eva made herself resume braiding. "Did you name your dog after Orphan Annie's dog?"

"Uh huh."

"What's Johnny like?" Eva twisted a handful of blond hair and grabbed another.

"He's nice and he's real big."

"He is?" Her fingers were getting tired.

"He's real smart."

Eva envisioned Johnny standing in front of a blackboard at Crescent College sharing his intellect with all those impressionable girls. "I'm sure he is." The predator guarding the unsuspecting sheep. How much smarter was he than those children?

"Here you go," Eva said finally as she tied the ribbon around the finished braid. "You want to see it?"

"Uh huh."

"Okay." Eva retrieved a hand mirror out of the vanity. "What do you think?" She held the mirror up so Trudy could inspect her work.

Trudy's eyes grew large. "Wow. That's pretty. Thank you."

"You're welcome."

She climbed down from the bench. "Can I show everyone?"

"Sure. Have fun."

In a flash Trudy disappeared. Suddenly, Eva felt terribly alone, and yet not alone enough. She held up her fist and shook it in the empty air. "You don't scare me, you bastard! You're not going to chase me out of here."

"You alright, Miss Dupree?" Nurse Cavanaugh popped her head inside the door. "I just wanted to check in on you before I left for the day, and heard you calling out. Do you need anything?"

"A good night's sleep."

The nurse shrugged her shoulders. "I can't help you there. I could use a good night myself. I'll ask Mrs. Turner to give you something. That would help, don't you think?"

"It might."

Nurse Cavanaugh waved a weary hand and said, "I'll take care of it for you before I leave. Bye, Miss Dupree."

"Goodbye Nurse Cavanaugh."

As tired as she'd been, she didn't want to spend another moment in the room. Like the past residents of the room, Eva too, was frightened of Jack. Or was it Johnny? She had to get out of the room. She had to think. Eva left and wandered down to the lobby to buy a newspaper.

"Good morning, Mr. Dye," she said as she passed the elderly patient she had met on the balcony that first morning.

He smiled and winked at her. "Good morning, Mrs. Dupree. He pointed to the glass pane doors facing the mountain. Would you like to join me outside for some sunshine?"

Before she could answer a colorful vase on the mantle caught her attention. *What the hell?*

"Not right now, Mr. Dye." Her voice sounded distant, distracted. "Maybe a little later."

He smiled and turned toward the door. "I'll take that as a promise."

"Okay." Eva approached the fireplace. On the mantle between a couple of Hummels and a Dresden doll dressed porcelain lace sat, the Ming Dynasty vase, the very one Roger Knight's mother had given him. The one that Mossell swore she would never give up. The one she wanted her niece to have if she died.

"Where did this come from?" Eva demanded of the admissions clerk.

The frazzled woman looked over her stack of papers. "I don't know. I think some patient left it here cuz she was so happy to go home."

"Of course," she said. But Mossell would never have left that vase behind—not as long as there was breath in her body.

It was time to get the hell out of here.

It grew late in the day. Rose finally showed up with her bag of clean ashes and some fresh giblets from the butcher.

As the maid cleaned the box, Eva called through the door. "Rose, I know this sounds crazy, but I believe there are some unsavory activities afoot here."

Rose stopped in the middle of a poop scoop and shook her fry strainer at Eva. "I could of told you that."

"How do you know?"

Rose dumped the ashes in the commode and rinsed out the pan. "The family I'm staying with was saying some unkind things about the hospital." She dried the cake pan off with a hand towel.

"Like what?"

"I don't want to get Mr. Brown in trouble, but he says lots of people die here that no one knows about." She emptied the bag of clean fireplace ashes into the enamel pan.

When she was finished with her toilet duty, she washed her hands and fixed Eva's scotch spiked hydrangea tea. "Here, drink this. It'll help you."

Eva took a long drink. "Rose, why don't you sit down? Get a drink if you want it. You still look a little tired."

"Really? Thank you, kindly. I do feel kinda tuckered." She pulled out an Old Heidelberg from its hiding place in the closet, and claimed a chair. Her eyes looked a little brighter than they had a few days before, but she looked as if she could still use another full-night's sleep.

"What else did you hear?" Eva asked.

"You won't laugh at me?"

"No, I won't laugh." Eva held three fingers up in the Girl Scout salute.

The maid hesitated, then finally said, "Their boy says the place is haunted." Rose took a very deep swig, then studied the label as if to memorize every important word. "Miss Eva, I got some things to say to you that you ain't going to like. But I want you to listen to me."

"All right, Rose. The floor is yours." After that opening sentence, Eva knew Rose was building up the courage to talk.

"I've heard some awful things about this hospital," the maid finally said.

"Why didn't you tell me before now?"

Rose picked at the label on her beer bottle. "Maybe I should have, but I figured it was most likely just rumors…and you know I don't like gossip." She hesitated, then continued. "Now, I don't tell you what to do very often, but you need to go home so your real doctor can take care of you. You ain't going to get any better here."

"I may not be the only one," Eva said. "Rose, I think Mossell's dead."

Rose caught her breath. "Miss Mossell? Why do you think that?"

"They said they took her to an isolation ward. I believe it's in that annex they keep locked. Then they said she went home, cured. I gave the nurse a card to mail to Mossell at her niece's home. Instead of giving it to the mailman, that nurse threw it away. Even worse, I found Mossell's Ming vase on display in the lobby. You know what she said about that vase. She'd never let it go. I don't know what's in the annex, but almost every night around eleven, I can hear the nurses pushing gurneys. When it leaves the annex, the gurney always has a dead body on it. One night I tried to listen through the door and heard someone moaning. Nurse Turner caught me and locked me in my room."

"You think spooks are moaning?"

"I don't know. I want to get a look inside to see what or who's there, but they keep it locked. If I only knew a way to get in."

Rose smirked. "I can show you how to open that lock. It ain't that hard."

Eva blinked. "You can what? Now, Rose, how would a good Christian woman like you know how to break into a locked door?"

Rose shrugged. "One time when you and Mr. Edgar were in Hollywood he called and asked me to look up something in his desk. He told me how to do it."

Eva gaped at her. "I never would have believed it. A sweet lady like you an expert lock picker."

"Honey, you ain't begun to discover my hidden talents."

"I should say not!" Eva marveled. "I'm certainly glad you're of good character, otherwise you could have cleaned us out years ago."

"Yes, I could've," Rose said proudly.

Suddenly, Eva looked at her maid with new admiration. Before this trip she had merely been the hired help. Now, Eva realized that this woman was clever, creative and scrupulously honest—mostly.

"Okay, Mrs. Capone, how do I get past that door?"

"Start by doing some paperwork," the maid said.

"What?"

"Don't you have some important papers the bank sent you here?"

Eva went to the vanity and pulled out a couple of stacks of papers held together with paperclips. Her eyebrows rose quizzically. "This is going to help me get into the annex?"

"Yes." Rose removed the two paper clips from the documents and held them up. "These will."

Rose straightened both clips, then bent them into the shape of a 'J'. She tried to bend the tip to angle in, but didn't have the leverage and dug the end of the wire into her fingertip. "Ow!" Rose sucked on her bleeding finger. "This isn't going to work. Miss Eva, I need to use the toenail clippers."

Eva rooted through the vanity and presented Rose with her manicure set rolled up in a cobalt velvet travel pouch. "Isn't this an odd time for a pedicure?"

"Reckon it is." She removed the pliers-style toenail clippers and grasped the end of the wire with it. "You bend a loop just big enough to fit in the keyhole. She showed off the finished products: one wire was altered into the shape of a 'J' with an extra bend at each end. The second clip had two additional bends at the top of the 'J'. "Here, I'll show you on the desk."

"Use one wire to press down on a little pin inside there. See? And the other to turn it like a key." Rose made it sound easy, but truth be told, she could have done with a couple of extra hands and a real key.

Eva looked at the desk as Rose maneuvered the lock. It was easy to see she didn't make her living breaking into desks. Perspiration beaded her forehead. She finally had the paperclip positioned just right. The lock emitted a faint click and the pin gave way. Rose took ten minutes before she pulled the top drawer open in victory. "It's just that simple." She removed a hankie from between her bosom and dabbed her sweaty face, then she put her picks back in the keyhole and locked it again. This time only took a single try. "Now it's your turn."

"That simple?" Eva rolled her eyes. "Rose, it took you ten minutes to get it. And you're the one who's supposed to know what you're doing."

"Now, Miss Eva, I don't go around breaking into things all the time. Only did it when Mr. Edgar told me to. Ain't done it in years." She turned back to the desk and returned her pick to the lock, popping the lock in only moments, then locking it again. "Go ahead and try it."

Eva inspected the lock. It didn't look all that different from the mechanism on her suite door...and the door to the annex. She inserted the first paperclip and then the second.

"Hold your right hand straight. And press your finger down just a tad. If it doesn't open, you might be pressing down too hard. And move that one back and forth like a tree saw until it catches. If it don't open in a couple of tries, take everything out and start over."

After several unsuccessful tries, Eva put her "picks" down. What was she doing? This wasn't what she expected to be doing while she was receiving treatments at the Baker Hospital.

Curious, Ivan joined them, sniffing the locks and pawing at the wires.

"I guess I don't have an aptitude for a life of crime. Maybe we should just forget this."

Rose clucked. "Now, Miss Eva, I've known you for an awful long time. You do just about anything you set your mind to. This ain't no different. You already told me about that night nurse locking you in the room. This new skill could come in right handy. Try one more time."

Eva sighed heavily and retrieved her tools. "One last try," she muttered. She inserted the clips, positioned everything just as Rose had coached her, and voila, heard the very faint click as it caught.

"You got it!"

"I did it!" Eva pulled the drawer open. The wood stuck and it took a good yank to open it all the way. Rather than being empty as she expected, the center drawer held a brown leather book—a diary. Gold leaf on the cover read , "Mile Stones-A Five Year Diary." At the bottom was the name "Mary Elizabeth Rankin."

Eva could feel her pulse quicken. Could this be the diary of the girl who was thrown from the roof? She grabbed it. A leather strap secured into a locked fastener kept Mary Elizabeth's secrets safe.

"It's locked," Eva said with disappointment. "Do you know how to undo a lock this small?"

"Sure do." Rose took the toenail clippers and cut the strap.

Eva's jaw dropped. "I can't believe you did that."

Rose dropped the book back in the drawer and dusted her hands together. "It didn't mean much to whoever left it. She didn't want it bad enough to take it with her." She closed the drawer and inserted the 'key.' "Remember, your job right now is to learn how to open that door and not get bogged down in other projects. Now you can read it any time you want to—" She paused and gave Eva a devilish smile. "—after you open the drawer again."

True. There'd be plenty of time to read the diary later. Once again, she inserted her makeshift keys in the keyhole. This time positioning the clips took no time at all.

"Looks like you've got it."

"I think I'll just continue to practice. Why don't you go on home?"

"Don't need anything else?"

"No. You look tired. Go on. I'm okay."

"I still feel a little peaked," Rose admitted. "I would like to go get some rest…If you really want to learn how to open that door in the hall, I'd practice on the doors in your room." She pointed to the door to the balcony, the main door and a door in the living area that stayed locked. "If you can bend the wire into a shape that opens those doors, it ought to work on that door out there. And you'll get to practice on the same kind of locks."

"Great idea."

Rose finished tidying up, packed up her bag and headed for the door. "See you tomorrow."

In her movies, Eva had played so many roles: wife, young mother, vamp, victim and once she even played a jewel thief—a thief who stole souls. In that role, she calmly picked the lock, which was never really fastened. Now that she was thinking about doing it in real life, her stomach twisted in knots. What if she got caught? Still, the staff wasn't being up front about Mossell. And she wanted to see what was really happening in the annex.

For practice, she once again inserted the paperclip in the desk's keyhole. This time Eva's motions were too exaggerated and didn't have her Christian maid's finesse at breaking and entering.

Damn. It seemed easy a little while ago while her coach was still around. But Eva kept after it. Finally, a faint click came from inside the desk and the drawer was unlatched. Yes! Eva pulled the diary out and set it aside for later, then returned her attention to the mechanism, which she struggled almost as much to relock.

In the background, The Glenn Miller Band played softly on the radio.

"Miss Dupree." The voice belonged to Nurse Johnston. Eva was so absorbed in working the lock, she didn't hear the door open.

Eva grabbed a fountain pen and looked up innocently as if she'd been making an entry in her diary.

"I brought you another glass of water. We need to keep rinsing all those poisons out of your system. I noticed you weren't drinking as much as you should have."

"Mmmm." Eva sipped the water. "Thank you."

The nurse stood there with her fists resting on her hips. "Go ahead and finish it, would you?"

Eva complied, polishing off every last drop of healthy Crescent Spring water, then handed the glass back to the nurse. "That was quite refreshing." She sounded like a soft drink commercial on the radio.

"You need anything else?"

Eva smiled sweetly. "No, I'm just fine. Thanks. I'm just going to write a couple of notes to some friends back home."

The nurse walked to the door and paused. "I'll be in to check on you in a while."

"Thanks, but I plan on getting to bed before long," Eva said.

When the door had been safely shut, Eva returned her attention to the drawer. Time and time again she practiced her newly acquired lock-picking. What had taken her ten minutes to accomplish on her first try only took four minutes, ten seconds on her second try.

Finally, she reduced it to a semi-respectable forty-five seconds.

Once Eva could pop the desk lock in under a minute, she reconfigured her picks to fit the larger door locks. As with the desk, starting out was slow. At first the pick didn't fit properly. A kink here and a bend there, and finally the lock submitted to her. Click.

Eva smiled. *Success!* She closed her eyes and released the breath she'd been holding unconsciously.

Tonight she would learn the annex's secrets. What seemed impossible only a few hours earlier, now rested just within her reach. She tried a couple more successful test runs on her aft door. As the door lock clicked, her heart pounded hard. The time had come to carry out her plan.

Eva showered and prepared for bed as she would any other night. Once she climbed into bed, she assumed a bleary-eyed expression and pressed the call button.

A few minutes later Nurse Johnston answered the hail. "Is something wrong?" The nurse looked weary and sounded short of patience.

Eva smiled sweetly and raised her eyebrows innocently. *I might be overplaying this scene.* "Nurse Johnston, could I have one more glass of water before I go to sleep? I'm tired and thought I might get to bed early tonight."

Eva could see the dubious look on the nurse's face. No crisis? No screams? No insanity? "Sure."

A few minutes later, Nurse Johnston returned with another glass of cold Eureka Springs water straight from the Crescent Spring. She also had a little white pill in her hand. "Mrs. Cavanaugh made a note on your chart that you've been having problems sleeping. This might help."

Tonight you bring me something to make me sleepy.

"Thank you." Eva pretended to take it, but cheeked it instead of swallowing. She gagged. It was the bitterest thing she'd ever tasted. She just concentrated on getting rid of the nurse. All tucked into bed, she put on a sleepy face. She took a few drinks, thanked the nurse and then nestled back into her pillow.

"You want me to turn off the light?" the nurse asked.

"Please."

The nurse flipped off the switch and said, "Sleep tight."

As soon as Nurse Johnston closed the door, Eva spit the gooey pill onto her nightstand. In the bathroom, she tried to rinse the vile aftertaste out with a glass of water. When that didn't work, she twisted the cap on her can of Pepsodent Dental Powder, and tapped some onto her toothbrush. After she scrubbed the drug from her mouth she went back to her suite door and practiced her new skill a couple more times.

Eva waited a few minutes for the lull between the time that the patients needed attention and eleven o'clock, the hour when the nurses retrieved the bodies from the annex. When all hall activity had ceased, Eva sneaked into the hall. She'd have to work fast. The annex door was in center of a 'T' where two hallways met. She'd be in plain view of not only anyone going down either corridor, but also, everyone getting off of the elevator.

She looked around nervously, stuck the paperclips in the lock and began fumbling with them. Suddenly she heard noises everywhere. Patients down the hall coughing, people whimpering, nurses shuffling papers at their station. The sounds and sensations from the keyhole were much more subtle here, almost imperceptible, than they'd been in her room. Finally, after what seemed years, she felt the 'click'.

Hurriedly, she pushed the door open and then pulled it shut, slowly, quietly. The layout wasn't at all what she expected. Instead of opening into a ward, it was a long doglegged hall that emptied into a series of shoebox-sized rooms. As she approached the rooms, the smell hit her: that fetid hospital odor, a dreadful blend of bodies rotting from the inside out, alcohol and cleaning supplies—that horrible stench that Trudy spoke of the other day. Eva certainly picked the wrong night to forget her oil of wintergreen.

This wasn't the ward that protected these vulnerable patients against infection. This was the ward that protected the living patients from the dying ones. Hadn't everyone from Norman Baker to the receptionist *implied* that no one ever died at the Baker Hospital.

Eva's breathing quickened and her heart pounded so loud she feared Nurse Turner could hear her at the nurse's station.

Stay calm. Stay strong.

Through the closed doors Eva could hear the groans and cries of the failing, albeit slightly muffled. Groping along the walls in the subdued light she could feel that each door had an observation window located slightly below face level. Through the glass inserts Eva made out fine streams of full moonlight filtering past tiny exterior windows on the east side of the annex. Eva's shoulders relaxed a little. The bed silhouettes showed unoccupied beds. At the far end of the hall, Eva found a room with a human silhouette. What horrors awaited her?

Eva hesitated then pushed the door open. A male patient was tethered to an IV bottle; it had ceased to drip. The man hadn't moved an eyelash since Eva first glanced through the window. She gasped. By the moonlight she could the see colorless patient had fixed his dilated stare on the door; clearly he was dead. By the looks of him, he died waiting for a nurse.

In the room next she found a woman in a fetal position. She reeked of rot. Eva's queasy stomach almost brought all that healthy Eureka Springs water spewing out all over the floor. What Eva wouldn't give for a little dab of that wintergreen oil! The patient groaned, reaching for Eva with a skeletal hand. Eva took the emaciated hand into hers. Eva could feel every line and curve of each bone.

Eva patted the boney hand ever so gently. "I'm so sorry."

Was this Eva's own future? Was she going to die just like these poor people? Eva no longer cared whether Mossell was in there. She just wanted out of the death ward. She stepped back from the bed, but the woman held fast. She opened her mouth—a silent scream. "Help me," she mouthed. Then her grip nearly broke Eva's hand in two. In a voice that could have punctured an eardrum she screamed, "Have mercy on me. Kill me!"

That death grip felt like the Creature of the Night's hand on her throat during that last night of filming *Caught in a Web*. Strangled and frightened, she tried to pull away from the creature. With a strength she couldn't find ten years earlier, she yanked free and dashed to the door.

"I'm so sorry," Eva repeated, exiting the room.

As she reached for the annex doorknob, it rattled. Someone was coming in. Eva didn't move, didn't breathe. From behind the door, Eva heard Nurse Turner's angry voice, "What's this doing opened?"

Oh, shit!

The other nurse on duty was going to be in a world of trouble. Johnston would be receiving an earful when Nurse Turner got back to the nurse's station.

Not believing this was happening to her, Eva stepped back flat against the wall. If Nurse Turner came in, she might be hidden in the shadows. But to her horror, Nurse Turner didn't enter the annex.

Instead, she pushed the door firmly shut. The click of Nurse Turner's key locking the door was like a jail cell locking. Eva was trapped with those suffering unspeakable pain, and those who no longer felt pain.

She stilled her own breathing long enough to press her ear against the door. The echoes of Nurse Turner's heavy nurse's shoe against the wood floor grew fainter. Finally everything was still. Certain that Nurse Turner had left to castigate her coworker, Eva reached into her robe pocket for her paperclips. In the utter darkness Eva groped for the doorknob. Her hands ran along the cool smooth wall until she felt the corner and, at last, the door frame. There she located the deep indention of the keyhole.

She sighed. *Thank God!*

How hard could it be? Even in her room she had to open the locks by feel.

Kneeling, she held up her picks and felt for the opening. The first paper clip slid into the lock easily, but her trembling hand bumped the second wire against doorknob and it slipped from her grip onto the floor.

Oh, God, no! Not now.

As she frantically groped for it, she felt a rush of icy cold. Goosebumps ran up and down her arms and legs. Eva had the feeling someone was standing behind her and she glanced over her shoulder, half expecting to see the dead man's corpse standing behind her, but to her relief she was quite alone. Her fingers ran along the oak planks of the floor.

It's got to be here. Her hands swept the floor finding only dust and a coin that felt like a penny. It had to be right next to the door. She'd heard it hit. Finally after what seemed like hours, her fingers moved over a fine piece of wire—her paperclip.

Thank you, God!

Her moment of victory was short lived. As she picked up the wire, every hair on her body electrified. She *wasn't* alone. A hand ran through her hair slowly, sensuously. Her stomach knotted. Cold breath brushed her cheek as a male voice whispered in her left ear, "I want you."

Jack Swann!

Her heart pounded so hard she thought it would explode. Something catapulted out of the gloom and whizzed past her.

She bit back a scream to whisper, "Who's there? What do you

want?"

From the woman's room came a shriek. "Kill me! Someone make it stop! For the love of God, kill me!"

For what seemed like an eternity, Eva leaned against the annex door, paralyzed. Finally she willed herself to move again. She had to get out of there!

Time after time with the dying woman screams battering her brain, and her fingers shuddering, she worked the paper clips. Time after time the lock resisted. Again, the wire slipped from her fingers with a ping. She fumbled around the floor, feeling for her illusive way out. She touched the wire, bumping it slightly. It disappeared forever between two wooden floor planks.

Eva collapsed, sobbing, overwhelmed by tears of despair.

"Oh, dear God!" Eva buried her head in her hands. "Please help me."

As if in answer to her prayer the latch clicked, and the door eased open a few inches. *A miracle or something more sinister?* It didn't matter. Eva jumped up and ran into the hall. She forced herself to stop and close the door quietly, not slam it, cutting off on that woman's pathetic screams. Trembling and with tears rolling down her face, Eva fled for her room without bothering to relock the door.

In her suite, she took a long shower, but no matter how much water and soap she used, she couldn't seem to get the smell of death off of her skin or out of her nose. She had barely dressed in her nightclothes when, Nurse Turner quietly opened the door.

Eva hurriedly leaped into bed and pulled the covers over her.

Turner touched Eva's throat counting her pulse. Eva feigned waking up, slightly startled.

"It's alright, Miss Dupree. I just wanted to make sure you were alright. My, your pulse is elevated."

Eva pushed the nurse's hand away. "Of course it is. You nearly scared the life out of me!"

The nurse pulled the corners of her mouth back. "I'm sorry. I really didn't mean to frighten you. Go back to sleep."

Eva settled back into the bed, muttered something indiscernible and pretended to return to sleep. She lay still until she heard Turner's footsteps fade toward the nurse's station.

With Turner gone, Eva pulled her knees to her chest and sat rocking. Ivan curled up quietly next to her. He emitted no purr; he made no sound at all. He just leaned against her, warming her ice-cold skin.

Eva saw nothing, felt nothing except Ivan's warmth and the intense pounding of her own heartbeat. Over and over she relived the death grip of the woman in the annex and the hand brushing her hair.

Still trembling, she said, "Ivan, I heard that voice again. He said, 'I want you.'" He opened the door." She drew a ragged breath. "Oh. God I'm so scared."

She glanced at the girl's diary on the oak desk. What did Jack Swann want from her? Eva had read about women who suffered violent sexual assaults from unseen entities. Or could Jack have meant he wanted her mind? The idea of demonic possession scared her even more than metaphysical rape.

She released her knees and pulled Ivan into her lap. His motor began cranking up. She hugged him to her. Though she had never imagined turning to Ivan for protection; his body warmth felt like a shield between her and the supernatural force that threatened her.

Ivan nuzzled her hand. His long, lush fur warmed her fingers. Absently, she rubbed his chin. "Thanks, Kitty."

She sat in the bed thinking about the voice whispering in her ear. How was she ever going to sleep? Then she remembered the pill she'd spit out on her wooden bedside table. She took a sip of water, dropped the mushy pill in her mouth, swallowed it, gagged, and followed with another drink of water, which all immediately came up again as pain from her kidney stabbed through her. She tried to aim for the bronze trash can Rose had set beside Eva's bed. Rolling away from the edge of the bed, Eva wrapped herself into a ball, breathing shallowly until the pain eased.

A vision of the future flooded her...pain going on and on...her once beautiful body wasting away until she looked like that living corpse in the annex. She would be robbed of every dignity. Even control of her bodily functions would be ripped from her. And finally, when they laid her in the casket, she wouldn't bear the slightest resemblance to her former self. Her favorite dress would hang around her like a flour sack tailored for someone of a highly grander scale. She doubted Edgar would even recognize her in Heaven.

She sat up and blew her nose. She ought to be like the characters she used to play, facing death with courage and grace. Except their courage was a lie, because they never actually faced death.

Reality was in that annex. The images of her future brought such terror, she began crying again.

The cat rolled over on his back giving her that coy, rub-my-tummy look. The last time Eva tried it she found that he was no cat, but a Venus Flytrap, his claws closing around her like the petals of the carnivorous plant. But this time when she ran her fingernails slowly from his chin to his belly, his paws closed around her hand without claws, just those soft pads with tufts of fur sticking out.

"Ivan, are you petting me?" she asked.

If he was, he wasn't confessing.

She sighed. "I guess Rose will officially be the one to take care of you soon. Of course, she does that now. I'll leave her some money so you won't have to go hungry."

They curled up together in the bed. Ivan shifted his position, dozing with his head hogging the pillow while Eva stared into the darkness outside her window.

Eventually Eva drifted off to a troubled sleep and dreamed about her different movies. There were no directors to yell cut and interrupt the horror. The scenes played out in glorious lurid color. Interspersed within the snippets from the past were horrors from the present, more terrifying than anything conceived of for the screen.

Once again the Creature of the Night pursued her. In the movies those silly rubber fingers extended rigidly past his fingertips. By today's standard their movies were primitive—no voices, no sound effects, and no color. Her own witchy portrayals looked ridiculous next to the frightening green witch from the recently released, *The Wizard of Oz*. But after all these years in her dreams, images of the Creature still haunted her.

Eva shot straight up in bed. She heard something move in her room. Whatever it was, it wasn't Ivan. Silhouetted with light seeping in from under the door, Eva could see the cat standing next to her—his ears laid flat against his head, staring at the empty air beside her bed.

Her radio was on and in the background she could hear the Tommy Dorsey band playing *"This is No Dream."*

> *"This is no dream, that's what my heart keeps saying.*
> *"This is no dream, this is real.*
> *"Stars dance above, heavenly music's playing;*

"This must be love the way I feel…"
"You don't know how much you can suffer until you fall in love.

Finally, exhaustion trumped fear and Eva slipped off to sleep again. That escape was short-lived. Later she woke to a whispery voice, "Chickadee, wake up." The voice sounded familiar.

Eva grabbed the cat and clutched him to her. Ivan hissed violently. Eva moved closer to the headboard. She felt nauseous and the air felt heavy, making it hard to breathe.

"Hi, ladybug." Mossell hovered above her bed. "Mind if I have a seat? I'm afraid I'm tired and a little stiff." Not waiting for an answer, she but plopped down in the middle of bed, superimposing herself on Eva. Instantly, Eva's lungs froze and her muscles seized.

"Don't you have anything to say to an old friend?"

Eva's throat felt paralyzed, too.

"Sorry." Mossell moved off the bed and to a chair. Then to Ivan she said, "What's got your tail ruffled?"

He growled in response.

She smiled wryly. "You'd think he'd remember me. That's gratitude for you."

Eva lay limp, struggling to breathe. Finally she managed to say, "So they did lie about you going home."

"Is that what they said? Yep, they lied. I'm still here. I'm down in the basement. And I'm cold as the lettuce you're going to have in tomorrow's salad. Come to think of it, I'm sitting right next to it."

Eva blinked. "To what?"

"To lettuce. I always hated lettuce."

Ivan hissed at her again.

"Ivan, is that any way to treat your old buddy?" Mossell asked.

Eva couldn't tell if this was real or a dream. "What are you doing here?"

"I came to warn you to get the hell out. You hear me? Go home. Don't die here, too. You don't want that Dr. Statler to do an autopsy on you. I've never had a man handle me like that way. I wonder if his mother knows what he does to us dead ladies. Really. If I'd been alive, I'd have slapped him…or married him. I haven't decided which, yet. Whatever. You need to leave, ducky."

"I can't," Eva said sadly. "I need the treatment. If I don't get it I'll die."

"To hell with the treatments. Get out of here, girl. I mean it."

The figure, whatever it was looked like Mossell, but not exactly.

Her skin had taken on a filmy appearance. And she filled the room with a rotting stink.

"Do you smell something?" Eva asked.

Mossell sighed. "Yeah, sorry, budgie. That's me. Baker doesn't have a freezer big enough to store all our bodies, so he puts us in the big commercial refrigerator. You can't expect me to keep well in there; it's just not cold enough."

"God, let me wake up from this dream!" Eva buried her face in her hands.

Mossell patted Eva's hand. Her touch felt like ice. Eva cut loose a siren scream.

Nurse Johnston came tearing into the room. "Miss Dupree! Are you—my goodness. It's cold in here. I wonder where that draft is coming from."

The nurse touched Eva's cheek. "You feel like you've been sitting in an icebox. And did you vomit? I'll replace that blanket and get you an extra one."

Eva grabbed her arm. "Don't leave me," she begged. "I don't want to be alone. I had a horrible dream. I'm dying. I don't want to die, Nurse Johnston. Please, I don't want to die."

Nurse Johnston pried her arm free of Eva's grasp. "Miss Dupree, I'm going to get you something for your nerves. I'll be right back."

Despite the tranquilizer, Eva couldn't sleep. She trembled in the dark—owl-eyed, hearing sounds she hoped weren't really there. She remembered when she was a little girl just after her father's death. She'd lie in bed unable to sleep. Sometimes she heard his footsteps moving down the hall to go to the bathroom as he had done thousands of times. When Eva told her mother, Mamma would smile sadly, and hug her tightly. "Baby, he's not in the house." Petting Eva's hair as she would comfort a whimpering puppy, Mamma said, "Daddy's not ever coming back. It's your imagination. Now, go back to bed."

Tonight felt just like the old days. Except the sounds she heard back then were made by Daddy, her protector. Much as those nightly footfalls terrified her, she knew her father would never hurt her.

Here at the Baker Hospital, she felt no such security. Eva climbed out of bed and flipped on the light.

DAY NINE—*Friday, September 8*

Miss Dupree, it's time for our treatment." Nurse Turner entered the room with her ominous little white tray.

Eva covered her head with a pillow. Damn her, she thought through a veil of sleepiness. After staring up at the ceiling and listening to the radio until dawn, she couldn't stay awake, not even for another second. Now, just as she had finally dozed off Nurse Turner wanted to torture her.

The nurse set the tray down on the bedside table. "One of the fourth floor nurses called in sick today. I'll be your nurse again this morning."

"Wonderful," Eva said sleepily. "Since it's 'our' treatment, I'll let you have the pleasure of being on the receiving end."

Nurse Turner scowled. "You know I can't do that. How are you feeling this morning?"

"Not very well." Eva put her hand against her side. "It's really hurting today."

"Where is the pain?"

Without removing the pillow from her face, Eva pointed at her side.

Nurse Turner pressed around the abdomen.

Muffled, Eva groaned. "That's the spot."

"How about here?" Turner asked.

"Yes. That hurts, too. No. That's not too bad. No, that's fine." She lunged up sending the pillow airborne. "Oh, my God. That hurts!"

"I'll notify Dr. Hutto." Nurse Turner opened the tray and checked the syringe for bubbles. "I know you don't feel well, but we need to get on with your treatment. Go ahead and roll over. This one is in the hip."

Now, she was fully awake, and wholly aware of the pain. Any motion at all felt like she was being stabbed from the inside out. "Nurse, let's wait until this passes."

Nurse Turner stood there holding the syringe like the Statue of Liberty. "Waiting won't change anything. Please, Miss Dupree, turn over."

"No, Nurse Turner, I will not! Put your needle down. A half an hour won't make any difference."

Nurse Turner set her weapon in the tray and clanked on the lid. "As you wish."

Eva dropped her head onto the bare mattress. "I need a hot water bottle," she moaned.

Nurse Turner nodded. "I'll be right back." She picked up her tray and left without another word turning the light off behind her.

While the nurse was gone, Eva struggled to the drawer where she kept the booze and took a long pull straight from the bottle, emptying it. Then Eva picked up the pillow from the floor and returned to bed.

The nurse soon returned with the hot water bottle.

Eva snuggled up to the warmth. Slowly, the pain washed away until she was empty and spent. The emptiness faded into nothingness as she finally slept.

Eva awoke with a start, worn-out and feverish, but at least free of pain for now. Gooseflesh crawled across her body. It was back; that sensation of someone watching just out of sight. Her heart hammered. The room felt like a freezer. She dared not move, nor look around. She longed to be home in Dallas in her own bed— even if it meant dying.

Beside her, Ivan sat up and hissed.

"Hey, morning glory, wake up." An icy hand shook her.

Eva bolted up in the bed.

It was Mossell again, or rather that dreamy image of Mossell. The smell was back too.

"Don't do that!" Eva yelled. She fought down nausea. "Go away!"

Mossell sniffed. "Now that's a fine how-do-you-do. You used to enjoy my company."

"That was before I started going insane. Now, I'm having a conversation with a dead person."

"Munchkin, you're not insane. This *place* is insane." She plopped down on the bed beside the cat. "Hi, Ivan."

The cat backed away, growling deep in his throat. With back arched, tail fluffed and one fully armed paw in the air, the cat dared her to come closer.

Even though she was dead, she reconsidered. "I thought we

were friends. All right...here. How about a bit of lunch tomorrow for a bribe." Mossell dropped a tiny shrimp between his front paws.

Ivan sniffed it and looked away.

Mossell sighed. "I guess he's not fond of dead people. Speaking of that, what did Ivan do when you got the ashes out of the furnace the other day?"

"He wouldn't use them," Eva said.

"That's cuz it's in poor taste to take a shit on dead people—even for a cat."

Eva stared at her. "What do you mean?"

"That was Annabelle Nichols, or rather what was left of Annabelle, you put in his poop pan that morning. Of course, you didn't know her; she died before you got here."

"These damn drugs are doing this to me," Eva said. She reached for the call button.

"It's not the drugs. It's really me, sunshine." Mossell reached down to touch Eva's hand again.

Eva moaned, "Don't do that! How could those have been human ashes?"

Mossell rolled her eyes. "I guess those drugs *have* made you a little slow out of the starting gate, Tootsie Roll. Baker keeps us dead ladies in the big refrigerator until he's pumped our families for all the money he can. Then he sends a note of condolences saying we died. Don't you remember those letters you signed?"

"What letters?"

"The letters. Remember? They say something to the effect of: *I'm doing great. Feeling much better, but treatments are expensive. Send more money.*"

Eva thought for a moment. Because of her hurried admission Eva couldn't recall signing a letter like that herself. But... "That does sounds like a letter I found misfiled in the Letters of Recommendation folder when Mr. Statler was admitting me."

"All us rich broads signed them, sugar buns," Mossell told her. "After we kick the bucket, Baker sends out those pre-signed letters until he's milked our families for as much as he can get. Then he sends them a note telling them we checked out—permanently. He gives them the choice between coming all the way to the Middle of Nowhere, Arkansas, to claim the body or allowing him to 'make the arrangements.' They always write back and say, 'You make the arrangements.' I mean, who wants to trek all the way out here for a great aunt, for heaven's sake? The hospital then gives us a less-than-dignified funeral pyre in the furnace next to the laundry...That's why Ivan refused to use the ashes. Even Ivan has the decency not to desecrate a body, or what used to be a body. So you've got to get out of here before these treatments kill you."

"But I can't. Except for lack of sleep, I think I'm feeling better. Or rather, I was starting to feel better"

"You need to go home. There's nothing wrong with you."

"Yes there is, Mossell. I still have these horrible pains in my side."

"I mean nothing that they can treat here, lovey," Mossell said. "I'm telling you, poppy, you need to get out of here. They're wasting your money." Mossell drifted closer to her.

"Mossell, could you please move more that direction?" She waved her hand in the direction of the door. "I feel like I'm going to throw up."

"Sorry, doll face. It's one of the hazards of dying. If only he'd keep the refrigerator a little colder. You're going to die if you stay here, peaches. Those phenols are murder on a healthy body." Mossell frowned. "How can I prove this to you? I want you to see what's going on. Really see."

"I've seen it," Eva said. "I snuck into the annex last night."

"Ah, now you know what really goes on after the sun goes down." Eva nodded.

Smiling, Mossell said, "I have to go. Tata for now. Oh, and strawberry, don't eat the watermelon today. It's way too ripe." The glowing figure faded. Only her smell remained.

Eva looked down at Ivan's untouched piece of a shrimp. Cold slid down her spine.

Moments later Nurse Cavanaugh walked in. She grimaced. "What's that smell? Oh, that's awful! It smells like something died in here." She rushed to the window, opened the curtains and raised the window. She fanned the air toward the window with her hand. "No wonder you've been nauseous. I wonder if the cat killed something and hid it. We need to find it and get rid of it."

"I wish you could." Eva shivered.

She pressed a hand to Eva's face. "You're a little warm today. Maybe I should take your temperature."

Eva nodded. "My side's really been aching."

"I'll be right back."

Eva dozed briefly, waking to hold the thermometer between her lips. She felt queasy and hung over from the sleeping pill she had taken that morning. Every movement felt as if she were under water pressing against a current. Even the nurses seemed to move in slow motion. Nurse Cavanaugh returned with a warm red rubber hot water bottle wrapped in a towel, but Eva already had a heater, a furry one. The nurse had to move Ivan to place the water bottle next to her back.

Later Nurse Cavanaugh slipped back into Eva's suite. "Are you feeling any better?"

Eva gave her a wan smile. "The pain has passed for now. Thank goodness. I'm tired. I don't sleep well in here." She sat up and stretched a little.

The nurse patted the cat now sitting at her feet. "I see you have your little heater with you. I bet he's even better than a hot water bottle, don't you think? He doesn't cool down after a few minutes."

"Although he does tend to abandon me when someone new offers to pet him..."

"So he does, " Cavanaugh said. "Oh, Trudy says, 'Hi'. She wanted me to give this to you." She reached into her pocket and pulled out another folded note on lined pulp paper.

Pleasure warmed Eva as she took the paper. What did Trudy have to say this time? "Naturally, you'll come back in a little while for the response."

"Of course." Cavanaugh smiled. "With all this coding and decoding, you'd think you two were planning a war."

Like the other messages, this one gave her the code number and a list of coded letters. However, it was special because she had illustrated it with a smiling star. The eyes had long eyelashes and two dots for a nose. After decoding the communiqué, Eva learned that Trudy wanted to visit Ivan. Eva responded for the cat by proxy, signing for him with a little paw print.

Eva dozed as Trudy sat on the wood floor, teasing Ivan with a piece of string the nurse had given her. He rolled over on his back with his paws suspended up in the air—claws fully extended. He was quick, so quick that Trudy could seldom sneak the string past him without snagging a big one, a catfish. Sometimes he'd reach up and grab it with his mouth. Every now and then she'd pull the string up and plant a kiss on his forehead or his nose. He'd draw back a little, but if she stopped, he'd come back for more. Trudy played with the cat for about thirty minutes before the nurse took her back to her own room for a nap.

Eva slept until Turner returned with her lunch. "Here's your meal." The nurse set the tray down on her bed table.

The morning's pain had ceased and she'd been left with a mild ache and a fairly hardy appetite especially since she hadn't eaten any breakfast. And for that matter, neither had Ivan. She grabbed the napkin containing her silverware and began unrolling it.

Nurse Turner removed the dish cover and a puff of steam drifted up to Eva's face, obscuring her vision for a moment. "Mmmmmm. That smells good. What is it?"

Next to her the cat hissed and backed away, his ears pinned flat against his head.

"Spaghetti with Shrimp. Mr. Baker had it brought in as a special treat. And a nice ripe piece of watermelon."

Eva's stomach lurched. Her fork slipped from her hand—and with it her hunger. "Suddenly I don't feel well."

The head nurse touched Eva's cheek. "You're still a little warm. You are having a difficult day. I'll get you something for the nausea."

"Could I just have some broth?"

When Rose arrived early that afternoon, Eva told her, "I broke into the annex. It was terrible. I found a dead man and a woman who was in horrible agony. Rose, I never want to go through that. I felt so bad for that lady. She begged me to kill her—and somehow I know she's dead now."

Rose eyed her. "Who's dead? I thought you said that lady was still alive."

"*Mosell* is dead. Rose, she's been coming to me. At first I thought it was a bad dream. It wasn't."

Rose propped her hands on her waist and nodded her head. Maybe her boss lady was going insane.

Eva continued. "I couldn't find Mosell anywhere in the isolation ward. I thought I was going crazy because she's come to me several times to tell me to leave the hospital, but she smells bad and you can see through her."

Rose clenched her hands together. "Jesus, help us."

"Oh, God!" Eva held out her trembling hands. "She's real. Last night Mosell gave Ivan a piece of shrimp and said we'd have some for lunch today. And we did. She said not to eat the watermelon because it was over ripe; it was. Rose, her touch felt cold as snow. I hate this place."

"Lord, have mercy." Rose closed her eyes. The moment of truth had come. "I should have told you this sooner: Mr. Brown told me if I wanted to keep my job I should get you to go home cuz this is a place where a lot of people die. He said when the Baker Hospital opened up two years ago there was only five funeral parlors. Now there are eight. And Mr. Brown's little boy tells me that Mr. Baker burns the bodies in the furnace."

The color drained from Eva's face. "Oh my, God! When you were sick, I got ashes out of the furnace outside. Ivan went berserk and wouldn't go near the pan. When I told the lady you sent to help out—I think Zola Mae was her name—when I told her where I got the ashes, she panicked and said she wouldn't touch a dead person. Last night Mossell, or whatever that was, she said the ashes belonged to someone named Annabelle. Rose, I need a drink. I hope you brought a fresh bottle."

Rose quickly fixed Eva a drink, sans the ice and handed it to her boss.

Eva stirred it in her traditional manner with her finger, licked the liquid from her digit, then took a deep drink. "Anesthesia."

Rose sat on the settee next to her boss, and took Eva's hands firmly in her own. "Miss Eva, you have to get out of here."

"All right." Eva let out a deep breath. "I'll see about getting myself released."

While Rose continued to straighten up, Eva got dressed. "I'll be back," she said closing the door behind her.

It was time to go on a little fishing expedition. Except this kind of fishing was for information and she was both the bait and the hook. Eva made her way to the ground floor, past the lobby and finally into Norman Baker's formal office.

"Mr. Baker," the secretary said through the intercom. "Miss Dupree wants to speak with you."

The door opened and Baker emerged. Today instead of the white suit he wore an eggplant colored suit with a white shirt and lavender tie and, of course, the horseshoe tie tack. It still felt odd, almost embarrassing to see a man wearing purple.

"Please come in." He led Eva inside an amethyst cavern. In the corner an upright piano waited for someone's fingers to bring it to life.

"You play?" She nodded at the piano.

"No." He headed to a turret in the back of the room that held a massive mahogany desk. Royal purple and lavender drapes adorned the window behind him, and the walls were papered in a busy like-shaded pattern. Above his desk hung a chandelier, original to the old Crescent Hotel. The lighting was suitable for a party, but hardly acceptable for paper work, so he had modified it The Baker Way. The electric cord of a green office lamp had been wired into the chandelier and dangled only a few feet above his head. Occasionally, it flickered off for a few seconds and then stayed on for a minute or two before repeating the cycle.

Reminders of his hometown hung on the wall next to his desk: a City of Muscatine pennant and another green and white pennant with a color painting of a radio station dwarfed by two enormous radio towers. It said "KTNT—America's Most Beautiful Radio Station - Muscatine, Iowa." There was a framed newspaper photograph of him standing before a massive crowd of people, with a headline "Baker says 'My cure works.'" A small table covered with an Indian blanket added a sense of expensive tacky to the office.

Baker circled his desk, a hexagonal monstrosity. He dropped into a swivel chair. He almost wore the desk, sitting on the inside, surrounded by it, like a mahogany stop sign with a hollow center. Eva guessed it must have measured eight feet in diameter.

Stacks of papers laid on four of the six desk surfaces. Each angle had three baskets: In, Out and Work to be done. The front of the desk was completely obscured by another hand-woven Indian blanket.

"Mr. Baker, I need to talk to you," Eva said.

She pulled a chair close to the desk and sat down. Close but not at it. With no overhang, she couldn't sit next to it without bumping her legs against the sides. It said a lot about him—made him unapproachable. The desk seemed to imply what Eva had already picked up about the hospital owner, that he was in control, powerful, distant and solid.

Eva mentally counted the working surfaces. "I've never seen a six-sided desk before."

Baker's chest puffed up. "I had it custom made. It helps keep me organized. I have several businesses: my Nuevo Laredo radio station XENT, the hospitals, Tangley Calliaphones, the Tangley catalog…

and several others. This desk allows me to work on several projects at one time without getting the paperwork mixed up."

"It fits so perfectly in this room. Did you have it made for this office?"

Baker adjusted his glasses. "No, I've actually used this desk for many years. It's interesting: When I first saw this suite and realized that my desk would fit in so perfectly, I knew I was preordained to own this building." Above him the light flickered again. He looked up, annoyed.

He flipped the switch on his intercom. "Miss Mussen, I'm having problems with my lights again. Have the goddamn janitor get in here and fix this once and for all."

He turned back to Eva instantly replacing the clinched jaw with an easy smile, as though someone flipped a light switch to 'cordial.' "Now, Eva, how can I help you today?"

How could he help her? How should she word this? On the elevator ride down to the lobby, she had perfected her 'speech.' In his office, she'd forgotten her lines and her mind had gone blank. On top of that, her hard wooden chair put pressure on all the wrong places and woke up the evil little guy with the pitchfork. She pushed herself upright against his desk. For dramatic effect she visibly pressed against her back and groaned a little. To hide her nervousness she moved to the windows behind his desk and gazed out at the mountain.

His eyes, piercing behind his glasses, followed her.

Pulling the drape aside for an unimpeded look she asked, "Do you ever get tired of this incredible view?" When she turned back to face him, her eyes grew wide and she gasped at the sight of a forty-five caliber machine gun hanging from a nail under his desk. What was *he* doing with a machine gun? What *is* going on around here?

Baker noticed her alarm and her eyes fixed on his weapon. He smiled and said, "Don't be alarmed. The gun doesn't work. No firing pin. It's from my collection. Sometimes, having something like this to discuss helps some of our male patients feel more at ease. I just keep it here as a conversation piece."

"Oh," she said, unconvinced. She sat down again.

"Now, Miss Dupree, what did you want to talk to me about?"

Before she could answer a breathless sandy-haired maintenance man came in with a ladder. He was the same young man who had cut down Mr. Janowitz's body. "Excuse me, Mr. Baker. Mrs. Mussen said you were having problems with your lamp." He stopped short. "Sorry, sir. I didn't realize you had someone in your office."

"It's all right," Eva said. "I can see that this would be very annoying."

The light flashed again.

"Go ahead and fix it," Baker said to the janitor.

"Yes, sir." He tipped his workman's hat to Eva and set up his ladder next to the desk. "I'll be back in a few minutes. I need to get some new wire."

"I'm sorry for the disturbance." Baker steepled his fingers. "Now, how may I help you, Miss Dupree?"

"I received a note from my stepdaughter telling me about a family emergency. Since I'm feeling so much better I'd like to go home."

Baker's brows knitted together sympathetically. "I'm sorry about the family crisis, but I'm delighted you're feeling so much better. Let's see what we can do." He pushed his chair back and stood up. "I'm afraid I'm going to need more information. Excuse me. I'll be right back."

He left her alone in his office. While he was away, she jumped up, dodged the ladder and ran behind his desk where the oak three-drawer file cabinet stood. She recalled he placed the woman's letter she had found on admission in the middle drawer, but she couldn't remember what part of the drawer he returned it to. Rifling through the manila file folders labeled in pencil she found Supplies, Payroll, Building Expenses, but nothing that looked like patient's files.

Baker was gone about five minutes, long enough to scan each accordion and manila folder. The letters Mossell described weren't there. Out in the hall, Eva heard footsteps and male voices as they approached the office. She scrambled back to her chair, crossed her legs and leaned back. Her breathing deliberately slowed. Her head came to rest on her fist, bored.

Taking long steps, Baker came in and resumed his seat at his desk. More footsteps followed his own. Eva turned to at the sound of Dr. Hutto's voice. "Good afternoon. Mrs. Dupree. Mr. Baker tells me you've got a family emergency." He held a patient's chart tucked under his arm.

"Yes, that's right."

The doctor turned to Eva. "Mrs. Dupree, you are progressing magnificently. I see improvement each time I examine you, but you still have some carcinoma in your kidney. Because of that, you will need a few more weeks of treatment. I plan to reevaluate your condition in another week. If you leave now, there is a good chance that the cancer will return, mainly because it wouldn't have been completely removed from your body. If that happens, it will most assuredly be worse than before you came here. I'm afraid I can't, in good conscience, authorize your release yet. Your Baker Hospital guarantee will be voided."

Eva made her voice urgent. "But I need to get home. There's been..." Lines were so much easier when she had a script! "...a death. I need to care for my stepdaughter's, uh, baby while she deals with her husband's loss."

"I'm sorry, Mrs. Dupree."

"*Miss* Dupree," she corrected.

"If I let you go home now, you'll just get sicker. You've been here this long. What difference will another couple of weeks make?"

"They'll make a helluva difference to my stepdaughter." Eva liked snarling at Dr. Hutto. "All right, Doctor. Have it your way."

"Not his way, dear lady," Norman Baker said smoothly. "But the way it must be for your own good."

"Of course. May I see my file?" she asked.

Baker hesitated. "What are you looking for?"

"I need to get my niece's address off of the emergency contacts list. I have to write her. Maybe she can help Esther out until I get home to help."

He rose and checked the contents of the file cabinet. "I'm afraid it's in my private office in my penthouse. I keep the files of my more famous clients there as an added precaution...to protect their privacy."

Oh, really? "Of course." She smiled and picked up her purse. "I supposed you are right about this. I don't want to set myself back. Thank you for your time, Mr. Baker, Dr. Hutto. You've both been very helpful."

She fumed in frustration all the way to her room.

On her bed she found one more of Trudy's messages. Unfortunately, she didn't feel like going to the trouble of decoding the message. She looked at the note. Every letter was so carefully drawn. Trudy had gone to extra special trouble to write this note. She even formed her "E" correctly instead of backward as she had in her other notes.

Angry as Eva felt, she pulled her decoder out and decoded the message. Finally, deciphered, it read, "I feel so good I'm going home."

Eva stared at her translation. "Trudy's going home?"

She had mixed feelings about it. On one hand Eva was delighted and excited for the little girl. Certainly Trudy looked like she was feeling better. Her bruises had vanished and she had more energy than she did when Eva first arrived at the hospital. But on the other hand, Eva had come to enjoy the silly messages. She'd miss her. Without Mossell around, Eva looked forward to the youngster's frequent visits and her cryptic messages. Her absence would create a huge hole in her day.

A little while later Trudy knocked at the door. She stood there in a red and white gingham jumper and a white blouse. She looked like she was ready for her first day of school. "Hi, Miss Eva." She immediately homed in on Ivan. They met each other halfway. He sniffed her hands and then sat down next to her.

"Hi, Trudy. It's wonderful you're going home. When are you leaving?"

"Today."

So soon? "Wow, that's quick."

Trudy nodded. "Uh huh. They got my train ticket already. Mommy's coming to pick me up in a little while. We'll get to sleep in a sleeper car and everything."

"That's wonderful. You'll be home by tomorrow evening."

"Uh huh."

"Are you excited?"

The girl grinned. "Uh huh. I talked to Mommy last night on the phone and she's already on the train coming here. I tried to tell you this morning, but you were sleeping and Nurse Turner said I could play with Ivan if I didn't bother you. I wish Ivan could go with me."

Eva watched Ivan snuggle with her. "I know he wishes he could too. But his job is to take care of me."

"I know."

"I have an idea. Why don't we ask Nurse Cavanaugh to have some tea sent up here and we'll have a little going away party?"

Trudy clapped her hands together. "Oh yes! Can we get four cups?"

Eva thought for a moment. "Sure. But instead of giving Ivan tea, I bet he'd rather have a cup of chicken broth."

"Uh huh!"

Eva pressed her call button.

In a few moments Nurse Cavanaugh appeared. "Trudy, you're not bothering Miss Dupree, are you?"

"Nuh uh. We're going to have a tea party."

"You are?"

Eva smiled. "Nurse Cavanaugh, we'd like to celebrate Trudy's going home. Can we have three cups of tea and a cup of chicken broth? Oh yes, and a round of cookies. Whatever the cook has that's fresh."

"I'll see what I can do."

About twenty minutes later the nurse delivered the refreshments: three servings of tea and a cup of chicken broth in real china and four peanut butter cookies.

"You ladies are going to have fun, don't you think?"

"Sure are," Trudy said with a big smile.

When the nurse left Eva went to her stockpile of alcohol. She added a little to her cup of tea. The cup was so full she had to lean down and sip it so she wouldn't spill any.

"What's that?"

Eva smiled. "This is special Eureka Springs water that makes you feel better. You already feel better so I need to catch up with you. Let's not tell the nurses about it, okay?"

"Okay. My friend says he wishes he could have some."

"He does." Eva leaned over and pretended to pour it in the cup.

The little girl put her fists on her hips. "He knows that trick. You're not going to give him some?"

"Why not?" This time Eva did pour some in the cup. After all, once Trudy returned to her room, Eva could drink it herself.

After they finished the cookies, Eva asked, "Would you like a tidy new braid so you'll look pretty when you see your mommy?"

"Uh huh."

Eva patted the vanity bench. "Hop up here.

Eva combed her hair out and divided it into thirds.

As she braided, Trudy started on a vocal roll. She told Eva about all the things she would do when she got home. She covered friends she'd see, going to church, starting school, her dog Sandy, and having all her brothers and sisters to play with. Whew. Finally the little girl took a breath.

Before long the grown-up braid was finished, the tea and cookies were consumed.

Nurse Cavanaugh appeared at the door. "Trudy, Mr. Baker just heard from your mother. She's at the train station. Mr. Bellows is going to take you there in just a few minutes. Your train leaves at five. That's exciting, don't you think?"

"Uh huh." Trudy hugged Eva hard, then ran over to kiss Ivan one last time. As she stood in the doorway, she stopped and turned around and cocked her head like she was listening to someone. "Johnny says he'll take care of you real good after I'm gone."

Eva swallowed hard. Again she felt sick. Of all of the departing messages Trudy could have left her with, her imaginary friend staying to watch Eva's every move was certainly the least welcome.

Nurse Cavanaugh took Trudy's hand and whisked her out the door. The little girl waved a final goodbye, then disappeared into the hall.

Eva suddenly felt chilled, and more alone than ever. She grabbed her last fresh hankie and climbed back to bed. A tear eased down her cheek and dropped onto blanket, lavender, of course. No longer could she be strong. She covered her face with her hands and sobbed. She wept for Edgar and Mossell and Annabelle. She wept for Rose, who needed the job so badly, and even for Ivan, who would soon lose his happy home. But mostly she cried for herself, and her enchanted life that somewhere along the line became cursed. She cried for her lost career. Finally, with all of her tears spent, she slipped into a troubled sleep. But for once she slept through the whole night.

DAY TEN—*Saturday, September 9*

Eva opened the center desk drawer and removed Mary Elizabeth Rankin's diary. It seemed to call Eva to pick it up—to read it.

Ivan jumped up on the bed, head-bumping the hand holding the book. At times like these, it took less time to pet Ivan than to ignore him. Scratching him absently, she opened the diary at random.

Mary Elizabeth had been an artist. She didn't just write about her day, she embellished it with doodling and little illustrations.

On November 17, 1932, the girl wrote, "I know I should be studying more for my math test, but it's hard to keep my mind on fractions when all I can think about is Mr. Swann. He's so keen." A cartoon depicted a balloon with numbers in it. The balloon had a mouth with a tongue sticking out.

November 28, 1932 "I'm doing so bad in math. I just can't understand all those formulas. Math is stupid, anyway. When I get out of school I just want to get married and have some babies. Then I won't need fractions or formulas. But if I fail the math course, Father will take me out of school and send me back to Omaha. I don't want to go back there. The boys back home are all so immature. Maybe I can ask Mr. Swann for some help so I don't have to go home."

December 4, 1932 "I told Mr. Swann I just can't understand what he's talking about. He told me to stay after class so he could give me some one-on-one help. Did he! He said I'm too nervous about my class. I need to relax. Then he gave me a back rub. I don't know what that has to do with math but I hope he keeps doing it. I wonder if I can get him to kiss me."

December 6, 1932 "Oh God! Mr. Swann finally kissed me tonight. He was helping me understand word problems and then he just reached over and pressed his lips against mine. I felt like electricity was shooting through my body. I thought I was going to explode. I never did understand what he was talking about, but who cares? If this keeps going I won't need any math for the rest of my life." She followed the entry about her math professor with a formula of her own. ME+JS=Love. A string of hearts encircled his name.

December 19, 1932 "While I was waiting for Father to pick me up, Jack came by to wish me a Merry Christmas. He gave me the best Christmas present ever and it wasn't a scarf. It started with another back rub but my back wasn't all he rubbed. I bet when school lets out, Jack's going to ask me to marry him. Who knows?" This illustration showed a pair of initialed hearts intertwined.

December 24, 1932 "It's Christmas vacation. It seems like it will never be over. I miss him so much. I bet that's the way Errol Flynn kisses." This cartoon heart was crying.

January 10, 1933 "Today's my first day of school. I'm really starting to love math. After everyone went to sleep, Jack snuck in and spent almost the whole night here. He said he's never met anyone like me. He showed me how much he loved me all night long. He left right before Mrs. Wilson came by to wake me up. He's afraid someone will find out. I can't wait until we get married."

This date had a rough sketch of Jack Swann's face as seen through the eyes of an enamored teen. He had a long thin face and dark hair, slicked back like patent leather. His lips were full, sensuous, kissable and dark gentle eyes. This was how Mary Elizabeth saw that pervert, her killer.

Eva stared at the eyes. Somehow in her primitive sketch the girl managed to capture everything she fell in love with. But something smoldered behind those eyes—a hardness. Maybe Eva simply filled in the blanks with adult experience, and the knowledge of what a short, sad future awaited the girl. But something in those vague, dark two-dimensional eyes terrified her.

January 15, 1933 "Jack and I made love again tonight. He was wonderful. I can't pay attention in school. He's all I can think about."

January 16, 1933 "I think I caught a bug. I hope it doesn't make Jack sick. I think I'm going to bed so I can dream about how wonderful he is." This time the heart looked sad and had something spewing out of its mouth.

January 17, 1933 "I threw up all morning so I didn't go to class today. I hope he comes by to see me."

January 19, 1933 "I'm feeling a little better. He came over and kissed me all over. Mrs. Jack Swann. Doesn't that sound wonderful?" The words, "Mrs. Jack Swann" appeared over and over again, each with different embellishments.

As Eva read she found herself unconsciously tracing her forefinger along the graffiti carved into the desk, "I love Jack." Suddenly cold air engulfed her and the hairs on her arms stood to attention. She jerked her hand away from the graffiti and placed it against her chest. This must prove the specter was Mary Elizabeth's Jack Swann. She wanted to put the diary down, but something inside her compelled her to continue reading.

"January 23, 1933 "I feel awful and my 'Auntie Flo' didn't come this month. I think I'm pregnant. I bet Jack is going to be so excited when I tell him. Mrs. Jack Swann. That sounds great, doesn't it? He makes good money. So I'll be able to stay home and have lots of babies. I'm going to tell him tonight. It's a crescent moon. It will be so romantic to tell him about our baby under a crescent moon at Crescent College. I think that is an omen." She had drawn the two intertwined hearts surrounded by six little bitty hearts. Above them was a sickle shaped moon wearing a smile.

Her entries ended. And so must have her life.

An omen, yes. Not a good one. Regardless of whether her death was at his hand or her own, the scythe-like moon cut her down—four stories.

Mary Elizabeth had locked her diary inside the desk.

"She must have kept the key someplace else," Eva said to Ivan. She ran her fingers across the strap that Rose cut. "She never intended for anyone else to read it. The poor kid expected it to end with, 'And they lived happily ever after.' Hell, she didn't even get to live unhappily ever after."

Eva could only imagine how happy the girl felt carrying the child of the man she thought she loved—how happy she would have been. Ironic that the unmarried woman with the lover who didn't really love her found herself in a motherly way so easily. And Eva, with a husband who wanted children, was barren. It wasn't fair.

Another one of those sayings her mother loved to throw around came to mind. "Life isn't always fair."

Suddenly she forgot the diary. *It* had returned...that sense of being watched—eyes boring through the back of her head. She held the book in trembling fingers as she read the final entry again. Did that dead man watching from the corner believe she was Mary Elizabeth or did he simply want to torment someone—anyone?

She closed the diary.

Between Mossell's stinky unannounced visits and Trudy's friend—Johnny or Jack or whoever he really was—stalking her, Eva had to get out of here. If they wouldn't release her she'd find another way. She'd close the place down if she had to. She'd dig up some evidence and get it to the authorities. She'd have to devise a way to get into his penthouse again.

She went to the gift store and thumbed through the rack of sheet music. Some of it was classical. A couple of pieces were more popular music.

"Do you have anything here for Mr. Baker's Calliaphone?"

The clerk, who had been reading through a pile of get well cards, looked up over her glasses. "No. I heard there's some music in the bench. If there's nothing exciting in there, I have a selection of piano music for people who may want to play the grand in the lobby. You might be able to use it."

"I see."

Eva rummaged through a box full of piano music, found a couple of pieces that appealed to her and charged them to her room. They were pretty simple pieces. She'd be able to sight read them without much trouble.

No one was near the grand piano, so she claimed it. Once seated on the bench she started limbering up her fingers. Over and over she played scales—up half a note; down a half note.

Though no one was around, it felt like she had an audience. Behind her a grotesque BatOwl creature carved into the fireplace mantle seemed to watch every movement of her fingers with his exaggerated owl eyes. The creature had the wings of a bat, symbols of good luck and happiness, and the face of the owl, which symbolized wisdom. Right now she could certainly use some wisdom. A pair of wings to fly her back to Dallas would come in damned handy, too.

If she could somehow get into Baker's private file cabinet, she might find out the truth.

She continued to run cords until her fingers felt limber and ready to play.

Finally, when she feared those lingering in the lobby could tolerate scales no longer, she took Mr. Brown's elevator to the fourth floor, climbed the stairs to the penthouse level door, and knocked.

The same guard she met the week prior opened the door with his machine gun in hand. "What do you want?" he demanded.

She gave him her most winning smile. "I would like to play the Calliaphone."

He studied her. "You're the lady who was up here with Mr. Baker last week."

"Yes. I am. I just wanted to play the Calliaphone for a few minutes."

The guard hesitated only a moment. "Sure. I don't think he'd mind. He loves to hear people play it. Come on."

Up in the Calliaphone turret Eva checked the music inside the bench. It had a modest selection. The first song was "Take Me Out to the Ballgame," followed by a "Mighty Fortress is Our God." She pounded out a rendition of "Sweet Georgia Brown." The she took the music out of her sack and played a little Tommy Dorsey and, to please Rose if she really could hear it all the way in town, even some Louie Armstrong. They all had a weird circus sound. Her final selection to her carnival in the air was *Bicycle Built for Two*.

As she played, the door flew opened and Baker came up to the room. He smiled widely when he saw her, as if she were showing off his first-born. Maybe she was. Eva returned the smile as she finished up the final three lines and the last chorus.

"You can express yourself so well with music," Baker said.

"I enjoyed the Calliaphone so much the other day, I wanted to do an encore performance. Once I leave here, I'll never have the opportunity again. I hope you don't mind. It's such a, uh, happy sound."

"Mind?" He beamed at her. "Dear lady, it truly is music to my ears. It's a rare treat to hear such an accomplished musician doing this instrument justice." He paused and his voice dropped to the compassionate tone of a funeral director. "I was sorry to hear about the loss of your family member. Please accept my deepest condolences."

"Thank you....Mr. Baker, I have to admit, I have really become fascinated with this most extraordinary musical instrument. I should like to know more about it and how you came to invent it. Perhaps we could get together this evening."

"What a delightful idea! I'm afraid I won't be free at dinnertime. How about lunch? Would one o'clock be acceptable?"

She smiled broadly as her character in, *The Black Widow* did. "That would be perfect." She collected her sheet music and placed it back in her bag. "I'll see you...in just a little while."

Eva returned to her room to rest before her lunch date. When she rose, she looked for just the right outfit.

When she went through the closet, Eva realized she'd brought too many clothes. She pushed the dresses aside to go through them one by one. For the first time she noticed a wood-framed panel screwed into the wall at the back of the closet. She eyed it a moment—how curious—then shrugged and began pulling the outfits across the hanger rod. She held up her robin egg blue sleeveless dress. As stylish as it was, sleeveless wasn't appropriate after Labor Day. She passed up several other choices of gowns, pajamas and robes.

Finally, she homed in on a cheerful silk georgette spackled with dusky lavender flowers on a violet background. The lavender and violet would most likely help Norman Baker relax and get him to open up with some information.

She put on some makeup, taking a few seconds to hide the lines under her eyes with a dab of lighter Max Factor pancake. Checking her work, Eva turned her head from side to side. What a contrast from the makeup she wore when she was the young and "beautiful" Eva Dupree. If her fans had actually been on the movie set, they really would have run away screaming. There her blue cheeks and lips, red eyelids and nose made her look more like some macabre clown. On the big screen in all the subtle shades of gray, and with the viewer's imagination, those blue lips appeared luscious red and those red eyelids a healthy flesh-colored.

She added final touches, making herself a lovely mature leading lady, or the mother of the leading lady. She'd need Nora Charles' looks and her Thin Man husband's cunning to not only get Norman Baker's private files, but also pry more information out of him about what was happening at the hospital.

Eva waited at the door to the Baker penthouse. Inside Greta and Bruno sounded the canine intruder alarm, shaking the entire end of the building with their barking.

Norman Baker opened his penthouse door. "Right on time. Please come in."

Eva smiled and entered the apartment. "Hello Greta; hello Bruno." She patted the dogs respectively on the head. "I still can't believe they are so big. I had a dog when I was young, but I bet she didn't weigh twenty pounds."

"I've always liked big dogs," Baker said patting Bruno's bottom.

"A friend of mine used to have a large dog," she said as she sat down. "I think he was a Doberman. He would bring home orphan kittens in his mouth. This dog just loved those baby cats. He'd carry them around and lick them." She laughed revisiting the scene in her mind. "You could tell they hated smelling like dog spit."

Baker laughed, too.

Overhead a yellow canary joined in. Then he began singing a lengthy musical solo. Eva looked in the direction of the melody.

"That's Jim," Baker said. "He's my canary."

"He's lovely. How long have you had him?"

"About six months. I love the way canaries sound. He relaxes me."

"Why didn't I see him here before?"

Jim broke in and graced the pair with another stanza.

"I think he was down in my office that evening. Sometimes he's there, sometimes up here. It depends on my mood. Occasionally, he adds a special touch to my radio programs."

Eva recalled the first time she listened to Norman Baker on the radio. As his program began, a funeral dirge swelled from the keys of an organ while little Jim sang to a completely different drummer. She had thought the funeral march and the canary were an odd combination.

She sat down at the couch that faced the east side of the valley. Below them a few people hurried through the belfry, down the path and then into the Catholic church.

"You're lucky," she said. "It would be wonderful waking up to this view every morning of the rest of your life. There's something stimulating about the air and the water here. Something—healing."

"That's why I opened the hospital here," he said. He took his cigarette package out of his breast pocket and lit one. "It gets back to what I told you the other day about believing that you are not sick and how important that is to getting well. Not to mention the curing power of the water. I've seen people come in with horrible holes in their skin—the flesh rotting away—and after a while the treatments close those wounds. They leave literally a whole person. Speaking of healing, you look like you are feeling better."

"As a matter of fact I do feel better," she said. "I still get those intense pains, but they are not as frequent as they were."

"See? As I promised you are going to get well."

"Yes, I believe you're right." Eva tried to sound enthusiastic.

"Then you have already won the battle. The treatment simply guarantees it."

"That's so profound," she said.

He smiled. "Sadly, that philosophy is wasted on most people. They just don't believe they have the power to change their condition."

The dogs started a round of barking followed by a knock at the door.

"Ah, that must be our lunch." He put out his cigarette and answered the door.

While he was directing the steward where to place the tray, she walked over to a desk against the wall. It was a traditional desk with only one working surface, but many sets of drawers. Discretely she tested the drawers. They were latched.

"Are you hungry?" he asked.

"Starved," she answered over her shoulder

"I asked the chef to prepare this especially for you. The recipes came from my cookbook." He seemed to beam.

Oh, no! "Is that the same cookbook I saw for sale in the gift shop?"

"You're very observant, Eva."

"You remember, my old job was to observe human reaction and mimic it. In my mind I try to capture everything: the ambience..." She nodded to the window. "The scenery." She ran her hand across the top of the desk. "The furniture." She gently tugged at the top drawer. It was locked. "Recalling things I've seen and done once helped me feel what I needed in order to play a scene." She smiled. "It's a habit I started a long time ago. Even after I quit acting I continued to be an observer." She moved toward the table and added, "Ummm, this looks delicious."

He described each dish as she tried it. "This is Cranberry Fruit Salad. It has apples, cranberries, dates and pears with just a dab of honey. Everything's ground except the pears and they're finely chopped."

"My, this is delicious." For once Eva didn't have to lie about one of his menu items.

When they finished, the server dished out something brown that resembled something else brown. "This is Mr. Baker's Croquettes," the servant announced proudly. "It has soybean curd, butter, soybean flour, soybean milk, green pepper, onion, celery, curry powder and bread crumbs."

"How tasty!" *Yes, it tasted—absolutely vile.* The croquettes must have been stored too close to Mossell, she thought. "Did you come up with these recipes yourself?"

"Many of them I concocted myself. Some I acquired from chefs I've met."

When he wasn't looking, she snuck Greta a piece of croquette. The Great Dane sniffed it and walked away, apparently unimpressed as well. Bruno, however, followed behind her and snatched it up in one bite.

"Would you like some grape juice? I had the chef prepare it fresh especially for you."

"Yes, thank you." Daintily she downed it. "That was delightful. May I have just a smidge more?" Several times he got up to fill her drinking glass, but not once did he leave the room.

She smiled. She had hoped as much water as he'd been drinking, he'd have to go to the bathroom sometime.

"What will you do when you get back home?" he asked.

She thought about it for a few moments. "I don't know. Things have changed so much."

"Why don't you get back into films?"

"I might. But I'd have to move back to Los Angeles. I've become rather fond of Dallas. Maybe I'll start teaching music again. I don't know. It's been very hard for me to look ahead. Now, I guess I'll have to."

"You'd be smashing in films—Texas accent and all."

"Thanks, Mr. Baker. But I'm not twenty years old anymore. Producers like their leading ladies young. It's not like the old days when thirty-year old Mary Pickford could play a twelve-year old. I doubt that I could get much more than a bit part."

"You'll never know until you try."

"That's true." But would she want to? "What plans do you have for the future, Mr. Baker?"

"I just want to keep healing people as long as I can," he said.

"Are you still planning on buying that hotel in Mineral Wells?" she asked.

"That's my hope. I'm supposed to meet with Hal Collins on the sixteenth of this month about buying the Crazy Water Hotel. The water there is supposed to have a healing effect on even lunatics. Mr. Collins is interested in franchising the Baker Hospital."

"Are you always here? It's almost like you have a ball and chain around your ankle. Don't you ever get to go vacation and enjoy yourself?"

"I have many pleasures," he told her. "And sometimes I manage to get away…not very often, though. Most of the time when I leave its still hospital business. Saturday I'm going to Little Rock to meet with Mr. Collins."

"Little Rock? That's a long way away, isn't it?"

"Not so far. I can drive down there in a day."

She smiled. "I'm sure that time will fly by in your car. That is the most amazing car I've ever seen. It looks like it belongs in a Flash Gordon serial."

"The Cord is only limited by the roads, and unfortunately," he said wryly, "some of the roads between Eureka and Little Rock are very limiting."

"Speaking of something that's ahead of its time, did you really invent the Calliaphone?"

He smiled broadly and his eyes gleamed behind his glasses. Had Baker been a peacock he would have strutted and shown his feathers. Instead, he sucked in his stomach a bit and held up his chest. "Yes, I did."

"You might like to see this." He went over to rummage through his desk drawers. Finally, he retrieved a brochure. Before he returned to Eva he locked the drawers and pocketed the key.

He handed her the pamphlet. There was a photo of an instrument—a small red organ with round brass whistles. She could read the faceplate in the picture. It said, "Tangley Calliaphone." In fancy print below it read, "The First New Tone in Forty Years."

"You actually invented this? But I thought calliopes had been around for years."

"*Calliopes* have been—almost a hundred years. But where a calliope operates on steam, which needs a bulky, dangerous boiler, the Tangley Calliaphone operates off of compressed air. Also, calliopes have one volume level—loud—the Calliaphone is more versatile," he said. "They have different voicings—loud enough for circus and carnivals, and soft for theaters and dance halls. Although I don't play, I understand it can be challenging. I was surprised you caught on as quickly as you did," he said.

"How are you feeling this afternoon?" he asked.

"A little tired." She rubbed her side.

Eva reached down and gave Bruno one last bite of croquette. When they finished their meal, Baker picked up the dishes and placed them in the sink. As he returned to her he explained, "An orderly will drop by in a little while to straighten up and take the dogs for a walk.—Would you like some more juice?"

"Thank you. That would be lovely. I had no idea how differently fresh juice tasted. It's so much more robust than juice from a bottle..." She stopped mid-sentence. Eva was suddenly overcome with a cold chill as if something passed right through her. The air grew foul.

Eva glanced in the direction of Baker's desk and found Mossell semi-reclined like a nudie French postal cards from the 1920s. She tapped on the desktop. When she saw that she had Eva's attention she pointed at the top drawer.

Baker frowned and looked around. "Do you hear something?"

"No," Eva said.

Baker inhaled deeply. "What's that?"

"What's what?"

He sniffed around the room, in the direction of the desks. "That smell. My God. Where's it coming from?"

Suddenly Greta saw or sensed Mossell's presence and barked a couple of times. She growled a deep-in-the-throat and I'm-going-to-rip-you-open growl. Mossell smiled and dissolved into the low light. That sent Greta into a furious display—biting and snarling at the empty air. She tried to lunge onto the desk.

"Greta! No!" Mr. Baker jumped up from his seat.

Greta backed up and dropped her ears, but continued to stare at the invisible Mossell.

Baker yanked the dog back by the collar. But Greta had other ideas. She twisted, then lunged forward, causing Mr. Baker to stumble and knock over his grape juice. It splashed on his white linen jacket in an interesting impressionistic design in his favorite color.

"Dammit!" As he dabbed the purple stain with a napkin, he said, "Eva, will you excuse me?"

"Certainly."

He climbed the stairs to his bedroom. "I'll be right back."

Eva looked over at the empty desk. "Take your time." She eased over to the desk. "I'll just enjoy this gorgeous view."

As soon as she heard the door close upstairs, she tried to open the desk drawers. *Damn.* All of them were locked. She tried to jimmy the top one with a steak knife, but the lock wouldn't budge.

Above her, the floor creaked as Baker moved around the room. The groaning boards sounded mysterious, almost ghostly. When he seemed to be moving toward the stairs, she ran back to the table and grabbed her glass, trying not to look flustered.

"I'm sorry," he said.

"Please don't apologize. Are you going to be able to get that stain out?"

"I'll have to have my cleaning lady work on it."

"Try soda water. The carbonation lifts most stains right out." She smiled. It was a trick she learned from her friend Desdemona. It took red wine stains out almost every time. The knowledge came in handy since they snuck into so many wild Hollywood parties.

"Really?"

"It works just ducky." She casually sipped her own wine glass of grape juice.

"I'll have to send someone to a liquor store in a little..." He was interrupted by the phone ringing.

"Now what?" Baker sighed and picked up the receiver. "Yes." He listened for a moment. "Can't you handle it? All right. Yes. Yes. All right, I'll be right down."

He slowly replaced the receiver. He sighed again and muttered under his breath, "Dammit!" He removed his glasses and polished a smudge on the lens with a clean corner of his cotton napkin. "I'm sorry this has happened again, Miss Dupree. There's a problem that requires my personal attention." He tried to smile. "There's always a problem. I'm afraid as pleasant as the company is, I must cut this afternoon short. Will you forgive me? Perhaps we can continue our conversation another time. Perhaps I can take you into town."

She smiled and feigned regret as well. "Of course, Mr. Baker. I am disappointed as well." She rose and headed for the door. "But this will give me another evening to look forward to." She held out her hand. "Good afternoon, Mr. Baker."

He kissed the back of her hand. "Good afternoon, dear lady."

Eva descended the stairs from the penthouse and headed down to the lobby. "Son of a bitch!" she said under her breath. "So close. So damn close."

Rather than return to her room she decided to take a long walk—to think. On the far side of the grounds she found an untended flowerbed. Magenta fall-blooming tea roses blended into a thicket of tall weeds and scrub brush. She broke a rose off and sat under a tree a few feet away.

"Every time it looks like something is going to work out, it all goes to shit," she said to herself.

She sniffed the rose. It smelled like her mother's living room with the bouquets of homegrown rosebuds in mason jars. Again she pressed it to her nose. If she thought wishes came true, she'd wish to go back to those happy years on the farm before Papa died. It was a simpler time. No con games. People meant what they said. And people made an honest living doing an honest day's work. Real work, sweating and struggling; not sitting around a movie set pretending or telling lies about a prognosis or a diagnosis or a treatment.

She recalled scraping her knee when she was about five. Mamma held her and rocked her until the tears stopped flowing. In those days there were people who loved you and those who didn't; there were people you trusted and people who weren't trustworthy. You never got those people mixed up.

She inhaled deeply.

Without realizing it, she plucked most of the petals from the bloom.

She went over her options. There were few. Go home and die. She plucked a petal. Stay and watch patients cheated and still possibly die. Pluck another petal. Neither desirable options. Every alternative ended with, "And you die." Kill the flower just a little more.

By then it was too late. She had stripped the once magnificent blossom; only a bare stem remained.

"I don't want to see anything die needlessly. Not even you," she told the flower. She set it down gently in the overgrown garden.

She'd lost track of time. The sun had disappeared behind the building and cast a yellow glaze on the trees and washed the sky with vivid evening watercolors. Down below, the bell from the Catholic church chimed calling the faithful to six o'clock mass.

Rose would have already come and gone by now. The room would be straightened up and Ivan would be anxious for his evening snack. As the sky transformed from blue to gray and then finally black, she decided it was time to head back to her suite.

She hadn't made it more than four or five steps than her old nemesis, the coal miners, returned with picks hacking their way through her kidney. Her body twisted as the ground rose to meet her. Never had the attacks been so rabid and persistent. She fell over among the stones waiting for what seemed centuries for the pain to pass.

Eva tried to pull herself to her knees, but the miners struck her with the slightest motion. She fell back to the rocky ground, helpless to move.

"Someone will come," she told herself. She called out, but nobody heard her. She lay there until the waning moon rose above the mountain. Still nobody came. Never had she felt more abandoned, not even the night Edgar died. She propped herself up against a pine tree. Why weren't they looking for her? If she hadn't shown up, wouldn't they send someone out to find her?

Hopefully, Rose had come to feed Ivan. Eva looked up at the darkened windows of her suite. On the balcony she could see a lone woman dressed in white-probably a nurse taking a cigarette break. When the woman moved next to the rail, Eva gasped. Her breathing quickened. "Mary Elizabeth! No!"

The pale figure climbed on the rail and let go.

"No!" Eva screamed from the depth of her soul. "No!" She sobbed uncontrollably.

The specter, with her white gown flowing behind her like angel's wings, plummeted toward the ground, but before hitting, her form simply faded away.

Poor Mary Elizabeth, still tortured by the man in room four-nineteen. Condemned to repeat her suicide over and over again. Was God punishing this poor child for taking her own life or for her carnal transgressions? Or was God punishing Eva for her pride?

Eva gathered her strength and pulled herself up the slope. Finally, feeling like an old castoff dishrag, Eva struggled to her feet. With each step an invisible pick drove into her side. When she reached the base of the stairs, things were just as they had been that first night at the Baker Hospital—no Mary Elizabeth, no blood, no sanity.

Eva crumbled to the steps and collapsed again, spent. Shortly, a few visitors left the building and descended the steps. After that everything seemed to move as fast as a time-lapse movie. She was vaguely aware of someone picking her up and placing her in a wheelchair. Finally the nurse gave her a shot, then helped her into her bed.

To sleep. Per chance to dream.

Much later in the night, Eva awoke to the sound of a gentle tap-tap tap-tap somewhere in the room. When she opened her eyes, the rapping stopped. The room had the same icy bite as when Mossell dropped in for her visits, but the air wasn't tinged with that rotting-Mossell smell. She lay there for some time, and hearing nothing, allowed herself to slip off to sleep again.

Tap-tap, tap-tap.

Eva opened her eyes. Despite the painkillers, her side and back still ached as if someone had pummeled her with a baseball bat. But the sharp pitchfork pain that had tortured her at the slightest movement, had subsided. Slowly, Eva sat up in bed, and turned on the night lamp. Ivan lay next to her like a miniature Sphinx, his gaze firmly fixed on the closet.

Tap-tap, tap-tap.

Eva reached to her night stand, grabbing the first thing she could feel. It was Edgar's photograph in the silver frame. She carefully set it back down and reached for the next object, a Baker Hospital water glass.

Tap-tap, tap-tap.

Tap-tap, tap-tap.

"Stop it." She flung the glass, water and all, at the closet door where it exploded in a spray of glass splinters and water droplets. "Let me sleep!"

Tap-tap, tap-tap.

"Son-of-a-bitch! Just one night; just let me sleep for one bloody night!" Remembering the broken glass, she slid on her slippers. She yanked the closet door open hoping to see a mouse or a rat, but found only empty air and her hanging clothes. After waiting a few seconds but hearing nothing more, she turned to leave.

From inside the closet wall came tap-tap, tap-tap.

Tap-tap, tap-tap.

She closed her eyes and whispered, "Please, stop."

Tap-tap tap-tap.

She threw up her hands. "What the hell do you want?"

Behind her the wall thumped again. A miasma swirled around her then gelled into a more solid form. An elderly woman with white hair piled atop her head and pale saggy skin poked her head through the wall inside the closet.

Terrified, Eva turned to escape and ran into the doorframe. She staggered back then ran out of the closet, slamming the door behind her. She kicked off her slippers and couldn't jump back into bed fast enough. Eva wrapped her arms around her legs, and rocked back and forth. With tears rolling down her cheeks, Eva cried, "No more. No more. Please, no more."

"Hello, dear." The hazy, translucent woman floated through the closet door into the bedroom. "I'm Theodora." She adjusted her gold wire-rimmed glasses to get a better look at Eva. Leaning on a translucent cane, the figure appeared to stand no taller than five feet. She looked thin and frail. "I know all this popping in and out must be a tad unsettling to someone who still has a pulse. This hospital is full of my, uh, ilk. How do you like my room?"

Eva's heart hammered in her chest and she could barely breathe. She swallowed hard. "Your room?"

"Lovely, isn't it?" The woman's presence sucked away all the warmth, just like Mossell, but the elderly lady had such a warm smile, and no rotten corpse smell. She held up two shriveled fingers. "I stayed here for a little over two months. When was that? When the hospital first opened in Eureka."

"You're dead?" Eva stammered.

The lady paused as though giving the question some thought. "I 'spose so."

Eva took a deep breath. Nothing should surprise her anymore.

Ivan maintained his Sphinx stance and his wide-eyed owl expression focused on the transparent woman. He remained alert but relaxed.

Eva trembled. "Please don't hurt me," she begged, tears streaming down her face.

"Oh, dear," the old woman said. "I don't want to hurt you. A pretty young lady like you needs to learn to relax."

Eva drew an uneven breath. "What do you want?"

"You want to get into Mr. Baker's room. I know how to do it."

Eva stared at her. "You do?" Was Eva really having this conversation?

"Through the closet."

"The closet?" Eva echoed.

Theodora's eyes twinkled with mischief. "Mr. Baker has secret passages all over the hospital to help him get away if those boys from the American Meatcutters' Association—I think that's what he calls them—if they ever caught up with him. The passageway in the closet leads to his penthouse."

"How do you know?" Eva asked.

"I confess, I'm a bit nosey," Theodora said. "I investigated some noises I heard inside the wall and found a passageway from my room to his. All you have to do is pull off that board. There's also a passage in Mr. Baker's office. There's another one in the basement that leads to Spring Street. I imagine there are others I don't know about. It's fun; like a mystery."

"Yes, fun," Eva said weakly. "Mossell, another visitor of similar ilk, as you put it, smells like, well, a rotting corpse. Why don't you?"

"Oh that." She waved a dismissive hand. "They burned my body right after I died. There's nothing left to smell."

"Are you trying to even the score with Norman Baker because you died here and he burned your body?"

Theodora laughed. "No, I've got nothing to get even about."

"But your cancer treatments didn't work?"

"No, but they sure tried to save me. The nurses were nice to me. The food wasn't bad except when the chef used recipes from Mr. Baker's cookbook. Even Mr. Baker treated me like a queen."

Eva found herself relaxing some. "Why are you still here? Why didn't you, uh, move on or go to Heaven or whatever."

The eyes grew nostalgic, as if looking at a photograph. "I like it here. My husband, Rupert, died in the war—you know, the War to End All Wars. I didn't have any other family. If I hadn't come here I'd have died alone in a smelly hospital ward with no one to visit me. Here I had friends…still do."

Eva's eyes grew wide, recalling the chair at the end of the hall rocking without an occupant. "You're Mrs. Taylor's friend?"

Theodora smiled broadly. "Yes, I am. We all meet in the rockers at the end of the hall to watch the sun set. Come join us sometime."

Strange. Theodora seemed so…normal.

"You'll forgive me if I visit in my corporeal form, won't you."

"Of course. We can't all be perfect." Her image became more translucent. "Have fun, dear. I hope you find what you're looking for. Oh, one more thing. I just wish you'd clean up the cat doots more often. The bathroom has an…well, an unpleasant aroma." Theodora raised her translucent eyebrows cryptically. "I'll just leave you alone. Taa taa." She vanished.

Eva waited until the room warmed up and then crunched through the broken glass in front of the closet.

She tried to pull the wood panel with her fingers, but it had been nailed tight.

DAY ELEVEN—*Sunday, September10*

The next morning Rose showed up a few minutes before Eva received her belly shot. On tonic days, Eva had instructed her to sleep in. But with the intestinal injection, Rose knew she could expect drama. Waiting in the sitting area, Rose heard Nurse Cavanaugh put the syringe back in the metal tray with a soft metal clink.

"I'm going to throw up," Eva said weakly.

The nurse handed Eva the emesis basin. "I'll be back in a minute with some ice water." She closed the curtains the rest of the way, gathered up all of her torture implements and left, turning off the lights behind her. A few minutes later, she returned briefly to bring the promised water pitcher, then left her patient in Rose's competent hands.

Rose wiped the perspiration beading across Miss Eva's upper lip and her forehead with the moist washrag. From her own past experience, Rose knew the cloth probably felt an odd combination of soothing cold and icy pain. After giving her boss lady a sponge bath to combat the low-grade fever, Rose handed Miss Eva a glass. "Here take a sip of this. There isn't anything that's better for a fever than an ice-cold glass of Eureka Springs water."

Eva said, "I want to die."

Rose's lips thinned. "That's not the kind of talk Mr. Edgar would want to hear." She patted Eva's hand, causing her to wince. Rose shrugged. Even that gentle gesture must have stung Eva's fevered skin. "Now, let me rinse off this washrag for you."

After a short nap Eva opened her eyes and watched Rose in silence. The maid sat silhouetted next to the open window puffing on a Kool. A ribbon of smoke curled up from the glowing embers. Caught by the breeze, it disappeared the same way the ghosts in this place did after their visits. Rose flicked a long line of ashes into the ashtray. In the maid's lap, Ivan quietly dozed. Absently, she stroked his fur with her free hand.

Rose is right. She's always right. After a short nap, Eva felt much better. Her fever had broken but her shot site ached some and her kidney pain continued to nag her. She struggled to sit up.

When Rose saw Eva move, she displaced Ivan, tapped out her smoke and rushed to the bedside. "How you feeling?"

"Tender, but better."

Rose wore that look on her face again. That expression that warned Eva it was either time for a lecture or something that tasted bad. Since Rose had a cup in her hand, Eva knew it was going to be the latter.

"Try this tea." Rose handed her the cup. "It will make you feel better."

Like Rose's cigarette smoke, the steam from the cup rolled into air and evaporated. Hot herbal tea didn't sound appetizing, but what Rose usually spiked it with made the drink tolerable.

Eva sipped her Scottish whiskey and hydrangea tea, occasionally setting the cup down on the graniteware rolling table. She'd never paid much attention to the table before; a chunk of blue stripe against white enamel had been gouged out of the corner possibly from someone dropping something heavy on it.

"Have you decided what you want to do?" Rose asked.

"I'm torn," Eva answered. "I just don't know. Part of me says, 'Stay.' Part of me wants to go home. I guess I want to know what's really going on here before I make up my mind."

"Did you find out anything yesterday?"

She shook her head. "Mr. Baker invited me to his penthouse, but the desk was locked and he never left the room long enough for me to get into it."

"How are you going to find out now?"

Eva gave the maid a coy smile. "An idea came to me while I was sleeping, but I'm going to need your help."

Rose cocked her head to the side. "Is this going to be like one of those *Thin Man* mysteries you drag me to?"

"Something like that."

Rose rubbed her hands together. "Now Miss Eva, you know I'm a church-going woman. Are you going to ask me to do anything I'm going to have to ask forgiveness for later?"

"No, you're just an accessory. I'll be the one who has to confess to breaking in."

Rose exclaimed, "You want to do *what*?"

"I need to get into Baker's penthouse." Eva pointed straight up at the ceiling.

Ivan jumped on the bed to join in on the conspiracy planning. Rose stroked the cat's head nervously as Eva unfolded her plan.

"How are you going to get back in there?"

"I believe I've discovered an escape passage in the closet." She repeated Theodora's information.

"You're fooling!" Rose went to peer inside the closet.

Eva dragged herself out of bed and retrieved the brass letter opener from her papers on the desk. Joining Rose in the closet, she tried prying off the panel with the opener, but she could not force the point behind the panel frame.

Rose took the letter opener. "You stand back and rest, Miss Eva. I'll get it."

As Eva watched, Rose worked the point under the corner of the board until she had forced a tiny space. She repeated the process until all four corners had pulled away from the wall. Finally, she shoved the opener blade all the way in there and twisted, creating a wider and wider gap. Before long, she pried the panel loose, revealing an opening barely large enough for one of them to crawl into.

Rose eased her head through the opening. "Oh my!"

"What's wrong?" Eva asked. "What do you see?"

"Nothing. It's pitch dark. I'm going to have to do this by Braille."

The hole swallowed the rest of the maid's body. "I'm feeling around and I found a ladder. Ow. It's certainly a crude one."

"Where does it lead?" Eva's heart was pounding. *Are we really doing this?*

"Can't tell exactly. It goes straight up."

"Baker's penthouse. Rose. Come back here. You're too old to be climbing ladders in the dark."

"Thank you kindly, Miss Eva." She popped her head back out. "Remember you said that next time you want me to get something out of the attic. You need to rest some more before you spend any more energy."

"Rose come out of there. I don't want you getting hurt."

"I'll be down in a minute," Rose promised.

Eva could hear boards creak as Rose climbed. The maid knocked at the wall and was answered by the booming bark of dogs. Quickly, Rose climbed back down. Covered with dust and cobwebs, she slithered out of the opening. She ushered Miss Eva out of the closet. Closing the closet door behind her, Rose motioned to Miss Eva to get back into bed.

Grabbing the cloth, she swabbed Eva's face as if nothing had happened.

Eva couldn't wait to hear about the reconnaissance mission. "Well, what did you find?"

"It's dark as the streets of Hell in there," Rose said. "You're going to need something to light the closet up with."

"Can you pick up a flashlight in town?"

"Yes ma'am."

"What else?" Eva urged her on.

"It feels like there's a door at the top of the ladder." Rose made a motion like she was opening a trap door. "Don't think there's a latch on it cuz I felt it move when I pushed it. But, brother, those sound like big dogs, and not very friendly either."

"He told me they weighed over a hundred pounds each. They're huge. What do we do about them?" Eva frowned at the ceiling. "Even though they like me, I doubt that they'll just let me waltz in there and open his desk."

Rose placed her hand over her mouth and nose like a mask. "Don't they have some of that stuff that makes you sleep during surgery?"

"Rose, remember the Baker Hospital brochures? They don't do surgery here."

"I might be able to find something to take the fight out of them at the pharmacy."

Eva's eyes grew wide. "We don't want to kill them. Just put them out of commission for a little while."

Rose opened her mouth to say something, then stopped.

"What Rose?"

"It's silly, Miss Eva. Absolutely loony farm silly."

"Try me."

Rose tittered. "What if we got the dogs drunk?"

Eva stared at her maid, speechless. "You want to get Norman Baker's dogs intoxicated?"

"Sorry, Miss Eva. It was a foolish thought."

Eva grinned at her. "Foolish thought, hell. Rose, that's bloody brilliant!"

"You've got your scotch. But how do we get them to drink scotch?" Rose wondered aloud. "As Miss Mossell would have said, 'I imagine they're too smart to drink paint thinner.'"

"What if we put it in some food?" Eva asked.

"Did those dogs look that hungry to you?"

Eva tapped her cheek with her finger as she recalled the Great Danes. "One of the dogs turned down food I tried to sneak to him when I dined with Mr. Baker. And it would only take one alert dog to give us away.

"Instead of putting it in food, we could prepare a canine cocktail," Rose suggested. "I could brew up some chicken broth and they'd be sure to drink that."

Eva nodded. "That's perfect!"

"Now, what'll we deliver the drinks in?" Rose asked.

Eva grinned wickedly. "What about this?" She held up an enamel white bedpan.

"Miss Eva, you do have an evil streak."

"So you tell me. All right. We give them a doggie daiquiri." Eva frowned again. "Supposing we actually succeed and get the papers tomorrow, we'll need to get them to the FBI as soon as we can. Can you take the train to Little Rock?"

Rose blinked. "Little Rock? You want me to travel to Little Rock?"

"Yes. I don't trust the authorities in Eureka Springs. Besides, he's going to be in Little Rock next week. If they tried to arrest him *here* with all the guns he's got, people are going to die. If they closed in on him away from here, they wouldn't put any patients in danger."

Rose nodded reluctantly. "I'll check the train schedule."

Eva jotted down a few items on a Baker Hospital scratch pad. "Here's your shopping list." She went into her purse and handed Rose a twenty. "This should cover it. Oh and Rose—"

"Yes, Miss Eva."

"Get cheap booze for the dogs."

"Yes, Miss Eva." Rose scanned the inventory. "You left off a flashlight and batteries."

"Of course." Eva handed her the pencil.

Rose licked the point and scribbled down her two items. "You already out of Haig and Haig?"

"I have some left, but I could use some more just to be safe. I don't want to run out while you're gone."

Rose double-folded the list, picked up her purse and slid the paper into the inside pocket. Eva marveled at Rose's hand bag and its organization. Like a magician's hat, at any given moment Rose could reach in and pull out whatever she needed. Granted, it must have weighed forty pounds, but she carried everything she could possibly need like her bottle of medicine, that strong-smelling rheumatism cream and her New Testament, in case she had to wait somewhere.

DAY TWELVE—*Monday, September 11*

Rose was a morning person. At home in Dallas, she enjoyed watching the sun come up, and reading her Bible before heading off to work. This worked well because Miss Eva hated mornings. Once Rose arrived at work, she could get her prayers out of the way, feed the cat and brew a fresh pot of coffee long before Miss Eva stirred.

As she would do at home, Rose arrived at the hospital before the sun broke above East Mountain. On this crisp first day of the week, as she carried her special load toward the trolley stop, she took a moment to watch the waking sky. Darkness, which for millennia represented all that was evil, transformed into gray. A coral haze appeared in puffy clouds at the top of the mountain. Maybe this was how the Second Coming would begin.

The entire eastern sky filled with clouds whose undersides wore a magenta lining, like a flock of flamingoes. Vanishing misty swirls of gray parted, revealing a cyan sky above a mauve cobweb of clouds. Surely, the good Lord Jesus had arranged this morning to let her know that soon all would be right in her world.

Rose shifted her load, which weighed considerably more than in days past. In addition to carrying her purse and her tote bag, a tawny wicker fishing basket bumped against her behind, suspended by a leather strap hanging across her shoulder. When the trolley finally arrived, Rose paid her fare and struggled to the back of the car. Inside the basket, chicken broth in a one-quart canning jar bobbled back and forth. After she took her seat, Rose tightened the jar lid. If it came loose and contents spilled, their entire plan would unravel.

At the hospital Eva smiled at Nurse Cavanaugh. "I'm going into town in a little while," Eva told her nurse. "I think I'm going to have my maid come in and give the place a thorough cleaning. Tell housekeeping not to bother changing the linens. Rose can do all that. I'll have her come down and get them when she arrives."

Cavanaugh smiled back. "You're finally getting out? That's wonderful. You'll have such a good time, don't you think? But…first things first." Cavanaugh set a pair of Baker Hospital fruit juice glasses on the rolling table. "Drink down today's treatment. I even brought your fruit juice so you don't have to ask for it."

The tarry-colored Cure looked revolting as ever. "Can I have a cup of coffee first?"

"Not till you've taken your medicine." Cavanaugh crossed her arms, waiting for Eva to drink up.

Obviously she had no chance to spike the elixir today. Eva braced herself, chugged the tar treatment, and hurriedly followed it with the orange juice chaser. The syrup tasted even worse than the castor oil her mother used for every ailment and as a punishment for sassing. If Mamma had given her the Baker Cure the first time she talked back, she never would have sassed again.

As Rose fed and cleaned up after Ivan, Eva dressed.

"How do I look?" Eva asked.

Rose put down the fry strainer, chuckling. "Miss Eva, you look ridiculous. So ridiculous that I believe you could start a new fashion trend."

Indeed she did look silly. She had the hem of her dress belted around her waist, which shortened its length to above her knees. But she teased, "You keep up that sassy talk and I'm going to have to dock your pay."

Rose sniffed. "Honey, I keep reminding you, something from nothing's still nothing."

"Is that your subtle way of asking for a raise?"

"Nothing subtle about it. This is too much work for an old woman." Rose began to empty her canvas tote bag. The contents looked like a random collection from a thrift store grab bag: two flashlights, ten "D" cell batteries, a pint of gin, Ivan's potty ashes, a fisherman's vest, screwdriver, hammer and a pocketknife.

"If we pull this off, there will be a big bonus in your next pay envelope," Eva promised. "If we fail, you can see me at the jail on visiting days."

"Lookey what I found at the hunting and fishing shop." Rose held up a pair of flashlights. "These are..." She stretched her arm full length to read the steel label riveted to the outside. "...Ray-O-Vac Black Rubberized Number 611 Flashlight..." She squinted trying to focus on the minute silvery engraved characters. "...approved for mine use. Figured you traipsing through secret passages is close enough to being in a coal mine. That fancy rubber-coated handle should help you to hang onto it. And this..." she held up a battery, "is the first leak-proof 'sealed in steel' battery."

Eva picked up the bottle of gin. "Why'd you get this?"

"Mr. Baker will know somebody's done something to his dogs if he comes home and finds them smelling like a drunk on a Saturday night. You need something he won't smell too much on their breath...like gin. Had a talk with the counter man at the package store. Told him I needed something for my nerves and didn't want my boss lady to know when I take a taste."

"Rose, you astound me! How did you even know to ask for something like that?"

"Honey, you gotta give me some credit for being young once. I didn't always have these gray hairs that both you and your husband and this mangy cat gave me." The corners of her mouth curled up and she gave Ivan an affectionate scratch under the chin. "My mama lashed me more times than I can count for coming home with a smell of whiskey in my mouth. If you want Mr. Baker to think his ponies just got an attack of the good-for-nothings, you just need to put the gin in that chicken broth."

"I'll certainly defer to your expertise. I'm glad you're on my side. What else do you have there?"

Rose held up an oversized heavy cotton khaki fishing vest. "When you start a fashion trend, every well-dressed woman this fall will be wearing a fisherman's vest with plenty of pockets to carry all your accessories." She unbuttoned a small flat breast pocket and held it open. "This one is the perfect place to keep your 'keys'."

Rose gathered up items from around the room and stowed them in one place. She tossed a white bath towel over the stash, just in case someone came in. She, then, retrieved Eva's bedpan from her night stand and the enameled basin used for giving bed baths. Before she handed the pan over to Eva, Rose scrubbed out the bedpan with hot water and bath soap. "We don't want the puppies getting sick, do we?" Finally, she added the kick to broth, then returned the O-ring and the glass lid to the jar, and forced the bail wire latch into place. She shook it, and inspected the seal. "Here ya go, Miss Eva. Canine cocktail." The jar and bedpan took their place in the fishing basket. The boards above their heads creaked as Mr. Baker moved across the floor. The lumbering thumps and thuds of the dogs followed his footfalls.

While they waited for him to leave the penthouse, Eva hid in the bathroom just in case one of the nurses came into the room. Rose, acting as lookout, stood by the door, with it ever so slightly ajar.

After what seemed like forever, Rose dashed into the bathroom. "He just headed for the elevator."

Eva put on the fishing vest and slid the tackle basket over her shoulder, taking a moment to adjust the strap. Quietly, she ducked down and eased into the crawlway. It was dark as a cave, and the air smelled stale and dusty. She sneezed a couple of times.

"Bless you," Rose called up into the hole.

Eva switched on the flashlight, and prayed none of her translucent friends would show up to cheer her on. The crawlway only measured two by three feet. It was like being trapped in a coffin. For a moment she couldn't breathe. "I don't know if I can do this."

"You'll be okay. Just do it."

In the yellowish flashlight beam, she could the see a false ceiling at about six feet above her. She could also make out the outline of the trap door, her destination.

Still crouching, she pivoted on the balls of her feet. Suddenly, a sticky film of spider web encased her face and hands. Yelping and flailing at her head she stumbled and fell against the wall.

"Miss Eva, you alright?"

Still swiping her with her hands, Eva groaned. "I'm caught in a spider web." She continued to brush at her cheeks and forehead." She shivered. "It feels like spiders are crawling all over me."

Rose popped her head in the opening and shined her own flashlight on Eva. "No creepy crawlies on you. I'm going back to my lookout post. Get back to your rat killing. You're fine."

Easy for her to say. Eva shivered as she wiped away the web clinging to her eyelashes. *Act brave. Act brave.* Ironically, those were the words she told her character while filming *Caught in a Web*. She inhaled deeply, intent to focus on her task. This time she shined the light around before she moved. Eva moaned as she grabbed the first rung.

Rose stuck her head back through the opening. "What?"

"I feel like I'm smothering."

"Do you want me to do it?" Rose offered.

Eva stared at the trapdoor. With Rose's ample frame, Eva doubted she could squeeze through the tiny hatch. "I'll be okay. Just give me a minute."

She stood up and tested the ladder. Bolted together, not nailed, and fastened to the wall, it was sturdier than it looked. After drawing a deep breath she said, "I'm ready."

Eva placed the flashlight in the belly pocket of her vest. She wrapped her fingers around the rough wood rung. Then, one step at a time, she climbed upward. In her basket, the canning jar bobbled back and forth against the bedpan, making a terrible racket she was sure the entire hospital could hear. "I need two extra arms to hold the flashlight and handle the bedpan," she called down the shaft.

"I'll pick you up an extra pair next time I'm in town," Rose called up.

When Eva reached the top, she wrapped her left arm around the ladder. Carefully, she pushed the trapdoor open with her head. *Perfect.* As soon as the opening was wide enough, she pulled the bedpan from the basket, then shoved it through. Above huge feet thundered toward her. She quickly grabbed the jar, and popped the latch open. Pushing the door open wider, she tapped around to find the pan, poured the cocktail, pulled back her fingers and dropped the trapdoor.

A thought froze her. She whispered down, "Rose, what if he comes back before the dogs go to sleep? I won't be able to retrieve the pans."

"You stay up there and pull out the pan as soon as the dogs are done. I'll stand by the door and keep watch. I'll let you know if he's headed this way."

Eva repeated the delivery process, delivering the enameled emesis basin. Only one set of feet was visible through the opening.

Eva pointed the flashlight at her watch. How long does it take to drink broth? Once they drank it, Eva figured she should give the gin ten to fifteen minutes to take effect. Anxious to get the bowls back, she sequentially tapped her fingers on the splintery rung. Her left arm was starting to ache.

Below her, Eva heard the suite door slam.

"Oh, Lord Jesus, help us. I think I hear him!" Rose called up to Eva still perched on the ladder.

Eva opened the trap door and pulled in the bedpan. By that time Rose had pushed her head and shoulders through the closet opening.

"Catch." Eva dropped the pan and splattered Rose with the residual Pooch Punch.

Eva had to climb up a step higher to open the trap door enough to see the other pan. The dogs had pushed it several feet away. Still no sign of the Great Danes. She reached farther and farther until she finally caught it with her fingertips. By this time she could hear his keys clinking against the lock. She grabbed the basin, dropped down and let the trapdoor fall just as the door opened.

Eva's heart pounded so hard in her chest she knew everyone in the hospital could hear her "Tell-Tale Heart." She quickly descended the ladder.

Rose dropped the emesis basin inside the pan. "You all right, Miss Eva?"

"He came in as I closed the trapdoor but I don't think he saw me."

"I thought you said he followed a regular schedule?"

Eva shrugged. "He does. Until now I could set my watch by him."

"Now what do we do?"

"We wait. Maybe he spilled something on his suit. He sometimes wears white suits, you know they show everything, and he is very meticulous about his appearance."

They waited nervously. After what seemed an eternity they heard Baker's footsteps descend the stairs and walk past the suite toward the elevator.

"What if he comes back?" Eva asked.

Rose looked thoughtful. "That won't be a problem. I have to clean your room."

She left and returned shortly with a broom, a mop and a bucket of mop water. "I have everything I need to get your room spotless."

Eva narrowed her eyes. "So?"

"So, if anyone comes your direction, I'll just pound on the ceiling with the broomstick."

Eva grinned. "Perfect."

Rose took her position at the door and Eva stepped into the crawl way.

She cracked the trapdoor open just a few inches. Nothing. She scratched the floor with her fingernails. No response. She opened the door even wider. Still no reaction. Finally she pushed it open all the way. Over in the corner catching afternoon rays through the windows Greta staggered to her feet, but after a few tottering steps, she plopped down.

"I'm sorry, Greta."

Eva climbed out of the hole and eased next to the desk. She tested all the drawers. Every one of them was locked tight as a safe.

Was he so distrusting that he had to lock drawers in his own apartment? Apparently so. But then again, maybe he had reason to be. Eva laughed at something Edgar once told her about Roger Knight, *"Just because he's paranoid, doesn't mean there isn't someone out there who wants to do him in."*

Eva had a feeling she was just one person in a long line who had reason to question the motives of Norman Baker.

She kneeled down, eyeballing the locking slot in the top drawer on the right side. Eva removed the paper clips from her vest, slid them into the lock and pressed down. The second pin slipped in and she twisted it. Before she could turn it, the spring popped back into place.

"Damn!" She tried again.

Suddenly she was overwhelmed by an old familiar feeling. That tightness in her midsection, and a burning in her kidney that felt like something was being welded to it. "Not now. Not now."

But yes, now. She doubled over.

Even through the pain, she eyed the lock. She forced herself back upright. Her hands shook, making it nearly impossible to slide the wire into the lock.

Concentrate. Press.

She recalled Norman Baker's own words about the mind having the ability to heal. "Ice" she said to herself. "It feels like ice. Nice cool ice."

In went the second paperclip.

"There's no pain. Only coolness."

Click. The charmed third try opened the latch. She grabbed the handful of files and sorted through them. No, wrong drawer. She carefully put everything back as close to the way she found it as she could. However, the fourth drawer reaped benefit. Jackpot! She found eight or nine personal files. She skimmed letter after letter from patients who swore Baker's Cancer Cure had lifted them from the Valley of Death. Each file contained from one to three letters. She pulled out three of the files: hers, Mossell's and Annabelle Nichols, whose ashes scared Ivan out of his fur. Then she glanced through the other files. The files with fewer than three letters meant that Baker must have already contacted the relatives for funds. Those would provide the best evidence. The relatives could verify receiving the letters and authorities should be able to match them up with the bodies in the refrigerator. She took single letters out of a couple more files.

Thump-thump-thump.

Rose's signal. Baker was returning.

She closed the drawer, dropped the files down the hole and climbed down through her escape hatch. Once again she heard the keys fumbling in the door.

She shut the trapdoor and quietly climbed down the ladder.

Rose stood just outside the closet clutching the files to her bosom. Corners of white typing paper and orchid paper, which obviously came from Baker's office, peeked out of the folders.

Once she had her feet on the floor, Eva crumbled to her knees. "I had an attack while I was up there."

"You should be feeling better now cuz we got the goods," Rose said.

Eva trembled and smiled weakly. "Help me lie down."

Still clasping the files, Rose helped her remove the fishing vest and tossed it on the floor of the closet. She wrapped her other arm around Eva, and led her slowly to the bed where Eva collapsed like a ragdoll.

Rose took the files into the bathroom and returned in a few minutes with a neatly assembled pile of paperwork. "Where do you want these?" On the way back to the bed, Rose kicked the closet door shut.

Eva pointed at the nightstand, where Rose hid the evidence underneath *Film and Screen Magazine*, a couple of get well cards and the copy of Ida Mellen's book.

Eva pulled the sheet over herself about the time the nurse's aide opened the door with an armload of sheets. "Oh, Miss Dupree." She placed a startled hand over her mouth. "I thought you were in town."

"I started feeling badly, so I came back early."

"I was going to change your bed."

Eva held the sheet tighter at her throat. "Not now. I told the nurse I didn't want housekeeping today. I just want to sleep."

"She must have forgotten to tell me. This won't take but a few minutes. We can't have our patients sleeping in dirty beds, can we, Sugar?"

Rose tried to take the linens. "Let me have those. I'll take care of it when Miss Eva's feeling a little better. You go have a cigarette break."

The young woman tightened her grip on the sheets. "If anyone found out, I could lose my job. I got two little boys."

"I'm sure they're very handsome boys." Rose patted her hand and whispered something in her ear.

The woman gave Eva a glance that could have curdled beer. "Really?"

Rose glanced Eva's direction and nodded.

"You won't tell anyone, will you?"

Rose put her finger to her lips. "Promise." She took the sheets and laid them on the desk. "Run along."

Once the aide left, Rose plumped her boss's pillow.

"What did you tell her?"

"I said you had a bit of a temper and you'd threaten to have her transferred to the morgue."

Eva sighed. "By the time that rumor gets done circulating, people will think I boil babies for breakfast."

"Not for breakfast; maybe dinner."

"Thanks. Just call me Mrs. Dracu." She bared her teeth.

"Weren't you her once?"

Dropping her head back into her pillow, Eva said, "I believe I was."

"Ain't it something?" Rose shook her head. "All those rumors true."

A thought hit Eva. "What if Mr. Baker notices those records are missing? With that board off the wall, he could easily tell I took them."

"Not when I get done, he ain't." Rose went into the closet and retrieved the vest. Then she put the panel back in place and gently tapped the nails into place. In no time the room had returned to normal: the back of the closet boarded up again, fishing vest returned to her tote and the clean bedpan and basin to the night stand.

"Reckon I didn't get the place as spotless as you expected. My apologies."

"Looks like I'm going to have to find myself a new maid."

Despite the fact that Eva was obviously teasing, Rose's expression dropped.

Eva said quickly, "Rose, you are a woman of many talents. Of course, I'm going to have to replace you, since I'm promoting you to a manager at Foxworthy Oil."

"A manager? You're not fooling an old woman, are you?"

"I doubt that any of those roughnecks could have come up with and executed a plan as perfectly as you did."

"Manager. Now, don't that beat all?"

"Maybe you should leave me one of the flashlights just in case the lights go out."

Rose pulled it back out of her tote and set it on the night stand. She disappeared back into the closet, returning with the dustpan and broom she had borrowed to clean the room. She finished tidying until the room was spotless. Quite a feat after all the dust Eva had tracked in from the crawlspace.

"Well, this manager has tidied up. I doubt anyone would be able to tell anything. If anything happens, you just get that innocent look you're so good at, and tell him someone must of come in here before you got back from town. You might want to change back into your nightgown."

Once Rose had left, Eva sat calmly in bed and listened to the radio. She flipped the pages of *Modern Screen Magazine,* she sang under her breath the lyrics of *A Foggy Day in London Town.* "*I was a stranger in the city; Out of town were the people I knew. I had that feeling of self-pity—What to do? What to do? What to do? The outlook was de-cid-ed-ly blue; But as I walked through the foggy streets alone, It turned out to be the luckiest day I've known.*"

As she sang the words, she wondered, *is this an omen? Are things really going to get better?* Maybe they were already better and she just didn't know it.

After dinner Eva asked for a sleeping pill, which she pretended to take, but cheeked it and waited for the nurse to leave before she spit it out.

She waited until Nurse Turner had checked on her for the final time and all the activity in the halls ceased, and then took out the flashlight. She also dug out the file folders. Sliding the folders under her covers, she turned on the flashlight. Eva felt like a little kid reading after her parents had gone to bed. Her papers were not the first to occupy this folder. The folder name had been erased and re-eased. Her name, written in pencil, was probably the fourth or fifth printed there. Eva wondered what happened to the other tenants of the folder. Did they live or die? Were they at work today earning a living or lying in a cemetery, as Baker had once said, silent as an oyster.

She first opened her own folder. One by one she went through the ten or so sheets. She was surprised that she recognized all of the paperwork. Admissions form, releases, next of kin notifications, form approving cremation, and a religious preference sheet, and finally a breakdown of medical costs. It included the additional twenty-five dollars a week for Ivan's room and board described as Special Requirements.

In Mossell's folder was a carbon copy of the letter to Mossell's niece Beulah Murphy, just as Mossell had described to Eva.

It read:

> *Dear Beulah,*
>
> *I've been at the Baker Hospital for three weeks and I'm enjoying it so much. I'm feeling stronger than ever, but I've been told I need at least a few more weeks of care before I can go home. Since you are handling my finances in my absence, could you please send Dr. Baker a check for $200. That should be enough for future expenses.*
>
> *I love you. Send my love to the kids.*
>
> *Aunt Mossy*

"Aunt Mossy?" Eva laughed as she repeated the signature.

The air grew icy and rank and a voice next to the bed asked, "What's so funny about that?"

Eva jumped away from the smell. "I wish you wouldn't do that!"

Ivan shrank to the foot of the bed, folded his ears flat against his head, and spit.

"Just think of all the joy I bring to your miserable life whenever you talk to me." Mossell moved in closer to the cat. "I can't believe you're acting this way around me. It's such a shame to let death come between such good friends."

Her words sent the cat slinking backward even farther.

"Ah, you found the letters. See, I told you he was a crook. Baker guarantee. What a con."

Eva held up the onionskin carbon copy of the letter. "I haven't had a chance to go through the others, but I did find a letter like that in your file."

"See, what did I tell you, pansy? You need to get those to the FBI or the postal inspector or whoever.

Eva nodded.

"That's a good girl."

Eva placed her hand over her nose. The smell brought back memories when she was a little girl and her beloved mutt Wilbur disappeared. When she ran across the smell in her Dad's field she thought it was a coon or a fox. But it was Wilbur, covered in bugs and worms, looking like he was sinking into the ground, bones sticking out of stiffened fur. Her mom tried to tell Eva that Wilbur was in Heaven. That rotting body wasn't really him any longer. But any time she caught a whiff of death, it made her sick—sick in her body, sick in her soul.

She groped for the emesis basin and filled it.

Mossell moved back. "Sorry about that, gumdrop. The smell's Baker's fault, too. If he'd just fix that damn refrigerator."

A rattling at the doorknob caught their attention. Eva fumbled to turn off the flashlight and shoved the folders under the covers. Mossell disappeared in a gray haze.

Turner opened the door and reeled back, hand to her nose. "It's got to be that cat! None of the other rooms smell like this."

Eva's heart was racing as Turner leaned over to take her pulse. Eva jolted upright as she had on so many nights here.

This time it was Turner's turn to be startled. "Good Lord, Miss Dupree. Do you have to do that each time I check on you?"

Feigning innocent fear Eva clutched fists to her breast. "If only you wouldn't sneak up on me when you come in. Can't you just knock?"

"I don't knock because I don't want to wake you."

Eva noticed the bulge of the flashlight under the blanket. She shifted her leg a little to camouflage it.

The nurse tucked the sheet beneath the mattress, and while doing so, leaned over to sniff Ivan, who curled up next to Eva.

On her way out, she popped her head in the bathroom and looked puzzled.

Eva felt like she was back at the farm with her mom again, waiting until Mamma was in bed so she could read. She'd take a kerosene lantern under the covers, but between the fumes and heat from the lamp, she could only read in short spurts. The flashlight was a vast improvement. With it, she could read until dawn.

A few minutes after Turner left, Eva returned to her research. She flipped through Annabelle Nichols' file. There were dated carbon copies of letters asking for more money, but no undated originals.

When she could no longer keep her eyes open, she hid the files in the top drawer of the desk. She returned to bed and snuggled up with Ivan.

While exhausted she couldn't stop reliving those moments in Baker's penthouse. Over and over again, she heard the keys clinking on the other side of the door as she raced to reach the hidden passage. Then her mind switched to home and all the things being neglected there. Before she could focus on any of them for long, however, her thoughts jumped back to Eureka Springs. Was she doing the right thing?

Next she imagined Norman Baker in prison, his prison suit striped purple and white instead of black and white. He also wore a crown of thorns. He held a chalice, which he offered to her. Even in his agony, he handed her his gift of life. With the image of the sacrificial Baker etched into her mind, she opened her eyes.

She stared at the white plaster ceiling above her. She just wanted to sleep. But sleep escaped her. And as all the doubts and fears circled in her head, a misty form appeared above her. She froze. Oh, no...Not more specters.

The apparition floated above her for a while, then slowly dropped down, engulfing her. She tried to scream but her throat closed tight, barely even letting her breathe. Ghostly fingers ran down her cheek, then, to her terror, the cold moved to her ear and whispered, "I want you."

A moment later the thing disappeared as suddenly as it appeared. Her throat released. She clapped her hands over her mouth to keep from screaming and bringing Nurse Turner in, but when the urge to cry out passed, she pulled herself upright against the head of the bed, switched on the light, cuddled Ivan, and spent the rest of the night rocking back and forth in her bed.

DAY THIRTEEN—*Tuesday, September 12*

Today was the dreaded shot-in-the-gut day. It always rolled around so quickly. After her treatment, Eva slept. Her body seemed to be adjusting to the medicine; instead of suffering from nausea and fever the entire day, she felt queasy for a little while, then felt just a dull discomfort.

Before Rose arrived, she wanted a chance to go over those files a little closer. After all, she needed to know what she was getting ready to turn over to the FBI.

With the bathroom door closed, she sat on the toilet and flipped through the folders and then placed them on the floor.

Ivan, sitting on the windowsill next to the toilet, supervised the investigation. He pawed at her arm...gently at first. As she continued to ignore him, the demands became more direct, patting with claws fully extended. Eva reached over and gave him an absent scratch under the chin. Apparently that wasn't good enough for him. He spun around and took a running dive at the folders, scattering papers and onionskin copies all over the bathroom floor.

Ivan's drive for affection was one of his most endearing qualities, as well as one of his most maddening ones.

She picked up the cat, gave him a kiss on the top of the head and set him outside the door. After she'd exiled him, she gathered up the papers and filed them back in their, hopefully, proper folder. Mossell Louise Knight, Eva Grace Dupree, Annabelle Velda Nichols, Stefan Janowitz, Mary Catherine and Gertrude Elizabeth Trent—a rather interesting collection of names. And paperwork that didn't make sense: onionskin carbon copies of letters asking for more money, an original request for additional funds that was dated a month before, and all kinds of miscellaneous correspondence.

But was this, as Sherlock Holmes said, the smoking gun? It didn't seem that incriminating to her, but she'd let the FBI sort it out.

Tapping the bottoms of the folders against the floor made the paper piles inside nice and neat. As soon as Rose arrived Eva could get rid of the evidence.

Rose came and left in record time. She changed Ivan's sanitary pan and set out his food, and left in fewer than ten minutes. She and Eva exchanged only a dozen words the whole time, but their looks, glances and nods communicated volumes.

Originally Eva was going to have Rose take the papers to the Carroll County Sheriff. But now Eva feared word would somehow get back to Baker that she had broken into his penthouse and raided his private files. It just didn't seem wise to enrage a guy who dangled a Tommy gun by a nail under his desk. No, she'd have to get the papers directly to the FBI.

Rose pretended to shop, until all the customers had left and the clerk was occupied in another part of Wofford's Eureka Pharmacy.

It was a pleasant store that smelled of bitter pharmaceuticals and spicy herbs. Shelves filled with clear, brown, and cobalt medicine bottles and jars completely covered one wall for the entire length of the drug store. Tiny palm trees in small pots perched atop the rows. The other wall with showcases and tall displays contained all sorts of personal necessities and gift items. Shorter showcases doubled as counters. In the center of the store a tall wheel display rack held hundreds of greeting and postal cards. Tucked away in the back of the pharmacy Rose found the telephone booth.

Stalling for time Rose, picked through the greeting card rack. Every one of the postal cards had a linen finish. Many of them showed scenes from around greater Eureka Springs. Not surprisingly, they also had a nice selection of Baker Hospital cards.

Once the other customers had cleared out, Rose sat down inside the phone booth amid the lingering scents of cigarettes and chewing gum, and closed the folded door. She fished a handful of coins from her purse and began feeding the pay slot. The phone clicked and dinged. She slid off her heavy shoes and wiggled her toes. It felt so good to sit down and take the weight off of her tired old dawgs. Hopefully, it would take a while to reach the FBI. While she waited for the operator to answer, she lit another Kool. Despite the privacy of the enclosed booth, when the operator came on, she leaned forward to almost touch the mouthpiece and she pressed the earpiece tightly against her ear. Quietly she asked the operator to connect her with the FBI in Little Rock.

As the operator instructed, Rose fed the phone some more, then took a deep puff off her cigarette, flicking ashes in the ashtray.

Finally a young nasally female voice answered with, "Federal

Bureau of Investigation."

"I need to talk to your head officer," Rose said.

"Bob Waller is the special agent in charge of the Little Rock field office. He's in a meeting. I'm sure one of our other investigators can help you."

Rose clinched the earpiece all the more firmly. "No ma'am. I need to talk to the head man."

"That won't be possible. Why don't you tell me what you want? I'll find someone."

Rose hesitated, glancing out the booth window to make sure there wasn't anyone who could overhear her through the door. "It's about a man whose taking advantage of widows."

"You'll need to call your local police about that."

Eva had already briefed the maid with responses. "I understand using the post office makes it a federal offense. He's using the mail and we have the proof."

"And who's this man?" the woman asked.

"Norman Baker of the Baker Hospital and Health Resort." *So there*, Rose added in a thought.

"Just a minute."

While waiting for the director, Rose finished her Kool. She looked at her pack. Only one smoke left. She'd have to pick up another pack.

Finally Bob Waller, special agent in charge of the Little Rock Field Office of the FBI came on the line and after hearing what she said, to her relief replied that, yes, he wanted to take a look at the evidence she had.

It had been a very long afternoon. Even with the belly shot this morning Eva found it hard to sit with nothing to do. She'd read her film magazine for a minute, but she couldn't keep her mind on the article about Shirley Temple. Who cared about the pint-size starlet anyway? It's a sin that a ten-year old could enjoy that much success.

She considered what it must be like to make a film today. So different from her years in front of the camera. She thought about all those pages and pages of lines, and having to worry about how to say it, not just the words, but the way they said them: the tone, volume, and her pronounced east Texas accent. She remembered the day Roger Knight cancelled her contract. He'd gotten a new starlet—younger, blond, and willing to do anything—and she knew that really meant anything—to get the part. For Roger the timing was perfect. He'd gotten tired of trying to get Eva to play out a love scene—actually a lust scene. So, the arrival of the sound era gave Roger the perfect opportunity to dump her without raising any eyebrows unnecessarily. After all, he couldn't produce a talking picture with a leading lady who sounds like a Walt Disney duck with an East Texas drawl.

Of course, in those moments when Eva faced the truth, she had to acknowledge the fact that the films she made with Roger and Edgar were hardly *Birth of a Nation* or even *Metropolis*. If DeMille's *Ben Hur*, with its expensive Technicolor scenes, was a five-star movie, her favorite role *Caught in a Web* was a two. Her pictures were popular, but hardly art.

Sitting alone in her room didn't help. Her nerves were frayed worrying about Rose. Every time Eva thought about her, she thought of something that could go wrong. Rose could get on the wrong connection, someone could rob her, the officials could simply choose to ignore her.

Eva tried listening to the radio, but even news of the new war in Europe couldn't distract her from the abysmal wait ahead of her. She had to find something to do beside let the minutes drag by. She made her way to the vanity and ran a brush through her hair. "Maybe we should go outside and enjoy this beautiful day," she said to Ivan. "Want to join me?"

He held up his head, blinked deliberately and yawned.

"Have it your way." She left the door ajar so Ivan could join her if he had the mind for it.

It was an active day on the observation deck. Everyone who was anyone, or rather, still alive, was catching some sunlight. There was a whole new group of faces...some looking tired and hopeful, others clearly just waiting to die.

The sun had crested above them and was just beginning its afternoon descent, casting short shadows in front of them. This time of day the greenery on East Mountain looked surreal, like a painting. Soon she'd be trading in her mountain sunsets for either a limited view of her modest flower garden, or of course, there was a possibility that her view would be limited to the inside of a casket. Eva decided that even if just for a little while longer, she would make it a point to enjoy this scene in all its glory.

She hesitated in the doorway. Cooper Reilly sat in one of the rocking chairs chatting with a new patient.

She now understood how Ivan felt when he stood in the door whipping his tail as he decided whether he really wanted to explore the deck or stay in the safety of the room. She, too, felt torn between going out on the deck and hiding in her suite.

She sighed wishing she could give Cooper a chance. He appeared to be such a kind man. Ivan certainly liked him. Edgar's cat had always been a good judge of people. The cat had hated a gardener she hired the year before. He'd hiss and scratch any time the man wanted to get friendly. The workman seemed nice enough and knew his flowers, but she found out he'd done time on a chain gang for murder.

So Ivan's endorsement of Cooper was not without its merit. Still, Eva didn't feel like plunging into a new relationship; not yet. Edgar had been gone such a short time. And even if she wanted to spend time with Cooper, it might be brief. Very brief, since the Baker Cure appeared to be little more than snake oil. Quietly she closed the door.

She needed something to do...something to keep her mind busy at least for a while. It had been a few days since she practiced piano. Her hands could use a good workout. She pulled the sheet music from the vanity.

She made her way down the north stairway and through the lobby. As always, patients had gathered next to the disused fireplace, visiting. Like the patients who met on the balcony, some read, a lady embroidered, another knitted and one man read his ham radio magazine, *QST*. Others gossiped. Some of them she recognized from the fourth floor balcony.

She pointed at the grand piano with the roll of music in her hand. "Do y'all mind if I get some practice in?"

Her question was answered by a chorus of, "That's fine," "Be my guest," "Please do," and "We'd love to hear you play."

She smiled and set up the music for Glenn Miller's *Moonlight Serenade*. She wiggled her fingers to limber them, followed by playing. She played a C cord then a series of scales up and down the keyboard. The off-pitch keys set her cringing. The piano needed tuning badly.

"Miss Dupree, could you play something cheerful?" Mr. Dye snapped his Kodak Brownie Flash. The flashbulb exploded a pop and crackle.

Normally, she'd play scales for a full thirty minutes to thoroughly cover all fifteen major keys, but she could see that her audience was becoming restless.

"Sure," she answered. "But I'm afraid I mainly know hymns. I don't know a lot of popular pieces." She played "Jerusalem," an old Church of England hymn she'd learned from the bishop's organist a few years earlier, and sang along.

> *"And did those feet in ancient time,*
> *Walk upon England's mountains green?"*
> *"And was the Holy Lamb of God*
> *On England's pleasant pastures seen?"*

A grumpy old man sitting alone interrupted her concert. "I didn't come down here to listen to no church service."

"Oh, Mr. Thadeus, don't spoil it for us," pleaded one of the women sewing on a quilt. "If you don't want to hear her play, you can go to the bowling alley."

"Hmmrf." He stood up and shuffled away from his wicker chair next to the piano.

Eva stood up herself and rummaged through the sheet music stored inside the bench seat. "I'm not the world's best sight reader," Eva confessed, "but if I find something you like I'll give it a try. Let's see, we have *Happy Days Are Here Again*."

That was something almost everyone could enjoy. Quickly everyone joined in singing the old Ben Selvin song. *Baby Face* followed *Happy Days* and then *Begin the Beguine*, and *Pennies From Heaven*. The singsong moved along as fast as Mr. Baker's 1937 Cord Convertible. As each song ended, they all laughed and applauded.

Every few minutes Mr. Dye would blind her with the flashbulb from his Kodak camera. It was certainly distracting, but not nearly as bad as the old open powder flash Eva had to suffer through during publicity shots. That was like standing next to an explosion with a flash of fire and a puff of smoke and burning through her sinuses. Roger Knight always waited until they were finished filming a scene to take the stills because, in a poorly ventilated set, it took forever for the smoke to clear and sometimes it triggered attacks of wheezing and gasping in some of the cast.

The woman who had been knitting left, missing a few songs. A few minutes later she came out of the gift shop with some sheet music of her own. "Mrs. Dupree, would you play this for me?"

"I'll try." She scanned the music and ran through the first few cords. Although not nearly as smoothly performed, Eva valiantly attempted the song Judy Garland performed in *The Wizard of Oz*. Apparently, her lack of polish didn't bother her audience. They oohed and aahed and cheered when she completed, *Somewhere over the Rainbow*.

Just as she finished playing the last notes, someone asked her, "Did you lose something?"

She turned to face Cooper who held a contented Ivan in his arms. "I found him on the observation deck alone. I think he wants his mama." He made no effort to release his charge.

"What was he doing there?"

"I think your door blew open. He started crying so I thought I should help the little orphan out." He and Ivan sat down in the vacant chair next to the piano. "Don't let us disturb you. Finish your concert."

She smiled. "Do you have a request?"

He thought about it. "How about *I'll Be Seeing You*?"

"I'm afraid I don't have the music for that one." And she didn't know whether or not she was sorry.

"Miss Eva, would you play this one?" Another woman handed her some more newly purchased music.

"Sure." She took it and glanced at it. She swallowed hard. *Thanks For the Memory* by Shep Fields. Edgar had loved that song. How would she ever get through it? "I don't know if I can play this one very well. It's a very difficult piece."

"Nonsense," the lady countered. "My husband's a lousy pianist and he can play it. If he can play it, you can. Please. It would mean so much. I really miss him."

She made herself smile. "I'll try."

Next to her, Ivan started to wiggle in Cooper's arms. He loosened his hold and allowed the cat to jump to the piano top and watch Eva from above.

It used to drive Eva crazy when the cat climbed up on her piano at home to watch her play, but eventually she got used to the furry, but appreciative audience. More recently, on days when he chose to let her practice solo, she missed him.

As she played the first few notes, Ivan peered at the keyboard, following every movement of her fingers. He reached down with his paw and swatted at her, claws safely retracted, when her fingers moved tantalizingly near his perch.

She completed the notes of the introduction.

"Thanks for the memory," Mr. Dye sang very off-key. *"Of candle-light and wine, castles on the Rhine, the Parthenon and moments on the Hudson River Line, How lovely it was."*

Midway through the first stanza, Eva's fingers began to falter. Her eyes filled with tears. She should have said no to the request. Suddenly, in a room full of people she felt so very alone. Then Cooper leaned over the keyboard. He lost a bar or two of melody, but filled in the musical void with clumsily played notes and encouraged the audience to join in with his own voice. Although he didn't play the full arrangement; he played the melody line with his right hand. His pace was not as smooth as Eva's but he managed to maintain the mood and allow her to gain her composure.

Eva slid to the side, giving him room to sit beside her on the bench. And even though Cooper struggled unevenly through the song, no one seemed to mind.

Then a familiar feeling overtook her, and she couldn't tell if she was choked by some unseen force or her own sadness. Like the helpless feeling she felt in her suite, she was enveloped by a cold breezy sensation.

Still feeling distant, the song progressed with blended voices, some better than others, *"We said goodbye with a highball, then I got as "high" as a steeple, But we were intelligent people, No tears, no fuss, Hooray! For us."*

Next to her, Mr. Dye took a photo with a sizzle of the flashbulb.

And just like in her room the Arctic feeling abandoned her as quickly as it had come. Her voice regained, she tentatively joined in on the last verse. Cooper moved away, letting her once again assume control of the keyboard.

"Thank you," she said to Cooper as she rose from the bench. "I couldn't have finished it without you."

"I know." He smiled and gave the cat a quick pat.

Her hands grew tired and Ivan grew restless...the perfect explanation to excuse herself. She and Ivan returned to her suite. It would be a long night of worry about Rose's upcoming trip.

If everything went according to plan Rose would take the seven a.m. train to Little Rock. To make it to the Arkansas capital, she'd have to transfer trains at least a couple of times. While the trip wouldn't have been a problem for Eva, herself, she worried about an older Negro woman traveling alone. There was always someone that wanted to abuse or take advantage of colored servants. To up the ante Rose would be carrying valuable cargo: the letters. If someone robbed her, the loss wouldn't be what little money she had on her, but the evidence. How safe or successful her mission was, Eva wouldn't know until Rose returned, tomorrow night at the earliest. Tomorrow would be a very long day.

DAY FOURTEEN—*Wednesday, September 13*

Rose looked at the scrap of paper with the address. Yes, this three-story building was 367 March Street. In her imagination, the Federal Bureau of Investigation office was a grand marble building with antebellum columns—a place where the pursuit of justice takes place. Her perfect world federal office had a foyer filled with fedora-wearing men in dark suits guarding the place with Tommy guns. The reality was a plain red brick office that was, well, a dump. She guessed she'd seen a few too many gangster movies with Miss Eva.

Eva enjoyed movies and dinner out but not alone. After Edgar died, she drafted Rose to come along. Even to restaurants. Once when a restaurant wouldn't let Rose eat in front, Eva bought the strip mall and raised the rent so high the diner closed.

But how would the FBI treat her?

Rose took a deep breath and braced herself to fight if necessary. She leaned against the red brick and pulled off her shoe. A small pebble fell out, and hit the pavement with a tick. Her feet ached and her knees throbbed.

As Rose massaged the arch of her foot she wondered what had possessed her to agree to this trip. Would she ever learn to say no to Miss Eva? Probably not.

A decade ago, when Rose's daughter, Tessie, died suddenly from an asthma attack, Miss Eva insisted that she take all that time off. Rose was surprised to find her pay envelope on the kitchen table with the regular amount tucked inside. She was even more surprised when she went to the funeral parlor to make the arrangements for Tessie, and found an anonymous white woman had already paid for her burial spot. Naturally, Rose found the plot on the outskirts of the cemetery, in the colored section. But Tessie had been given a lovely marble headstone with a cherub carved into it, with the inscription, "Mother's little angel" etched into the bottom. Rose cried when the undertaker showed her the stone.

"I always called her My Little Angel," she told him.

Eva never admitted to the deed, but Rose had never looked at her boss' wife quite the same way again.

Rose took a deep breath and stepped into the building. It was a welcome refuge against the pounding September sun. She checked the directory next to the elevator.

Clutching her canvas bag tightly to her breast, she climbed the stairs and found the office she wanted at the end of the second story hall. The words "Federal Bureau of Investigation—Little Rock Division" were painted in black on the smooth side of textured glass.

Rose straightened her dress, dabbed the sweat off of her upper lip with her hankie and opened the door. Behind the reception desk sat a young white woman about twenty-five. She tapped a cigarette into an ashtray and looked up at Rose.

The receptionist sat behind a desk painted dog turd brown, talking on the telephone.

"Yes, Frankie. I understand." She glanced up at Rose, but kept talking. "I don't care if she is your mother. I don't have to put up with her saying that about me."

Rose continued to stand and wait patiently.

"I'm sorry she doesn't have your daddy no more."

Once again she looked at Rose, placed her hand over the mouthpiece and said, "I'll be with you in a few minutes."

"Yes ma'am. So that's official FBI business, is it?" Rose asked nodding at the phone.

The receptionist wrinkled her over-plucked eyebrows. Staring at Rose, she hesitantly continued her conversation. "I gotta go Frankie. There's someone here that needs help...No. I don't think she can wait. I'll call you back in a little while. All right. Bye." She looked at Rose. "Now, what do you want?"

"I need to talk to..." She glanced down at her notes. "...Special Investigator Waller."

The receptionist looked Rose up and down. "He's in a meeting. One of our other investigators can help you."

Rose clutched her bag all the more firmly and looked over her reading glasses. "No ma'am. I need to talk to the headman. I'm here for Miss Eva Dupree. He's expecting me."

The receptionist had white blonde hair—shoulder length with waves all the way down to the ends. She wore too much lipstick and powder that was a little too dark for her pale skin.

"I need to see the man in charge," Rose repeated.

"What would you like to see him about?" the receptionist asked.

"I have information."

The receptionist tapped in the phone receiver with her finger-nails. "What kind of information?"

Rose pulled it next to her chest. "I'll discuss *that* with the head investigator."

"Special Investigator Waller is in a meeting right now. Investigator Rogers is available to talk to you. I'll get him."

"And who is Mr. Rogers?" Rose's left eyebrow rose dubiously.

"He's the deputy investigator's assistant. I'm sure he'll be able to help you."

"Told you that Mr. Waller's 'pecting me. I'll wait until he's free. How long will that be?"

Irritated, the receptionist tapped her long red fingernails against the desk. "Look if you can just tell me what you need I can help you better."

"Miss…" Rose looked at the nameplate on the woman's desk. "Miss Klegg, I have some evidence for a case that has interested the FBI for a decade. Those papers aren't leaving my hand till I give them to the man in charge. Ain't leaving until I unload these papers." Then to arouse a little sympathy, Rose added, "If I gave this to someone besides Mr. Waller, my boss lady would have my hide…and yours. I'll wait. Your boyfriend is waiting." Rose nodded at the phone.

Clutching her purse tightly, Rose went over to a row of uncomfortable oak straight-backed chairs. It might take some time before the head investigator showed up. She pulled out her tattered pocket New Testament and began to read the Gospel of Mark.

Miss Klegg picked up the phone and called her friend back. Apparently they resumed their conversation at the exact place they left off.

Rose took off her shoe and massaged her sore foot. Why would she go to all this trouble for her measly paycheck?

Rose looked up from her Bible. The secretary kept glancing her direction. Finally, Frankie must have said something that grabbed her attention because she started talking into the phone at twenty miles an hour and motioning exaggeratedly with her free hand.

Rose waited until the receptionist became wrapped up in her conversation again, then went to get a drink from the Colored drinking fountain. She looked around and finally found the door with "Special Investigator Bob Waller," painted in black on the glass. Rose walked over and knocked on the door.

"Yes?" came the answer from within.

She opened the door to find a large middle-aged man with a balding sandy head behind the large oak desk in the center of the room. A plume of smoke rose from the half-smoked cigar imbedded between his stubby fingers. His feet were propped up on the desk and crossed at the ankles. His pants had ridden up exposing a patch of hairy leg. His suspenders fell loosely at his side. Behind him his suit coat and charcoal fedora hung from a coat rack. Across from his desk a couple of men in similar dress sat in uncomfortable straight back chairs. One drew deeply from a cigarette and the other chewed on a cigar from the side of his mouth.

"I need to see Mr. Waller," Rose said firmly.

"I'm Bob Waller." He placed the cigar in the square glass ashtray and let it smolder.

The air smelled thick and stale and the room looked like it was filled with a Houston fog.

"I'm Rose Freeman."

"You don't say? Someone threaten to hang a friend of yours?"

She set her jaw. "I spoke to you yesterday. I'm here for Miss Eva Dupree of Dallas. I got some evidence concerning the Baker Hospital in Eureka Springs. If you're not interested, I'll just send these papers to your Moline office. My boss lady tells me they've been after this man for ten years. They'd be right interested in this evidence."

"Sit down, Mrs. ..." Waller motioned to the man with the cigarette to vacate the chair.

"Freeman. Rose Freeman." She sat down and set her heavy leather purse on the desk with a sound thunk. "Miss Dupree is a patient at the Baker Cancer Hospital in Eureka Springs. She believes that there are, as she put it, dubious activities afoot there." Rose rummaged through her purse and handed him a white Baker Hospital envelope labeled in Eva's elegant script, "FBI".

Rose handed him the stack of manila folders. It contained a letter from Mossell to her niece, contact information for the niece, letters from Eva to her niece and carbon copies of letters from the other patients.

Waller opened the envelope and began to read:

To Whom It May Concern,

I am presently a patient at the Baker Cancer Hospital in Eureka Springs, Arkansas. I have been here for over two weeks and have *noticed some irregularities. I believe I have information that will help you successfully prosecute Norman Baker for mail fraud.*

I could not contact any of the local law enforcement because I can't be certain that they are not loyal to Norman Baker, the hospital owner. Assuming the worst, I've sent my servant, Rose Freeman, to deliver to you the letters that Baker sends out. Maybe this evidence will be helpful.

The Baker Cancer Hospital has a treatment guarantee. When certain patients check into the hospital, usually wealthy widows with no immediate family, Mr. Baker makes them sign three letters that state to the affect, "I am feeling much better; send more money." He keeps these in a private file in the event of the patient's death. Upon their passing away, Mr. Baker sends out the first letter to the person who is responsible for the lady's finances. Usually, the family member responds by sending the appropriate funds. Then other letters are sent out. When those funds are also received, Mr. Baker finally mails a letter saying that the dear loved one has unfortunately passed away. What would you, as a loving family member, like him to do? You can either make the difficult trek to Eureka Springs to coordinate the funeral or Baker could handle the arrangements himself.

Since these families are all the way across the country, and the relative always distant, the answer is inevitably, "Please go ahead and handle the arrangements."

The bodies are then loaded into an onsite furnace and cremated.

This has apparently been going on since he opened the hospital here in 1937.

If you choose to pursue this case, I advise you to contact the American Medical Association and the Muscatine office of the FBI and perhaps the Iowa State Board of Medicine. I'm sure they'll have lots of interesting tidbits about Mr. Baker.

He has armed security guarding the hospital grounds and an excellent vantage point atop the Baker Hospital. Norman Baker, himself, keeps a machine gun under his desk and two very large dogs in his penthouse as protection. If you attempt a straightforward arrest at the hospital, there is a good chance that innocent patients or hospital personnel will suffer.

Mr. Baker has confided in me that he will be in Little Rock on September 16 to talk to Mr. Hal Collins from Mineral Wells, Texas about a franchise deal. This would be the perfect time to confront him without risking innocent patients and staff."

Waller paused for a moment and reread that paragraph. He smiled broadly. "We've got him. But we're going to have to really push it." He returned to the letter.

> *He would not be a difficult man to spot. He traditionally wears a white suit with a lavender shirt and drives an ostentatious orchid-colored Cord Convertible. This vehicle stands out in a crowd to say the least.*
>
> *As incredible as this sounds, this is not a hoax. If you do not believe me, contact the American Medical Association. Norman Baker proudly discusses his run-ins with them. I'm sure some of the physicians around Muscatine would verify my claims.*
>
> *I will be happy to give you whatever help I can. My housekeeper, Rose Freeman will act as my messenger, as I cannot have any direct communications with you.*
>
> *Sincerely,*
> *Eva Dupree.*

As Waller read through the letters, he glanced up at Rose with more interest. "And you know all about what's happening in this hospital?"

"Yes, sir. I do," she answered.

He stood up. "I'll have to ask you to step out of the room while I make a few calls. Would you care for a cup of coffee?"

"That would be mighty fine," she said.

Rose sat in the lobby smoking and drinking a cup of coffee so strong it would have removed that pretty lavender paint from Mr. Baker's car. Through it all Rose sat patiently and read her Bible. She would exercise the patience of Job, as she always did. And if that didn't work she'd kick their white hinnies all the way back to Muscatine.

After she sat there for over an hour, Waller finally opened his office door.

"Miss Klegg, get Cooper and Rickey in here right away." He looked to Rose and said, "Please don't leave yet. I'm still looking into this. It won't be much longer now."

She nodded silently and returned her attention to the Gospel.

A few minutes later a tall slender older man dashed into Waller's office. A little later, his opposite, a short stumpy young agent, ran in and slammed the door behind him.

Rose set down her Bible and lit another smoke. She was running low. She'd need to pick up another pack before she took the long train ride back to Eureka Springs.

Finally the dumpy fat man opened the door. "Mr. Waller would like to see you, now."

She put her Bible back in her bag and put out her smoldering butt before following him.

Once again Special Investigator Waller offered her one of those uncomfortable seats. He returned to his own desk. "Thank Mrs. Dupree for me. As you know, we've been investigating Norman Baker for several years. As a matter of fact, we had lost track of him for a while. We've looked for him everywhere but with Amelia Earhart. We'll need to go over this new evidence."

Eva sat alone on the fainting couch in the living area of her suite. This was the longest day she'd spent at the Baker Hospital. A few minutes earlier the nurse brought her a glass of ice so she could drink some miraculous Ozark Mountain water. She did drink some of that cleansing water, just adding a generous helping of Scottish whiskey to sterilize the glass.

Nearby, Ivan suddenly announced with a low, gritty yowl that he wanted to play a game. He galloped into the bathroom at full speed, sliding, and when his brakes failed, smashed into the tub with a crash. Shaking his head, he dashed out into the middle of the living area, bucked like a bronco, spun in a semicircle and flopped down at her feet expecting a belly rub with a rub hither look on his face.

She took a drink. "I know that expression." She drained the glass. "You want to show me your Venus Fly Trap. I'll pass."

He held his head up as if to say, "You know you wanna."

Eva grabbed the pigeon feather laying on the end table. She tickled his chin with the feather. As she expected, the trap closed around the teaser and took it away. It now belonged to him. Using his claws fingers, Ivan gnawed on the tip of the shaft.

If Edgar was here there would be an animated game of chase. Tonight there would be no rousing romp—at least not one with her as an active participant. However, that didn't mean she couldn't entertain him. She feigned a grab at the feather, but he jumped up, with his prize in his mouth, and dashed off.

The game was effectively over and the drink glass empty except for a couple of cubes of ice. Eva decided that the ice was lonely, so she poured another drink to keep it company. She made sure the scotch was well hidden. Couldn't have the nurses confiscating her only escape from reality. She polished off a third drink, and leaned her head on the arm of the fainting couch. Instead of feeling better, the room seemed to spin around.

"I told you that shit'll kill you, *schatzi*."

Eva didn't have to open her eyes. "Go away."

"I'm proud of you."

"Great." Eva said brusquely.

"And, snuggie, what did you do with the papers?"

Eyes still closed, Eva answered, "Rose took them to the FBI in Little Rock."

"Delicious. He'll live to regret cheating me." She smiled broadly.

"Mossell, you stink and I'm getting ready to throw up."

The ghost faded away, and Eva slept the rest of an uneventful night, snoring softly on the fainting couch.

DAY FIFTEEN—*Thursday, September 14*

Thursday was like any other day at the Baker Hospital, except that Rose was absent. She ought to be arriving in Eureka Springs late in the afternoon. Until then, Eva simply had to wait and worry.

Unfortunately, Ivan's toilet couldn't wait till later, so once again she had to perform the maid duties herself.

Late in the afternoon Rose came dragging in. Uncharacteristically, she dropped her overnight bag next to the door. Perspiration had collected on her brow and dripped down the back of her neck. Eva could tell the trip had taken a toll on her.

"This is too much for an old woman to go through," Rose sighed.

Eva helped unload her by taking her purse and leading her to the armchair. "How'd it go?"

Rose flopped down in the easy chair, leaned back and dabbed her brow with her already moist hanky. "Got to get me some new feet. These ones aren't working so good."

"You thirsty?"

"Yes, ma'am. I'll get some water."

"Not water. Something better. Stay there." She went into the bathroom and returned with something draped by a towel. Eva held it from the bottom and ripped the drape away like a magician revealing the disappearing bunny. Beneath the hand towel was an aluminum Baker Hospital water pitcher holding a bottle of Old Heidelberg and packed to the brim with ice cubes. She popped the cap off with the church key and presented it over her arm with the finesse of a Brown Derby waiter. Condensation rolled down the bottle and dripped onto the wood plank floor.

"I believe," Eva said, "this was a very good year—whatever year it was."

"Miss Eva." Rose wiped the sweat from her top lip. "That's about the most scrumptious looking thing I ever seen." Closing her eyes, she drew a long drink from the bottle, sighing with satisfaction. "That's mighty good."

"You earned it."

Ivan trotted over, sniffed a drop of water, then licked it up. Rose invited him to join her by patting her lap. Not being able to resist such an invitation, he jumped up on the chair.

Eva fixed herself an icy scotch and water and sat down."

"Well, what happened?"

"Talked to Head Special Agent Waller. He's the one over the Little Rock officers. Says they'd been working on the Baker case for several years and you did the right thing by sending the evidence to him. Didn't say much except that he'd go over our letters. Said that the information about Mr. Baker coming to town was right helpful. He asked a couple of questions. Then a bunch of them agents got together and asked more questions. He said they're going to keep an eye out for him."

Eva nodded. "He won't be hard to find."

"Not in that big ol' purple car," Rose agreed. "And once he and the other man sit down in the restaurant, they'll surround him and arrest him."

"Guess we'll see in a few days how badly they want *Doctor* Baker." She sarcastically emphasized the word "doctor."

"That's sure enough." Rose took another swig.

Eva couldn't help but feel disappointed. She'd hoped Rose would return with tales of how they grilled her for information, demanded detailed descriptions of Baker or his car, or wanting more information about who he was meeting. But Rose's recollection was brief and to the point. And it sounded like her meeting was too. Waller would look into it. Period. No promises, or tipping his cards, if he had any.

DAY SIXTEEN—*Friday, September 15*

"Miss Dupree?"

Someone gently shook her.

"Miss Dupree," Nurse Cavanaugh said urgently. "You need to wake up. I can't find your cat. You need to look for him, don't you think?"

Eva sat up. "What?"

The nurse held up her robe. "The hall door to your suite was ajar when I came to check on you. I did a quick look around the suite and didn't see him. I brought your coffee."

Eva felt the same dread she did before her belly shot.

"After you've found him, come back and I'll give you your treatment. If I lost my dog I wouldn't be able to sit still for a moment."

Eva downed the coffee in a single gulp, not even tasting it. Seconds later she had jumped into her clothes and dashed out the door to the deck.

"Has anyone seen my cat?"

A new patient whom Eva had never seen before said, "Oh, is that your cat? He's really pretty."

"Where'd you see him?" Eva quizzed the woman.

She was an older lady and tapped her chin as she thought. "I was sitting right here, because I don't have anything else to do while I'm getting better, ya know. Anyway I was watching this big red and white cat play around in the dirt...right down there." She pointed to the ground below. "He headed off that way, ya know." She pointed south. "He acted like he had a list of things to do today. He was a big cat."

Eva barely took time to thank the lady. She flew down the stairs and started searching to the south of the hospital building through waist-high weeds. The knife-sharp blades nicked one finger.

"Ivan!" she called.

She spotted a trail, and crossing her fingers, followed it up and down several slopes until she heard a familiar male voice.

"Ivan, you scoundrel," Cooper yelled.

Eva stopped and listened.

"Give me that...No, you can't have it. You have to give it to me."

Stealthily, she moved closer to the voice, but stayed concealed in the high grass and tall scrub. Finally, she could make out Cooper's form. He was wearing a wool newsboy cap and a fishing vest that looked a great deal like the one she donned for the great Baker Caper. Next to him lay an open metal tackle box. In his hand he held a fishing rod. He had his arms back, poised to cast his line into a small stock pond—only he didn't. Instead, the lure flew a foot from the shoreline where the water was just a few inches deep.

A furry white and red streak splashed into the water after the lure. Just before Ivan reached it, Cooper tugged, sending the lure airborne once again.

Eva gasped, imagining the barb biting into the cat's paw pads. But something made her continue watching in silence. Catching the lure, Ivan swung his chest around and trapped the bait in his paws.

"I've got a big one," Cooper said. "He's a fighter. He's a big one. Funniest catfish I've ever seen." He tugged some. "You're a strange cat, Ivan. I've never seen one of your kind that liked water. And you fetch. You're more like a dog than a cat. You think your mama got friendly with a golden retriever?"

He continued his one-sided discussion. "I don't know how you found me, all the way down here. I need to make sure you get back to the hospital safe. Don't want anything to happen to you. You may not know it, but you're one lucky cat, Ivan," Cooper confided. "Eva Dupree takes good care of you. She's a nice lady. Sure wish she'd look at me the way she looks at you. At least you'll be my friend. I guess that will have to do."

Once he made landfall, Ivan secured his prey with teeth and claws. Victorious and with droplets of pond water streaming off his fur, he tried to trot away; but he quickly came to the end of his line. Cooper seized the opportunity, gave the pole a yank, and reeled it in. Ivan took chase, hopping and pouncing all the way back to Cooper.

"Ha! You got cocky," Cooper said. "Remember, you're prey's never really caught until he's in your stomach." He released a little line and let the cat bounce and leap for his toy.

"You've got some good reflexes there, you scoundrel. I've been letting you have it easy. From now on you'll have to work for it."

About that time Ivan jumped full-bodied onto the fly. He hooked his claws into it and refused to let go. Even Cooper yelling and making silly noises couldn't distract him from the horsehair fly.

Cooper tugged a few more times, but Ivan held fast to the lure. "I caught a big one! Okay, Scoundrel. You win. It's all yours."

As if to acknowledge Cooper's surrender, the cat bit down on the bait.

That was too much. "Ivan don't!" Eva charged out of hiding.

Cooper spun around. "What's wrong?"

"I don't want him getting hurt!"

Cooper smiled. "He's fine. The last thing in the world this cat is, is hurt. Look." He yanked on the line again.

Ivan tightened his grip with his claws, bit down and growled.

Walking toward the cat, she asked, "What about the hooks?"

Cooper looked hurt. "You think I'd use a hook when I play with the cat?"

As if he were playing with a large catfish, Cooper waited until Ivan relaxed, then snapped the fly out of his grasp and reeled it in. The cat chased it to no avail. With the lure dangling tantalizingly from the tip, Cooper presented it to Eva.

"See, it's perfectly safe. I couldn't hurt a cat, especially your cat. After I met you and Ivan I made a special fly just for him. This is the first chance I've had to let him try it out."

She turned the red and white horsehair lure over in her fingers. She really didn't know anything about fishing flies. However, this one had nothing sharp in it. "You went to all the trouble to make this just for Ivan?"

"Sure. He'd get hurt if I used a real lure." He nodded to the cat still eyeing the tip of the fishing rod. "I'm sorry I alarmed you. Would you like to sit down?" He shook the dirt off the canvas and offered her his folding fishing chair. "I'm afraid it's a little dirty. Would you like something to drink? I'm afraid my selection is limited." He pulled a bottle of red French wine out of a submerged minnow basket. "I don't even have a glass," he apologized. "I wasn't expecting company. I know it's a little early for wine, but it's all I have."

He twisted in the corkscrew, pulled the cork and took a sniff. "It seems okay. Want some?"

Wine wasn't scotch, but maybe some could help her relax. She nodded and he handed her the bottle.

She took a sip. "This is wonderful!"

"It's a Rhone Valley red. It's probably going to be the last we'll have from that area now that Germany is shopping for property in

France."

She took another sip and passed him the bottle. "I may have to teach you to drink scotch."

"Your scotch may eventually be unavailable as well. When I get back to my office, I think I'll try to make some connections."

"The war in Europe must be very difficult on you," she said.

He took a long drink and grimaced. "Yes. My company had just gotten back on solid footing after prohibition. I'm thinking that before the French give the Germans the keys to their country, I'd like to import some of the grapevines. If I can't have their wine, perhaps I can start a vineyard and produce some of my own."

He looked so down-to-earth that Eva had a much easier time seeing him in a vineyard than as a hoity-toity importer of wine.

"You know, it's ironic. Here I am staying in Carrie Nation's hometown—a woman who would have had me tarred and feathered because I bring fine wines to people." He cast the fly next to the stock pond where the grass had been trodden down by livestock. Ivan followed and pounced on it.

"You seem awfully fond of Ivan."

"He's a remarkable cat. He acts like a dog."

"I guess he does." Eva smiled.

Once again Cooper cast the special cat fishing lure out to be pursued by an enthusiastic Ivan. "A cat saved my life once."

She took another sip of wine. "Really? How?"

"I'd have been a third generation navy officer, but when the Great War started I joined the army instead. I was in France and the Spanish flu was killing our guys in the trenches faster than those Hun bastards ever had. While I was out on patrol I got sick and crawled into a barn. The farmer's wife brought me soup and herbs, but left me out there where it was very cold. This tiger-striped cat laid on top of me, purring and keeping me warm. That cat didn't leave my side until I was well, then she went on her way. I never cared for cats before that, but I have a feeling I'd have died if I hadn't had such a good nurse." He nodded at Ivan. "You have a good nurse, too."

She thought about it. "I do at that... You have kids?"

He shook his head. "My wife Pearl died in childbirth," he said quietly. "I lost them both. I was in France at the time."

"I'm so sorry. I didn't know. You never remarried?"

Cooper made eye contact with Eva for just a moment, then

looked away. "Didn't find anyone I thought Pearl would approve of." His voice trailed off, and he reeled in Ivan. "How about you? Any children."

She pointed at the red-tailed cat. "Ivan. He was really my husband's cat. Like you, I didn't like cats. But Edgar loved him, and now it's up to me to take care of him. But...funny. Since I've been here, the cat has actually taken care of me." She handed him the half-drunk bottle of wine and stood up. "I better catch my nurse and get back to my room. I haven't had my treatment today. Nurse Cavanaugh wanted me to find Ivan first."

He took a last swig before returning the bottle to his empty minnow basket. He took her hand, kissed it quickly and stepped back. "Have a pleasant day, Eva Dupree."

"And you, Cooper Reilly."

DAY SEVENTEEN—*Saturday, September 16*

The days after Rose's FBI meeting dragged by, till finally it was Saturday. Today Norman Baker would conduct his business meeting in Little Rock. Until he returned, if he returned, Eva would try to keep herself occupied. With her daily treatment behind her and Rose gone for the afternoon, Eva picked up Ivan went downstairs to the lobby.

"Where's Mr. Baker?" Eva asked the clerk in the reception area just double checking.

"I understand he's out of town on business. I'm not sure when he'll be back."

"I'm sure that's true," Eva muttered under her breath.

"What was that, Miss Dupree?" the receptionist asked.

"Nothing. Just thinking out loud."

Eva wandered aimlessly around the lobby. She found a quiet corner with a good vantage of both the entrances and the staff offices. She had the best seat in the house. If anything happened to Norman Baker, Eva and Ivan would know that something was amiss before anyone else except for privileged staff. She opened the new book that Rose picked up while she was in Little Rock, a book of poetry by T. S. Eliot called *Old Possums Book of Practical Cats*. Holding it in her hand, Eva sighed. Rose seemed determined to turn her into a cat lover. At least the poems were entertaining and the rhythm pleasant. Since no one was around, she started reading quietly to Ivan. It would be good practice just in case she decided to get back into acting. Ivan seemed to enjoy her recitations. He laid across her lap, purring softly to the cadence of the words.

On the other side of the lobby, Mr. Dye played checkers with another patient. She called, "Who's winning?"

A much older gentleman with a gaping facial sore grinned.

"I'm afraid Mr. Alevetti is giving me a rather sound thrashing," Mr. Dye confessed.

Alevetti's red pieces had four kings. Mr. Dye had only one left. "I love it, but I'm afraid checkers has never been my game."

She got up and moved closer to the game leaving her book to

hold her observation post.

"By the way, Miss Dupree," Mr. Dye said. "The other day when we had the sing-song I took a couple of photos of you. I took them down to Gray's Photography to develop. I'm sorry. I'm afraid some of them didn't turn out so well. I guess they damaged the negative during processing or maybe my camera's leaking some light. Maybe it's time to buy a new one. Would you like them anyway? I did get a nice shot of you and the cat playing a duet."

He handed the stack to her. "That's very kind of you." Eva glanced at them briefly before slipping them into her pocket. "They're just fine. Thank you."

He turned back to the game in time to watch his opponent do a triple jump, wiping all but two of his pieces from the board. In another move or two the game would mercifully be over.

Sparing Mr. Dye the embarrassment of a witness, Eva went back to her spot.

As she read the poems to Ivan, she accumulated a larger audience. A few older ladies stopped to listen, then a few more joined them. Her acting experience had not been in front of an audience; she found herself stumbling through "The Naming of Cats," worried she wasn't pronouncing the names right. She struggled through a few more of the poems, and discovered with relief that her audience didn't seem to care that the words weren't well rehearsed.

A few minutes later, Cooper quietly joined the assembly.

During her delivery of "Mongojerrie and Rumpelteazer", Mr. Bellows, the hospital administrator, ran past them into Dr. Statler's office, slamming the door behind him.

Voices rose, words indistinct but their tone frantic. Before long, Dr. Hutto charged in, the tail of his white lab coat flying behind him. One-by-one higher administration entered the office. And the turmoil within seemed to grow more frantic.

Eva's stomach tightened. This must be it. She looked around at the patients lounging in the lobby. She felt jubilant and sad at the same time.

A few minutes later, an off-duty Nurse Turner, wearing a housedress, joined the ruckus. Her face looked ashen and her stern expression had been replaced by anxiety.

Eva giggled. *"Is that Turner in red polka dots?"*

The small assembly stared at the closed door.

"I'll be damned," Mr. Alevetti said, scratching the top of his head. "Who'd of thunk? Nurse Turner's a human."

"I wouldn't go that far," Mr. Dye said.

They stared intently at the office. *What next?*

"Wonder if Dr. Baker's going to join 'em?" Cooper wondered aloud.

"Don't count on it," Eva said in a voice just above a whisper.

After a few minutes Nurse Turner flew out and shot up the stairs. The news for the hospital staff must have been very bad.

"What's going on?" Mr. Dye asked.

"Beats me," his game partner said. "That broad's blown her wig." He chuckled. "It's fun to watch her sweat for a change. She got that one 'xpression. Don't never smile. Wouldn't you want some of that nookie? You'd freeze your dong off." He faked a shiver.

Mrs. Hundley gasped, "Really, Mr. Alevetti."

"C'on, Mrs. Hundley, can you imagine any man surviving nookie with that?"

As Mr. Alevetti and Mrs. Hundley bantered back and forth, two groups of men in dark suits armed with Tommy guns entered through both east and west entrances. The banter cut off abruptly. Everyone stared at the men. It was surreal. Machine guns and G-men stalking threateningly around the hospital, staring at patients and opening and closing office doors.

This is real. Did I do the right thing?

Eva held onto to Ivan who shrunk back into her arms. He wasn't the only one.

Mrs. Hundley broke into tears. "What's happening?"

At the same time the elevator door opened spilling frantic Nurse Turner out into the lobby. She froze when she saw the armed men.

"Attention everyone," one of the men said to the patients. He tried to sound calm, but he came off sounding like a drill sergeant. "You all need to go back to your rooms for now."

"Why?" Mr. Alevetti asked.

Nurse Turner said, "Just go to your rooms." Her voice sounded more like a plea than her usual authoritative tone. Her voice quavered reflecting the fear showing in her face.

Eva smiled to herself. She felt no sympathy for the Duchess of Ice. Now Nurse Turner would experience the fear every cancer patient in the hospital experienced, especially those like Eva, forced to stay in haunted rooms.

Nurse Turner herded Eva and the other patients into small groups and showed them to the elevator. Their faces reflected the same fear as a calf awaiting slaughter. "Someone will be up to check on you in a few minutes," the head nurse assured them as the elevator doors closed.

"What's going on?" Mr. Alevetti repeated to Andy, the elevator operator.

He didn't have time for an answer. Andy opened the doors. "Here's your floor, sir."

Mr. Alevetti shuffled from the elevator at the second floor leaving Eva, Ivan and Cooper alone with Andy.

"I think I know," Eva said to Cooper. "Come to my suite and I'll tell you."

She offered him a scotch and water. There were a few almost melted ice cubes in her bucket and she dropped them in his drink. This afternoon she'd take hers without.

She told him about what she had seen in the locked ward and the letters.

"I'll be damned. That son-of-a-bitch!" he said. "I wasn't so sure about him curing cancer, but I didn't think he'd resort to robbing the dead."

Eva returned to the suite's living room where they sat wordlessly for a few minutes, looking out the window. The moment was interrupted by a loud knock at the door.

Eva opened it to find a man in hat and suit with a clipboard.

He glanced at the door number and jotted it down, "You are...?" he asked.

"Eva Dupree. And you are...?"

"Dupree. Oh yes. You're here for treatment of stomach cancer."

"Kidney.

"Kidney," he repeated. He looked at Cooper. "And your name?"

"You first," Cooper said. "What's going on?"

"Special Agent Lee McKean, FBI. I'm afraid we're closing down the hospital. Mr. Baker has been arrested for mail fraud. You'll need to make arrangements to return home. There are agents in the lobby that will assist you."

The agent looked over Eva and her suite. "Did Mr. Baker have you sign any letters?"

"I've already turned over that information to Special Agent Waller."

McKean nodded knowingly. "You're the one Special Agent Waller mentioned. He'll be here soon. He'll want to speak to you." He looked at Cooper. "What are you being treated for?"

"I came to the health resort for some rest."

"I see. No letter?" McKean asked.

"No. I signed no letters."

Gazetta stormed through the deck door to the suite. "Eva, did you hear? They arrested Mr. Baker, Dr. Statler and Mr. Bellows."

"Gazetta Smith, this is Mr. McKean with the FBI."

"Jeepers! Just like at the picture show. What's going on?"

"Gazetta, Mr. Baker has been arrested for mail fraud," Eva said. The explanation stopped there.

"Dr. Baker was arrested?" she repeated incredulously. "My God! What'll happen to me?"

Guilt shot through Eva. She hadn't thought about what affect his arrest would have on his patients. She looked away from Gazetta.

"You'll go back home and get treated by a real doctor not a snake oil salesman," the agent said.

Gazetta sank into a chair. "Oh my God, I'm going to die now. I was feeling so much better. But I'm going to die now." She turned to Agent McKean. "Why couldn't you leave him alone. He wasn't hurting anyone."

"He committed mail fraud, ma'am."

Gazetta gaped at him. "Mail fraud?"

"It's a federal crime to mail fraudulent material through the mail. His brochures contained deceptive photographs and false statements."

"I'd heard he sent letters to the families of dead patients asking for money," Eva said.

"We'd heard reports, but no evidence has ever turned up to support that."

"What about the new evidence you just received?" Eva asked.

The agent looked puzzled. "I don't know about any new evidence."

She looked over at Gazetta, who sat trembling. Suddenly Eva felt nauseous. *What have I done?*

"I need to see the agent in charge, Bob Waller, right now."

"Okay. He said to let him know when we found you anyway." McKean grabbed Eva by the elbow, led her to the elevator and down to the lobby where Waller was shouting orders to G-men and directing the local law men as well. While she waited for him to take a breath, she retrieved Mossell's Ming vase from the fireplace mantle.

During a brief instant of silence, McKean said, "Sir, this little lady needs to talk to you."

"I'm a little busy, but what can I do for you?"

"I'm Eva Dupree."

He hesitated and then recognition crossed his face. "Mrs. Dupree. Yes. You've been a tremendous help in our investigation."

"Mr. Waller, rumor has it that Mr. Baker stored some of the bodies in the refrigerator in the basement. One of those bodies belongs to a friend of mine, a Mrs. Mossell Knight. She wanted me to speak with her niece, who is her only relative. She had specific instructions for the disposition of her body."

Waller raised his hand like he was motioning to a waiter and immediately spoke to the man who appeared. "Rogers, this is Mrs. Dupree."

"Miss Dupree," she corrected.

"Miss Dupree. She believes he may have stored some bodies in the basement. Also, when the mortuary comes to pick them up, make sure Miss Dupree has an opportunity to instruct them on what to do with…"

"Mrs. Knight."

"Yeah. Mrs. Knight's body."

"Right, chief." He nodded to Eva, then turned to a flock of feds standing in a circle comparing notes. "Wright, Clayton, Engstrom." He tilted his head in the direction of the stairs.

Obediently, they ambled over.

The lobby stairwell was the most direct passage into the bowels of the building. There was nothing remarkable about the single floor basement beneath the hospital: concrete floor, bare, unpainted walls and hallways wide enough for push carts and gurneys. Since the building was originally designed as a hotel this level handled the laundry and supply receiving.

A young Mexican woman with a faded purple Baker Hospital scarf tying back a cascade of wavy black hair leaned against a wall, smoking. As the investigators approached her she flicked a half-inch of ashes on the floor .

"Where's the refrigerator?" Rogers asked her.

"Which one?" She took another puff on her cigarette.

"One big enough to hold bodies," Rogers said.

"Oh, that one. I never seen 'em, but I hear people talk. It's straight down there, all the way."

"Will you show us?" Rogers asked.

"Nope. Not going near no dead folks. Mr. Baker told us if we ever went near there, he'd fire us before we had a chance to blink."

"Sounds promising," Rogers said.

"What's your name?" Eva asked her.

"Maria."

"It's okay," Eva said gently. "Maria, these men are with the government. Mr. Baker's been arrested. He can't hurt you. They've come to close the hospital down."

"You're closing it down?" She stared in dismay at the G-man. "Dios mio. What am I going to do? My mamma, she is sick. Mr. Baker gives us food." Her eyes grew wild. "We're going to starve now."

"Will you show us where it is?" Agent Rogers asked.

She didn't. Instead she swore at them in Spanish and left them standing in the hallway.

Exploring the bowels of the building they opened room after room. Off the main corridor they found the pharmacy where the doctors concocted the Baker Cure, the telephone switchboard room, and finally as they neared an open garage door at the end, the laundry room.

Sweltering humidity hung like fog. It was like breathing liquid air. The sweat-soaked workers had stripped to the waist.

Rogers asked them about the refrigerator, but they all stared at him with their arms folded or with fists perched angrily on the hips. Finally, one woman stepped forward. She led them back into the corridor through a chamber that looked to Eva like something from a Frankenstein movie: tables and drains, a stainless steel counter holding heavy surgical instruments: scalpels, chest cutters, spreaders.

Eva's knees weakened when she recalled Mossell's description of her autopsy. This had to be where it happened.

The laundress whispered in Eva's ear, then hurried back toward laundry.

Eva caught Rogers' eye. "Mr. Rogers, she told me I should go upstairs because she has seen men armed with machine guns down here."

Rogers sent Eva back to the laundry. "I'll have someone come get you when it's safe," he said. He and his men took out their pistols.

As Rogers promised, a G-man came for her after the danger had passed. He said that despite their concerns, the guards gave up without shots being fired.

Before Eva even entered the basement's commercial refrigerator, she smelled that ever familiar, yet potent Eau d' Mossell. Inside the unit she found the agents all had handkerchiefs over their noses. One of them had thrown up. It was a giant walk-in industrial refrigerator with a heavy insulated door. The single light provided little illumination, but it was enough to see the outline of the bodies on steel racks with white sheets covering them.

"This is definitely the place," Rogers told her. "I wasn't sure I believed you before. I apologize for doubting your story. Clayton, go upstairs and find the medical examiner. Tell him we have some stiffs for him." He glanced at Eva. "I mean we have some bodies."

The medical examiner, determined quickly that the seven elderly females in the cooler died of natural causes.

Eva pointed at one body. "That lady over there was my friend Mossell Knight. She wanted special arrangements."

"When the mortuary comes to pick up the bodies, I'll make sure you have a chance to talk to them. Can you identify any of these other bodies?"

She shook her head. "No. I don't know any of them."

She left quickly and returned upstairs.

Later, a line of hearses arrived and true to his word Rogers summoned Eva.

"The driver tagged Mrs. Knight. He said you can go to the office and make whatever arrangements you want."

Eva returned to her room to find Ivan staring at the Ming vase. She gave him a quick pat on the head, grabbed the vase, and took the trolley downtown to Morton Funeral Home where she met with Mr. Morton and his wife.

"Yes," the lady attendant said. "The sheriff said you would be coming in to make arrangements for Mrs. Knight."

Eva handed the mortician the vase and filled them in on Mossell's final wishes.

He turned the vase over in his hands. "This is a beautiful piece.

Where did it come from?"

"It's been in her family for several generations."

"It's certainly large enough. It should do nicely."

"Good. I'll pick up the remains tomorrow. I'm going to send them to her niece. I wanted to write a note and tell her what her aunt meant to me." Eva handed him a check for his services. "It's the least I can do for her. She helped me right a terrible injustice."

Mrs. Morton nodded knowingly, although she had no idea what Eva was talking about.

As long as she was out, Eva took the trolley to the train station to purchase tickets so she and Rose could return home. The hospital closing created a long line. It would be tomorrow afternoon before they could leave. Next she stopped by Basin Liquors and picked up a new fifth of Haig & Haig Scotch and a bag of beer. It would help her get through this one final night.

When Eva returned to the hospital, she went back down to the switchboard. It was in a small room with a single operator, a middle-age woman who was frantically trying to answer calls from concerned staff, patients' families, government officials, mortuaries, and medical suppliers.

Eva stood patiently for some time and then broke in a brief moment between calls. She gave the operator the phone number for Mossell's niece and returned to her suite. The operator would notify her when she'd connected with her party. A few minutes after she reached her room, the floor nurse alerted her that Beulah Knight was on the line.

Eva picked up the phone at the nurse's station. "Beulah, this is Eva Dupree, a friend of your Aunt Mossell Knight."

There was a long silence on the other end of the line. Finally the woman said, "Hello, Mrs. Dupree. What can I do for you?"

"Your aunt recently passed away at the Baker Hospital."

"I know."

"You do?"

"Of course. Dr. Baker called me himself to tell me."

"He did?"

"Of course. He wanted to know what I wanted to do with the body and her personal effects."

"He did?"

"I told him I didn't want anything to do with that evil old bat."

"Oh." Eva paused for a moment. "Mossell once told me she wanted to be cremated and placed in a Ming Vase."

"Yes, Uncle Roger's vase. Well, do whatever you want. You can keep the damn vase and throw her ashes in a cesspool for all I care. Same thing I told Dr. Baker. He said he'd have her cremated for us."

"Beulah, Mossell said you were the one handling her finances while she was being treated."

"I did it as a favor to Uncle Roger, so he wouldn't have to deal with her."

"Did Mossell send you any letters asking for money for treatments?"

"Yes. A month ago, she wrote and asked me for money. I sent what she asked for."

"Have you received a letter from her more recently?"

"No, but Dr. Baker sent me a letter of condolence. Is that what you mean?"

"That was nice of him. Yes, I guess that's what I meant." Even though it wasn't. Puzzled, Eva thanked Beulah and hung up.

Before she returned to her room, Eva went to Norman Baker's main office on the first floor where Special Agent Waller and another investigator were still going through his files. Waller would pull a folder out, glance through it and either place it in wooden box or put it back on the file cabinet.

"Mr. Waller, I wanted to ask you some questions."

"Miss Dupree, I'm a little pressed here," agent Waller said. His suit jacket had been tossed aside. His pistol and leather holster contrasted frightening against his white shirt. "What do you need to know?" He added another folder to the box he was taking.

"I sent you some folders that came out of Mr. Baker's private office." She hesitated. "I'm beginning to wonder if I made a mistake. I'm not sure that he did the things I accused him of."

Waller closed the drawer of the old oak cabinet and opened the next one. Grabbing an armful of brown folders, he tossed them on Baker's mahogany desk. Some individual papers flew out and settled to the floor. The agent plopped down in Norman's chair to inspect his files.

Eva continued. "It was concerning sending letters to families of dead patients asking for more money for treatments. One of the patients told me he had all the rich widows sign previously typed letters saying that she's getting better but she needs more money. The patient told me he only sends these to the family after the person has died. Then, when he's milked them for as much cash as he can, he tells them that their aunt, or whoever, died."

Midway through the story, Waller looked up impatiently over his wire-rimmed glasses.

His stare intimidated her but she continued. "Then he burns the bodies in the furnace out on the side of the building."

"Yeah, we heard that too."

"I sent you all those letters I found in his private files," she reminded him.

"Yeah."

"I'm not so sure he does that," she admitted.

"Look lady, you picked one helluva of a time to change your mind," Waller said. "The truth is, we've heard complaints like that before. Never found a shred of evidence that he did that. It'd be pretty easy to prove something that stupid. Did he do a whole bunch of other things? He sure as shit did. The Food and Drug Administration says his cure is a nostrum. Worthless. The truth is the only thing we can nail him on is mailing his brochure. So that's what we're doing."

"That's all. Mailing a brochure is all he's done?"

"I didn't say that. I said it's all we can prove right now. But it's enough to hold him on."

Eva looked around at Baker's office. Once immaculate, it was in shambles. His drawers stood open; files lay scattered; and his normally clean crystal ashtray overflowed with ashes. Ordinarily Norman Baker would have been outraged.

Shoulders drooping, Eva turned to leave.

"Mrs. Dupree," the agent said after her, "if it makes you feel any better, you didn't get Baker into trouble. He did that all on his own. As a matter of fact, the evidence you sent didn't pan out. The letters were useless to us. But we've been planning this raid for a long time. The one thing you did was help us take him without killing him and a lot of innocent people. If we arrested him here with all the machine guns he and his men pack," he reached under the desk and held up Baker's Thompson, "there'd be a lot of dead people. Not just Baker and his bodyguards, but my agents and nurses—and patients. We'd be swimming in blood. Maybe even yours. You may have saved a bunch of lives, including Norman Baker's. Personally, I'd just as soon mow that egotistical quack down, but I didn't want anyone else getting caught in the crossfire."

Above them something crashed and someone wearing heavy shoes, presumably an agent, clomped across the floor. Both Eva and Waller glanced up for a moment.

Then, amidst the chaos, Eva recalled two more victims. The dogs! "Norman Baker has two Great Danes in his penthouse. They're guard dogs."

"We may have to shoot them."

"You won't have to do that," Eva said urgently. "I believe his house boy Chester, can handle the dogs."

"I'll have someone locate him."

"Thanks." Hesitantly, she took a last look around Baker's office and left.

On the way up the stairs to her room she fell to the floor. That damn kidney pain, jabbing and stabbing at her. Reminding her how sick she still was. She waited for the pain to run its course and subside. It eased some, but didn't let up completely. She struggled to reach the next floor and then staggered to the elevator.

She made it past the fourth floor nurses' station and to her room. Arriving there she found Rose taking a nap on the fainting couch. Ivan snoozed on her stomach, unaware that he was riding up and down with each breath. Next to the closet sat Eva's partially disassembled travel trunk, a Wardrola. Rose must have already heard the news and started the formidable job of packing. From the look of things, Eva's seldom worn outfits had already been put away.

"Hey." Eva shook Rose's shoulder, then sat on the edge of the couch. Although the stabbing had subsided, it was still there. God simply exchanged the pickaxe for a paring knife.

Rose sat up, forcing the cat to the floor. "What time is it?" she mumbled. "What's happening?"

Eva glanced at her rose gold Rolex. "It's almost seven. Five till. The FBI is closing down the hospital. They arrested Baker in Little Rock today."

"Sorry Miss Eva. Must have dozed off." Rose brushed her hand groggily across her forehead. "Yes, the nurse told me what happened. Reckon you got what you wanted."

Eva chewed her lip. "I'm not so sure I did the right thing."

Rose sighed. "This is fine time to decide that."

"Yes, I know." Eva sighed too. She dug through her purse and pulled out the train schedule. "I have two tickets to Dallas for late tomorrow afternoon. Why don't you head back to the Brown's and get packed and settle up with them. Meet me back here first thing in the morning and we can organize everything here."

Rose tidied Ivan's sanitary pan. When she finished she grabbed her purse and left Eva sitting on the couch with the cat.

Down at the fourth floor nurses' station, Nurse Johnston was running around frantically. Mr. Pryor, a quiet patient Eva had seen on occasions out on the observation deck, sat in a wheelchair beside the nurse's desk.

"You ready to head down. Mr. Pryor?" Nurse Johnston asked.

The patient nodded weakly.

"Where's Nurse Turner?" Eva asked as the nurse jotted down a few notes.

"She's been arrested."

"Nurse Turner was arrested, too?"

"Oh yes. Her, Dr. Statler, Mr. Bellows, Dr. Hutto, and I'm not sure who else...What do you need?"

"I want some ice."

"The refrigerator is over there. I'll be busy for a while. Can you get it yourself?"

"Sure." She broke open the ice trays and emptied them into her bucket."

"Don't forget to fill them with water," the nurse called behind her as she wheeled her patient toward the elevator. "Oh yes. I'm afraid tonight if you want something to eat, you're going to have to go down to the dining room. With so much of the staff unavailable..."

In her mind Eva translated "unavailable" as "arrested."

"...I'm not going have time to get it for you."

"Okay."

Nurse Johnston disappeared into the elevator with the patient.

Eva followed instructions and returned to her room, where she fixed herself a scotch and water. She didn't plan to hide her drink this evening. What could the nurses do about it anyway? Throw her out? Not likely. While she was at it, she iced down the beer she bought in town just in case one of the few lingering patients dropped by.

Hoping it would deaden the kidney pain, Eva grabbed her fifth of Haig & Haig Blue Label and headed down to the dining room. The only time she'd been in there was when she'd attended a talking movie several days earlier, and then it wasn't set up for dining.

The enormous room was deserted save a few patients sitting together near the kitchen. The room was quiet and the mood was glum. Why shouldn't it be? She asked herself. Now all these people are going to die. No hope.

In addition to the wisteria wallpaper, the lavender crisscross curtains covered the arched floor to ceiling windows. Next to the window was a mirrored buffet that held silverware, napkins and glasses.

How grand this room must have been in the days of the Crescent Hotel! She could imagine a small orchestra playing a Strauss waltz about where she was seated. She could almost see the ladies in their floor-length gowns with the yards and yards of fabric flowing gracefully like a mountain creek. She looked into the mirror and smiled. What a shame she and Edgar hadn't had an opportunity to make it here during those days.

Finally the waiter asked her to order, she simply asked for a half-filled glass of water and a bowl of soup.

As the waiter returned with her glass the last of the patients filtered out of the dining room for the lobby. When the waiter left, she filled the glass with Blue Label and lifted one high to the memory of her old friend, Mossell.

"This one is for you," Eva said to the wall.

"Thanks, angel," a voice behind her said.

Eva didn't have to see who it was. She could tell without turning that Mossell had come back for a visit.

"Well, well, pigeon," Mossell said. "Look what you've done. You managed to get his whole place closed down. That's something the AMA tried to do for a decade. Congratulations."

Eva sniffed the air. "Gads, Mossell. I thought by now you'd smell better."

"They haven't done anything with my body yet," the ghost said.

"I instructed the mortuary to cremate you and place your ashes in the Ming Vase."

"How thoughtful of you, Eva."

Eva? That's the first time Mossell's called me by name. "I thought you'd be pleased."

"I'm delighted, tomato. I'd always hoped I'd get to spend eternity keeping Roger from his dearest mother's vase. And you managed that too. Poor Roger. He so wanted to put Mommy's ashes in it. Since they are almost ready to put me in the furnace, I thought I'd come tell you goodbye. There's no point in me hanging around any longer."

"I'm going to miss you," Eva told her.

"Well, chowder, you didn't miss me much when you left the location of *Caught in a Web*."

"What are you talking about? I barely knew you then!"

"But you knew my husband." Mossell's eyes narrowed and her brows knitted angrily.

"Of course. He was my director."

Mossell laughed. "Among other things."

"What are you suggesting?"

"I'm not suggesting, butterscotch. I know that you and Roger did some poontang. Personally, I think you could have done better. You were such a pushover."

Eva held her hands up. "Wait just a minute. I've told you before, I didn't sleep with Roger. I could barely stand to be in the same room, much less screw him."

Mossell's glowing figure intensified slightly. "You're lying. He left me for you."

Eva wished she could shake Mossell. "I was nice to him. I had to be; he was my director. But that was *it*. I never spent time on his casting couch. Or any other casting couch"

Mossell sniffed. "How do you explain Edgar? You slept on his casting couch."

"Really, Mossell, I loved Edgar. I never *ever* went to bed to get a job."

"Then why did Roger tell me he was going to marry you?"

"Maybe he was using me as an excuse." Eva realized frost escaped her mouth as she spoke. "I'm sorry you think I would have betrayed you."

"You can't betray someone you don't know and you didn't know me. You still don't, lamb chop." Her lip curled. "You just thought you did. You broke up my marriage. Roger left me because he wanted to marry you, you little tramp!" The almost new bottle of scotch exploded on the table beside her. Shards of glass flew everywhere. Liquid raced across the table and dripped to the floor. "And now, peaches, without the Baker Hospital, you're going to die, just like the rest of these poor chumps."

Eva felt frozen in her chair. "What do you mean? You said Baker's cure doesn't work "

Mossell bared her teeth and laughed unpleasantly. "Oh, it works all right. At least sometimes. Didn't you notice you were feeling better? But you're not completely well yet, are you? So, now what little bit of cancer that's still in your body will grow and grow until you die an agonizing death—just like I did. I died in searing pain, alone. No family, no husband. You did that to me. And, joy of joys, you did it to yourself, too. So, now my little veal cutlet, you too are going to die alone with just a mangy cat. Lovely, isn't it?"

Eva felt faint with that same gut-punch feeling she had when the doctor first told her about her cancer. "Mossell, why would you do this?"

"Because one husband wasn't enough for you. You had to cast that spell on Roger. He left me for you and then you dumped him like yesterday's trash. And that's just what you are, you green-eyed prostitute. You'd sleep with anyone to get a part!"

She's crazy. That wicked old ghost is nuts. She's going to kill me!

Above Eva the dining room's crystal chandelier vibrated. It escalated to shuddering. The flame-shaped bulbs exploded, showering tiny glass shards down on her. In seconds the remaining crystal began to shake violently. Eva stumbled out of the way just a fraction of a second before the fixture ripped from the ceiling and crashed to the table she'd just fled.

"So now, without Baker, you're going to die, *cabrita*." Mossell leaned back, laughing from deep within her gut. With Mossell's glossy, greenish decomposing skin, Eva felt like she was Dorothy in *The Wizard of Oz* and the Wicked Witch wanted Eva's shoes.

"You've managed to shut down your only chance for survival and after all these years I've finally paid you back." Mossell gave Eva another toothy grin.

"Why would you do this to Mr. Baker?" Eva shook and felt nauseous.

"Because I didn't get well. Like everyone else, he let me down. So he's going to go to prison and you'll die the same slow lingering death I did. I thought you both should know what it felt like, sugar." She smiled broadly. "I took care of both of you. Or should I say, you took care of both of you. And in just a few minutes, my earthly shell will be cremated and placed in Mommy's Ming vase. I'll have almost everything I want." She blew Eva a kiss. "Goodbye, sweet pea. Have a good life, or should I say, 'Have a good death.'"

The mirror behind Eva cracked in a spider web of broken lines, leaving her face a distorted mosaic of fragments. The cold air disappeared just as the windows next to her blew up sending a spray of glass shards her direction.

And as the air gradually cleared, Eva realized that Mossell was gone. She stared around her. Broken glass lay everywhere. The chandelier dropped down atop the fragments of her scotch bottle. Mossell had set her up.

The waiter ran over and helped Eva up from the floor. "What happened? Are you alright? Did we have an earthquake?"

Eva leaned against him, trembling and crying. "I'm going to die," she cried. "Oh, no. I'm going to die."

The pain in her gut hit her with a vengeance, sharp and savage as Mossell's hatred. She wanted to curl up on the floor under the table. No. Not here. Somehow she stood and brushed the glass from her skin, but she couldn't walk. Eva leaned on the waiter gasping for breath.

She didn't remember the waiter apologizing about the chandelier. Neither did she remember him finding a wheelchair and rolling her back to her room. She couldn't recall how she found herself huddled on the floor of her suite, trembling. As Mossell had accurately predicted, she would die alone—so alone even her scotch was gone. She could do nothing more except wash the glass out of her hair, pack her clothes and wait for the inevitable.

Eva dried her hair with a hospital towel.

She looked at her hands. They were covered with fine bloody lines like dozens of little paper cuts. She hadn't noticed them down in the dining room when Mossell had unleashed horror movie hell on her. Now they stung like streaks of fire. So did the peppering of tiny stabs on the side of her face. Luckily she'd kept her eyes covered during Mossell's attack.

She folded her arms across her stomach. God her side hurt!

She rummaged through the closet looking for another bottle of scotch, but found none. Nothing but the six bottles of Blatz Old Heidelberg cooling in the sink.

"What the hell!" Alcohol was alcohol. She popped open a bottle with the church key and sat down in her easy chair. "God, this tastes like pig pee." Of course, she didn't know what pig pee tasted like.

Did anyone, really? Drink enough, she knew, though, and she wouldn't care what it tasted like.

After the third Old Heidelberg, she didn't...but it had not dulled her anger at Mossell. "You old witch!" It came out sounding like "wish." "If I'd known you were such a vindictive old tart, I'd of shlept with your old man jush to say I'd done it." She took another slug. "He left you cuz you were such a mean nasty old broad. I can't blame him."

Ivan jumped up on the arm of the chair.

She stroked him. "Ivan, ol' buddy, it seems we've come full circle. A few weeks ago, you and I sat on my couch and I was dying and alone. And then I was feeling better. And now I'm dying and alone again. Life reeks."

She took a long deep swallow of the Old Heidelberg, finished the bottle and reached for a fourth. "Maybe I can drink myself to death."

Before she knew it she downed all but one of the bottles. She sat on the floor with the empties lying around her. Unable to stand up, she scooted next to her bed and brought her knees up to her chest to help ease the aching in her side.

"She played me like a fiddle," Eva said to Ivan, whose tail lashed with the shrill rising of her voice. "Like a catgut *fiddle*." Picking the cat up, they met nose to nose. "'Course, you don't have anything to worry about, Ivan, cuz catgut's not really made from a cat's gut. It's made from some other unlucky animal. But I can't remember which."

He wiggled free and moved just out of her reach.

"Or maybe she played me like a beer bottle." She picked up an empty bottle and blew across the top like a flute. "That sounds awful. Maybe the Baker Chamber Orchestra would let me play a beer bottle solo." She broke into a giggle, but the giggle quickly dissolved into tears.

Then she thought more about Mossell's words. Baker's potions did help some people. Not anymore. Not her. He trusted her and she betrayed him, and herself. Poor Norman Baker would spend the rest of his life in prison unable to help anyone, including her. She'd end up like Mossell.

"Look what I've done. I'm a murderer. All the people here are going to die cuz of me."

Suddenly the feel of the room changed. Even through her alcohol-induced haze she felt she was no longer alone. He was watching her—Jack the baby-rapist. Well, maybe Mary Elizabeth was a willing victim, but Jack Swann was the older, wiser teacher and he abandoned her, maybe even murdered her. Either way, he was responsible for her death.

She felt something cold brush her face. The icy air circled her, easing up her spine, surrounding her. She threw her bottle at empty air. It bounced against the wall and fell to the floor, shattering into several large pieces. "Take that you, baby-raping bastard!" She commanded her legs to run away but they refused to obey. The tears came harder. She was trapped in a useless dying body and subject to Jack's perverted will and desires. Icy fingers caressed her cheeks and ran across the lines of her jaw. Nothing would stop his advances, just the same way that the girl's protests fell on deaf ears.

"Stop it!" she yelled. "Go away! Leave me alone!"

The cold lingered for one last moment, then left her with a cool biting sensation on her lips and the chilling words, "I want you."

She tried again to stand up but once more failed. Then she spotted the last beer and crawled over to it. "One last drink and then it's over. All over." Eva guzzled it down.

She crawled around her room, but found nothing sharp or poisonous or deadly enough to kill her and once again found herself beside her bed. Now, though, a more urgent need than suicide hit her. She had to go to the bathroom. She felt about to burst a kidney or her bladder.

She knew she couldn't make it to the bathroom so she pulled the bedpan out of the bedside table. As she peed, the stabbing in her abdomen went from a paring knife to a cleaver to hatchet and back to the pickaxe. She groaned. She was dying. Right here on the bedpan. Right now.

She could see the headline, "Has-Been Silent Screen Star Dies Taking a Piss," or would it say, "Bedpan Kills Hollywood Has-Been, uh, What's Her Name."

Then suddenly the pickaxe went away...gone...completely. The pain had disappeared. Unlike in days past when it eased but always left faint residual pain or pressure to remind her she was still a prisoner of her disease. But this time she was free, completely delivered.

She pushed the bedpan aside and pulled her clothes back on as best she could. Exhausted, spent and so terribly drunk, she fell asleep on the floor.

DAY EIGHTEEN—*Sunday, September 17*

"Miss Eva." Rose shook her gently.

Eva groaned. Her head seemed to be swelling and compressing like a bellows.

Rose knelt down and placed a strong arm around Eva's waist. "Baby, you need to help me get you in bed."

She pried open one eye and instantly slammed it shut again. "Oh, God...turn off the sun."

"Got connections with the Almighty, but they're not that good. Now, try to stand up and I'll take you to bed."

"I drank too much," she told the maid.

"I should say so. You got swacked." Rose looked around at the beer bottles littering the floor. "It looks like you held quite a soiree in here. What possessed you to drink all that beer? I didn't think you ever liked it."

"When I drank a toast to Mossell. She showed up one last time and told me that the treatments do work. But now there won't be more treatments. I've stopped them. I'm going to die. So I got good and drunk. Rose, she used me to get even with Mr. Baker and stop my treatments to get even with me, too."

"Well, he wasn't any angel. Those letters didn't belong to an honest man." Rose hoisted Eva up onto the bed.

"Mr. Waller said they were worthless, carbon copies, but nothing current. They couldn't use them." Eva flopped into the bed. "Mossell was angry because he couldn't save her." She leaned back into the pillows and slid her feet under the covers. "I was her pawn."

Rose went to the bathroom and then returned with a damp cloth. She bathed Eva's face and arms as she had done so many times since she became ill.

"Funny," Eva said. "I'm sick to my stomach from all the beer and my head feels like it's been shot out of a cannon, but the burning and stabbing in my gut has stopped."

"Just get a little sleep." She evaluated the mess. "I'll clean up."

"Don't you have one of those concoctions for hangover?" she moaned.

DEATH UNDER THE CRESCENT MOON

"Of course. But what would you learn from your experience if you got off so easy?"

Eva closed her eyes. "You're fired."

"Yes, Miss Eva." She picked up the bedpan from the floor. "Shall I empty this, Miss Eva?"

Without opening her eyes, Eva nodded. She heard running water in the bathroom and the toilet flushed.

Rose approached Eva holding a piece of toilet paper. "How do you feel?"

"I wanna die."

"Not your hangover. Your side. How does it feel?"

Eva tried to think. The thundering in her head made it hard. "It stopped hurting sometime last night."

"You mean after you took a piss?"

Eva shrugged. That hurt like hell, too. "Yes, I guess so."

"How many bottles of beer did you drink?"

Her head pounded too hard to figure that. "Count the dead soldiers."

Eva heard Rose counting under her breath, then: "You drank six beers...and now your belly doesn't hurt?"

"I think I'm going to puke," Eva said. "Does that count?"

"I mean your side."

"No, Rose, my side doesn't hurt."

"Remember I said those doctors in Dallas didn't know what they were talking about. Looks to me like you passed some stones."

Eva forced her eyes open. Rose held a paper with several tiny rocks lying in the center.

"You've had the last treatment you need, Miss Eva," Rose said. "Those beers cured you. When my preacher at the Macedonia Church had stones he'd drink beer until he peed them out. During Prohibition he had a terrible time getting his medicinal brew. That's when I learned about hydrangea tea. Praise God for beer and hydrangea! Now have a glass of water."

Rose finished packing Eva's belongings while her employer slept off her binge. As she folded the last few blouses she heard Eva yawning from the bed. "You finally decided to join the land of the living?"

"Maybe."

"Saw Mr. Cooper downtown this morning. He wanted me to

pass on the message that he'd like to have dinner with you before we leave this afternoon."

"Tell him, not today. I've got a headache."

"I will not tell him that!" She closed the trunk.

Eva sat up and stretched. She felt her side and back. Still no pain! "Whatever it was, it's not there now. All this time and money was wasted."

"No it *wasn't*," Rose said. "If you hadn't come here, you never would have sat down and drank a whole bag of beer. You'd of sat around your house sufferin' until it grew too big to piss out. God had a reason for makin' you do everything you did. Even Miss Mossell was part of his plan. The important thing is: you came to the hospital sick and now you're going home better. That's all anyone can ask."

Eva considered Rose's wisdom and nodded.

"And you met that fine man here, too. He's mighty fond of you."

Eva sighed. "Rose, Cooper is a very nice man. But, you know I'm not interested."

"If you aren't, you should be." Rose shook her finger in Eva's direction. "Now, I'm not one to tell you how to live your life…"

"Since when?"

"But perhaps he's the kind of man that Mr. Edgar would want you to spend time with. I left one of my suitcases at the Brown's house. What do you want me to tell Mr. Cooper when I see him at the station?"

Under Rose's hard stare, Eva could only say, "All right. I'll meet him there. But Miss Matchmaker, I'll meet *you* down at the train station at three o'clock."

"Good, girl." Rose went into the bathroom and returned with another glass of water. "Now, here. Drink this."

Eva sighed deeply. "Now that I've passed the stone, why do I need to drink water? I thought I was done with all that."

Rose handed her the glass. "You wanted my secret cure for a hangover headache. This is it. Just keep drinking water until you quit feeling the explosions."

"Water?"

"Yes, ma'am. Trust me."

After Rose left, Eva sat on the floor and started going through the knickknacks she accumulated during her stay. She had an assortment of cards and letters from friends and church members wishing her good health. She also had a couple of new fountain pens and a bottle of purple ink.

"Miss Dupree?" Nurse Johnston stood at the door holding an envelope. "This came for you in the mail."

"Thank you," Eva said, taking the envelope.

"There's something else. Here's where you can reach Harry Hoxsey." She handed Eva a slip of orchid-colored paper. "He's the man Mr. Baker bought one of the Baker Cure formulas from. As a matter of fact he has a clinic in Texas. Anyone who wants to continue with the treatments can still get them at the Hoxsey Clinic in Dallas."

"Thanks."

"I'm letting all of the patients know," Johnston said. "I've seen too many people come in here sick as a dog and leave healthy, especially with carcinoma of the skin and blood."

"Not all of them, though."

"No. Of course not all of them. But enough to know how sad it will be to close the hospital down. Maybe he'll win in court. I hope." She headed for the door. "I need to get these to the others before they leave. When you're packed, let me know. I'll have your bags sent to the station. If I don't see you again, Miss Dupree, good luck. I hope you're feeling better soon. "

Still cross-legged on the floor she opened the envelope...and smiled when she recognized the childish handwriting. Trudy's. It read:

> "Dear Mrs. Dupree,
>
> "I like being home. I missed my dog and my brothers and sisters. How is Mr. Kitty? I miss him. I wish I could have took him home with me. I hope you get to go home too real soon. Here's a secret message. XOXOXOXO
>
> "Trudy"

At the bottom of the paper was another message written in Orphan Annie's secret code. Eva took the letter and tossed it in her purse. She'd decode it later.

She went through some more items acquired during her stay. Among them she found Annie's Telematic Decoder Badge. She dropped it in the envelope with Trudy's letter before she closed her handbag. It would be a long ride back to Dallas. Decoding Trudy's message would give her something to do—a pleasant diversion.

Eva glanced at the desk. *What to do with Mary Elizabeth's diary?* The poor child never intended for anyone else to read her most intimate thoughts and hopes. It didn't seem right to take it back to Dallas, but leaving the diary for the whole world to read was equally wrong. Eva returned the leather book to the drawer where she'd first found it.

"I hope you find peace, Mary Elizabeth."

Eva fished out her trusty paperclip desk key and maneuvered the latch until it clicked. A quick tug let her know the drawer was once again locked. But that wasn't good enough. She rummaged through the middle drawer for something that could permanently lock that drawer. There wasn't anything of use, just the dog-eared copy of *Gone with the Wind* and a pencil with a broken lead tip and an eraser that someone had chewed off. Human teeth marks marred the yellow paint. Ewww.

With all her strength, Eva jammed the pencil tip all the way into the keyhole and pulled up, breaking it off flush with the lock. She smiled. No one would be able to get to that diary unless they tore the desk apart. Mary Elizabeth's shame would remain a secret, at least for the foreseeable future.

Eva returned her attention to the loose contents of the trunk. She picked up the photographs that Mr. Dye took during the sing-along at the piano last week.

She had only paid them a token glance the day he gave them to her. This time she looked more closely. In the first shot, five patients crowded around the piano, their mouths wide open singing joyfully. There was a cute one of Ivan reaching for the keyboard. It looked like they were playing a duet. Just to look at the pictures, she'd never guess that many of those people were dying. In a couple of shots she was alone, caught up in the song. One had her mouth wide open. In another she wore an intense expression as she sight-read a musical passage. Then she came to the pictures of her with Cooper. He stood next to her holding Ivan. His face looked smudged, as if the lens had a fingerprint on it. Finally, she came to the one that Mr. Dye snapped during *Thanks for the Memory*, the shot that Mr. Dye complained the film processors ruined. Cooper had joined her on the bench and Ivan was perched on the piano desk staring down at the two pairs of hands. This time the picture was hidden by pale streaks. Something looking like smoke obscured the other side of her face.

She remembered the chill that touched her about then.

Suddenly her heart lurched. If she used her imagination, she could see a face in that pale patch, that looked like...Edgar...his lips brushing her cheek.

Her eyes filled. Was it possible? "Edgar, was that you?" The longer she stared at the photo, blurry as it was through her tears, the more it looked like him. Had the song, their song, brought him? Perhaps it had...to give her the goodbye kiss he missed that afternoon in the Dallas Hospital.

The trolley dropped Eva off at the front of the train station. She clutched a large cardboard box.

The station was small by Dallas standards, with walls made of the same limestone as the Baker Hospital. A steady stream of people filed through the building on their way to the loading platform. It was much busier than when she first arrived. She found Rose sitting alone on a wood bench, ignoring the bustle around her. She had her Bible in her hands, her mouth moving as she read the words under her breath. Ivan's carrier sat at her feet with one of her feet on it. If anyone tried to take it, she would know immediately. A frightened meow would unleash the wrath of the Rose.

"You hungry?" Eva asked.

Rose looked up from Psalms 33.

"Let's see what they have for supper."

"Fine by me." Rose picked up the cat's travel cage, grunting a little with the cat it weighed a hefty twenty-five pounds. She set the cage down again. "Maybe I'd better not. This is awful heavy for a woman my age."

Eva suspected something else really concerned her. "They'll let you in. I'll just tell them you have to give me my medicine. After all, I'm too sick to keep track of all those pills."

Eva opened the door to the station café. There in a dark corner in the back she spied Cooper, seated alone at a booth. The rumble of collective conversations and clinking plates made Eva raise her voice to be heard. "Want some company?"

He stood up. "If you mean *your* company, yes?"

"That's what I meant." Eva motioned for Rose to take a seat. "Sit down," she said as Rose hesitated. When the maid was settled Eva carefully set the carton next to her and joined Cooper in his bench.

He eyed the carton. "Been shopping?"

"No, just taking care of a few arrangements for a friend."

"Speaking of friends, it's a shame Mossell didn't make it. I miss her," he said. "She was a very funny lady."

"I'm afraid she wasn't much of a lady." Eva patted the box. "I know you're going to think I'm crazy, but..." Eva gave Cooper the quick synopsis of the Mossell Story, including her visitations and the glass-shattering conclusion from the night before.

Cooper's brows rose. "She had me fooled. I thought she was just a pleasant little old lady. I guess you're well away from her."

"I'm not yet."

Cooper blinked. "No?"

Eva opened the box and pulled out an exquisite blue and white Ming dynasty vase.

"It's lovely. What does it have to do with Mossell?"

Eva ran her fingers across its curved corners. "It's her vase."

"You mean it *was* hers," he corrected.

"No, 'is' is accurate. The Ming contains her mortal remains." She patted the top of the urn. "This priceless vase belonged to Mossell's former mother-in-law, who she hated. She kept the vase just to spite her ex-husband. I had Morton Funeral Home place her ashes in it just as she requested."

"Miss Mossell would be happy that you made the Ming her eternal resting place," Rose said. "But I'm confused. Why'd you follow through with her wishes when she betrayed you the way she did? God forgive me, I'd have flushed her bones right down the toilet."

"Rose, you're just going to have to learn to be more forgiving. Or more creative." Eva grinned wickedly. "I'm returning the vase, remains and all, to its rightful owner, Roger Knight. They can make each other miserable. They deserve to be together for eternity. It'll be good practice for all the time they'll spend together in Hell. The mortuary used a special glue to seal the vase. If he wants to get rid of her, he has to break the vase. That would be a pity, wouldn't it?"

Rose clapped her hands together. "You have a mean streak I admire, Miss Eva."

After their meal and a drink, they returned to the terminal.

To pass the time until the train arrived Eva dug into her purse and pulled out the decoder and the note from Trudy. As instructed, she turned the code to "11", working through letter after letter.

"My special friend wanted me to tell you this."

"I-W-A-N-T-Y-O..."

She froze, unable to go farther. Cold ran up her back and her arms, raising goose bumps. In her left ear, the same voice that haunted her at the Baker Hospital, whispered, "I want you."

"Oh God," she whispered. "What do you want, you bastard?"

Well, she might as well find out. Maybe it would help her be rid of him. She finished decoding the message. "I-W-A-N-T-Y-O-U-T-O-L-I-V-E. I-W-A-N-T-Y-O-U-T-O-B-E-H-A-P-P-Y. -I-L-O-V-E-Y-O-U-G-O-O-D-B-Y-E. -J-O-N-A-T-H-O-N-E-D-G-A-R-F-O-X-W-O-R-T-H-Y"

Her eyes welled. She suddenly remembered what Gazetta said about ghosts, that sometimes they could not finish what they wanted to say, that they didn't have much energy for communicating. "Edgar, it was you all along? You've been here with me?" She thought of all those nights she spent in terror when she needn't have. It was Edgar who watched over her, and opened the annex door when she was trapped. "I'm so sorry I didn't realize..." The tears spilled down her cheeks.

Across the aisle, Ivan scratched at the wire windows desperately and cried a most plaintive meow.

"Goodbye, dear Edgar," she whispered. "I miss you."

She pulled out the photos Mr. Dye had taken. Edgar really was there. She recalled the cattails Cooper had brought her. Had Edgar coached him? Was this Edgar's way of saying the time had come for her to move on with her life? Was Cooper the one she should move on with?

Her thoughts were interrupted when the public address system announced that the train for Dallas was boarding.

Cooper roused from his nap and kissed her hand. "They've announced your train. I guess this is goodbye."

She glanced down at the pictures. "I really wish we could have spent more time together."

His brows rose in surprise. "Do you mean that?"

"Yes." And she did.

"Really?"

"Yes, Cooper, really. You could say I've had an epiphany."

"Then excuse me just a minute." He hurried away, but returned shortly. "I hope you don't mind. I turned in my ticket for a seat on the train to San Diego via Dallas."

October 24, 1959
The Crescent Hotel—Formerly the Baker Hospital
Eureka Springs, Arkansas

The 1959 Cadillac Seville drove up to the back parking area of
what had once been the Baker Hospital. As it had twenty years ago,
the Statue of Liberty still stood vigil next to the building's entrance,
welcoming each newly arriving patient...or guest. The bellhop opened
the car door on the passengers' side and offered his hand to Eva in
the front seat and then opened Rose's back seat door. After the
bellhop loaded the luggage onto his cart, Eva and Rose followed
him inside while Cooper parked the car.

"Oh my!" Eva scanned the lobby. "What a difference a couple
of decades make."

"It certainly has changed," Rose set down her heavy leather
purse and pressed her weight against her wooden cane with the
ivory handle. She wore a yellow Christian Dior hat and a fourteen
karat gold and diamond cross necklace with matching earrings.

Eying the cavernous lobby, Eva had a feeling she'd arrived in
the Land of Oz, or maybe she had returned to Kansas after escaping
from the Lavender City.

Inside it looked so normal. Oak wood planks and burgundy
carpet covered the floors. Last time she'd been in this lobby, the
walls had been washed in brilliant colors and silly signs hung on the
wall. The amethyst shades had been replaced by nondescript flow-
ered wall paper and the ceilings painted white. The large columns
that had once worn coatings of purple, stood more conservatively
elegant in dark stained wood. The hokey signs had vanished with
Norman Baker. Bulky upholstered chairs and sofas replaced the lavender wicker furniture.

Instead of nurses and orderlies scurrying around, uniformed
porters paraded about the lobby. And fully loaded luggage carts
replaced the wheelchairs once so prominent in the great room.

"I guess the building isn't the only thing that changed." Eva
primped her hair. The silver streaks that had highlighted her waves
two decades ago, had expanded, taking over her head. Only a single

lock of chestnut strands remained over her left eyebrow. Her face had filled out, as had the rest of her body. And deep smile lines betrayed the last two happy decades.

The registration desk was a massive fixture that had at one time been the hospital check in. Eva checked in, then she and Rose wandered into the center of the lobby to wait for Cooper. Beside them the bellboy waited silently for the party to be reunited.

Just standing in the building evoked so many memories like little pigtailed Trudy and her tea parties, and spying on Cooper as he secretly played catfishing with Ivan. She took a deep breath to check the fear closing her throat: the agonizing shots that made her so sick, and icy sensations that woke her from a sound sleep. Unconsciously Eva pressed her hand against her back. She could almost feel the throb of the kidney stone more than twenty years after the fact.

"Who knew this place had such beautiful dark wood?" Rose asked.

The door opened and Cooper walked in carrying a wooden box by a suitcase handle. Row of one-inch air holes encircled the container. A pink nose pushed as far as it could to sniff the strange surroundings. From inside the box came a passionately protesting meow.

Cooper Reilly looked so dignified in his snowy white hair. He was thinner than he had been in the old days, both in physical frame and his hair. Wearing a pair of black framed glasses he watched the crowd for his family.

Eva waved at him with the hand holding their room key.

He smiled and joined the ladies, greeting his wife with a peck on the cheek.

Cooper too, examined the room. "I can't believe this was the Baker Hospital. The only thing I recognize is the admissions desk."

"...And the shape of the windows," Rose added. Remembering the old days, "I was always glad I didn't have to wash all of those."

"I don't see Nurse Turner chasing anyone down with horse needles," Cooper said watching a couple of guests hurry past them. "Thank goodness. She used to scare the crap out of me."

"Trudy's already here," Eva said. "I woke her from a nap. She'll join us at five."

They entered the elevator, followed by the bellboy with the luggage cart. Eva said, "Fourth floor, please," to the elevator operator.

Rose stood up straight and smiled. "This is the first time I've ridden the elevator here."

They exited the elevator, and by rote Eva headed toward her old suite—four-nineteen. At the far end of the hall, at the intersection of three hallways, was the entrance to the annex which had been the ward for the Baker Hospital's dying patients.

Eva stopped and stared. Her stomach tightened. The new owner of the Crescent Hotel had turned the ward into small sleeping accommodations. The door that had once barred the way to the death-bed ward had disappeared. An open hallway twisting around ninety degrees led guests to the low-cost rooms.

Although Eva wanted to see what the new owner had done with the place, she turned to the right, and made her way back to her old suite. There would be plenty of time to explore the changes later.

"See you in a while." Rose made a left turn and inserted her key into the lock and closed the door behind her.

Before entering her own room, Eva approached the end of the hall. Next to her door was the steep stairway leading to Norman Baker's penthouse. The desk had told her nobody was scheduled to stay there tonight.

Eva inserted the key in the lock. "At least tonight will be quiet," she said to Cooper. "No Clydesdales tromping around above us." She turned the knob, but hesitated before pushing the door open.

"You okay?" Cooper asked.

She took a deep breath and forced a smile. "I guess I'm a little nervous. I never knew what I'd find when I opened the door."

She pushed the door and found an unremarkable hotel room. It looked strangely familiar, yet alien. Stepping inside, Eva found once again, things had been moved around. The bedroom and the sitting area had switched. As in the lobby, typical hotel-style wallpaper covered the walls. The once brilliant purple pigment coating the baseboards and door frames had been replaced by warm, natural wood.

The bellboy unloaded the suitcases and a cardboard box from the cart. "This is the best room in the hotel." He opened the drapes exposing a view of East Mountain and rows of pine and juniper trees in the foreground, "Can you believe this view? I've worked here a couple of years and I still haven't gotten used to it."

He took a couple of steps toward the open door. "Do you need anything else?" The bellboy gazed at the ceiling, thumbing at the chinstrap of his scarlet hat.

Cooper set down the carrier, pulled a couple of bills out of his pocket and passed them to the bellboy. "After you deliver Mrs. Freeman's bag, we could use ice, four glasses and four champagne flutes and a wine bucket."

"Yes, sir." He glanced at the folded bills. "Thank *you*, sir." He grabbed the ice bucket and disappeared out the door.

After the bellboy closed the door, Cooper removed a turkey roaster from the box and untied the string holding it shut.

"Would you put the litter pan in the bathroom, dear?" Eva asked as she opened the door to the carrier.

A pink nose emerged, sniffed the air, then out came a white cat with auburn patches on the head and an auburn tail. Odd eyes, one ice blue and one amber, cautiously scanned the room.

"Here, Ivana. Want to potty?" Eva moved a more petite version of Ivan to the black and white tiled bathroom floor.

While they waited for the cat to conduct her urgent business, Eva examined the room. Something's missing.

"The desk is gone." Eva sounded disappointed.

Cooper scanned the suite. "They must have moved it to another room."

She shrugged. "Or gotten rid of it." She pictured the desk at the dump with "I love Jack" peeking out from beneath the trash. "How sad." Hopefully, no one ever discovered Mary Elizabeth's diary.

Of course, also missing was the old Tangley radio that kept her company on those long, lonely nights. Eva opened her suitcase and pulled out her brand new Emerson transistor radio. "I guess we won't get to listen to the Viking Accordion Band today," Eva said, her voice dripping with mock sadness. She turned an a.m. radio on and adjusted the dial until she found a station playing Elvis Presley singing about a "Hunk a Burnin' Love". She grinned at Cooper. "This song's about you."

At five o'clock sharp Eva answered a knock at the door. It was a slightly tentative knock, more of a tapping rather than a rapping. Eva expected a pigtailed teenager wearing penny loafers and pedal pushers. Whoever this woman was, she wasn't wearing pedal pushers. Expressive eyes the shade of bluegrass gazed down on Eva. Soft honey curls tumbled down past the woman's neck. A pencil skirt hugged her slender body and a shawl collar blouse gave her a sophisticated look. In one hand she clutched a scrapbook. The other arm was stretched out in anticipation of a hug.

"Mrs. Dupree?"

Eva raised her eyebrows dubiously. "Trudy?"

They embraced as tightly as their goodbye hug so many years earlier. This Trudy smelled of Chanel No. 5. Eva felt the bra beneath Trudy's blouse. *A bra? Of course, she's wearing a bra!* This isn't six-year old scared and lonely Gertrude any more. This Gertrude stood tall and straight, and self-assured.

Eva looked her up and down. "My, you have changed."

A familiar smile, only framed in Victory Red lipstick spread across Trudy's face. "Well, you haven't changed a bit. You look wonderful!"

Cooper rushed to the door. "Is this really my little Gertrude?"

Trudy blushed. "Of course, I am. I'll always be your little Gertrude, Mr. Cooper. I'll spare your back and not ask you to swing me around. But please, everyone calls me Trudy now."

"Fair enough. You forgo the swing and I'll call you Trudy."

"I will take a hug." She wrapped her free arm around his neck.

"Come in. Come in," Cooper said.

Trudy looked around the suite. "This is your same room, isn't it, Mrs. Dupree?"

"Trudy, you're an adult now. You can call me Eva."

"Okay." She continued scanning the suite. "It looks so different." As she inspected the room, her eyes fell on Rose, who was already seated. "And you must be Miss Rose. I guess we never met, but Mrs. Dup...I mean Eva, told me all about you. I'd know you anywhere."

Rose set down her drink. She grabbed her cane and began to struggle to her feet.

"No." Trudy reached down and touched Rose's shoulder, giving it an affectionate squeeze. "Don't get up." She sat down beside Rose on the settee.

"Would you like something to drink?" Cooper asked. "Lemonade?"

Trudy smiled. "I'm afraid I'm past the lemonade stage, Mr. Cooper. Do you have anything a little more grown up? What are you drinking?"

Cooper ran down the list of beverages they had with them. "If you'd like something with less punch we can ask room service to bring you a coke."

"Thanks. I'll have some Bordeaux."

Ivana peeked her head out from under the love seat as if to test the water, or in this case, the stranger.

"What do we have here?" Trudy asked. "Is this Ivan? I didn't know kitties lived that long."

Eva stroked the cat's soft fur. "This is Ivana. She looks a lot like Ivan," Eva said. "But we had to say goodbye to him about five years ago. Kidney disease. He was seventeen. That's an *old* cat. The house just wasn't the same without him."

Ivana took slow, uncertain steps and sniffed Trudy's leather pumps. Trudy ran the tips of her fingers through her fur. "She feels so soft. Just like Ivan."

Eva smiled sadly, then nodded at Cooper. "A couple of years ago while we were in England, we learned about a cat from Turkey called a Turkish Van. The breeder let us take this little girl home because she had the wrong color eyes. We still miss Ivan, but we've enjoyed her. Ivana acts so much like him; she's very active. Ivana is such a funny cat."

Cooper handed Trudy a wine glass containing a rich red burgundy wine.

She swirled the red wine in her glass. Then took a sniff. Finally she took a sip. "This is wonderful."

Cooper looked like a proud daddy. "It's from my vineyards in California. 1954 was a very good year."

"I'll say," Trudy agreed.

"What do you do, Miss Trudy?" Rose asked.

"I'm a nurse in a children's ward at St. Louis City Hospital. I love it."

"I bet your experiences at the Baker Hospital gave you the foundation to be a wonderful nurse," Eva said.

"Let's just say I have more empathy for the kids than I would have had otherwise. I wanted to emulate Mrs. Cavanaugh. She always treated me so kindly. She used to come into my room and cheer me up when I missed my mommy. I hope I never turn so jaded that I treat patients like Mrs. Turner. She scared me as much as the shots did."

"She certainly lacked in the bedside manner department," Eva said. In her mind Eva replayed the click of the latch the night Nurse Turner locked her inside her room.

"Did I hear you got a new job, Rose?" Trudy asked.

"Yes, Miss Trudy. When we arrived back in Dallas, Miss Eva promoted me to a property manager at Foxwothy Oil. I had to make sure those roughnecks had a place to lay their heads after working so hard. When they moved the drilling operations to another location, I had to find housing. I also got to crack a few heads when they tore things up." She hit the floor with the bottom of her cane. "That happened a lot more then you'd imagine. Those boys were *wild.*"

"After working hard all her life, Rose finally gets to be a lady of leisure," Eva said. "We hated to lose her. We never had to worry logistics while she was in charge of the housing. Now we're breaking in a replacement."

"They gave me a gold watch when I retired a few months ago." Rose extended her hand to show off the shiny timepiece around her wrist. As she did, Ivana jumped down from Eva's lap and bumped Rose's hand with her head.

"She's so sweet," Trudy said.

Eva took a piece of Crescent Hotel stationary and wadded it into a ball. "Does this bring back memories?" She threw the paper ball on the floor.

With rocket speed, Ivana tackled the paper, sending it sailing across the hardwood floor. Ivana spent several minutes kicking it around the room, before finally bringing it back to Eva in her mouth.

Eva handed the soggy paper to Trudy. She tossed it to the floor and the game began anew.

"I remember Ivan spent the longest time doing this." Trudy threw the paper against the wall where it ricocheted across the room. "I can't believe she acts so much like him."

"The breeder says a lot of the Vans like to fetch," Cooper said. "We're so glad. It's like bringing Ivan back to life."

"I finally have a cat too," Trudy said. "And a dog."

Rose asked, "Do you have any children of your own?"

"I was getting ready to mention them, two so far. Alta Grace—she's four and J. D. just turned two."

"Are those pictures?" Rose pointed at the picture album laying on the couch next to Trudy.

Trudy smiled shyly. Although the face had matured, her mischievous grin hadn't changed. "Yes. I thought you might like to see what the kids look like. Also, I have some pictures that Mr. Dye took at the Baker Hospital. He mailed them to me after I went home."

Eva dragged her chair closer to the settee. Cooper stood behind them and looked over Eva's shoulder.

Trudy opened the red leather photo album. Two blonde headed kiddoes stared out of the pages. The little girl looked a lot like Trudy had the first day Eva had met her. Page after page showed adorable children doing cute kid things. Trudy showed them some shots of her husband, David, so handsome and brave in his firefighting gear. In the photo without his helmet he had a flat top.

"Who's taking care of David and the children?" Eva asked.

"David is working this weekend and the kids are having a slumber party at Grammy's house."

Trudy kept flipping pages until she came to a photo depicting a six-year-old pigtailed Trudy playing Monopoly with Mr. Janowitz and Gazetta Smith. Little Trudy held a huge wad of money in her tiny hands. Dark shadows circled her eyes. The back of Cooper and Eva's heads could be seen in the photo's background.

"I remember that day!" Eva exclaimed. "That was the day after I arrived."

"I do too," Trudy said. "Mr. Janowitz let me win at Monopoly that day. He was such a nice man. What happened to him?"

Eva's stomach tightened and she felt queasy as she revisited the image of Mr. Janowitz's lifeless body turning suspended from his robe belt.

"I'm afraid he didn't make it," Eva said quietly.

"So what do you do now Mrs. Du…I mean Eva? Did you ever get back into acting?"

"No. I liked it better behind the camera. After I left the hospital I started writing horror novels and screenplays under the name Evan Reilly."

"Really?"

"My favorite novel, *Phantom at Midnight*, was made into a movie starring Bella Darvi a couple of years ago."

"That's boss," Trudy said. "What's it about?"

"A woman stuck in a haunted hospital."

"Gee. Eva" Trudy laughed. "Whatever was your inspiration?"

Eva pulled out her own photo album. "Here are some publicity shots from *Phantom at Midnight*." Eva pointed to a picture a patient sitting upright in a traditional hospital bed wearing a harried expression. The sick woman's hair and makeup were impeccable. "That's Bella, she was the star. In the story she was haunted by the people who had died in her hospital bed."

Eva turned the page showing a photo of what looked like the Baker Hospital, but the windows along the first floor, were boarded up. Next to the photo Eva had scribble the date 1944.

Cooper pointed at the photo. "I took Eva back to Eureka Springs for our fifth anniversary. We stayed at the Spring Hotel in town, but had to come see what had happened to the Baker Hospital."

While only pictured in black and white, one could still see the once beautiful gardens had fallen heir to a thriving crop of weeds. Only the Statue of Liberty stood in wait for a day when life returned to the old building. The old building looked as lifeless as the corpses that had once been stored in its basement refrigerator.

"That must have been depressing," Trudy said examining the rest of the photos from that roll.

"We took this one through a loose board near the front door into the lobby," Eva said. "It felt so strange to peer inside that hole. It's what I'd imagine a shipwreck to look like," Eva said. "It was so quiet. So dead."

In the photo only slivers of sunlight filtered past the wood planks into the tired old building. The once Grand Lady of the Ozarks had been like so many of the silent stars Eva had once known. So vibrant in their day, only to become decrepit and abandoned. And so the once stunning Crescent Hotel, garbed in clownish purple and lavender, faded to a mere caricature of her formerly elegant self.

They flipped through the book and finally came to pages of pictures from Eva's weeks at the Baker Hospital. She and Cooper were seated at the piano.

"Did Mr. Dye take these?" Trudy asked.

Eva nodded. "Yes he did. What a sweet old man. I wonder what happened to *him*?"

"I never heard from him again after he sent the photos," Trudy said. "I guess even if he survived the cancer, he's probably not with us any longer."

Trudy turned the page the picture that showed a close up of Eva with a white smudge next to her face.

"What's that?" Trudy asked.

"I don't know." Eva turned the page this time.

"Here's another picture from the fourth floor balcony that day," Cooper said.

The next shot was a mostly white cat airborne and reaching for a bird flying just overhead.

"Is that Ivan?" Trudy asked. "I just loved that kitty. After David and I got married, I finally got our cat, Jasper. He's a tiger striped kitty."

"That's wonderful, Trudy," Eva said. "I imagine he's great with the kids."

"Sometimes you can tell he'd rather the kids lived on Mars, but he manages. And they just love him."

Eva turned the page.

"Hey," Trudy took the book out of Eva's hands. "Who's that?" She pointed at a photo of much younger Eva with her arm around the waist of a tall, distinguished man standing next to an oil derrick.

"That was Edgar, my late husband."

Frantically Trudy turned more pages. "I know him."

"He died a couple of years before I came to the Baker Hospital."

"Eva, I *know* him." She cocked her head to the side. The ends of her mouth eased up.

"He was your invisible friend?" Eva said knowingly. After all, she'd figured this out twenty years ago.

"Uh huh. He showed up around the same time you arrived at the hospital. Remember how horrible those shots in the intestines were?"

Eva's stomach tightened. "I'll never forget that pain."

"I was all alone. But Jonnie kept me from being scared. We even had tea parties. He always used to tell me how much he liked you."

Eva remembered. "How could I forget?"

"He would hold my hand while Dr. Hutto or Mrs. Turner gave me those shots."

"Do you know why he didn't tell you his name was Edgar? I always wondered about that."

"Yeah. The day I left he told me he didn't want to make you cry anymore."

"Something, or somebody visited me several times while I was at the Baker Hospital." Eva's hands trembled. "I was so scared. I didn't realize it was Edgar. I wish I'd known." She wiped a tear from her cheek.

Cooper, who still stood behind Eva, squeezed her shoulder reassuringly.

"Johnny, I mean Edgar, came to me only once after I went home. He wanted me to give you a message before you left the hospital. I don't even remember what it said."

"I do." Eva opened the photo album to a page holding an envelope. She handed Trudy a yellowed piece of tablet paper.

Trudy read Eva's translated message written just beneath Trudy's coded letters. "Oh yeah. I'd forgotten. We used to write those notes to each other in code."

Eva handed her the Orphan Annie decoder. "It was one of the high points of my hospital stay. I missed your messages after you went home."

Trudy ran her finger around the edge of the decoder, then spun the dial. "I can't believe you kept this."

"How could I not?"

"Did you ever hear from your Edgar after you left here?" Trudy asked.

"No, that note from you was the last I ever heard from him. I stopped feeling that presence around the house. I guess he felt it was okay to move on."

Trudy handed the decoder to Eva, but Eva closed the young woman's hand around the toy. "You keep it. Teach your kids to use it. Maybe they can go to work for the FBI as decoders."

"Thank you. They'd like that." Trudy pocketed the Orphan Annie Decoder. "Hey, whatever happened to Miss Mossell? She was such a funny lady."

Eva told her every last detail about Mossell's betrayal and her last terrifying visit. "It's funny. If she hadn't broken my scotch bottle, I might not have passed those kidney stones. She might have saved my life, even if it was the last thing in the world she wanted to do."

Eva raised her eyebrows and an evil smile crossed her face. "I kept my promise to her, and had her remains placed into her ex-husband's priceless Ming vase. So I sent the vase, ashes and all to her ex, Roger Knight."

Eva snickered. "Roger called me and thanked me for returning his mother's vase. He said he'd been so excited about getting it back, he'd had problems sleeping."

"I bet he had some exciting times after that," Rose said grinning.

"Yes, indeed. They deserved each other." Eva punched her fist against her flattened hand. "I even heard through the grapevine that weird things started happening in Roger's home. A couple of years later, he offered me a movie role as a grandmother. A grandmother? No thanks. But he read my book and got me in touch with a producer who eventually made *Phantom at Midnight*."

"I can't believe Miss Mossell turned out to be so vindictive. She was nice to me," Trudy said. "Do you know what ever happened to Mr. Baker? He was kind of a strange bird."

"Agent Waller at the FBI kept me updated on the trial," Eva said. "A federal grand jury indicted Mr. Baker, his sister Irma, his attorney, Dr. Statler and hospital administrator Mr. Bellows...and who else...oh yes, Dr. Hutto, for mail fraud for mailing out his "Cancer is Curable" booklet. That's all. They couldn't prove the cure didn't work. Mr. Baker appealed his conviction to the U.S. Supreme Court but lost. He had to pay a four thousand dollar fine and spent four years in Leavenworth. Mr. Bellows served two years and Dr. Statler served one. Apparently Mr. Baker had put all his assets in his girlfriend's name, so once he went free he still had plenty of money. He tried to open a new research hospital in his hometown of Muscatine, Iowa, but couldn't get the permits.

"He and Thelma Yount, I think that was his girlfriend's name, retired to Florida to live on railroad tycoon Jay Gould's three-story sailboat in Miami."

Eva turned pages in her photo album until she found a newspaper clipping from a Muscatine newspaper. "Here's his obituary."

Trudy scanned the article. "He died of jaundice on September 9, 1958," she read aloud. "His body was returned to Muscatine for burial in Greenwood Cemetery. The man who once commanded attention from an audience of thirty-thousand failed to draw more than twenty-five mourners to his funeral. The mortuary had to hire six pallbearers to carry him to his grave because no one else could be found."

"Sad isn't it?" Rose said. "Even his own brother didn't go to his funeral."

"This isn't a time to be sad," Cooper said handing everyone a champagne flute. "Let's toast life." He filled the glasses.

"Okay." Trudy held up her glass. "I toast to surviving leukemia,"

"To surviving kidney stones," Eva said.

"Surviving depression," Cooper held up his glass.

"To just surviving," Rose added.

Ivana jumped up on the chair next to Eva holding the paper ball. "To absent friends, and new friends," Cooper said.

They all sipped their bubbly.

"Oh my, Mr. Cooper," Trudy said. "This is the best champagne I've ever had."

"Nothing but the best for my dear friends." He held up his own glass. "To my bride of twenty years. And to Norman Baker, regardless of whether or not he was a scoundrel, he brought us all together and made this day possible. And to you, Edgar Foxworthy wherever you are, for lending me your wife's company."

"Hear, hear."

Trudy closed her eyes and relaxed her face. "A lot of them are still here, you know. I can't see them anymore, but I can feel them."

"Is Edgar here?" Eva asked hopefully.

"No." Trudy shook her head.

"What about Miss Mossell?" Rose asked. Her eyes darted around the room nervously.

"She's gone. But several of them are still waiting for their cancer cures. I think some of them just liked the way they were treated at the Baker Hospital or maybe at the Crescent Hotel."

The evening moved so quickly. Before long dinner in the dining room turned into an after dinner drink and then bedtime.

"Here's my phone number," Trudy handed Eva a slip of paper. "I'll be driving back to St. Louis in the morning. I'm sure Mommy will be ready to hand the kids back to me." Trudy hugged Cooper again and gave Eva a kiss on the cheek.

Eva took the number and held on tightly, then followed Trudy to the door. "Maybe next time we can meet in Dallas. You and the whole family can stay at our house. It's not as interesting as the Baker Hospital, but we can find something fun to do."

"That would be great." Trudy smiled. "I'd love you to meet David. He's such a doll." She hesitated. "Although the kids can be a handful. After five minutes with my little ruffians, you'll either exile us to the garage or move out."

"We've endured much worse than noisy kids," Eva said. "Trust me. We'd survive."

Rose picked up her heavy leather purse and her cane, and ambled toward the door. "Goodnight, Miss Eva, Mr. Cooper. It's too late for an old woman. I'm heading off to bed."

"'Night, Rose," Eva said. "See you at breakfast. Sleep well."

Rose closed the door behind her.

"Well, Miss Dupree…" Cooper pulled his wife's silver hair off her forehead. "Did I ever tell you what a crush I have on you?"

She smiled. "Yes, Mr. Reilly. I believe you did."

"Happy anniversary, Eva. I love you."

"I love you too, Cooper. Thank you for bringing us back."

He pulled a fresh icy bottle out of the champagne bucket and grabbed a couple of clean flutes. "Why don't we dance under the stars?" he asked moving toward the door to the balcony.

She picked up the transistor radio and turned it on. "That sounds like a wonderful idea." Some Big Bands were playing.

He took Eva's hand and led her out to the balcony where they first met. The sky looked like brilliant diamonds against a veil of black velvet. Directly across from them, East Mountain only appeared as a black silhouette obscuring the stars. Above the mountain, a crescent moon had just risen over the mountaintop.

She set the radio on a picnic table and turned up the volume. The music ended and a new song took its place.

As they sipped champagne, they watched the town below. White lights of homes and businesses sparkled in the icy air. Car headlights crept along windy roads. Everything felt surreal—a blend of old and scary memories and new and pleasant experiences.

A cold wind rushed through the guardrail bars, so icy and sharp it seemed to cut through Eva's dress. She shivered.

After a pause for the radio news and some commercials, the first few notes of Glenn Miller's *Moonlight Serenade* eased out of the tiny radio speaker.

"May I have this dance, Miss Eva Dupree?" Cooper bowed and extended his hand.

"Why Mr. Reilly. I'd be honored." Eva curtsied, the kind of formal curtsy one reserves for the queen.

He placed his hand around her waist and felt her trembling. "I'm sorry. You're cold." He pulled her close to him and Cooper wrapped his arms around her shielding her from the breeze.

Abandoning the dance, they simply stood next to the guardrail and swayed to the rhythm of Glenn Miller's classic notes. As he had done so many times before, Cooper serenaded Eva with the lyrics of 'their song.' As the final notes faded away, they kissed.

"I love you Eva."

"And I love you, Cooper."

They smiled and embraced. Eva closed her eyes, leaning her ear against Cooper's chest. She had experienced a few perfect moments in her lifetime, when every element, was, well perfect. She drank in every sensation: the music, his touch, his warmth against her body and the cold against her face, his breath against her cheek, and the sound of his heartbeat.

In her free ear she felt a cold puff of air. Then gently, quietly a soft, sad female voice whispered in her ear, "Why don't you jump?"

Afterward
The Real Norman Baker

Norman Glenwood Baker and the Baker Hospital really existed. The major events in *Death Under the Crescent Moon* involving him and the Baker Hospital and Health Resort actually occurred. Baker was born in 1882 in Muscatine, Iowa, and he died in 1958 in Dade County, Florida. Even the most bizarre aspects of Baker's personality depicted in this novel are true. Yes, he really wore and decorated everything in shades of purple, including his $7000 1937 Cord Convertible. He made his initial fortune with the invention of the Calliaphone, a calliope that operated on air pressure rather than steam. His financial empire included a magazine, a10,000-watt radio station in Muscatine with the call letters KTNT (Know The Naked Truth), the Tangley mail order catalog, and the Baker Hospital chain. He worked behind a six-sided desk. (Half of the desk still sits in the lobby of the Crescent Hotel.) I embellished Baker's life and idiosyncrasies very little. I didn't have to. His life was so quirky, I just let Baker tell his own story.

Baker had a catalog store that sold the same model of radio Eva listened to in her hospital suite. The catalog also sold a wild assortment of household merchandise, including canaries. Baker's radio station frequently played the commercial playing the death dirge in D flat accompanied by the vocalizations of Baker's real life pet canary, Jim. (Yes, really.) Sadly, as far as I know, no recordings of his Know the Naked Truth show survived.

In the book Eva listened to KTNT on several occasions. The music described in the novel came from station schedule published in the Eureka Springs newspaper, *The Echo*. I must confess that I was not clever enough to come up with the Viking Accordion Band. Apparently, these happy minstrels performed regularly for adoring KTNT audiences.

Baker operated the Baker Institute, a Muscatine, Iowa cancer hospital from 1929 until 1936. With the American Medical Association threatening to shut down the Institute, Baker purchased the defunct Crescent Hotel/Crescent College for Girls for $30,000. (Construction of this state-of-the-art hotel originally cost $250,000 in 1886.) The medical tycoon invested another $50,000 on renovations. His modifications included a network of secret passages to enable his escape from the FBI or the American Medical Association (or the American Meatcutters Association as Baker liked to call it) should they ever raid the hospital. (These passages were thought to be simply legend, but were discovered during recent restoration.)

Baker kept two enormous dogs for protection from the FBI and AMA. In a break from fact, they were reported to be St. Bernards, not Great Danes. (And remember, never, *never* give your dog or cat alcohol. It's toxic to pets; it's not safe and it's not funny.)

Norman Baker's quotes within the pages of this book came almost verbatim from his own brochures, catalogs, authorized biography, court transcripts and contemporary newspapers and magazine articles. Contrary to popular myth, he didn't represent himself as a physician. Articles in the Eureka Springs newspaper always addressed him as Mr. Baker, not Dr. Baker. He kept the AMA at bay by hiring licensed doctors and never permitting surgery at his hospital. While chief physician Dr. J. L. Statler, hospital administrator R.A. Bellows, Dr. W. S. Hutto and head nurse Mary Turner all worked for Baker, I fictionalized their roles. (Dr. Hutto shares my husband's last name and initials. How weird is that?) All of the Baker Hospital patients depicted in *Death Under the Crescent Moon* are purely products of my imagination, but most of the spirits mentioned herein still haunt the Crescent Hotel today.

On one trip to the Crescent to conduct research, my husband's video camera captured an electronic voice phenomena (EVP) in the area that was once the hospice ward. You can listen to it by going to *www.dustyrainbolt.com*. I personally experienced the hanging ghost in room four-twenty-four. And Theodora, who resides in Eva's suite (room four-nineteen), had a little fun with us one weekend.

Some people think Norman Baker was evil, taking advantage of dying people and their families. Others believe he was a lifesaver. In Baker's hometown he was known for feeding the poor and making utility payments for families going through difficult financial times. Whether Baker was saint or sinner depends on who you talk to, and whether the patient lived or died. I believe he had the essence of both running through his veins.

Was the Baker Cure snake oil or did it save people? It's hard to say. It was brought out at his appeals trial that the Cure appeared to be effective in combating some forms of cancer. Norman Baker "purchased" the "Baker Cure" from Harry Hoxsey of Illinois, a formula Hoxsey got the cure from his grandfather. The FDA banned the Hoxsey Cure from being used in the U.S. in 1960. Holistic practitioners today still believe in the curing power of the Hoxsey cure, which is still available at a Hoxsey clinic in Tijuana, Mexico. Go to my website (www,dustyrainbolt.com) if you want to read the ingredients of Hoxsey elixir.

Eva's description of Baker's fate after his arrest is factual, but her part in the arrest is fictional. He *was* arrested in Little Rock to protect innocent patients from becoming caught in the crossfire between the heavily armed hospital guards and the G-men.

The Baker's obituary excerpt Eva read to Trudy was taken from the September 11, 1958 issue of the *Muscatine Journal & News Tribune*. You should be able to view more of my research at www.DustyRainbolt.com.

If you stay at the Crescent Hotel, and if you're lucky (or unlucky—depending on how you look at it) you may experience some of the other gentle spirits mentioned in the book: the girl on the balcony, Theodora, the mischievous lady in room four-nineteen, the sad man in four-twenty-four, the "I want you" man in the spa suites on the third floor, the nurse pushing a gurney from the third floor annex, another nurse pushing a wheelchair on the second floor, the Irish stonecutter Michael in room two-eighteen, and the man in black on the stairway. There are other spirits there as well. Don't forget to check out the ghost tour. You might get to see some of my old friends there. Who knows? You might even get to meet Norman Baker.

Happy haunting,
Dusty Rainbolt

Norman Baker's Obituary

Published in the
MUSCATINE JOURNAL & NEWS TRIBUNE
Muscatine, Iowa, Thursday, Sept. 11, 1958

Norman G. Baker, 74, one-time radio, doctor and a pioneer Iowa radio broadcaster, died Tuesday at Miami, Fla., where he had made his home in recent years. Death was due to jaundice. —His body is to be returned to Muscatine for burial and is scheduled to arrive early Friday. It will be taken to the Fairbanks Home for Funerals, where arrangements for services are pending. —Baker was a son of John and Mary Francis Baker and had spent a large part of his life in Muscatine. He is survived by two brothers, Paul Baker, Muscatine and John Baker of Los Angeles, a sister Mrs. Myrtle Plum of Iowa City and adopted sister, Mrs. Mabel Kerr of Mercedes, Tex., along with several nieces and nephews. He was preceded in death by his parents, a brother and four sisters. —Baker was a colorful figure during his residence in Muscatine. He wore purple shirts and white suits and owned an orchid colored car in an era when black was the standard color for automobiles. He became identified with the radio broadcasting industry in the 1920s with station KTNT, later engaging in broadcasting from Mexico after his station license in Muscatine was suspended. He had engaged in a number of business enterprises, including the manufacture of Calliaphones, operation of a restaurant, gasoline station and in association with others of a cancer hospital. —Baker ran for governor of Iowa on the Farmer Labor ticket in 1932 and unsuccessfully sought the Republican nomination for US Senator in 1936. —His cancer hospital was eventually closed by state officials, and another was established in Arkansas and conducted for a time. —The hospital led him into repeated court appearances before the hospital was closed. He was also involved in a federal court action with the American Medical Association, tried in Davenport, in which he was the loser. —Baker moved to Arkansas in 1938. In recent years, he is reported to have lived on a three-story houseboat in Miami. He sought in 1946 to return to Iowa and establish a Baker Research Foundation but his request for approval of a nonprofit organization to operate hospitals was turned down by the Iowa Secretary of state. —Throughout his career he had contended he was unjustly treated by governmental authorities. In 1940 he was convicted at Little Rock, Ark., on a charge of using the mails to defraud in the advertisement of a cancer treatment. He served a four-year federal prison sentence.

About the Author

Dusty Rainbolt, ACCBC, is an award-winning cat writer according her answering machine. She's the author of the humorous science fiction novel, *All the Marbles*, and co-author of *The Four Redheads of the Apocalypse* series (written with three other redheaded authors). She's also the author of *Cat Wrangling Made Easy, Ghost Cats: Human Encounters with Feline Spirits* and *Kittens For Dummies* (yes, one of the famous Dummies series). Dusty, who is editor-in-chief for AdoptAShelter.com, writes the monthly feline advice column, "Ask Einstein." Dusty serves as the vice president of the international organization, Cat Writers' Association. Over her writing career, Dusty has received 18 Muse Medallions for Excellence (the Cat Writers' version of the Pulitzer) and 34 special writing awards.

About the Artist

Dell Harris is back on the sci-fi/fantasy art scene with this fantastic cover. Check out his art at www.facebook.com/atomicdogstudio.

Yard Dog Press Titles As Of This Print Date

A Bubba In Time Saves None, Edited by Selina Rosen

A Glimpse of Splendor and Other Stories, Dave Creek

A Man, A Plan, (yet lacking) A Canal, Panama, Linda Donahue

Adventures of the Irish Ninja, Selina Rosen

The Alamo and Zombies, Jean Stuntz

All the Marbles, Dusty Rainbolt

Almost Human, Gary Moreau

The Anthology From Hell: Humorous Tales From WAY Down Under,
        Edited by Julia S. Mandala

Ard Magister, Laura J. Underwood

Bad Lands, Selina Rosen &,Laura J. Underwood

Bad City, Selina Rosen & Laura J. Underwood

Black Rage, Selina Rosen

Blackrose Avenue, Mark Shepherd

The Boat Man, Selina Rosen

Bobby's Troll, John Lance

Bride of Tranquility, Tracy S. Morris

Bruce and Roxanne Save the World... Again!, Rie Sheridan

The Bubba Chronicles, Selina Rosen

Bubbas Of the Apocalypse, Edited by Selina Rosen

Chains of Redemption, Selina Rosen

Checking On Culture, Lee Killough

Chronicles of the Last War, Laura J. Underwood

Dadgum Martians Invade the Lucky Nickel Saloon, Ken Rand

Dark & Stormy Nights, Bradley H. Sinor

Deja Doo, Edited by Selina Rosen

Diva, Mark W. Tiedemann

Dracula's Lawyer, Julia S. Mandala

The Essence of Stone, Beverly A. Hale

Extensions, Mark Tiedemann

Fairy BrewHaHa at the Lucky Nickel Saloon, Ken Rand

The Fantastikon: Tales of Wonder, Robin Wayne Bailey

Fire & Ice, Selina Rosen

Flush Fiction, Volume I: Stories To Be Read In One Sitting, Edited by
        Selina Rosen

The Four Bubbas of the Apocalypse: Flatulence, Halitosis, Incest, and... Ned,
        Edited by Selina Rosen

The Four Redheads: Apocalypse Now!, Linda L. Donahue, Rhonda Eudaly,
        Julia S. Mandala, & Dusty Rainbolt

The Four Redheads of the Apocalypse, Linda L. Donahue, Rhonda Eudaly,
        Julia S. Mandala, & Dusty Rainbolt

The Garden In Bloom, Jeffrey Turner
The Golems Of Laramie County, Ken Rand
The Guardians, Lynn Abbey
Hammer Town, Selina Rosen
The Happiness Box, Beverly A. Hale
The Host Series: The Host, Fright Eater, Gang Approval, Selina Rosen
Houston, We've Got Bubbas!, Edited by Selina Rosen
How I Spent the Apocolypse, Selina Rosen
I Should Have Stayed In Oz, Edited by Selina Rosen
Illusions of Sanity, James K. Burk
In the Shadows, Bradley H. Sinor
International House of Bubbas, Edited by Selina Rosen
It's the Great Bumpkin, Cletus Brown!, Katherine A. Turski
The Killswitch Review, Steven-Elliot Altman & Diane DeKelb-
    Rittenhouse
The Leopard's Daughter, Lee Killough
The Long, Cold Walk To Mars, Jeffrey Turner
Marking the Signs and Other Tales Of Mischief, Laura J. Underwood
Material Things, Selina Rosen
Medieval Misfits, Tracy S. Morris
Mirror Images, Susan Satterfield
More Stories That Won't Make Your Parents Hurl, Edited by Selina Rosen
Music for Four Hands, Louis Antonelli & Edward Morris
My Life with Geeks and Freaks, Claudia Christian
The Necronomicrap: A Guide To Your Horoooscope, Tim Frayser
Playing With Secrets, Bradley H & Sue P. Sinor
Prophecy of Swords, M.H. Bonham
Redheads In Love, Linda L. Donahue, Rhonda Eudaly, Julia S. Mandala, &
    Dusty Rainbolt
Reruns, Selina Rosen
Rock 'n' Roll Universe, Ken Rand
The Runestone of Teiwas, M.H. Bonham
Serpent Singer and Other Stories, M.H. Bonham
Shadows In Green, Richard Dansky
Some Distant Shore, Dave Creek
Stories That Won't Make Your Parents Hurl, Edited by Selina Rosen
Strange Twists Of Fate, James K. Burk
Tales From the Home for Wayward Spirits and Bar-B-Que Grill, Rie
    Sheridan
Tales from Keltora, Laura J. Underwood

Tales Of the Lucky Nickel Saloon, Second Ave., Laramie, Wyoming, U S of A, Ken Rand
Texistani: Indo-Pak Food From A Texas Kitchen, Beverly A. Hale
That's All Folks, J. F. Gonzalez
Through Wyoming Eyes, Ken Rand
Turn Left to Tomorrow, Robin Wayne Bailey
Wandering Lark, Laura J. Underwood
Wings of Morning, Katharine Eliska Kimbriel
Zombies In Oz and Other Undead Musings, Robin Wayne Bailey

Double Dog (A YDP Imprint):

#1:
Of Stars & Shadows, Mark W. Tiedemann
This Instance Of Me, Jeffrey Turner

#2:
Gods and Other Children, Bill D. Allen
Tranquility, Tracy Morris

#3:
Home Is the Hunter, James K. Burk
Farstep Station, Lazette Gifford

#4:
Sabre Dance, Melanie Fletcher
The Lunari Mask, Laura J. Underwood

#5:
House of Doors, Julia Mandala
Jaguar Moon, Linda A. Donahue

Just Cause (A YDP Imprint):

Death Under the Crescent Moon
Dusty Rainbolt

Non-YDP titles we distribute:

Chains of Freedom
Chains of Destruction
Jabone's Sword
Queen of Denial
Recycled
Strange Robby
Sword Masters
Selina Rosen

Three Ways to Order:

1. Write us a letter telling us what you want, then send it along with your check or money order (made payable to Yard Dog Press) to: Yard Dog Press, 710 W. Redbud Lane, Alma, AR 72921-7247

2. Use selinarosen@cox.net or lynnstran@cox.net to contact us and place your order. Then send your check or money order to the address above. *This has the advantage of allowing you to check on the availability of short-stock items such as T-shirts and back-issues of Yard Dog Comics.*

3. Contact us as in #1 or #2 above and pay with a credit card or by debit from your checking account. Either give us the credit card information in your letter/Email/phone call, or go to our website and use our shopping carts. If you send us your information, please include your name as it appears on the card, your credit card number, the expiration date, and the 3 or 4-digit security code after your signature on the back (CVV). Please remember that we will include media rate (minimum $3.00) S/H for mailing in the lower 48 states.

Watch our website at
www.yarddogpress.com
for news of upcoming projects
and new titles!!

A Note to Our Readers

We at Yard Dog Press understand that many people buy used books because they simply can't afford new ones. That said, and understanding that not everyone is made of money, we'd like you to know something that you may not have realized. Writers only make money on new books that sell. At the big houses a writer's entire future can hinge on the number of books they sell. While this isn't the case at Yard Dog Press, the honest truth is that when you sell or trade your book or let many people read it, the writer and the publishing house aren't making any money.

As much as we'd all like to believe that we can exist on love and sweet potato pie, the truth is we all need money to buy the things essential to our daily lives. Writers and publishers are no different.

We realize that these "freebies" and cheap books often turn people on to new writers and books that they wouldn't otherwise read. However we hope that you will reconsider selling your copy, and that if you trade it or let your friends borrow it, you also pass on the information that if they really like the author's work they should consider buying one of their books at full price sometime so that the writer can afford to continue to write work that entertains you.

We appreciate all our readers and *depend* upon their support.

Thanks,
The Editorial Staff
Yard Dog Press

PS – Please note that "used" books without covers have, in most cases, been stolen. Neither the author nor the publisher has made any money on these books because they were supposed to be pulped for lack of sales.

Please do not purchase books without covers.